# THE SCORE

KERRY KAYA

Boldwood

First published in Great Britain in 2021 by Boldwood Books Ltd.

Copyright © Kerry Kaya, 2021

Cover Photography: shutterstock and depositphotos

A CIP catalogue record for this book is available from the British Library.

Paperback ISBN 978-1-80162-922-5

Large Print ISBN 978-1-80162-921-8

Hardback ISBN 978-1-80162-920-1

Ebook ISBN 978-1-80162-923-2

Kindle ISBN 978-1-80162-924-9

Audio CD ISBN 978-1-80162-915-7

MP3 CD ISBN 978-1-80162-916-4

Digital audio download ISBN 978-1-80162-917-1

Boldwood Books Ltd
23 Bowerdean Street
London SW6 3TN
www.boldwoodbooks.com

*For Tanya*

# 1

For well over an hour, Mark Creasey's blood-curdling screams had resonated off the walls of a remote Portakabin in Stratford, East London. Having been forced down into a kneeling position, his face had swollen to twice its usual size and was battered, bruised and slick from the blood that spilt down his cheeks from a series of deep, ragged gashes.

'I don't know anything.' His voice was thick and the words were slurred as they poured out of his mouth. 'Honest to God, Rosco, I don't know who took your gear, it wasn't me, I swear it wasn't.' His head rolled to the side and he lifted his arm to reach out for a brunette woman who was standing towards the rear of the Portakabin. 'Tell him, Kit,' he pleaded with her, 'tell him I don't know anything about the hijack.'

Amusement danced across Rosco Taylor's face and, turning his head, he threw the woman in question a wide grin. 'Can you believe this?' He kicked a bloodied Stanley knife across the far side of the cabin, pulled a handgun out from the waistband of his dark trousers and slammed it into the side of Creasey's head. 'Can you believe the actual audacity of this bastard?'

A deep sense of dread ravaged throughout Kit's body and, tearing her eyes away from the tortured man's face, she swallowed deeply then gave a slight shake of her head.

Creasey's shoulders sagged and as he began to sob, his breath constricted in the back of his throat. 'I don't know anything,' he cried. 'Please, Kit, I'm begging you, tell him that I don't know who took it.'

As Rosco smashed the butt of the gun against the bridge of Creasey's nose, the sickening crunch of bone splintering was as deafening as the man's harrowing screams. 'Who took my fucking gear?' Rosco's nostrils flared and spittle flew out from the corners of his snarled lips. 'And trust me, you treacherous bastard—' in quick succession, he smashed the butt of the gun down a second and third time, '—unless you start talking you're a dead man fucking walking.'

As he slipped into a much-longed-for unconsciousness, Creasey's head slumped onto his chest. It was only the fact he was being held up by two of Rosco's foot soldiers that stopped him from dropping to the floor faster than a whore's knickers.

Rosco began to pace the length of the cabin. He was a large man, with a thick bull neck, cropped hair and a flabby belly that rippled as he moved. His chest continued to heave and his breath streamed out ahead of him. Right from the very beginning his gut instinct had told him that whoever was behind the stolen drugs had to be someone with a lot of muscle behind them, had to be someone a lot bigger than the little bastard bleeding out on the linoleum floor. Yet the nagging voice at the back of his mind told him that, despite the fact it was common knowledge Creasey was scared of his own shadow and that he didn't have the nous nor the power to try and tuck him up, he had to know something; he had to know who was responsible.

From the floor, Creasey began to groan and bubbles of blood-stained mucus billowed from his nostrils with each and every ragged breath he took.

Toying with the gun in his hand, Rosco gave an irritated sigh and, slumping down heavily onto a chair, he placed his forearms on his knees and leant forward. 'What d'ya reckon?' he asked, turning his bloated face to look at Kit.

The fact Rosco had even asked for her opinion caused a surge of relief to flow through Kit's veins. Her expression didn't waver as she took her time lighting a Benson & Hedges cigarette. 'I think,' she said after blowing out a thin stream of blueish grey smoke, 'that you need to deal with this and fast. Make an example of him.' She glanced down at Creasey. 'Show them that you mean business, that you won't be messed with. Think of it as sending out a warning to anyone who thinks they can get one over on you.' She stepped over a puddle of congealed blood and came to stand in front of the man she despised, the same man she shared a home with, and even more so, to her disgust, shared a bed with. Not only was Rosco old enough to be her father, but night after night he pawed at her with his greedy hands, and despite the fact that being in close proximity to Rosco made her skin crawl, she stood close enough to speak privately in his ear. 'If you let him walk out of here alive then people will think that you've lost your nerve, that you've gone soft, that you're running scared.' She watched his expression cloud over and, reaching out to touch his forearm, her scarlet-coloured fingernails were a stark contrast against the expensive white shirt he wore. 'And we both know that you're not running scared, don't we?'

As he nodded his head, Rosco chuckled out loud, the gap between his teeth appearing even more prominent as the tip of his yellow-coated tongue poked through. From where Kit was standing, she could smell his rancid breath, the onions and garlic he'd eaten the day before mingled with the stale stench of tobacco and alcohol. 'Do you wanna know something, Kit? You really are one hard-nosed bitch, ain'tcha, darling, and to think' – he slapped his hand against his chest and grinned – 'I was all for letting the little bastard walk out of here.' He stood up, pulled her into his arms and kissed the top of her head, savouring the scent of her floral shampoo. 'But I guess that's why I married you,' he said with a wink. 'At the end of the day, me and you, we're cut from the same cloth, ain't we?'

His words brought bitter, acrid bile flooding into Kit's mouth and she hastily swallowed it down in one large gulp. 'Of course we are.' She forced herself to grin up at him.

The stark reality, of course, was very different. Kit had only ever truly loved one man: her elder brother, Austin. She adored him, always had done, and despite his faults she fully believed that she always would. Stealing a glance towards Mark Creasey, she felt a sudden urge to break down and cry and wanted nothing more than to allow the hot, salty tears to slip freely down her cheeks. After all, she was the one who had all but signed his death warrant. But she wouldn't shed a tear, she was determined of that – at least not yet, anyway, and more importantly not in front of Rosco.

Stalking forward, Rosco kicked out at Creasey's prostrate form. 'I'll send them a warning, all right,' he growled, aiming the gun at the unconscious man's head and pulling the trigger.

The gunshot was deafening and it took all of Kit's strength not to jump. Digging her fingernails into the palms of her hands, she forced herself to look down at what was left of the broken, bloodied mess of the man who had once been her brother's best friend.

Closing her eyes, a memory of herself as a child sprang to her mind. For the majority of her childhood she'd followed Austin and Mark around like a lost puppy, begging them to let her join in with their games and it wasn't until they were in their teens and puberty had hit that they stopped letting her tag along. All of a sudden, having his little sister following him around cramped Austin's style. She'd even had a crush on Mark for a while, fully believing that they were destined to be together, that they were kindred spirits. All he'd had to do was glance in her direction and her tummy would flip over and her cheeks would flush bright pink. She'd fully believed that she would marry him one day. She'd cried for weeks when Mark had told her in no uncertain terms that he saw her as Austin's little sister and nothing more.

Ten years on and she was fighting down the urge to cry again, only for very different reasons. She'd had no other choice, she told herself. To keep Austin safe, she'd had to sacrifice Mark; she couldn't afford for him to talk, and knew from experience that all it would take was one wrong word and Rosco would put two and two together, come up with five and learn of Austin's involvement in the stolen drugs haul. As much as she loved her brother, at this very moment in time she wanted to brain him. Austin had never been able to see the bigger picture. It was a particular trait of his, a dangerous trait, and ever since she'd found herself tied to Rosco, through his association to her, her brother thought of himself as untouchable. The very notion was ludicrous. Rosco had no qualms when it came to murder. Family or not, it made no difference to him – something he enjoyed pointing out to her on a daily basis, such was his mindset.

She took a final drag on her cigarette and as she inhaled the smoke deep into her lungs, her hands ever so slightly trembled. 'Are we done here, Rosco?' she asked. Stubbing out the cigarette, she made a show of glancing at her Cartier wristwatch.

Rosco looked up. The sickening grin he gave made Kit's stomach churn with repulsion. 'Yeah, you get off; I'll sort this out.' He jerked his thumb in Creasey's direction.

She returned the smile and, forcing herself to move across the Portakabin, she planted the briefest of kisses upon his cheek. 'I'll meet you back at the club, then.'

Rosco waved his hand to dismiss her and, taking this as her cue to escape, Kit inched closer to the exit. Her hand on the door handle, she turned her head in time to witness the two foot soldiers bundle Mark's corpse onto a length of thick polythene.

'Oh, Kit, one more thing.'

Kit's breath caught in the back of her throat as she turned her head.

'Tell Aus that I want a word with him.'

Her heart began to beat faster. 'Aus,' she repeated back.

'Yeah, Aus.' Rosco gave a menacing chuckle. 'You know, as in your brother, Austin. Let's see what he has to say for himself.' He stabbed a stiff finger forward. 'It wouldn't surprise me if the little scrote had a hand in this.'

'Of course, I'll let him know.' Kit's voice was a lot higher than she'd intended and, giving her husband one final forced smile, she stepped out of the Portakabin and walked briskly across the deserted forecourt. Once seated inside her car, the full severity of the situation hit home and the tremor that she had been so careful to conceal intensified until her entire body shook with fear. In the rear-view mirror, she watched the cabin door swing open and, twisting the key in the ignition, her heart began to hammer inside her chest so fiercely that she had to rest her hand upon it. Pressing her foot down on the accelerator, she sped out of the car park, leaving behind her a plume of gravel and dust.

It wasn't until she had driven at least two miles down the road that the tears finally came, blinding her vision in the process. She swallowed down the painful lump in her throat, swiped the back of her hand across her eyes, pulled the car over to the kerb then slammed the palm of her hand over her mouth. Deep, raucous sobs engulfed her and, thumping her fist against the steering wheel, she fought the urge to scream out loud.

From inside her handbag, her mobile phone rang and, rummaging inside, she located the device. Austin's name flashed up on the screen. Cancelling the call, she switched off the phone and tossed the device back into the designer bag. As much as she loved him, her brother was the last person she wanted to speak to, at least at the moment, anyway. She let out a deep, shuddering breath and glanced up at her reflection in the rear-view mirror, then, wiping away the tears and traces of mascara from underneath her eyes, she pulled her brown hair up into a ponytail.

Once she had composed herself, she flicked the indicator and pulled out onto the road, contemplating her marriage. Right from the very start she'd known that marrying Rosco would come at a price, and equally she had known that by becoming his wife she would at some point end up putting her own life on the line. It was inevitable, but if it meant keeping her brother safe from harm, then, no doubt about it, that was exactly what she was prepared to do.

**2**

---

Jutting his chin in the air, Fletch closed his eyes and embraced his first precious moments of freedom. After spending the last twenty-two years banged up, this day had been a long time coming.

From behind him the sound of heavy metal clunking broke his reverie and, glancing over his shoulder, he took a moment to stare at the closed iron gates. He was out, actually out; it was a heady thought.

'Oi.'

Fletch spun around.

'Are you gonna stand there all day?'

A slow smile spread across Fletch's face and, moving forward, he pulled his oldest friend, Stevie, into a bear hug.

'Fuck me, you look well.' Stevie beamed, and it was true: despite the tinge of prison pallor to his skin, Fletch had bulked up a great deal and in fact looked fitter than he ever had.

'I look like shit.' Fletch chuckled. 'And you know it.'

'Nah.' Throwing Fletch's bag onto the back seat of his car,

Stevie straightened up. 'It's me who looks like shit.' He reached up to touch the greying hair at his temples.

'You should be more concerned with this.' Jabbing his finger into Stevie's bulging gut, Fletch grinned.

'Yeah well,' Stevie's cheeks flushed pink. 'I've tried every diet going, meal replacement shakes, calorie counting – you name it, I've done it. I love me grub too much, that's my trouble.'

Fletch chuckled. 'Life must be treating you good, then, mate.'

'It is now. Fuck me, I didn't think I would ever see this day.' Stevie beamed.

'You're not the only one, mate.'

Stevie continued to grin. After a few moments he tapped the palm of his hand on the roof of the car. 'Come on, let's get you out of here. I want you to meet my wife and kids.'

Returning the smile, Fletch climbed inside the car, fastened his seat belt into place and glanced back at the prison, his home for the past twenty-two years.

'You're gonna love Jess,' Stevie said, 'and my two girls, they can't wait to finally meet you.' He glanced sideways. 'The little buggers had me up at six this morning; they wanted to make you a welcome home banner.'

As he laughed, Fletch's thoughts turned to his own two children. They were adults now and he'd missed out on their entire childhoods. Guilt plagued him and he had a sinking feeling that it always would. Over the years he had only managed to see them a handful of times, and then it had only been for an hour at a time. Still, they were never too far from his mind.

As they drove down the motorway, Fletch leant his head against the headrest and closed his eyes. Just over two decades he'd spent locked up, almost half of his life. Did he regret the crime he'd committed? Oh, he'd said all the right things, told the parole board that he felt deep remorse for taking a gun and shooting his own father to death, but he didn't, not really, and given half the chance he would do it all over again. If it hadn't been for their father then Fletch's brother, Spencer, would have still been alive.

'We're nearly there.'

Fletch snapped his eyes open. On either side of Upminster's high street was a parade of shops. Sitting in traffic, Fletch focused his attention on a florist's shop. It looked classy and the shop front was decked out in cream and gold. It was the name, though, that had caught Fletch's attention – Suzy's – the same name as the woman he still considered to be the love of his life and always would. Not only was Susan King beautiful but she had had a gentleness about her that Fletch had never known in any other woman. He'd loved her so much that he would have walked to the ends of the earth for her without question. After her husband's murder, she'd left England for a new life in Spain and, to his knowledge, had never returned. He'd thought about writing to her more than once over the years, but with no known address for her it didn't take a genius to work out that his efforts would have been fruitless.

For a few moments he was quiet, then, clearing his throat, he jabbed his thumb across to the florist's shop. 'Have you heard from Suzy at all?'

'Suzy?' Stevie exclaimed. 'Why would I have heard from her?'

'I dunno.' Fletch shrugged. 'I just thought that maybe she would have been in touch, that she might have wanted to see me, to, you know' – he looked away, his cheeks flushing pink – 'see how I was doing?'

Stevie screwed up his face. 'I thought she fucked off to Spain?'

'Yeah, she did.' Fletch sighed. Even as he'd asked the question he'd already known what Stevie's answer would be. During their last meeting, Suzy had more than made it clear that their relationship was over and that she had wanted to get as far away from him and the situation surrounding her husband's murder as she possibly could. Still, a compulsion inside of him had made him ask; he needed to know if she'd returned, if for no other reason than his own sanity. Other than his two children, Suzy had never been far from his mind. He still wanted her, would always want her; she owned a piece of his heart and it was as simple as that.

'How about Spencer? Do you still visit his grave?' Fletch asked, swiftly changing the subject.

'I try to, mate.' Stevie followed Fletch's gaze to glance over at the flowers displayed outside the shop in large plastic buckets. 'I go on his birthday, and on the anniversary of when he... you know...' He swallowed deeply, leaving the sentence unfinished.

Fletch sighed; at his brother's funeral he'd sworn he would never visit the graveside again, that he couldn't bear the idea of Spencer's corpse rotting under his feet, but now more than twenty years later he felt ready to visit his brother's final resting place, to finally say goodbye to him.

'I know your mum still visits, though.'

It was nothing less than what Fletch had expected. She'd told him herself that come rain or shine she paid a weekly visit to his brother, that she found the graveside peaceful and that she took comfort from knowing that by being there she was close to her son.

'I can take you over to the cemetery if you like?' Easing his foot off the brake, Stevie inched the car forward. 'It's only up the road from where I live.'

'I will do soon, mate,' Fletch answered, tearing his eyes away from the shop front. 'As soon as I've sorted myself out.'

\* \* \*

Flicking the indicator, Stevie turned in to a tree-lined avenue.

'This is me,' he stated as he pulled up outside a semi-detached house with a glossy green painted door and a large bay window that overlooked a well-kept front garden. 'Not that you wouldn't be able to tell.' He laughed. 'The banner the girls made for you this morning pretty much gives it away.'

A sparkly blue poster with childlike sloping writing that spelt out the words 'welcome home' was stuck to the front door. From what Fletch could tell, the house, not to mention the affluent area of Upminster, was a definite step up from the Dagenham estate where he and Stevie had both grown up.

'Looks nice. You've done well for yourself, mate,' Fletch said with a smile.

'Yeah, well.' Stevie unclipped his seat belt and opened the car door. 'Mortgage payments are a killer and working the doors doesn't exactly pay a fortune these days, but we manage. It's not like we've got any other choice, is it?'

Fletch shook his head, not that he knew anything about paying a mortgage. Over the years he hadn't even had the privilege of turning off a light switch, let alone paying a bill.

Opening the front door, Stevie called out, 'We're home.' He turned back to look at Fletch. 'Come on in.'

Two little girls ran into the hallway, their tiny bare feet pitter-pattering across the laminate flooring. After their initial shrieks of delight, they looked up at Fletch shyly.

'This one here is Megan.' Stevie hauled a little girl with blonde hair up onto his shoulder. 'And this,' he said, pulling a second girl two years older than her sister towards him, 'is Rachel.'

'Hello.' Fletch grinned, then, cursing himself, he whispered, 'I should have brought them sweets or something.'

'Nah.' Stevie dismissed the idea. 'They get enough as it is.' Placing the youngest girl onto the floor he asked, 'Where's your mum?'

Five-year-old Megan rolled her eyes theatrically and placed her hands on her hips, a gesture that she copied from her mother. 'In the kitchen, of course.'

'Come on.' Stevie jerked his head towards the narrow hallway. 'Come and meet the missus.'

Bad vibes were something that Fletch was an expert on. Locked up, he had learnt to listen to his gut instincts and read situations before they could escalate into something a lot more serious. His intuition had got him out of many sticky situations over the years and the atmosphere in the kitchen was no different: it was so thick that he could cut it with a knife.

'Jess?' There was a nervousness to Stevie's voice that Fletch immediately picked up on. 'This is Fletch, my best mate.' He raised his eyebrows and gave Fletch a wide grin.

Jess Williams's movements were stiff and, folding a tea towel, she carefully placed it on the draining board then slowly turned around. Across her face was a tight smile that was more for her husband's benefit than his friend. As she looked up at the stranger, a pink tinge crept up Jess's neck. Over the years she'd had more than one grainy photograph of her husband and his friend shoved underneath her nose but nothing could have prepared her for how normal he looked, nor how handsome he was. There and then she had to remind herself that he was a murderer and it hadn't been just anyone he'd murdered; it had been his own father. What kind of monster would even contemplate such a thing, let alone see it through? 'Hello, Fletch.'

Fletch smiled, then, remembering his manners, he thrust his hand out. 'Hello, Jess, it's nice to meet you at long last. It's good to be able to put a face to the name; he doesn't stop talking about you.' He jerked his thumb in Stevie's direction and grinned.

Jess stared down at the outstretched hand as though he were about to strike her with it.

'Jess.' Stevie nodded down at Fletch's hand. 'He doesn't bite.' It was said as a joke but there was no humour in Stevie's voice.

'I'm sorry.' She tentatively took his hand in hers, then, pulling away, surreptitiously wiped her palm down the side of her jeans as if she were wiping away a stain. 'It's nice to meet you too.'

'How about a drink?' Stevie rubbed his hands together then opened the fridge door and peered inside. 'What do you fancy, Fletch – a beer?'

'How about tea?' Shooting her husband a glare, Jess flipped the switch for the kettle to boil. 'I don't think this is a time for alcohol, do you?' Her words were loaded with meaning; the last thing she wanted was an intoxicated murderer in the house.

Fletch looked between husband and wife and, picking up on the tension, he gave a slight shrug. 'Tea's fine with me.'

Ten minutes later, once they were seated in the lounge with steaming mugs of tea in front of them, Fletch jerked his thumb in the direction of the kitchen. 'I don't think she likes me very much.'

Stevie dismissed the words with a wave of his hand. 'She's just a bit shy, mate, that's all; she'll be fine once she gets to know you a bit better.' It was a lie and they were both well aware of that fact.

Sipping at his tea, Stevie cleared his throat. 'What are your plans now, then, you know, now that you're out.'

Fletch sat forward, leant his forearms on his knees and gave a gentle smile. 'I'm gonna see my kids, mate, they're my priority. I haven't seen them in almost seventeen years, and every minute

I've spent away from them has near enough killed me, and I hear that I have a granddaughter.' He beamed. 'Lacey, Austin's daughter.'

As he made a clicking sound in the back of his throat, Stevie shook his head. 'I don't think that's such a good idea, mate.'

'I don't mean right now.' Fletch chuckled; he glanced up at the clock on the wall. 'I was thinking tomorrow afternoon, once I've clocked in with the probation officer, I'll go and see them.'

Stevie continued to shake his head. 'Like you said, it's been seventeen years, Fletch; you can't just rock up without giving them some sort of warning.'

Fletch's smile froze. 'They're my kids – what do they need to be warned for?' He sat up a little straighter and screwed up his face. 'I'm not fucking dangerous.'

'Of course you ain't – fuck me, I know that.' With a quick glance at the lounge door, Stevie lowered his voice. 'What I meant was, you said it yourself: you haven't been a part of their lives for a long time.' He slumped back against the plump pillows. 'Don't get me wrong, I get it, the thought of not seeing my two girls kills me, but...' He looked away, not wanting to look his old friend in the eye. 'Just wait a while, you know, sort yourself out a bit first and then get in contact with them.'

Fletch was saved from answering by the two little girls running into the lounge. They weren't much older than his son and daughter had been the last time he'd seen them. At the time, Tina had given him no inkling that it would be their last visit and despite his best efforts to keep in contact, his letters had gone unanswered and the only phone number he'd had for her was dead. His only consolation was that his mum, Stevie and Uncle Frank had all told him the same thing, that Tina had moved on with her life and had met a new man, and more importantly his children were happy. Although the knowledge didn't exactly ease the pain in his heart, knowing that another man would be raising his children, he'd had no other choice but to accept it. Under the circumstances, what else was he supposed to do? It wasn't like he could waltz out of prison, turn up on Tina's doorstep and demand answers from her.

## 3

Austin Fletcher was laughing so hard that he was doubled over and tears rolled down his cheeks. Just an hour earlier he'd collected in one of his debts from a man named Mickey Davis. It wasn't even about the money; it was the principle of the matter. Mickey owed him and it was as simple as that. Besides, he wasn't in the habit of letting people try and treat him like a mug, so why start now?

'I swear down...' Charlie Withers, Austin's friend, laughed. 'I thought he was going to shit himself.'

In an attempt to catch his breath, Austin placed his arm across his abdomen. 'Well, he did have a gun shoved up his nose at the time, and trust me,' he winked, 'the prick is lucky that was the only place I shoved it.'

Charlie roared with laughter. 'I'm more surprised you got that close to him; he stinks of piss.'

'Yeah, true, he did hum a bit.' Picking up his pint of lager, Austin wrinkled his nose. 'Here, have you heard from Mark?' He pulled out his mobile phone. 'Ten times I've tried calling him and it just keeps going straight to the answering machine. It's just, you know,' he glanced around the pub and lowered his voice, 'after what went down, it's a bit fucking weird that he's not answering.'

'He's probably shacked up with some bird.' Charlie dismissed Austin's concern. 'You know what he's like.'

'Yeah, I suppose.' He toyed with the device, pushed several of the buttons, and then gave it a shake. 'I can't get hold of my sister either, and no,' he said as Charlie lifted his eyebrows, 'don't even go there. Rosco, the fucking arsehole that he is, would kill him stone dead if he so much as looked at her in the wrong way.'

'Good point. Anyway,' Charlie studied Austin over the rim of the pint glass, 'how does it feel?'

'How does what feel?' Narrowing his eyes, Austin shrugged.

'Your old man.' He swallowed a mouthful of lager and indicated to the barmaid for a second round of drinks.

'What about him?'

Pocketing his change, Charlie turned his head. 'Your old man.'

'Yeah,' Austin answered, 'like I said, what about him?'

'Ah, I'm sorry, mate.' As the penny dropped, Charlie held up his hands. 'I thought you knew; I mean, I thought it was common knowledge. Everyone's been talking about it.'

'What the fuck are you going on about?' Slamming down his pint glass, Austin growled out the words. 'What's going on with my dad?'

Charlie sighed, rubbed the palm of his hand across his face then braced himself for Austin to kick off, which he did often and in spectacular fashion. 'He's out, mate, got out yesterday.'

'Do what?' Austin's face paled. 'Nah.' He shook his head. 'No way – if my old man was out, I'd know about it, Kit would know, and as for my nan, she would definitely have heard something and she's said fuck all to me.'

'He's out. I heard some geezers talking about it; they used to knock about with him years ago. At least, that's what I heard, anyway.' Charlie shrugged.

Austin continued to shake his head; the revelation was the equivalent of a ten-ton truck pinning him to the floor. He rubbed the palm of his hand over his jaw, his mind reeling. It had been seventeen years since he'd last seen his father, seventeen fucking years and not one bastard had had the decency to inform him of his dad's release from prison. His nan must have known, and if she didn't then Stevie would have been told – he and his dad were still as thick as thieves – so why hadn't they said anything? A sickening thought hit him: maybe it had been his dad's idea to keep schtum. Maybe after all these years he wanted nothing to do with his children. Perhaps his mum had been right after all; she'd always said his dad was a selfish bastard, that he'd only ever put himself first and that at the first opportunity he'd had it away on his toes and left them, albeit if you could call being handed down a life sentence actually willingly leaving them. He gulped down the remainder of his pint. There was only one way of knowing for sure if the rumours were true and that was to have it out with his nan and demand the answers from her if need be. 'I've gotta go.'

Charlie watched as his friend walked towards the exit. 'Sorry, mate,' he called after him. 'But I honestly thought you knew.'

As the probation officer's voice droned on, Fletch fought down the urge to rub at his temples. For the majority of the interview he'd tuned her out; in his opinion her voice was the equivalent of someone dragging their nails down a chalkboard.

'And that brings me to employment.' Valerie Winterbourne shuffled a stack of paperwork on the desk and looked up at him over the ridge of her half-moon glasses.

'Yeah.' Fletch's ears pricked up and he shifted his position on the chair. 'My mate, he works as a doorman in a club, you know, doing security, that sort of thing, and, well, he's already said that he can get me a job – it shouldn't be a problem at all.'

'A doorman.' Valerie continued to stare at him over the rim of her glasses. 'No, no, no, Mr Fletcher, that will not do at all.' She paused slightly. 'Can I call you Harry?'

Fletch gritted his teeth. Even after all these years, he still despised being addressed by his birth name. In his mind, 'Harry' went hand in hand with 'Bannerman', his father's surname. 'It's Fletch.'

Valerie steepled her fingers on the desk, her lips set into a thin line. 'You see, the thing is, Fletch, you have a criminal record; security work is out of the question.'

'Yeah, but' – Fletch spread open his arms – 'he's already said that I've got the job. I can start this week; I won't even have to wait a week in hand for my wages. I'll be paid after every shift I work.'

'No.' She gave him a condescending smile. 'I think this position would be much more appropriate.' She passed across a sheet of paper.

'It's a takeaway food shop.' Fletch looked up, his expression one of disgust.

'We like to call it an eatery.' Valerie smiled. 'Five eight-hour shifts per week, leaving two days off to rest.' She gave a high-pitched laugh that resembled a cackle. 'That should keep you out of trouble for the foreseeable future.'

'Nah, you're all right.' As Fletch rubbed his palm over the stubble covering his jaw, he turned up his nose. 'It's not really me. I think I'll look around for something else.'

Valerie tapped the sheet of paper. 'From what I've read in your report, you aren't really qualified to do much else – nothing that is legal, anyway,' she said, pursing her lips. 'You have an interview tomorrow morning. Ten thirty sharp.' She turned away from him to look at a computer screen. 'That will be all for now; you can shut the door on your way out, Mr Fletcher.'

Snatching up the sheet of paper, Fletch groaned. 'Thanks for nothing,' he grumbled beneath his breath.

\* \* \*

Jenny Fletcher was enjoying a well-deserved rest and, with her legs tucked underneath her, she settled down to watch *Countdown*, her favourite television show. She quite fancied appearing on the programme herself one day.

Hearing a key turn in the lock, she barely took her eyes away from the screen as she called out, 'Who's that?'

'It's me.' Her only grandson, Austin, appeared in the doorway to the lounge.

'Hello, darling.' Jenny pulled her feet out from underneath her and placed the steaming hot mug of tea she had balanced precariously on the arm of the sofa onto the coffee table. 'Do you fancy a cuppa? I've not long made a pot of tea.'

'No.' Austin shook his head.

She glanced back to the television and rolled her lips together in concentration. 'Come on, Aus, help me out, darling – I can only think of a six-letter word.'

Austin sighed and, stomping across the room, he switched the television off. His dad's release from prison was a far more pressing topic of conversation than *Countdown*.

'Hey, I was watching that,' Jenny said, her mouth falling open in shock.

'Is it true?'

'Is what true?' She turned her face away and closed her eyes, knowing full well what her grandson was referring to.

'You know what,' Austin growled. 'Is my dad out?'

'So he's contacted you, then?' she said with a sigh.

Crossing his arms over his chest, Austin shook his head. 'No, not yet.'

'Well, that's a good thing; it's your mum I'm worried about.' She lifted her face towards the ceiling and shook her head. 'I don't know how she is going to take the news, what with her...' She turned to look at her grandson. 'This could push her over the edge.'

'Fuck my mum,' Austin spat. 'Why didn't you tell me, Nan?'

'Keep your voice down,' Jenny chastised, her eyes riveting back up to the ceiling, her ears straining for any telltale signs that her grandchildren's mother was up and about. The last thing she needed was for Tina to get wind of her son's release. As it was, she teetered on the edge of normality; the drugs she'd sunk throughout the years had put paid to any kind of a regular life and, as much as she hated to admit it, the truth was glaringly obvious for all to see. Tina was an addict and there was no getting away from this fact. In the past she'd lied, stolen and begged to get the money for a fix, so much so that Jenny had taken to carrying her purse around with her at all times. The bottom line was Tina couldn't be trusted and as a result was treated as such. 'I don't want your mum to find out that he's out just yet; we have to break the news gently to her.'

'Tell you what?' a gruff voice from the doorway asked.

'That my dad was out?' Austin said, turning to look at his great-uncle Frank.

Frank shook his head. 'I told her,' he said, pointing to his sister, 'I told her that you and Kit had a right to know, but she wouldn't listen to me – she never bleeding does.'

'That's not true,' Jenny said, waving her hand in the air. 'I didn't tell you because' – tears sprang to her eyes – 'because I want you and Kit to have the chance of a normal life. I don't want you embroiled in the world your dad lived in.' Her eyes were drawn to the photograph on top of the mantelpiece of her youngest son, Spencer. 'Nothing good can come from that way of life.'

'A normal life.' Austin gave a bitter laugh. 'You do know Kit is married to Rosco Taylor, right?'

Frank rolled his eyes and pursed his lips. 'I'm saying nothing,' he said, holding up his hands.

A silence fell over the room and the ticking of the small carriage clock on the mantelpiece was suddenly loud to their ears.

'Well,' Frank said, breaking the silence. 'He's out and that's that and I, for one,' he said, pointing a finger towards his chest, 'will be happy to see him. He's been locked up for too bloody long, if you ask me.'

Jenny turned to look at her brother, her expression fearful. 'He's out,' she said, 'but for how long, eh?'

Frank and Austin shared a glance. Jenny had just hit the proverbial nail on the head. It was only a matter of time until Fletch found out the truth and when he did there was no saying what would happen as a consequence.

# 4

Sheree Murray was almost giddy with excitement. Quickening her pace, she puffed away on a Rothmans cigarette as she pushed her daughter Lacey's pushchair through Barking town centre towards the estate where she and her boyfriend lived.

Despite being kitted out in designer clothes, Lacey's outfit looked grubby and unwashed, which wasn't too far from the truth; Sheree had found the clothes on the bedroom floor that morning and after a quick sniff had deemed them acceptable enough for her daughter to wear. As for little Lacey's face, it was filthy, full of snot and Marmite as her mum, much to Sheree's annoyance, often pointed out. She'd have to stick Lacey in the bath. She might even drop in a dollop of bubble bath for her – obviously not the expensive stuff she kept for herself. No, something from one of the cheap gift sets her aunt and uncle had given her for Christmas a few years back, the stuff she wouldn't have been seen dead using.

She let herself into the flat and was met with the familiar scent of cannabis and Lacey's soiled nappies. Housework wasn't exactly Sheree's forte, but even she knew she had to get rid of the nappies before Fletch visited; she might even give the flat a few blasts of air freshener – if she even had any, that was – something else she would have to add to her ever-increasing to-do list.

'Aus?' She was breathless as she called out her boyfriend of three years' name. 'Is it true?'

As he slouched on the sofa, Austin shot her a brooding glance. 'Is what true?'

'Your dad.' Not taking her eyes off him, she unclipped the straps that secured their daughter into the pushchair and yanked her out by her arm. Lacey gave a protesting scream.

'Watch it.' Pointing an unlit joint in Sheree's direction, Austin's face clouded over. 'You're too rough with her.' He held out his arms and, grinning widely, Lacey's sobs subsided into little hiccups as she toddled into them.

Sheree rolled her eyes. Austin's love affair with their child grated on her nerves; the way he doted on her wasn't normal, in her opinion. If they weren't careful she'd end up a spoilt little fucker, much like herself – not that she would ever admit that fact out loud.

'Is it true?'

Placing the joint in the overfilled ashtray, Austin deliberately ignored the question and went on to make a fuss of his daughter, tickling her until her shrieks of laughter filled the flat.

'Aus.' Sheree's voice rose a notch. 'Are you listening to me?'

'What?' Tearing his eyes away from his daughter, Austin looked up.

'Is your dad out?'

He nodded his head and Sheree's pulse quickened. 'Right.' She looked around the cramped and cluttered lounge. Everywhere she looked was a layer of dust so thick that she could write her name in it. 'We need to get this place sorted out and quick.' She placed a finger to her lips, then began gathering up handfuls of clean washing that she'd dumped on the armchair days earlier but still hadn't got around to putting away. 'You need to get in there quick and go and see him before that sister of yours does.'

Austin screwed up his face.

'What?' Sheree demanded. 'You know what she's like; she'll stick her oar in and take over, and you' – she pointed a painted talon towards him – 'are his son.' She nodded down at Lacey. The child, much to her delight, was the image of her boyfriend; that alone should earn more than a few brownie points where his father was concerned. 'And it's you who has given him a grandchild, not Kit.'

'What are you talking about? He's as much Kit's dad as he is mine.'

Sheree rolled her eyes; it wasn't rocket science. Kit, Miss High and fucking Mighty, would muscle in with her looks, expensive perfume and her big tits, as per fucking usual, and take Fletch's attention away from them and that was the last thing Sheree needed. She wanted to be able to bask in Fletch's notoriety, for people to treat her with the respect she deserved. After all, she was the mother of his only grandchild and this fact alone was enough to earn her some serious kudos. Still, Sheree grinned, they had the one thing that Kit didn't. She reached down and plucked her protesting daughter from her boyfriend's arms. 'Bath time,' she said in a sing-song voice. The housework could wait for the time being. Making Lacey look not only presentable but also utterly adorable in the process was much more of a pressing issue.

* * *

Just days after landing the job in the fast-food restaurant, Fletch's cheeks flushed a deep shade of pink as he tossed the cloth he'd used to wipe down the shop counter into a bucket of bleach. 'Yeah, all right,' he said, crossing his arms over his chest. 'Have a good laugh at my expense; you might as well get it over and done with.'

'Ah, mate.' Stevie could barely conceal the smile that had inched its way across his face. 'You look... it's just—' He burst out laughing. 'It's the hat. I'm sorry.' He cleared his throat and tried once more to look serious. He managed to last all of two seconds before bursting out laughing a second time.

Snatching the paper hat off his head, Fletch rubbed at his temples. 'This is what I've been reduced to,' he groaned. 'I was better off inside; at least there they didn't make me dress up like this.' He leant his forearms on the counter top. 'I've got that probation officer Winterbourne checking up on me every five minutes and that's without him back there.' He jerked his thumb towards the rear of the property where the manager was doing a stock take. 'He's always got his beady eyes on me; I think he thinks I'm planning to rob the till or something.'

'Listen, Fletch.' Stevie's voice became serious. 'You knew it wasn't going to be easy and this,' he said, looking around the fast-food shop, 'it won't be forever. Think of it as a stepping stone, mate.'

'Yeah I know,' Fletch groaned, 'I just didn't think it would be this hard.' He tapped his fingers on the counter then leant forward. 'I've been thinking about what you said, you know, about waiting until I've sorted myself out before meeting up with my mum and the kids, and I think I've put it off long enough. I have to see them, mate. For the first time since being sent down, I'm this close to my kids.' As he placed a thumb and forefinger an inch apart to emphasise his point, the churning in Fletch's gut intensified. He'd missed his children to the point where it had almost driven him out of his mind. It was only the fact that time and time again they had told him Austin and Kitty were doing well without him in their lives that had kept him from completely losing his shit, even if the knowledge that they didn't need him had somewhat broken his heart to pieces in the process.

'Yeah, one step at a time, though, eh,' Stevie reiterated. 'You don't want to rush into anything. Anyway,' he said, changing the subject, 'I've come to invite you to dinner.'

'Dinner.' Fletch raised his eyebrows. 'How does Jess feel about that? I was under the impression that she didn't like me very much.'

'Jess will be sweet; in fact, it was her idea,' Stevie lied.

'Yeah, go on, then,' Fletch reluctantly agreed.

'Good.' Stevie rubbed his hands together. 'Tomorrow, Sunday lunch, all the trimmings.'

Fletch glanced down at his oldest friend's protruding abdomen.

Stevie sucked in his stomach. 'Yeah, all right,' he said with a wink. 'Maybe I'll leave out the trimmings.'

'Yeah, maybe you should,' Fletch called after him as Stevie made for the exit.

Across the street, Austin was sitting inside his car watching with interest as Stevie exited the fast-food restaurant. For the past hour he'd been tailing his father's friend and, noting that he wasn't actually carrying any takeaway containers, he narrowed his eyes. It was common knowledge that Stevie loved his grub so if he hadn't gone into the shop to buy food, then what exactly had he gone in there for? He snatched up his mobile phone from the passenger seat and tapped in his sister's telephone number. After three rings the answering machine kicked in and, resting his forearms over the steering wheel, he chewed on his lip.

'Fuck it,' he muttered to himself. Then, snatching the keys out of the ignition, he jumped out of the car, slammed the door closed behind him, locked up and made his way across the street.

\* \* \*

As he was about to sweep the shop floor, the bell above the door tinkled. Fletch looked up, a ready smile plastered across his face. The figure before him forced him to snatch the paper hat off his head for the second time in less than ten minutes.

'Hello, Dad.'

The tiny hairs on the back of Fletch's neck stood up on end and as a wave of shame flushed over him, he closed his eyes tight. Working in a fast-food restaurant wasn't the first impression he had ever envisioned for his son to have of him. 'Austin.'

For a few moments they stared at one another, then without saying another word Austin launched himself forward and threw himself into Fletch's arms.

They stood embracing for what felt like an age, neither of them wanting to break the spell.

After a few moments, Fletch broke away and, holding his son at arm's length, he looked into a face that was so like his own. From the light splattering of freckles across Austin's nose to the mop of dark hair, his boy was a mirror image of himself. 'You look well.' Tears glistened in Fletch's eyes as he pulled Austin close again and kissed the top of his head. 'It's good to see you, son. Fuck me, you don't know how many times I've dreamt of this moment.'

Taking the cuff of his sleeve, Austin swiped away the tears from his eyes. 'I wasn't sure that you would recognise me.'

Fletch chuckled. 'What's not to recognise? You're a carbon copy of me when I was the same age; you're like the spit out of my mouth.'

Austin beamed; all his life he'd longed to hear those words. 'It's good to have you back, Dad; I've missed you.'

'Same here, son.' Fletch took a step back to look at him. 'And I hear that I have a granddaughter.'

'Yeah.' Austin beamed. 'Here, take a look.' He rammed his hand into his jeans pocket and pulled out his wallet. Flipping the leather case open, he slid out a crumpled photograph. 'Her name is Lacey.'

Taking the photograph, Fletch's heart constricted inside his chest and he gave a gentle smile; she was a Fletcher all right and from what he could see she was also the image of his son. A part of him was relieved that he could see nothing of Tina in her. 'She's beautiful.'

'Yeah, she is.' Austin grinned.

'And how's Kitty?' Looking up, Fletch quirked an eyebrow. 'Is she okay, is she happy?'

'She's...' The smile slid from Austin's face. 'You've got a lot of catching up to do, Dad,' he said with a rise of his eyebrows.

* * *

As she sat behind her desk in the office above a strip club, Kit sipped at a glass of brandy.

On the desk in front of her was her mobile phone and, with her chin resting on her hand, her eyes were drawn to it. Over the past week she'd managed to avoid her brother and had ignored his telephone calls and promptly deleted his text messages, which in itself was no mean feat.

The sudden sound of voices coming from the corridor outside

her office made the hairs on the back of Kit's neck stand up on end. She would recognise her brother's voice anywhere. With a thud, she slammed down her glass and was already up and out of her seat before he could push open the door.

'Kit.'

She could hear the excitement in Austin's voice and as she clenched her fists into tight balls, a sense of panic engulfed her. She had to get him out of the club before her husband turned up. 'Not now, Aus.' She looked up at him, saw the lopsided grin spread across his face and resisted the urge to push him back out of the door. 'I'm busy.'

'Look who's here.' Oblivious to his sister's panic, Austin was animated as he gestured towards the figure standing behind him.

Ever so slowly, Kit turned her head. Shock resonated across her face and as she rocked back on her heels, she shook her head. 'No.' She stumbled back towards the desk. 'No, Aus.'

'It's Dad.' Austin continued to grin.

'I can see who it is,' Kit snapped. Gripping onto the desk so hard that her fingertips had turned a deathly shade of white, she took a series of deep, steady breaths, composed herself then turned back around. 'Get him out. I mean it, Austin; I don't want to see him.'

Austin frowned. 'But it's Dad.'

'I know who he is,' she screamed back at her brother, 'just get him out of here.'

Fletch held up his hands and backed away, the hurt in his voice when he spoke clearly audible. 'I think maybe I should leave.'

'No, Dad, don't go.' Austin looked from his father to his sister and, walking across the office, he stood just inches away from her. 'It's our dad,' he said in a low voice. 'He's finally out, just like we always wanted.'

Turning away from her brother, Kit closed her eyes and slammed her hand over her mouth in a bid to stop the sob that was lodged in the back of her throat from escaping. When she turned back to face him, the only telltale sign that her father's sudden appearance had clearly rattled her was the tension in her voice.

'I want him to leave. I want you both to leave.'

Fletch gave his daughter a sad smile. 'I'm sorry, Kitty, I should never have come here, at least not without warning you first. But I was desperate to see you, both of you,' he said, giving his son a wide smile.

Kit screwed up her face. 'It's Kit,' she said, her tone cold. 'I haven't been called Kitty since I was ten years old.'

Fletch held up his hands. 'Like I said, I'm sorry.' He gestured towards the door. 'I'll leave you to it, but for what it's worth, it's good to see you.' He tilted his head to one side as he studied his daughter. 'You look like your mum; you could easily pass for her when she was your age.'

The remark earned him a grunt of disapproval.

He looked around the office. He hated to admit it but he wasn't exactly overjoyed by the fact his daughter worked in a strip club. The sign out front had said it was a gentleman's club and, walking inside, he'd expected the club to be a modern-day spieler, not a strip club complete with floor-to-ceiling metal poles. Still, looking on the bright side, it was a job, he told himself. At least she wasn't on the dole, or even worse than that, working the main floor and taking her clothes off for men old enough to be her father – the very notion was enough to bring him out in a cold sweat. 'I can see that you've done well for yourself,' he told her, 'and I'm proud of you.'

Kit screwed up her face. 'It's a bit late for the caring father act, don't you think?' she spat. 'Twenty-two years too fucking late, to be precise. Now if you don't mind' – she nodded towards the door – 'I want you to leave.'

Once their father had left the office, Austin turned on his sister. 'What the fuck is wrong with you?' he said, spitting out the words. 'Our dad and you throw him out like that, like he's nothing, like he's the shit beneath your shoe.'

'What's wrong with me?' Kit roared back at him. 'Are you out of your tiny little mind? You brought him here,' she said, her voice rising. 'You brought him here to Rosco's fucking club.'

'You mean your club.' Austin's eyebrows knitted together. 'This place,' he said, looking around him, 'it was part of the deal, wasn't it? Your pay-off for marrying the bastard.'

A bitter laugh escaped from Kit's lips and she slapped the palm of her hand against her forehead. On paper it may have been her club but her husband still very much ran the show. 'You just don't get it, do you, Aus?'

'He's our dad; he's entitled to see us as much as we are him,' Austin protested.

'Don't you think Rosco is going to think him turning up out of the blue is a little bit suspect?' She stared at her brother, waiting for the penny to drop. 'The missing coke, Aus,' she growled, stabbing a finger against his temple. 'I know it was you; I'm not stupid and, despite what you might think of him, neither is Rosco.' She continued to glare at her brother. 'And now by bringing him here,' she said, flicking her eyes towards the door, 'Rosco is going to put two and two together and think that he had something to do with it. It's just a little bit of a coincidence, don't you think, that he should turn up here just weeks after the merchandise was stolen.'

'Oh.' Austin tilted his head to one side. 'I didn't even think of that.'

Kit threw her arms up in the air, exasperated. 'That's your

problem, Aus; you never do think. All you ever do is go in all guns blazing and sod the consequences.'

'Fuck Rosco.' Austin gave a nonchalant shrug of his shoulders. 'Who gives a fuck what he thinks anyway. Am I supposed to be scared of him?' He sniggered.

Kit shook her head. 'You've got a short memory, Aus.'

Austin glared. 'My memory is long, sis, trust me on that. I'm just not a little kid any more – big difference.'

As he made for the door, Kit called after him. 'You can't see what you've done, can you?' The fight was gone, leaving in its place a deep sense of foreboding. 'You really can't.'

Pausing beside the door, Austin kissed his teeth. 'See you around, sis.'

It was only after her brother had left the office that Kit slumped down onto a chair, held her head in her hands and began to sob so hard that her entire body felt as though it were breaking in two.

## 5

After tossing and turning for the majority of the night, Fletch had finally given in and climbed out of bed. Deep in thought, he absentmindedly sipped at a cup of black coffee. The bitter liquid had turned lukewarm, not that he appeared to notice, or care for that matter.

Over and over again, in his mind's eye, he went over the events of the previous day. The look on Kitty's face haunted him. He'd had no idea that his daughter seemingly despised him so much.

From the vague comments his son had made he'd gathered that life hadn't exactly been rosy for his children while growing up, and had wrongly assumed that by being out of the picture their lives had been all the richer for it. When Tina had suddenly stopped visiting or bringing the children to see him, his mum, Stevie and even his uncle Frank had all said the same thing: that it proved Tina had at long last taken his advice and had moved on with her life. As much as he'd argued the case that he should still be able to see his children, regardless of Tina's new-found happiness, the answer thrown back at him had always remained the same: Austin and Kitty were thriving, they were doing well at school and were happy, so why rock the boat and unsettle them for his own selfish reasons? It was only then that he'd relented. As it was, he'd been racked with guilt; the last time he'd seen his children, their pitiful cries when it had been time to leave had broken his heart in two. They had been far too young to understand the concept of prison and if he was being totally honest with himself he hadn't wanted them to. They were innocent; they shouldn't have been subjected to spending time among armed robbers and murderers, himself included.

He looked around the small box room that he occupied in a bail hostel, or halfway house as it was more commonly known. The room was so tiny he'd be hard pushed to swing a cat around, not that he'd want to, mind. He may have been a murderer but he wasn't a monster.

Wafting up from the kitchen, an overwhelming scent of eggs being fried hit his nostrils, and he wrinkled his nose at the unmistakable stench that mingled with mould and the stale sweat that came from the great unwashed he shared the hostel with. The place stank to high heaven and, considering he'd spent the majority of his life banged up inside with men who came from all walks of life, that was saying something.

Other than the usual toiletries, the room was devoid of any personal touches and consisted of a neatly made-up single divan bed, a chest of drawers with two cans of deodorant, two bottles of body wash, and a handful of loose change adorning the top. In his mind, the room didn't look much different to how his prison cell had looked. The only difference was that he was free to come and go as he pleased, within reason, of course – he still had a ten p.m. curfew.

By the time Stevie was due to collect him for Sunday lunch, stress lines were clearly visible around Fletch's eyes. A text message pinged on the mobile phone Stevie had acquired for him. By all accounts it was the latest gadget on the market, a must-have that the kids of today were scrambling to get their hands on. He wearily picked the device up. He still couldn't get to grips with the thing, and he cursed under his breath as his fingers clumsily tapped out a message across the smooth screen. More than half the message he'd typed was gibberish, letters either mistyped or words with letters missing. Giving up, he tossed the phone onto his bed, left his room and made his way down the steep staircase, past the reception desk and out onto the street where Stevie was waiting for him.

'You all right, mate?'

'No, not really.' From the corner of his eye, Fletch noted the CCTV camera above the hostel door and manoeuvred himself out of view. 'I've seen Austin, Kitty too.' He lifted his eyebrows, watching Stevie's reaction closely. 'Or Kit as she now likes to be called.'

Stevie visibly blanched. 'I thought you were going to wait a while, settle back into life on the outside first?'

'No.' Crossing over the street to where Stevie's car was parked, Fletch was barely able to keep his temper in check. 'That was your idea; I wanted to see my kids the day I came out, but you' – he stabbed a stiff finger in his friend's direction – 'you wanted me to wait, and now I'm beginning to wonder why that was.'

Stevie gave a nervous laugh as he dug his hand into his trouser pocket to fish out his car keys. Across his forehead, beads of sweat broke out. 'I just...'

'What,' Fletch hissed, 'you just what?'

'Come on, Fletch.' Stevie held up his hands and took a step away from the car. 'I was only trying to help.'

'No you weren't.' Fletch's eyebrows knitted together. 'You were trying to keep something from me.'

Stevie closed his eyes. 'Whatever you might think, I had your best interests at heart, I really did; we all did.'

'Who's "we"?' Fletch growled.

'Me and your mum.' He unlocked the passenger door with a sigh before taking a deep breath. 'We were only trying to do what we thought was for the best, honest to God we were; you have to believe that. We thought that if you knew the truth then it would just make the situation ten times worse.' He watched Fletch's eyebrows knit together and inwardly groaned. Him and his big trap; he never knew when to keep the bastard thing shut. 'And you still don't know the truth, do you?'

'No, but you're going to tell me,' Fletch said.

Moving around to the driver's side, Stevie opened the door and rubbed the palm of his hand across his face. 'All right,' he finally answered, 'I'll tell you.' Or at least he would tell the edited version. 'But I can tell you now you're not going to like this.'

'Just tell me.'

'Tina.'

Fletch's shoulders sagged. Everything and anything that had ever gone wrong in his life had always begun with the mother of his two children. 'Go on.' He climbed into the car. 'What has she done now?'

'I think you'd been banged up, I don't know.' Leaning back in his seat, Stevie rested his head on the leather headrest as he tried to think back. 'Maybe five or six years – the kids were still little, I know that much – and, well, she got herself involved with this bloke. To be honest it all happened so fast and before we knew it she'd moved him into her house.' He paused to catch his breath. 'Your mum still visited regularly back then, and at first everything seemed okay, the kids were doing great and Tina seemed happy—'

'But,' Fletch interrupted, sensing a 'but' coming.

'It all went downhill pretty fast.' He raised his eyebrows. 'Your mum turned up unannounced one day and, well, the house was like a shit tip, the kids were filthy and hadn't been fed and as for Tina,' he sighed, 'she was still in bed stoned out of her nut.'

'Drugs?' Taken aback, Fletch's mouth dropped open. 'No, she wouldn't, not Tina.'

'You name it, mate, and she was on it: speed, coke, E's, the whole fucking shebang. She was taking so many pills I'm surprised she didn't rattle when she walked. Seems this new bloke of hers was supplying it to her.' He looked away and rolled his lips together.

'Go on.' Fletch raised his eyebrows. 'I've got a nasty feeling there's more.'

Still in two minds just how much he should divulge, Stevie nodded. 'Austin.'

'What about him?' Fletch's breath caught in his throat and his heart began to race.

'I had my doubts, and I did confront her,' Stevie was quick to point out, 'but at the time, Tina, well, she was kind of convincing, she kept saying that he was accident-prone.'

'What do you mean by "accident-prone"?' Fletch frowned.

'You know.'

'No, I don't fucking know.' Fletch's voice began to rise. 'I wouldn't ask if I did, would I?'

Stevie shook his head. 'Knocks, bumps, you know, that kind of thing.' His voice lowered. 'He even had a couple of broken ribs at one point. She said he'd fallen down the stairs and I did ask him about what had happened but Austin clammed up. One thing I can say about that boy is that he is loyal to Tina; she is his mum, I suppose.' He shrugged. 'To this day, he still hasn't told me what really went down.'

Fletch exhaled loudly and brought his hands up to his head.

Talk about history repeating itself; he and his brother had been through hell and back with their own father, and he'd been determined that his own children wouldn't suffer in the same way as he had. 'What exactly are you trying to tell me, that Tina did that to my son, that she was abusing him?'

'No.' Stevie was quick to answer. 'I'm telling you that I don't know what was going on inside that house. It could have been her or it could have been this bloke she was seeing. I just never believed Tina's version of events; there were too many accidents for them to be an accident, if you know what I mean.'

Fletch clenched and unclenched his fists. 'What happened to the money?' he asked, raising his eyebrows.

'What money?'

'You know, the money,' he urged Stevie. 'All the dough that I left her?'

'I don't know.' Screwing up his face, Stevie scratched at his head as he tried to think back.

'There were five bin bags filled with cash underneath the floorboards in Spencer's room; there had to be at least three hundred grand there, maybe even more, I didn't exactly keep track over the years. I told Tina to take the lot and spend it on the kids. I know she bought the house in Rainham, but what happened to the rest of it?'

'As far as I know they never saw a penny of it. She most probably snorted it up her nose. Like I said, this bloke of hers started supplying, and I did wonder at the time where he was getting the cash from to start dealing. He was throwing money around left, right and centre at one point; from pretty much nothing, he built himself a firm and is still going strong today.'

'What, and you didn't think to tell me any of this?' Fletch turned to look at Stevie, his expression hard. 'I can't believe you've kept this from me. You're supposed to be my best pal; why didn't you tell me?' he demanded.

Stevie swallowed. 'It wasn't like that, mate,' he protested. 'I did what I thought was for the best.'

'Wasn't like that?' Fletch bellowed. 'Then what was it like? They're my kids – I had a right to know what was going down.' An image of his children flashed before his eyes and he shook his head. Austin and Kitty had only been seven and five when Tina had ceased contact. In his eyes, they'd still been babies and as their father he should have been there to protect them. 'I'm gonna wring her fucking neck over this. That money was for my kids; I specifically told her to spend it on them and make sure they had a good life.'

Stevie raised his eyebrows. 'Anyway,' he sighed, 'they ended up being taken into care for a while, until eventually your mum stepped up and took them in. That's where...' He stopped to think for a moment. 'I think that's where Austin's problems stem from.'

Barely able to get his head around the revelation he'd just been told, Fletch snapped his head around. 'What do you mean by that?' His blood ran cold and his voice was a lot higher than usual. 'What problems?' A vision of his younger brother sprang to his mind. When they were children, Spencer had been left suffering from a brain injury after their father had taken his fists to him. 'He seemed all right to me; he's nothing like Spence was.'

'No.' Stevie shook his head. 'I don't mean like how Spencer was; I mean anger problems. He went off the rails for a while and was pretty difficult to manage. Your mum had to get psychologists involved and everything; he ended up on medication to calm him down.'

'Why wasn't I told about any of this?' Fletch's face was a mask of anger. 'You're my best mate; why didn't you tell me what was going down?'

Stevie sighed and spread open his arms. 'What could you have done? You were banged up; there was nothing you could have done to help them from inside.'

'I still had a right to know.' Fletch patted his denim pockets, then, remembering he'd tossed the mobile phone onto the bed, he groaned. 'You should have told me. You had plenty of opportunities to tell me what was going on, but nah, you let me think that everything was rosy, that my kids were as happy as fucking Larry without me around, that they were safe with Tina.'

Stevie's heart sank. 'Come on, Fletch, don't be like this. I did what I thought was for the best, we all did.'

'What, keeping me out of the know was for the best, was it?' Fletch screwed up his face, the anger he felt clearly visible. 'It wasn't the best for my kids, though, was it? You of all people should have told me; I trusted you to keep me in the loop.'

Stevie didn't answer. What could he even say? He cleared his throat but before he could open his mouth to speak was interrupted by Fletch.

'Just drive me to my mother's house.'

'Why?' Stevie asked.

'Why do you think?' Fletch spat.

'What about the Sunday lunch?'

'Did you really just say that?' Fletch brought his hands up to his temples, amazed that his friend even had the audacity to ask him about food at a time like this.

'All right.' Stevie held his hands up in the air. 'Fair point, it was a stupid question.'

'Yeah, it was,' Fletch replied. 'A really stupid fucking question.'

## 6

Like most junkies, all Tina cared for was drugs, or to be precise, crack cocaine. The drug and her need to score on a daily basis was her only waking, conscious thought. Underneath the coat she had pulled around her thin frame, Tina's outfit left little to the imagination and the flimsy, black, sleeveless Lycra dress she had thrown on that morning barely covered her skinny body. Her legs were encased in sheer black nylon tights that had a ladder running from her thigh to her ankle, and her feet, which were peppered with faded track-mark scars, had been shoved into black, calf-length PVC boots, the heels so worn down that the PVC had peeled away to reveal the white plastic underneath.

Up ahead of her was a low-rise block of flats and, bypassing a dilapidated children's playground, the equipment rusting and long broken, she punched in a series of digits on the entry call system. The door sprang ajar and she trudged up a flight of steps, her feet heavy and her body weary.

The years had not been kind to Tina. The once vivacious woman she had been was gone and in her place was an emaciated shadow of her former self. Even her lank hair that had once been thick and glossy was now thin and sparse in places.

She tapped her knuckles on a wooden door, the paintwork chipped and peeling.

'Yeah,' said a voice as it opened a crack.

'It's me,' she answered, her voice high at the mere thought of the fix that awaited her.

She followed the man down a dimly lit corridor and, entering the kitchen area, her eyes were automatically drawn to the counter top. In a polythene zip bag was a handful of tiny white crystals and she licked her lips in anticipation.

'This is the last time, right. After today I don't want you coming back here; I can't do this any more.'

'I won't.' She dragged her eyes away from the crystals to look up at him. 'I promise, okay.' She slipped her hand into the pocket of her coat and took out a battered cigarette packet with trembling, nicotine-stained fingertips. Underneath her chipped painted fingernails was a thick layer of ground-in grime. 'I mean it,' she said, placing a cigarette between her lips and lighting up. 'I won't come here again.' Pushing her straggly hair away from her face, her voice took on a desperate tone and as she blew out a cloud of smoke, she began to cough. It was a deep, phlegmy, hacking cough that was enough to turn even the most hardened of stomachs.

'You should get that cough seen to,' he said, giving her a side-long glance.

Picking a flake of tobacco off her tongue, Tina nodded her head. 'I will do.' Even though they both knew that she wouldn't.

'I mean it, Mum,' Austin said as he handed over two tiny rocks of crack cocaine. 'You need to sort yourself out.'

With the rocks firmly clutched in her hand, Tina afforded her son a bright smile. 'I said that I would, didn't I, so stop with your fussing.' She grinned up at him.

Austin rolled his eyes. When it came to his mother, he'd heard it all before.

\* \* \*

Austin wasn't the only one rolling his eyes. In Brentwood, Essex, Kit was sick to the back teeth of listening to her husband's irate shouts.

She stretched out across the bed she shared with him, half of her straining to hear Rosco's one-sided telephone conversation, the other half of her wishing that he would shut the fuck up and leave the house.

He walked into the bedroom and she pulled the crisp white Egyptian sheet over her body. As far as she was concerned, the less her husband saw of her the better. The last thing she wanted was for him to jump back into bed; even the notion of any form of intimacy with him was enough to make her blood run cold.

'Problem?' she enquired, playing the ever-dutiful wife.

'Problem?' As he turned towards her, his face was almost purple with rage. 'Fucking problem?' He kicked the dressing table stool across the room, upsetting the contents arranged on the table. Bottles of perfume and cosmetics rolled to the floor, landing on the cream carpet with a soft thud.

'Cheers for that.' She rolled her eyes, threw the sheet away from her, clambered off the bed and then stooped down to pick up her belongings. 'I was only asking a question; you don't need to spit your dummy out the pram.'

Rosco's face clouded over and he narrowed his eyes. 'Speaking of dummies, did you tell that brother of yours that I want a word?

It's been over a week and the little bastard still hasn't shown his face.' He rolled his tongue across his teeth. 'And trust me when I say this, Kit: when it comes to him, my patience is thin.'

Kit's back stiffened. It was no lie; Rosco's patience had always been thin when it came to her brother. 'Not yet, I haven't been able to get hold of him.' She turned around, a smile plastered across her face. 'You know what he's like, he's probably been on a bender or something, but I'll try to give him a call today and let him know that you want to have a chat.'

'Chat?' Rosco scoffed. Studying her for a moment, he pointed a podgy finger forward. 'Make sure that you do.' He dipped his hand into his trouser pocket and pulled out a bundle of cash. Rolling off six fifty-pound notes, he threw them across the bed. 'There's three hundred nicker.' He nodded towards the dressing table. 'To replace any bottles I might have broken.'

As he left the bedroom, Kit glanced down at the red notes and, swiping them to the floor, she screwed up her face. 'Fuck you,' she spat underneath her breath.

\* \* \*

Whoever had said that patience was a virtue had clearly never been given news the likes of which Fletch had just received. Without giving pause, he jumped out of Stevie's car, stormed down the pathway to his childhood home, and thumped his fist against the front door.

'Fletch, wait up.' After locking his car door, Stevie rushed after his friend. 'You need to calm down,' he told him as he leant against the door frame in a bid to block Fletch from entering the house. 'Going in all guns blazing isn't going to help matters, is it?'

'Maybe I should keep schtum instead, would that be more to

your liking?' Fletch retorted as he thumped his fist against the wooden door.

Stevie's cheeks reddened at the remark. 'I know you're angry, but this isn't going to help.'

'Nah, you're right,' Fletch growled. 'The only thing that would help is for me to have my hands wrapped around Tina's fucking throat but until that time comes, which, trust me, it will, this will have to do.'

The door opened and before Jenny could even open her mouth to speak, Fletch had barged past her.

In the lounge, he came to a halt beside the electric fire, his eyes drawn to the collection of photographs of Spencer and himself as children that still sat proudly on top of the mantel-piece. Joining them were similar school portraits of his own two children. He peered closer, his heart constricting inside his chest. His own flesh and blood; he'd always believed that they were safe – instead they had been thrown to the wolves.

As he entered the lounge, Stevie raised his eyebrows in a warning and, taking the hint, Jenny closed her eyes and sighed. Ever since her son's release from prison, this was the moment she had been dreading.

'How many times did you visit me when I was inside, Mum?'

Jenny shook her head, confused by the question. 'I don't know, it must have been hundreds of times.'

Fletch turned to face his mother. 'And not once did you think to mention it to me that my kids were being abused?'

'It wasn't like that, darling.'

'No, then what was it like?' he asked. 'Because from what I can remember, every single time you visited me I asked you how my kids were doing and you' – he pointed a stiff finger forward – 'you told me they were fine, that they were happy. Do you remember?'

He tilted his head to one side to look at his mother. 'Do you remember, Mum?'

'Of course I remember,' Jenny told him, 'and I also know what you're like, what you're capable of, and I know exactly how hot-tempered you are and I didn't want you to go and do something silly and end up adding years to your sentence. And yes, I know that you're a grown man but you're still my son and that means I'm entitled to worry about you – that's my job. And as your mum, lying was the only thing I could do to protect you, to make sure you didn't spend every day and night locked up worrying yourself to death. If you'd have had just the tiniest inkling of what was going on out here with the kids, knowing there was nothing you could do to help them, you would have been worried sick, and I didn't want that for you.'

'I told her to tell you.' Leaning against the door frame, Frank shook his head. 'Time and time again, I told her to be straight with you instead of trying to protect Tina.'

'I was protecting my son,' Jenny retorted, 'not Tina.'

'Fucking Tina,' Fletch growled.

'Hey, that's enough of that.' Jenny wagged her finger. 'No matter what you might think about her, that poor girl has been through the mill and back all thanks to you. You might be my son and, yes, I would do anything to protect you, but that doesn't make you completely innocent in any of this. You ruined her, you tore her heart to shreds and she did her best trying to cope with two small kiddies all on her own so don't you dare stand there and say a word against her.'

'I didn't love her, Mum; you know I didn't.'

'That didn't stop you from getting her pregnant, though, did it?' Jenny chastised.

Fletch had the grace to look away.

'She was a lovely girl, and you could have done a lot worse for yourself. All she ever wanted was to be loved, but nothing she ever did was good enough for you, was it? If only you and Tina could have settled down then none of this would have even happened.'

With his fists clamped at his side, Fletch clenched his teeth. 'Why am I even surprised that you're taking her side? You knew I didn't love her, that I didn't want to be with her, but what did you do?' He spread open his arms, his voice rising. 'Come on, Mum, what did you do? I'll tell you what she did.' He looked between Frank and Stevie, fury reflecting in his eyes. 'She took Tina's side as per fucking usual, said I had to stick it out, it didn't matter how I felt about the situation, I had to stick it out with her,' he said, spitting out the words.

'She was pregnant,' Jenny cried. 'You couldn't turn your back on the girl; there was Austin to think about.'

'What, like you did, you mean?'

Screwing up her face, Jenny recoiled away from her son.

'Well come on, Mum, answer the fucking question. Like you looked out for Austin when Tina the druggie was abusing him?'

As she shook her head, Jenny's shoulders slumped. 'You don't know that it even was Tina.'

'No, so who was it, then?' Fletch tilted his chin in the air. 'If it wasn't Tina then who was it?' He narrowed his eyes. 'What's the name of this bloke she was seeing?'

Jenny, Frank and Stevie shared a nervous glance.

'Well, who is he?' Fletch roared.

'He was just some random bloke she'd shacked up with.' It was Stevie who answered.

'You said he runs a firm?'

'Yeah.' Stevie waved his hand in dismissal. 'I'm not talking about the sort of firm Billy King was running; this bloke is small-time, got a couple of heavies that run around after him, that's about the extent of it. Now look, come on, Fletch.' He held up his hands. 'None of this is your mum's fault, is it? She did her best, she took the kids in and looked after them, didn't she? She did her bit.'

Wiping the palm of his hand across his face, Fletch exhaled loudly and slumped down onto the sofa. 'I can't get my head around any of this. I really believed my kids were safe.' He looked up at his mum. 'Do they still live here with you?'

Glad to be back on neutral territory, Jenny came to sit beside her son. It was the closest they had physically been in the last twenty-two years without cameras or a prison guard watching their every move. She clasped his hand tightly in hers. 'Austin has a flat over Barking way with his girlfriend and their daughter,' she said gently, 'and as for Kit, well, she's married now, darling, and lives with her husband.'

'Married?' Snatching back his hand, Fletch leant his elbows on his knees and held his head in his hands. His mum might as well have kicked him in the gut, he was so shocked. 'My little girl is married, and I didn't even know.'

'It was a very quiet affair,' Jenny told him. 'Kit didn't want a big fuss; they didn't even have a reception or honeymoon.'

'But I still should have been there to give her away.' As he rubbed at the back of his neck, Fletch's shoulders slumped downwards. To say he was devastated was an understatement. Not only had he missed out on watching his daughter grow up, he'd also missed out on one of the happiest days of her life. 'I'm her dad; that was my job.' He dragged the sleeve of his shirt across his eyes and looked up, his voice ever so slightly breaking. 'Who walked her down the aisle? Was it you, Frank?'

'There was no aisle.' Jenny looked over at her brother. 'It was a registry office, darling. Like I've already said, it was a very low-key wedding.'

'So who is he?' Fletch asked as he looked around him. 'Who's the lucky man?'

A deathly silence fell across the room, making the fine hairs on Fletch's arm prickle. 'Well?' he demanded. 'Who is he?'

Stevie blew out his cheeks. 'Rosco,' he said with a scowl.

'Rosco?' Sitting upright, a jolt of recognition rippled through Fletch's body.

'Yeah, Rosco.' Stevie shot an apologetic glance in Jenny's direction; he'd given his word that they would keep Fletch out of the loop for as long as possible but seeing as his best mate had asked the question, he could hardly claim that he didn't know the name of Kit's husband. 'The biggest cunt this side of the water, if you ask me, but who am I to say anything? She wanted to marry him; she was hellbent on it, in fact. Beats me why – he doesn't exactly have a lot going for him.'

Rosco... the name reverberated inside Fletch's mind and he sat up a little straighter. 'Rosco Taylor?'

'Yeah that's him.' Stevie screwed up his face. 'How do you know him? You were already banged up when he first came on the scene.'

'Know him?' Fletch spat back. 'I was inside with the wanker – it was me who marked him. I was the one who gave him that scar on his arm.'

Stevie's skin turned ashen. 'I didn't know,' he muttered as he looked between Jenny and Frank. 'How were we supposed to know who he is?'

Fletch snapped his head up to look at his friend. 'I'm gonna kill him.' Sitting forward in the seat, anger pounded through his veins and as he clenched his fists, the muscles across his chest strained against his cotton shirt. 'I'm gonna do the ponce and this time I'll make sure that I slice more than just his arm.'

## 7

It wasn't often that Kit ventured over to her brother's flat but today she was making an exception.

After parking her Mercedes, she climbed out, clicked the fob to activate the central locking system and then made her way across the car park towards the block of flats.

The stench that came from inside the block was enough to make her wrinkle her nose in disgust. At the foot of the stairwell was a puddle of urine and as she ventured further up she had to step over strewn litter, a used condom and what looked suspiciously like animal faeces, although from what she knew of the inhabitants it could well have been human waste.

'How do you live in this dump?' she asked her brother once he'd opened the front door.

'Easy.' Austin grinned. 'It's cheap and that suits me down to the ground.' He slumped down onto a sofa, a rickety orange velvet affair that reminded Kit of a fifties throwback, and sparked up a joint.

'Doesn't Sheree ever clean this place?' Kit asked him as she gingerly took a seat on the edge of the stained sofa. From day one she and her brother's girlfriend had never hit it off. They were never going to become the best of friends, and she had a sneaky suspicion that Sheree was jealous of her, jealous of the close bond that she and Austin shared, not to mention her house, car, job, lifestyle; it must all seem so glamorous to an airhead like Sheree. If only she knew the sacrifices she had to make for her way of life.

She glanced around the room. It was so cluttered that every available surface had been crammed with what she could only describe as non-essential crap: the floor was littered with her niece's toys and what looked like half of her wardrobe. Whether the clothes were clean or dirty was anyone's guess. Thankfully, it didn't smell as bad as usual, and she wondered if Sheree or maybe even her brother had collected up the soiled nappies from the kitchen since her last visit and disposed of them.

Austin shrugged his shoulders. 'You know what she's like; she's more concerned with getting a spray tan or having her nails done.'

'Well, it's disgusting,' Kit told him. 'How can you bring a baby up in this shithole?'

'No more disgusting than having to share a bed with that cunt Rosco.' Austin pointed the joint towards her. 'Speaking of which, is he dead yet?'

'No,' Kit retorted.

'Ah well, I can live in hope.' He ducked down as his sister threw a cushion at his head. 'I bet he's going off his swede. The thought of someone getting one over on him must be driving him out of his nut.'

'You know full well it is.' She snatched the joint out of his hand and took a deep toke. Coughing as she exhaled, she passed it back. 'Where did you get this shit from?'

Austin grinned. 'Mickey Davis.' He shrugged his shoulders.

'He owed me some dough and in the end I gave him the option: he either gave me his grow or I blasted his head clean off his shoulders.'

'You're not thinking of selling this crap, are you?' she asked, still coughing.

'Nah.' He glanced down at the smouldering joint between his fingers. 'You're right, it's shit.'

'Where is it, Aus?' She gave him a pleading look. 'I know it was you. What have you done with it? Where's the coke?'

Austin raised his eyebrows and, after studying his sister for a moment or two, he lounged back on the sofa. 'You know at Nan's house, in my old room?'

'Yeah.' Kit narrowed her eyes. 'What about it?'

'Well, if you pull back the floorboards there's this space, it's big enough to actually crawl inside.'

'And?' The hairs on the back of Kit's neck stood up on end and she slammed her hand over her mouth. 'Please tell me you haven't hidden it at Nan's house?'

'It's the last place anyone would ever think of looking for it!' Austin laughed.

'Jesus Christ, Aus!' Jumping up from the sofa, Kit bellowed at her brother. 'Are you out of your fucking mind? You've used Nan's house to stash the coke?'

'Chill out.' Austin laughed. 'It's not like she's ever gonna find out, is it?'

'I'm not worried about Nan finding out; I'm more concerned about what Rosco's going to do when he gets wind of this. He'll kill her, you know he will, and then he'll come for you. He's going to destroy you over this; you do understand that, don't you?'

'And I bet he would love that, wouldn't he?' Austin's voice was thick as he inhaled the smoke deep into his lungs. 'That cunt has wanted to get rid of me for years.' He stood up, offered across the joint and as his sister took it from him, he slung his arm around her shoulders.

'I mean it, Aus.' Kit looked up at him. 'When, not if, he finds out about this, I won't be able to protect you any more. Everything goes out the window, the deal's over and he won't let the fact that you're my brother stand in his way. All you've done is given him the ammunition to get rid of you once and for all.'

'Relax, he's not going to find out.' He took the joint back and placed it between his lips. 'I've already got a buyer for it anyway, some little firm in Manchester.' He laughed out loud. 'They nearly chewed my arm off to get their hands on the gear.'

The very thought of her brother doing a drugs deal and selling on Rosco's merchandise brought ice-cold fear to Kit's heart. He rarely made it out of bed in the morning without having a zoot first, let alone had the sense to traipse halfway across the country and deal with a firm of Mancunian heavies. 'Just give it back to him, Aus, please, dump it somewhere and then tip him off.'

'Fuck off.' Austin laughed. 'And fuck Rosco; it's mine now. Well, mine, Mark and Charlie's.' He paused for a moment and tilted his head to one side. 'Here, you haven't heard from Mark, have you? No one can get hold of him.'

Kit's mouth was suddenly dry and, giving a slight shake of her head, she turned her face away then squeezed her eyes shut tight in a bid to stem the tears that were never too far away. She was still unable to erase the image of Mark's body from her mind. The way Rosco's foot soldiers had carelessly tipped her brother's friend onto the thick sheet of polythene sickened her to the core.

'I was thinking.' Austin scratched at his head. 'Do you think Dad might want in on the deal? I thought he might still have some contacts who'd be interested.'

'I thought you said you already had a buyer?'

'Yeah, I do.' Austin laughed, pulling his sister under his arm. 'But you never know, there might be someone out there who'll pay a lot more for it.'

Kit shook her head. Her brother was playing a dangerous game, one that she had a sinking feeling he wasn't going to win.

* * *

In quick succession, Rosco clenched and unclenched his fists. The cargo, or to be more precise, the missing cargo, was the only topic of conversation that came out of his mouth. The fact it had been stolen from right underneath his nose not only galled him but until now had also been what he'd considered as downright unthinkable. In fact, he likened it to something straight out of one of his worst nightmares. Not only was there a great deal of money involved but the firm he'd been dealing with were shady characters who, in any normal circumstances, he wasn't fool enough to want to cross.

'Whoever it is...' Dennis Maguire, Rosco's right-hand man, lounged back in a chair and gave a disgruntled shake of his head. 'They've gone to ground.'

'What do you mean, "whoever it is"? I know who it fucking was: that little scrote Austin. This has got that little cunt's name written all over it.'

Dennis sighed. For as long as he'd known Rosco, Austin had been the contention of his life, and was blamed for pretty much everything that went wrong.

Getting up from his seat, Rosco stormed across the office and slammed the door closed with such ferociousness that it almost came off its hinges. He rubbed at his temples; the constant pounding of the music that came from the club below was beginning to give him a headache. He lifted a balloon glass half filled with whiskey to his mouth, chugged back the contents, then wiped the back of his hand across his fleshy lips. 'Has he shown his face yet?'

Dennis rubbed the palm of his hand over the dark stubble that covered his jaw and shook his head. He was a good-looking man and years younger than Rosco. He was also much fitter and stronger than his boss. Shifting position, he toyed with the small gold cross that hung from a thin chain around his neck. Despite being of Irish descent and brought up as a Catholic, he wasn't particularly religious. 'No one has seen him, but...'

'What?' Rosco growled out.

'I've heard a rumour,' Dennis said, 'and it comes from a reliable source...' He paused for a moment, making sure that he had Rosco's full attention. 'It was a mate of mine, actually.'

'Yeah, and?' As he resumed his position behind the desk, Rosco leant back in his chair. 'Get to the point; I want the facts, not the drivel that goes along with it.'

Dennis cleared his throat. 'I've heard that the old man is out.'

Rosco's interest was piqued and, sitting forward, he steepled his fingers in front of him. 'Say that again.'

'I've heard that Kit and Austin's old man is fresh out of nick.'

'Yeah, that's exactly what I thought you said.' Slumping back in the chair, a crooked smirk spread across Rosco's face. Fletch: the name conjured up a memory from his distant past and his fingertips automatically reached out to touch the six-inch scar that ran the length of his forearm. The pale pink, hairless skin felt smooth to his touch. It was a stark, constant reminder of their last meeting. 'Well, well, well,' he said with a grin, 'looks like I could end up killing two birds with one stone after all.'

## 8

Tina was crying, as was usual when she was on a comedown. Tears slipped down her cheeks and, pulling the cuff of her coat over her hand, she wiped away a trail of snot from underneath her nose.

'My kids,' she wailed. 'When they were little, I loved them so much; they were my whole world.'

A woman with long, greasy, straggly grey hair nodded her head sympathetically. She was at least twenty years Tina's senior and was affectionately referred to as Mother Hen among the group of junkies and runaways that frequented a squat just off Longbridge Road in Dagenham.

'I mean, I really loved them,' she said with a hiccup, 'but they don't love me any more.' Her voice lowered to a whisper and her eyes darted around the room. 'Do you wanna know why not?'

Mother Hen sucked a greasy strand of hair into her mouth and nodded her head, eyes wide, relishing the idea of learning some juicy gossip.

'It's because of him.' She began to wail again, tears and snot mingling together. 'It's all because of him. He destroyed our bond, you know.' She crossed two fingers and then, using her free hand, tore them apart. 'Just like that, he destroyed everything we had.' She gripped onto the woman's arm, her bony, ice-cold fingers clinging on like a vice. 'He still watches me,' she said in a whisper. 'He follows me.'

As if on cue, the two women peered fearfully towards the open door; a large figure filled the doorway.

'Tina.' Stevie's face loomed into view.

'What do you want?' Even as her shoulders physically relaxed, a scowl was present across Tina's face.

'A word.' He stepped cautiously inside the room, conscious not to touch or lean against anything. 'Now,' he said with a nod of his head.

Doubled over as if she were in physical pain, Tina began to wail. 'No,' she cried, 'no, no, no.'

'Tina, get up.' Through gritted teeth, Stevie growled out the words. He turned to look behind him, spotted a face peering through the grimy window and lifted his hand in the air. 'It's okay,' he called out, 'she's had some bad news, that's all.' He turned back around. 'Tina, get the fuck up.'

'Does he know?' Still doubled over, fear was clearly audible in Tina's voice.

'No, not yet.'

She began to wail even louder and Stevie tentatively reached out his arm before screwing up his face and pulling his hand back. *Fuck touching her*, he thought to himself. *Let's face it, she could have been anywhere.*

'You have to help me.' From out of nowhere, she lurched towards him, her arms outstretched, her eyes wide and panic-stricken. 'You know how to keep him calm, how to keep him under control; he listens to you. He'll do what you tell him.'

'He's not a dog on a fucking leash, Tina.' Holding up his

hands, Stevie retreated away from her. 'I can't put a muzzle on him, can I?'

'He's going to kill me.' Her hands flew to her mouth. 'My babies,' she cried. 'If he finds out about the babies, he's going to murder me.'

'He already knows.' He watched Tina's eyes open even further until they were almost bulging out of her head and hastily rephrased himself. 'He knows some of it, okay; I didn't tell him everything.'

'You didn't tell him about...' She whispered out the words as if afraid to say them out loud.

'No.' Stevie was quick to answer. He glanced back to the house and stuffed his hand inside his trouser pocket, toying with the bundle of notes he'd taken out from a cash machine on his way over to the squat. Against his better judgement, he'd fully intended to give her some cash, tell her to make a run for it and start a new life somewhere far away, but on second thoughts he knew she would do no such thing. The temptation of seeing Fletch again would be too much for her to resist. 'Look, I'm just giving you a heads up on the situation, letting you know the score. He's seen the kids...'

'He's seen Kit?' The tears were gone and in their place anger flashed across her face. 'He's seen that little bitch.' She placed her hands on her hips and her expression was one that Stevie instantly recognised. He'd seen it so many times before: hatred. 'Oh, I bet she just loved that, didn't she.' She began to pace the length of the small patio area, jealousy raging to the fore. 'Oh, I bet she did, the fucking whore.'

'Hey, enough of that,' Stevie roared. 'Whatever you might think of her, she's still your daughter.'

'Daughter,' Tina screeched. She spat a blob of phlegm on an uneven patio slab, narrowly missing Stevie's shoes in the process.

'She's no daughter of mine and you can tell the little whore that an' all.'

Holding up his hands, Stevie backed away. 'Sort yourself out, Teen,' he said, 'for your sake as well as your kids.'

With those parting words, he stormed back through the squat. All the while, Tina shouted after him.

'It's all her fault,' she screamed. 'She did this to me, she did this.'

For the past hour, Fletch had been standing outside the club where his daughter worked on the off-chance that he might see her come or go. All he wanted was ten minutes of her time so that he could explain the circumstances that had driven him to murder his father. It was imperative that she heard the truth from his own mouth. Who knew what lies Tina could have fed her as a child, and he, better than anyone, knew just how manipulative and spiteful the mother of his children could be.

Every time the door to the club opened, his heart would beat that little bit faster. So far he'd seen four women come and go and as they had passed him by they had given him more than just an inquisitive glance. He suddenly wondered if he came across as a creep; perhaps they thought he was a punter. The very notion was enough to make his cheeks flush a bright shade of pink.

As she exited the club, Kit slung her handbag over her shoulder and made her way down the short flight of steps that led to the pavement.

'Kitty.'

On hearing her name being called, Kit turned her head. The image of her father standing before her was enough to make her want to roll her eyes, more so out of agitation than anything else. She'd already told him once that she didn't want anything to do with him. 'What do you want?'

Fletch gave her a gentle smile. 'Just to talk.' He gave a light laugh. 'I've been waiting here for more than an hour hoping to catch you.'

Kit swallowed down her anger and turned to walk away. 'I don't have time for this; I'm meeting someone.'

'Hey.' Fletch caught hold of her hand. 'All I'm asking for is ten minutes of your time; just hear me out, and if you still don't want to know, I'll understand and back off.'

Snatching her hand back, Kit scowled. 'And I've already told you I'm meeting someone. I'm not interested in having a cosy little chat with you, so do us both a favour and leave me alone.'

'He's not right for you, you know that, don't you?'

As she made to walk away, Kit narrowed her eyes and swung back around to face her father.

'I'm talking about your husband. I know him; I spent years banged up with the ponce. He's a slimy fucker, always has been, and you, my darling, deserve so much better than the likes of him.'

Kit's heart began to beat faster. She would never have admitted it out loud but she felt trapped by her marriage, so much so that at times she felt as though she couldn't breathe. 'I know exactly who and what my husband is, thank you, not that my marriage is any of your concern.'

Fletch's mouth dropped and he rocked back on his heels. 'You know what he's like and you still married him?'

A bitter laugh escaped from Kit's lips and as she leant towards her father, a flash of anger creased her face. 'Save the caring fathers act for Aus,' she said, looking him up and down with a sneer. 'Out of the two of us, he's the only one who'll actually fall for your crap.'

With those parting words, she turned on her heel and walked away. As he called out to her, she quickened her pace, afraid that the ice wall she'd put up around her heart may ever so slightly crack.

# 9

An hour later, Kit parked her car in a secluded car park on the outskirts of Epping Forest. Taking a quick glance around her, she switched off the ignition and stepped out of the car.

'Well?' Her eyebrows were arched as she walked across the gravel to where a man was leaning against his car at the far side of the car park. His hands were shoved into the pockets of his jacket and as she approached him, he straightened up.

'He fell for it hook, line and sinker, just like you said he would.'

Kit's shoulders visibly relaxed and as she pressed her fingers to her lips she closed her eyes. The effect was more than Dennis Maguire could stand and, grabbing her by the wrist, he pulled her closer to him.

'Are you happy now?' He wrapped his arms around her and kissed her forehead. 'I've done what you asked and told him that your old man is out.'

Kit nodded her head. Relieved would be a better word for how she was feeling. All she'd needed was for Dennis to plant a seed of suspicion inside Rosco's mind, and she knew from experience that seed would grow into something that resembled a paranoia that would fully consume him.

'I still don't like this, babe. You're playing a dangerous game.'

'More dangerous than this?' She pulled herself out of his arms and gestured between the two of them. 'More dangerous than you fucking the boss's wife?'

Dennis's eyebrows shot up. 'That's not what this is.' He searched her face. 'You know it isn't. I love you; you're not just some random bird I'm shagging.' He shook his head and gave a bitter laugh. 'You don't realise how much I'm putting my neck on the line to be with you. If you knew half the shit that's going on, it would make your head spin. I didn't plan for this to happen, but it has, and I wouldn't change that for the world.'

Rubbing the palm of her hand across her face, tears sprang to Kit's eyes. 'I know and I'm sorry,' she told him. 'I didn't mean what I said, you know I didn't.' She reached out and curled her fingers around his forearm and looked up into his handsome face. 'It's just my brother – I'm worried. I can't protect him; I can't wish all of this away. I can't turn back time and put that coke back.'

'Austin,' Dennis warned, 'is a loose cannon, he always has been, and if we're not careful he's going to bring us all down with him.'

'I can control him,' she spat back.

Dennis raised his eyebrows. 'You haven't done much of a job reining him in so far, have you?' Instantly he regretted his choice of words and as she glared up at him, he held up his hands. 'I'm sorry,' he said with a shake of his head, 'but you're not his keeper, Kit. You can't control what he does.'

'He needs to get things off his chest; he needs...'

'I get it.' Dennis pulled her close again and hugged her to him tight, relishing the feel of her body close to his. 'I'm just not so sure putting your dad in the frame was the right thing to do.'

'Rosco hates my dad almost as much as he hates Austin, if not even more; it's where all of this stems from.' She was thoughtful for a moment, 'Look,' she sighed. 'I don't like this any more than you do, but I have to divert him away from my brother. And you know what Aus is like; he doesn't think things though, he never does.'

'Yeah.' Dennis blew out his cheeks. 'And that's what worries me.'

'Don't worry.' She smiled tightly up at him. 'I'm going to take care of this. I'm going to take control of the situation.'

\* \* \*

Austin was becoming increasingly concerned. He snapped his mobile phone closed and chewed on his thumbnail. Where the fuck was Mark? No way would he just up and leave, at least not without taking his share of the cocaine with him.

Shrugging on his jacket, he slammed his way out of the flat and as he made his way down the stairwell, he kicked the discarded trash out of his path.

At the entrance he lit a joint, shoved open the door and made his way around the deserted children's playground to where he'd parked his car. As he climbed inside, turned the ignition and pulled out onto the road, he failed to notice the dark blue Range Rover on his tail.

\* \* \*

Charlie Withers was rolling a joint. The sickly-sweet scent of cannabis resonated throughout his bedsit, not that he appeared to care. As far as he was concerned it was more or less legal, so who gave a rat's arse if one of the neighbours grassed him up to the old bill. In fact, if the filth did turn up on his doorstep, he would tell them as much. He knew his rights and as long as he wasn't actually dealing there was fuck all anyone could do about it. Oh, he might get a slap on the wrist but that would be the extent of any police visit, should they even decide to actually turn up.

Licking along the length of a cigarette paper, he placed the joint between his lips, sparked up and exhaled a thick cloud of smoke.

A hammering at the front door made him frown and, clambering off the divan bed that doubled as a sofa, he swaggered across the small room and threw open the door.

'Fuck me, Aus, you've got a knock like a fucking copper.'

Austin didn't answer and, making his way inside, he flopped down onto the bed.

'What's up with you?' Taking a deep toke of the joint, he passed it across.

'Mark.'

Charlie frowned. 'What about him?'

Austin shook his head and passed the joint back. 'Where the fuck is he?'

'I dunno.' Charlie ran a hand through his blonde hair and shrugged. 'He's probably shacked up with some bird.'

'What, for two fucking weeks?' Austin bit back. 'You know as well as I do that he'd be bored out of his nut after a day.'

'Well, I dunno.' Charlie gave a second shrug. He flopped down beside his mate and tried to think. 'Maybe he just wanted some time out; he could have gone on holiday or something.'

'A holiday?' Austin screwed up his face. 'Get real.'

'Well, I don't know, it was only a suggestion.'

As he chewed on the skin surrounding his thumbnail, Austin was deep in thought. 'I'm worried,' he said.

'About what?' In all the years he'd known Austin, Charlie had never known his oldest friend to be concerned about anything, at least nothing that he admitted out loud to, anyway. Oh, he knew Kit's marriage to Rosco was something of a worry but even then Austin passed it off as a series of well-honed put-downs rather than came out and blatantly said he was feeling troubled.

'What if something's happened to Mark? What if...' Austin studied the dotted blood on the side of his thumbnail, not wanting to look his mate in the eyes. 'What if that fat cunt caught wind of what we did and comes after us next?'

'Are you being serious?' Charlie's voice rose a notch and his gaze flicked towards the front door. 'You said the plan was fool-proof, that Rosco would never find out.'

Austin raised his eyebrows. 'Yeah, you're right, I did say that.' He nodded towards the joint between Charlie's fingers. 'I've been smoking too much of that shit,' he said with a smile that didn't quite reach his eyes. 'It's making me paranoid.'

Charlie let out a sigh of relief. 'You fucking nutter,' he said, flopping down onto the bed.

He'd barely made himself comfortable when a hammering at the front door made them both turn to look at one another.

'Who's that?' Charlie asked.

'How the fuck would I know? It's your gaff,' Austin answered in a low growl.

Easing himself off the bed, Charlie made his way across the bedsit and, glancing back over his shoulder, he gingerly placed his hand on the door handle. 'Yeah, who is it?'

'Open up,' a gruff voice replied.

Charlie turned his head, panic clearly visible in his eyes.

'Open the door.' As quietly as he could, Austin slipped off the bed and reached out for the baseball bat Charlie kept propped up against the wall.

As Charlie pulled down the handle, the door flew open, smashing him up against the wall in the process.

'Where is she?' a male voice spat out. 'Where the fuck is she?'

Dropping the bat to his side, Austin's mouth fell open. 'Dad,' he exclaimed. 'What are you doing here?'

## 10

'Where is she?' On leaving his daughter, Fletch had driven straight to his son's flat. It was only by sheer chance that he'd been able to follow his son across town. His gaze lingered on the baseball bat in Austin's fist. 'Where's your mum?'

'She's not here.' Throwing the bat to the floor, Austin shrugged. 'Why would she be? This is Charlie's gaff, not mine,' he said, slumping down on the bed.

'I wouldn't have that skank in here,' Charlie piped up, then, remembering the skank he was referring to was in fact Austin's mother, his hands shot up in the air. 'No offence, mate.' He turned to look at Fletch. 'The last time I let her in, she stole a couple of PlayStation games.' He gave the games console a wistful glance. 'They were my favourite games an' all.'

Fletch ran his tongue across his teeth. Satisfied that Tina wasn't actually hiding out in the tiny bedsit, he allowed his shoulders to relax. 'Is she still living at the house?'

As he and Charlie shared a glance, Austin shook his head. 'Nah, Dad, she sold it years ago.'

'Right.' Fletch nodded. Everything made sense to him now.

After borrowing Stevie's car, he'd driven over to Rainham and parked up outside the house that his money had bought. He'd thought that the property had looked a bit too well kept for someone who supposedly spent most of the day out of their nut on whatever narcotics they could get their hands on. 'Where does she live, then?' He looked between his son and Charlie. 'If she's not living in Rainham then I'm guessing it's got to be somewhere local?'

Austin took a few moments to think the question over. 'Look, Dad,' he began, chewing at the side of his thumbnail again. 'Forget about Mum; she ain't well,' he said, tapping his fingers against his temple. 'Up here, she's not well.'

'From what I've heard, she's a junkie,' Fletch snarled back. 'Big difference.'

'Yeah, she is.' As he shot a glance towards Charlie, shame flooded through Austin; he still found it difficult to admit what his mother had become. 'She's an addict; she can't help the things she does. Like I said, she's not well in the head.'

Fletch nodded and, narrowing his eyes, he asked, 'And who's this bloke she was shacked up with?'

'He ain't important.' Getting to his feet, Austin steered his father towards the door. 'I'll give you a bell when it's time to shift the goods,' he said, looking over his shoulder and giving Charlie a knowing wink.

\* \* \*

With one half of her listening out for the front door, the other half of Jenny was listening to Tina as she alternated between crying one minute and ranting the next.

'You knew he would be back one day, darling,' she told her as gently as she could.

Fresh tears filled Tina's eyes and for a brief moment Jenny could see the young woman she had been before the drugs had taken hold, the same young girl who had loved her son, so much so that at times it had been painful to witness.

'But why now?' Tina cried. She pushed her straggly hair out of her eyes. 'If I'd known, if I'd had warning that he was coming back then I could have sorted myself out, I could have got my hair cut.' She reached up to touch the limp, greasy strands. 'I could have at least made myself look presentable for him.'

Shaking her head, Jenny reached out to clasp Tina's hand. It was far too late for any of that. Deep down in her heart, she had always known that her son had never wanted Tina in his life. From day one there hadn't been any feelings there, at least on Fletch's part anyway. He'd told her so enough times, and more than once she'd wondered if there had been another woman who'd caught his eye. 'I'll tell you what, why don't you go and run a nice hot bubble bath? It'd be a start. Go on.' She jerked her head towards the ceiling. 'I'll put some fresh clothes out on the bed for you.'

As she sniffed back her tears, Tina got to her feet. 'I did love him, you know,' she said, referring to Fletch, her voice childlike. 'If...' She screwed up her face, her expression filled with a mixture of anger and hatred. 'If that bastard hadn't swept me off my feet, if he hadn't fed me with empty lies and promises, I would have still been waiting for Fletch to come out; I would have stayed faithful to him. In here' – she tapped a finger against her chest – 'he was the only man I ever wanted.'

Jenny took a deep breath before answering; they had had this discussion so many times over the years. 'It wasn't your fault, darling,' she said, giving her the usual, expected response. 'Now go on.' She patted Tina's arm. 'Go and have a nice hot bath.'

As Tina made her way up the stairs, Jenny walked into the lounge and came to stand in front of the window.

'Wasn't her fault?' Frank's lips were pursed. 'Then whose fucking fault was it?' he spat out.

Still staring out the window, Jenny shook her head. 'Not now, Frank,' she told her brother.

'I blame you for this; you've mollycoddled that girl far too much and this,' Frank said, throwing up his arms, 'is the upshot.' He glanced towards the mantelpiece. 'It's those kids you should have been looking out for, your own flesh and blood, not her up there. She was nothing to us, Fletch was dead right about that; she's not family,' he said, jerking his thumb towards the ceiling, 'and I can tell you this for nothing.' He spread open a newspaper and laid it across his lap. 'When he finds out the truth, don't come running to me; don't say I didn't warn you.'

Fear clutched at Jenny's heart and as she turned to face her brother it suddenly dawned on her that the secrets they had kept quiet for so many years were about to be revealed and there was nothing she, or anyone else for that matter, could do to stop the truth from coming out.

## 11

'You don't keep a dog and bark yourself' had never been one of Rosco's mottos; he liked to get his hands dirty and did so frequently with vigour. Stamping his size eleven steel-toe-capped boot repeatedly down onto an unconscious man's head, he spewed out a tirade of abuse.

'You fucking cunt,' he screamed. 'You no-good fucking cunt.'

Witnessing his boss unleash his formidable temper was becoming pretty much an everyday occurrence for Dennis Maguire, and as he leant against the door of the Portakabin, his expression was one of boredom. The problem was he'd seen it all before and his gut instinct told him it wouldn't be the last time he would watch his boss kick seven bells of shit out of someone, either.

'You fucking bastard.' Rosco stamped his foot down once more for good measure and as he began to pace the floor, steam was virtually coming out of his ears. 'He knows something,' he spat. In quick succession, he kicked out at the comatose body; his heavy boots connected with the soft tissue with a sickening thud.

'He knows exactly what fucking happened; he knows who took my gear.'

Dennis glanced down at the broken body of the man who'd been driving the van on the night of the hijack. It had only been a matter of time before Rosco took his anger out on someone in his firm, starting with the driver. Even he could see the poor man hadn't stood a chance; there wasn't much he could have done to stop the hijack, not when he'd had a semi-automatic pistol shoved up his nose, other than let the thieves take what they wanted and then hope and pray they didn't finish him off afterwards.

Blood and brain matter splattered the walls and ceiling and the unmistakable iron scent of claret filled the air. 'I think he's dead,' Dennis said matter-of-factly.

Rosco stopped pacing. Still breathing heavily through his flared nostrils, he began to rip apart the buttons of his stained shirt, revealing his flabby belly that he made no sign of trying to hide. 'Get rid of him,' he barked out, addressing the foot soldiers who waited patiently for his instruction.

Watching as the men in Rosco's employment dragged the corpse out of the cabin and into a waiting car, Dennis handed over a jerrycan full to the brim with petrol. 'Once you've dumped the car, torch it.' He turned to look at the car in question, a brand-spanking new, gun-metal grey Audi, and gave a shake of his head. 'Pity really; it's a nice car.'

The men nodded in agreement.

Discarding his shirt, blood peppered Rosco's face and arms, and, taking a damp paper towel, he rubbed himself clean and pulled on a fresh shirt. Lighting a cigarette, he squinted as the curling smoke filtered above his head, stinging his eyes in the process. 'I want that little scrote brought to me.' He stabbed the cigarette in Dennis's direction. 'I want the bastard found and brought to me kicking and fucking screaming if need be.'

Dennis swallowed deeply, the only sign he gave away that he felt uneasy with Rosco's request. 'Which bastard would that be?' he asked. 'The father or the son?'

As he reached into his trouser pocket and pulled out his car keys, Rosco grinned; it was a sickening grin that reminded Dennis of a predatory wolf.

'The son,' he spat as he made for the door. 'I've got something a lot more fitting in mind for the father and, believe me' – he laughed – 'it's going to be fucking spectacular.'

\* \* \*

Opening the front door, Austin gave his sister a wide grin. 'Twice in one week – I am honoured.'

Kit rolled her eyes. 'Cut the crap, Aus.' She laughed. 'And just let me in.'

Walking through to the lounge, Austin flopped down onto the velvet sofa. 'Well,' he asked once Kit had taken a seat beside him. 'To what do I owe this pleasure?' He reached out to grab a large polythene zip bag from the coffee table that was filled to the brim with cannabis and began to build a joint. 'Because I'm ninety-nine per cent sure you didn't come all this way just for a toke on this shit,' he said, nodding down at the cannabis he'd taken from Mickey Davis in exchange for a debt he was owed.

Kit shook her head. She looked around the cluttered room; her niece's clothes were still present and flung into an untidy pile in the middle of the floor. 'Is Sheree out?'

'Yeah, she took the baby over to see her mum and dad.' He gave a half laugh. 'She's done me a favour, to be honest. There's only so much I can take of her in one day; her voice goes right through my head when she's on one and throwing a paddy, which, trust me, is often.'

'I take it we're talking about Lacey and not Sheree?' Kit raised her eyebrows.

'Yes, Lacey.' Austin cocked an eyebrow; there was no love lost between his sister and girlfriend, and he was the one stuck in the middle of them both. 'Sheree's not so bad once you get to know her. She's actually all right; her bark is worse than her bite.'

'I'll take your word for it.' In truth, Kit had no intention of getting to know her brother's girlfriend any better than she already had.

'Well, come on.' He licked along the length of a cigarette paper, flicked his lighter across the roach then tapped the singed cardboard on the coffee table before placing the joint between his lips. 'The suspense is killing – what do you want?'

'I was thinking...'

'Spit it out!' he joked. 'I ain't got all day. As you can see' – he gestured to his tracksuit bottoms and bare feet – 'I'm a busy man.'

Rolling her lips together, Kit looked her brother in the eyes. 'I want in.'

'What?' Exhaling a cloud of smoke, Austin screwed up his face. 'What are you talking about, you want in?'

'The coke.' As she spoke, Kit's voice didn't so much as waver. 'I want in on the deal.'

\* \* \*

Stevie was watching his friend closely. They were at his home in Upminster and after sitting his two daughters at the kitchen table with a large bowl of chocolate ice cream in front of them, he had closed the door to the lounge so that he and Fletch could speak in private.

'Every time I picture her face I get this feeling in here.' Fletch gestured to his chest. 'Do you know what I mean? Like I want to rip her head clean off her shoulders. All that woman has ever done is cause me grief; I wish I'd never clapped eyes on her.' He rubbed at his temples. 'If Suzy hadn't finished with me, I would never have even given Tina a second glance; I wouldn't have given her the time of day and you know it.'

Stevie raised his eyebrows and, blowing out his cheeks, he sank back against the cushions. Even after all these years Suzy was still the love of Fletch's life, and with the internet now at his disposal he wouldn't be surprised if Fletch had already tried to track her down. 'No matter how much you might want to hurt Tina, you can't. She's the mother of your kids; whether you like or not, that makes her untouchable, mate.'

'I already know that,' Fletch groaned, 'but it doesn't stop me from wanting to kill her for what she's caused, does it? How the fuck did she manage to get through over three hundred grand of my kids' money?' He let out a bitter laugh and shook his head. 'And all this time I thought that even if I weren't around at least they had some cash to fall back on – at least she could feed them, buy them clothes and toys. It's not as though she even had to pay rent or a mortgage; she had enough money to buy a house outright.'

'Yeah, I forgot about that. What will you do about the money now? I mean, by rights it was yours, wasn't it?'

'Nothing.' Fletch shrugged. 'I gave it to her.' He gave a bitter laugh. 'It's not like I can actually go to the old bill and report it as theft, is it? I didn't exactly come by the money legally to begin with.' He sighed. 'What would even be the point? It's gone, she spunked the lot; there's no way of getting it back now.'

Stevie was thoughtful for a few moments. 'So what are you going to do about Tina, then? Give her a swerve?'

'I don't know,' Fletch said with a sigh. He sat forward and chewed on his thumbnail as he studied Stevie's face. 'How close are you to Austin?'

Stevie shrugged. 'I've tried looking out for him over the years, not that he listens to much of anything I have to say. He's got too much of his old man in him,' he said with a wink. 'He does what he wants, when he wants, regardless of the consequences.'

Fletch gave a low chuckle. 'Yeah, he gave me that impression.' Leaning his forearms on his knees, his tone became serious. 'But I do want to talk to you about him.'

'Go on.' Stevie raised his eyebrows. 'I'm all ears.'

'I dunno.' Fletch shook his head. 'I just... I just get this vibe from him.' He opened out his arms. 'I can't explain it; there's something, but I don't know what it is, it's like...' He was thoughtful for a moment. 'Like he's into something, something big, like he's in over his head, maybe.' He shook his head. 'I don't know, it's something, I just can't put my finger on what it could be.'

Stevie nodded. 'You mean like we were at the same age. Fuck me, Fletch, we weren't exactly angels, were we? And let's face it...' He lowered his voice so that the two little girls couldn't hear what was being said; the last thing he needed was for them to relay the conversation back to his wife. As it was, Jess had already told him that she wasn't happy a convicted murderer had stepped foot inside the house and was spending time around their daughters. 'You roped me into disposing of a body long before you even killed your old man.' He shook his head. 'That was our life back then, that was how we lived, that's who we were.'

'That was different, and you know it.' Fletch's cheeks reddened at the memory of the murder he'd committed of his former boss, Billy King. At the time it had been a matter of life or death and he had chosen life. 'I just didn't want that way of life for my kids; I've never wanted that. I don't want them to live like I did. I don't want them following in my footsteps. I want more for them, I suppose. I mean, look at Kitty: I went to the club she manages and, fair enough, I'm not happy she works in a strip club, but she's doing well for herself. She's got an office and everything.' He laughed.

Stevie raised his eyebrows. The club actually belonged to Kitty; it had been a wedding gift, or a bribe, whichever way you wanted to look at it, but that was a whole can of worms he didn't want to open up just yet.

'I just want the same for Austin, I suppose. I don't want him taking the same path that I did. It's a slippery slope that leads to nowhere, mate, and once you're on it, it can only follow one of two paths: prison or in the ground.'

'Yeah, I get that.' Stevie slapped Fletch on the shoulder, all the while thinking that his mate was years too late. Whether he liked it or not, both Kit and Austin were already on the slippery slope to nowhere.

\* \* \*

Austin snapped his mouth closed and stared at his sister.

'Well?' she asked.

He gave a nervous laugh and shook his head. 'Why would I want to do that, Kit? Why would I let you in on the deal?'

'Because I'm your sister.' She laughed. 'And because you love me.'

'Who told you that?' he answered, tongue in cheek.

'Hey.' Kit threw the cushion at his head. 'And because I know about business. I haven't spent all these years with Rosco without learning a thing or two.'

Austin was still shaking his head. 'That's the problem, though – it's Rosco's gear, or at least was.' He laughed. 'And I don't want you involved; he already wants to see me dead, has done for years, and I don't want him turning on you too. I don't want that on my conscience. It's bad enough knowing that you're married to the man.' He caught hold of her hand, the tone of his voice becoming serious. 'And I know you only did that because of me; I know you don't love him, not in here.' He thumped his fist against his chest.

'Love him?' Kit snorted with derision. 'I despise him, you know that I do. What he did to us—' She gripped his hand even tighter and corrected herself. 'The way he treated you is unforgiveable; he tore our family apart, Aus. Everything that has ever gone wrong in our lives was down to him, so no, I don't love him,' she said, shaking her head. 'I never have, and I never will. I can only just stomach being in the same room as the bastard.'

Leaning back on the sofa, Austin continued to shake his head. 'I don't know, it's gonna be risky and, let's face it, Rosco will be the least of our worries. There's gonna be firms involved, real firms, Kit, men who wouldn't think twice about opening you up if this deal goes tits up.'

'I can handle it.'

Austin raised his eyebrows. 'You think you can, but you can't, not really.'

'I'm married to Rosco Taylor,' she persevered, 'and if I can handle him, I can handle anything that is thrown in my direction.'

Austin sucked his bottom lip into his mouth. Whether he liked it or not, his sister had made a valid point. She had to be a lot tougher than she looked; if nothing else, her marriage to Rosco was proof of that.

'Aus.' Kit leant in closer and clutched his hand. 'Trust me, I can handle this.'

'Okay,' he relented, 'but if at any time this gets dangerous, I want you out. I mean it, Kit – I want you gone.'

'Deal.' As she threw herself into her brother's arms, a knowing smile spread across Kit's face.

## 12

Nathan Bannerman was a nasty piece of work, something he relished in and used to his full advantage. He and his two younger brothers were considered legends among their peers and they instilled fear in the community where they ruled with an iron fist.

In a rented factory in South East London, the Bannerman brothers ran their drug empire. Every few months they moved property, staying one step ahead of the filth as they did so.

Every aspect of their business was run with precision. They only ever used burner phones, and rarely involved themselves in the day-to-day running of their business, preferring to let those further down the chain deal with any troubles that arose. At the end of the day, they were replaceable, as was everything else in the brothers' life, including their women. It wasn't often that they needed to get their hands dirty – the Bannerman name alone was more than enough to ensure that their business ran smoothly – but when they did, it was guaranteed to be spectacular.

Nathan was practically frothing at the mouth as he punched his fist repeatedly into the face of a man in his employment.

Around him, others watched the spectacle unfolding before them in silence, the majority of them too afraid that Nathan would take his anger out on them next if they dared question his tactics.

Earlier that week he'd been expecting twenty kilos of cocaine to make its way into his hands. He'd arranged to buy the charlie for a steal and was still waiting for the merchandise to manifest.

Convinced the man in question had somehow fucked up the deal, he'd decided before even entering the factory to make an example of him and as he continued to punch his fists into the unconscious man's face, he screamed out a tirade of abuse. After one final punch he stood back, pulled a handgun from the waistband of his trousers and took aim. The silence in the room reached a terrifying new level as those in close proximity scrambled to take cover.

'Leave it out, man,' a voice screamed out. 'He ain't done anything wrong.'

Nathan looked up and as his two younger brothers, Connor and Lee, egged him on, he stalked around the room looking for the culprit who'd dared question him.

'You ain't gonna stand there and take that, are you, bruv?' Connor laughed. Like his two elder brothers, he was a good-looking man. Standing at over six feet tall, he had dark hair and a muscular physique, all thanks to the many hours he put in at the gym. 'He's mugging you right off.'

Without saying a word, Nathan's hand whipped out and he grasped the neck of a young lad no older than fifteen and pulled him roughly towards him.

'What did you just say to me?' Nathan's lips were pulled into a snarl as he hissed out the words.

The boy whimpered and, clearly terrified, his voice when he spoke was high. 'I didn't say anything.'

Still grasping the boy by the neck, Nathan looked around him.

'Do I look like some kind of fucking mug?' He smashed the gun into the boy's cheek. 'Well, do I?' he screamed.

Eyes blinking rapidly, the boy frantically shook his head.

Throwing the teenager away from him, Nathan looked around the factory. Spread out across three workbenches, the contents from several overstuffed packages of cocaine spilt out, the white powder dusting the wooden bench tops and immediate floor area. Beside them, several large zip bags containing amphetamines had been emptied out and among the narcotics was the usual drug paraphernalia, several weighing scales that still held traces of cocaine, and bundles of small man-made envelopes and polythene bags. 'Phone, now.'

Burner phones were thrust towards him and, snatching the nearest one to him, he tapped out a series of digits and brought the device up to his ear. The call was diverted straight to the answering machine. He pressed recall and for a second time a messaging service kicked in. He launched the phone at the wall, and pieces of broken plastic flew out in all directions.

Giving the men in his employment one final menacing glare, Nathan nodded towards his younger brothers and as they made their way out of the factory, he stopped beside the unconscious body on the floor. Taking aim at the man's head, he pulled the trigger. The gunshot was deafening. Instinctively, he knew there would be no comebacks. The fear he instilled in those around him was enough to make sure that no one would dare go against him and call in the old bill. 'Get this shithole cleaned up and get rid of this useless prick,' he told the remaining men who were standing watching him, open-mouthed.

\* \* \*

'Rosco Taylor is trying to mug us off.' Getting into his car, it was Lee, the middle brother, who spoke. He was the quiet one out of the three, regarded as the thinker. He was naturally suspicious of everyone around him.

'The fat fucker wouldn't fucking dare,' Connor said as he leant through the gap between the two front seats to look at his elder brother.

'Con's right,' Nathan sneered, 'Taylor is small-time; he hasn't got the bollocks to try and pull a stunt like this.'

As he started the ignition, Lee narrowed his eyes. 'The merchandise is already two weeks late, and you reckon he isn't trying to mug us off. Have we got "cunt" written across our fore-heads or something?'

Leaning back in his seat, Nathan was thoughtful. 'Looks like we're gonna have to take a trip over the other side of the water, then, doesn't it?'

'Yeah.' As he looked between Nathan and Lee, Connor gave them a wide grin. He loved nothing more than to get stuck in and inflict as much damage as he possibly could. It was a blood sport in his mind, one that he excelled in, as did his two elder brothers.

Rosco was concerned and, after rejecting the series of phone calls, he absentmindedly placed the device on the desk and chewed on his bottom lip. Nathan Bannerman wasn't a man to cross and, after having already told one of the men in his employ-ment that he could expect the cocaine over two weeks ago, he still had the unenviable task of actually trying to locate it. The only reason he'd even decided to do business with the South London firm was because of their connection to the man he despised more than anything else in his life, and considering he loathed his wife's brother with a burning hatred that consumed his every waking thought, that was saying something. What a kick in the teeth it was going to be for Fletch when he found out he'd been doing deals with his own family, that they were allies. With a bit of luck, a war was on the cards – a cousins' war, to be precise. After all, it was common knowledge that Fletch had murdered their uncle, and from all accounts the Bannerman brothers had been close to George Bannerman, more so than Fletch, his own son, had ever been. When the shit well and truly hit the fan, he wanted a front-row seat. All he needed now was a bucket of sweet popcorn and then he'd be a happy man.

'Have you found that little scrote yet?'

'No,' Dennis answered. 'I went to his flat personally; his missus hasn't seen him in weeks.' Of course, it was a lie; Austin had pretty much told him to fuck off when he'd turned up on the doorstep and tried to persuade him to give the merchandise up.

Rosco continued to chew on his lip. Beads of sweat broke out across his forehead and he reached out for a glass of whiskey. He was drinking far too much of late and, after chugging back the contents, within moments, an all too familiar nagging pain began to grow inside his chest and he swallowed down bitter acid. He wouldn't be surprised if he had an ulcer or two, something else he blamed on his wife's brother. He shovelled three indigestion tablets into his mouth and chewed. Saliva mixed with traces of white powder from the tablets gathered at the corners of his snarled lips. 'Find him.' His fist tightened around the glass so tight that it almost shattered.

Dennis nodded and, standing up, he made his way across the office.

'In fact...'

With his hand on the doorknob, Dennis paused.

'Tell Kit that I want a word with her. If anyone can wheedle the little bastard out from whatever shithole he's hiding in, it'll be her.'

'I'm on it.' Closing the door behind him, Dennis took a deep breath. As much as he loved her, and he did, he really loved her, Kit was playing a dangerous game and if they weren't careful, she – or to be more precise, her brother – was going to bring them all down.

## 13

Having put off the inevitable for long enough, Fletch decided that he needed to bite the bullet and visit his brother's grave... alone.

On his way to the cemetery in Upminster, he made a point of visiting the florist's shop that he and Stevie had passed on his release from prison. Call him a sentimental old bastard but the fact it was named Suzy's appealed to him in more ways than one.

As he pushed open the door, he was engulfed in an earthy, flowery scent. The inside of the shop was just as classy as the outside: the walls were painted cream and the parquet flooring was spotlessly clean. On either side of the premises were three rows of wooden shelving that ran the length of the shop, each shelf stacked higher than the one below. Adorning the shelves were white metal buckets filled with an assortment of flowers that had been arranged in colour starting from the lightest to darkest. Standing in the middle of the floor was a table that held smaller, matching white buckets of lilies, and dotted around the shop were green, leafy plants in large ceramic pots. What they were, exactly, Fletch had no idea.

'Can I help you?' a young woman asked.

Fletch shoved his hands in his pockets and flashed her a wide smile. 'I need...' He looked around him, at a loss. What exactly was it that he needed? 'Some flowers.'

Sensing his awkwardness, Harriet gave a gentle smile. It wasn't the first time a man had entered the shop with no idea of what he wanted to purchase. 'Is it for a special occasion?' she prompted.

'No, not really.' He gave a sigh and began again. 'They're for my brother – I mean, for his grave.'

Giving him a sympathetic smile, Harriet gestured towards the metal bucket nearest to him. 'How about some oriental white lilies, white roses and then some green foliage to break it up?'

Fletch nodded. He watched as she began to gather the flowers. 'Are you Suzy?' he asked, jerking his thumb behind him to the sign above the shop.

'No.' Harriet laughed. 'Suzy is my mum.'

'Oh.' Deflated, Fletch's shoulders slumped. A tiny part of him had hoped that the Suzy in question was his Suzy, even though he knew it was a long shot. Suzy had fled to Spain after the murder of her husband, Billy King, and had shown no sign of ever wanting to return to England. She had also been childless.

'Harri.'

On hearing their name being called, both Fletch and Harriet turned to look in the direction of the voice.

'I made us both some tea.' Seeing the customer standing beside her daughter, the smile across Susan King's face froze and the porcelain cup she had been holding slipped to the floor, splashing hot tea over her in the process.

'Mum.' Harriet rushed forward.

'I'm sorry.' Hiding her face, Susan crouched down to pick up the broken pieces of porcelain.

'Careful, Mum.' Harriet joined her mother and began

mopping up the spilt liquid. 'I'm sorry.' She turned her head to look over her shoulder. 'Just give me two minutes to sort this mess out,' she told Fletch, 'and I'll get you your flowers.'

Rooted to the spot, Fletch opened his mouth to answer but was instead rendered speechless. All he could do was stare after Susan, or his Suzy as he'd always thought of her. In the twenty-two years since he'd last seen her, she'd hardly changed at all; she was still as beautiful as he remembered and was still after all these years able to make his heart skip a beat. As if on cue, he placed his hand upon his chest, silently willing his heart to continue thumping, all the while unable to tear his eyes away from the woman before him. He'd missed her so much that it physically hurt. Alongside his children, she had never been too far from his mind and he'd often wondered if she was okay, hoping above all that she was safe, that she was happy.

Involuntarily, he began to back away. His hand snaked out to grab the door handle and before he could even stop himself he'd flung the door open and begun to run down the street. From the look of things, Susan had been more than happy over the years; she'd made a new life for herself, one that he clearly had no place in.

* * *

Tina was looking much cleaner than she'd done in weeks. Wearing freshly laundered denim jeans and a pale pink sweat-shirt, she could almost pass for the young woman she had been when she'd first met Fletch. Until you peered closely at her face, that was. There was no getting away from her gaunt, thin face and hollow cheeks, nor the dark rims underneath her eyes. Her hair, which had been washed and blow-dried, was still thin and sparse in places. Even the foundation did nothing to hide her sallow skin. She looked exactly what she was: a junkie. Still, it was a start, she told herself, not that she had expected a miracle. There was only so much a bar of soap and a tube of foundation could do, after all.

'There you are.' Jenny stood back to look Tina over. 'You're starting to look better already.'

Tina smiled her thanks and, slipping on a pair of black pumps, she slung her handbag over her shoulder. 'I'm just going to pop out for a bit.' She rubbed her pale lips together. 'Thought I'd treat myself to a new lipstick.'

Jenny's face fell.

'It's okay, I'm not...' A flush of shame crept up Tina's neck and she lowered her voice until it was a whisper. 'I'm not going out to score, if that's what you were thinking.' Her thoughts turned to the crack pipe and the tiny rocks she'd stuffed underneath her mattress earlier that morning. 'Honest, I'm not,' she said. 'I'm going to sort myself out, I promise.' She fluffed out her hair. 'I want to change; I want my life back, and now that Fletch is home, I want him.' Her cheeks flushed pink and she looked down at herself. 'I just want him to see the old me and remember the good times we had.'

'Okay, darling.' Jenny gave a tight smile. From what she could remember, there hadn't been many good times. 'Well, this is a start.' She gestured towards Jenny's outfit. 'Now, don't be too long; I thought we could have an early dinner today so I'm going to make a start soon.' She looked Tina up and down a second time; she was nothing but skin and bone. 'And you look as though you could do with a good meal inside of you.' Her eyes twinkled. 'I'll even make your favourite, steak and kidney pudding with a dollop of creamy mashed potatoes on the side. How does that sound?'

Tina smacked her lips together. 'Sounds perfect.'

As Tina left the house, Jenny opened the fridge and took out a tray of meat.

'You never learn, do you?' Entering the kitchen, Frank slammed his empty mug down in the sink. 'She's got you wrapped around her little finger.'

Jenny ignored her brother and as she began to slice the beef into chunks, she concentrated on the task in hand.

'You wanna hope that Fletch doesn't turn up and catch her here, because if he does, all hell will break loose. You should have told him from the start that she was kipping here.'

'She doesn't just kip here.' Jenny placed the knife on the chopping board and looked up at her brother. 'She lives here; this is her home.'

'Home,' Frank muttered underneath his breath. 'My home, you mean. It's my name on the tenancy agreement; it's me who put a roof over our heads.'

'Which you never cease to remind me,' Jenny retorted. Her body bristled as she picked up the knife and resumed chopping the meat. 'If you want me to leave, Frank, then you only have to say the word and I'll go. It's about time I found a place of my own, anyway.'

Frank shook his head. They had lived together for more than thirty years, after Jenny and the two boys had fled from her violent husband, George Bannerman. 'You know that's not what I want,' he told her. The truth was he'd be lost without her.

Jenny sighed. 'I'm just trying to help, Frank. No matter what I do, someone will have something to say about it – I can't win.'

'I know.' Frank gently gripped his sister's shoulder. 'Just be careful of her,' he warned, referring to Tina. 'She's not the same girl she was all those years ago. She'd stab you in the back as soon as look at you, that one.'

'Oh, I know that.' Nodding her head, Jenny took the warning on board. 'I'm not completely daft, you know.'

\* \* \*

Tina turned the corner of the street. Just yards ahead of her was the shopping parade.

From the corner of her eye, she noted a car slow down beside her, and as it crawled along she could just about make out the colour and make. Her heart began to beat faster and, keeping her head down low, she quickened her pace.

'Oi.'

She could hear the anger in the driver's voice, and without even turning her head could envisage his expression.

'Oi.' The car door slammed shut and as he stormed around the vehicle, she broke out into a run.

'Leave me alone,' she cried, the stark terror his presence brought clearly audible in her voice.

He grasped a handful of her hair in his fist and flung her around to face him. 'Where do you think you're going?' he spat into her face.

Twisting her face this way and that, Tina cried out in fear. She could smell the booze on his breath mingled with the stale odour of tobacco. It was enough to make her want to gag. 'Let me go,' she cried.

With a handful of her hair still wrapped around his fist, he pushed his face even closer, spraying her in spittle. 'Nah, I don't think so.' A wicked grin spread across his face and as he dragged her towards the car, Tina began to scream. She knew no one would help her; too many people were afraid of him, afraid of the repercussions his wrath would bring to themselves and their families.

He bundled her into the passenger seat, pushed down the lock then slammed the door shut before calmly walking around to the driver's door.

As he got into the car, Tina rubbed at her sore head. A handful of hair had been ripped out from the roots and the loose strands clung to her sweater. 'What do you want?'

He turned to face her and the smile he gave in return chilled her to the bone and she gave an involuntary shiver.

'Well, it ain't you.' He looked her up and down; the smile was gone and in its place was a smirk. 'Trust me, that ship sailed a long time ago. I've got myself a younger model now, nice firm arse and big tits.' He cupped his hands and grinned. 'Much better in the sack an' all,' he said with a wink.

Tina swallowed down the bile in her throat. She could smell the faint scent of lemons that came from the air freshener hanging from the rear-view mirror and took a wild guess that her daughter had put it there. Rosco had never been one for what he referred to as 'women's shit'.

'What do you want from me?' Rephrasing the question, there was a tremor in her voice.

Rosco's fist, when it shot out, connected with the side of her face. 'What I want,' he spat at her, 'is to know where that boy of yours is and you, you dirty slag, are going to tell me exactly where I can find him.'

As his fist shot out a second time, Tina screamed so loud that she felt as though her lungs were on fire.

## 14

---

June Bannerman had a good figure for her age. She could still turn heads, and with her peroxide-blonde hair falling just past her shoulder blades in soft waves, at a distance she could easily pass for a woman twenty years her junior. When they were courting, her husband had used to call her a right little dolly bird, and the words still made her smile today. She'd always looked after herself, had June, and in her mind there was nothing worse than seeing a woman let herself go once she had a ring on her finger. Even now drivers would still beep their horns at her when they drove past in the street, a fact that secretly thrilled her to bits, even if her three sons, on the other hand, didn't share her sentiment.

She was immensely proud of her sons. They were good boys, hardworking and ambitious; they doted on their old mum and never missed their weekly visit, not to mention they liked to bung her a few quid just to make sure she had some cash in her purse. In all her life she'd never been so flush.

As they traipsed into the house, she gave each of them a warm hug and a kiss on their cheek. They were handsome devils and the image of their father; he'd been a handsome bugger as well, too handsome, in her opinion. He'd also been a womaniser; many a slanging match she'd got herself into in her younger years, all because some tart was giving him the come-on.

She turned her gaze towards a small table in the lounge. It held photographs of her husband and a pillar candle that she would light on a nightly basis. Her boys called it the shrine, but it wasn't, not really. After all, they didn't even know if Albie was actually alive or dead.

Twenty-three years ago, Albie Bannerman had walked out of the house and had been on the missing list ever since. A part of her believed that he had to be deceased to have stayed away for so long. If nothing else, he'd loved his sons and would never have willingly walked away from them. Another part of her, the jealous, suspicious and bitter part of her, fully believed he was living it up somewhere with a new woman and more than likely a new family in tow.

Over the years, Albie had never been too far from her mind. She would often imagine him to be living abroad, some place hot; he'd always loved to feel a bit of the old current bun on his back. Somewhere like the Costa del Sol – in fact, Marbella would be her guess. They had holidayed there a few times when the boys were young. He'd fallen in love with the area and had promised her that one day they would buy a villa there, a huge whitewashed one, with a wraparound balcony and a swimming pool. Maybe they would even sell up and make a permanent move.

'You all right, Mum?' her middle son, Lee, asked.

June tore her gaze away from the framed photographs to look at her son. 'Course I am, why wouldn't I be? I've got my three boys around me; what more could I possibly ask for?'

Lee flicked a glance towards the shrine. A new photograph

had been added since his last visit. 'Why don't you get rid of all this, Mum?' He jerked his head towards the table. 'It's morbid.'

'It's all I've got left of your father.' June's voice rose several decibels higher than usual. It was always this son, the middle one, who antagonised her. Within nanoseconds he managed to get her back up; he had too much of his uncle in him, that was the problem, and as much as she loved Lee, she couldn't help but notice traits in him that she despised. 'It's my way of remembering him.'

'Leave her be.' Nathan glared at his brother. 'They bring her comfort, ain't that right, Mum?'

'They do.' After lighting a cigarette, June gave her eldest son a wide smile. He'd always been the same, had her Nathan: thoughtful, caring, at least when you were on his good side, anyway. Oh, she better than anyone knew what her sons were like, that they weren't always the angels they portrayed themselves to be. How could they be? They were Bannermans; they had too much of their father's, not to mention their uncle's, blood flowing inside of them to be anything different. Right from the start she'd known that her boys were never destined to become bank managers. No, even as children they had been cheeky little toerags, and if they made their way in life by taking part in more than their fair share of skulduggery then who was she to complain? It wasn't as if they were murderers or anything.

'I agree with Lee. It's morbid; it gives me the fucking creeps.' As he lounged back on the sofa, Connor eyed the table adorned with photographs with a measure of distaste.

'Oi.' Nathan clipped his youngest brother around the ear. 'Watch it, bruv.'

As she puffed away on her cigarette, June grinned. Oh, she did love it when she had her boys all under the same roof; it reminded her of when they were children and her Albie had still been around. Life had been so much simpler back then. She missed those times and would give anything to be able to relive it all over again, even the times when the boys were fighting and bickering over a favourite toy, which was pretty much an everyday occurrence – so much so that she was amazed they got on so well as adults.

Her gaze flicked towards the photographs for a second time. If only she had her husband by her side, too; now that really would have made her day that little bit sweeter.

\* \* \*

Fletch and Stevie were in the Robin Hood public house in Dagenham. The boozer had been one of their old haunts back in the day and as Fletch looked around him he could see that not much had really changed over the years, at least not for the better, anyway. The carpet still felt sticky underneath his feet, the once-red chair covers had now faded to a dusky pink, and the tables were covered in chips and scratches. One or two even had folded beer mats wedged underneath the table legs to stop them from slanting or toppling over.

Standing over six feet in height, together Fletch and Stevie made an intimidating duo and as a result were given a wide berth by the regulars. As he paid for a round of drinks, Fletch pocketed his change then passed across a pint of lager.

'And he said he'd definitely meet us here?' Stevie asked, taking a glance at his watch. It was typical of Austin; he was already well over thirty minutes late. Stevie couldn't help but believe he'd be late for his own funeral.

'Yeah.' Fletch nodded and took a sip of his pint. Wiping away a layer of froth from his upper lip, he glanced around the bar. Crowded around a fruit machine were a group of men similar in age to his son. He watched them for a few moments, then turned his head away. 'Listen, when he gets here don't mention anything about Suzy.' His cheeks flushed a deep shade of pink; it was bad enough that he felt like an idiot without anyone else judging his stupidity. He'd spent the last twenty years of his life pining for a woman who had clearly never given him a second thought. No, Susan had obviously moved on quickly; her daughter alone was proof of that. 'Oh, and while you're at it, do me a favour and tell me what you think about Austin.' He gave a slight shake of his head. 'I think he's hiding something.'

Swallowing down a mouthful of lager, Stevie answered, 'You do realise he's a big boy now, don't you? He's not a little kid any more; you can't tell him what he can and can't do with his life.'

'I know that.' Fletch dismissed Stevie's words. 'But he's still my son and if he's involved in something heavy I want to know about it.'

Stevie raised his eyebrows and as the door swung open and Austin walked through, he was saved from answering.

'Here you go, son.' Fletch passed across a pint of lager.

'Cheers.' Austin swallowed down a large mouthful of the amber liquid and smiled across to his father and Stevie, or Uncle Stevie as he'd always thought of him. 'What's up with you two?' He studied them over the rim of his pint glass.

'Nothing.' Shaking his head, Stevie continued to smile.

'Yeah there is – you never grin at me like that.' He turned to look at his father. 'What's going on, Dad?'

Glaring at Stevie, Fletch sighed. 'Okay.' He held up his hands. From across the pub, the fruit machine hit jackpot and a series of pound coins hit the plastic tray attached to the machine with a loud clatter, much to the delight of the men crowded around it. 'I'm concerned,' Fletch said, raising his voice to be heard over the din.

'Concerned about what?' Austin looked between the two men; his eyes narrowed.

'Look, I know what's it like, we both do.' Fletch gestured to Stevie. 'Believe it or not,' he said with a small smile, 'we were young ourselves once.'

'Oi, speak for yourself,' Stevie interrupted. 'I'm still young, or at least young at heart anyway,' he said with a grin.

Fletch threw his friend a second glare. 'What I'm trying to get at is this: we've both been there, we've both had to step up and prove ourselves at some point.'

Austin's forehead furrowed. 'I'm still not getting it. What are you trying to say, Dad?'

Fletch began again. 'Peer pressure,' he said. 'I know how it all works and when I was inside I learnt a lot about it. I did this course, it was a sociology course actually...' He waved his hand. 'It doesn't matter; what I'm trying to get at is that I know how it works. They reel you in and, once they have you in their grasp, it's a constant battle to prove yourself; in order to survive, you need to climb up the ranks.'

'Climb up the ranks.' There was a hint of amusement in Austin's voice. 'What the fuck are you going on about?'

'Gangs.' Fletch lowered his voice. 'I'm talking about peer pressure from gangs.'

'Gangs?' Austin repeated back, his eyes widening as he finally cottoned on to what his dad was trying to get at. 'You think I'm in a gang.' He laughed.

Fletch nodded, his expression serious. 'Is that Charlie a member? Because if he is, I can have a word in his ear and tell him to back off. We can work this out together, me and you; I can help you get away from them. I know how they operate – they try and manipulate you. It's drummed into your nut' – he tapped a finger against his temple to emphasise his point – 'that once

you're in, you're in for life and all that old bollocks, but it doesn't
have to be like that. I can help you, son.'

'A gang,' Austin reiterated as he looked between Fletch and
Stevie. 'Fucking hell, Dad, I'm not fifteen.' He laughed. 'A fucking
gang – what would I be doing in a gang?'

'Are you saying you're not?' Fletch tilted his head to one side
and narrowed his eyes as he scrutinised his son.

'No.' Austin chuckled. 'Why the fuck would I want to be in a
gang? Fucking hell, Dad, give me some credit. Charlie's my pal –
that's it. We went to school together like you and Stevie did.'

'I just thought...' As he sipped at his pint of lager, relief was
evident across Fletch's face. It wasn't often he relished being in
the wrong but this was one of those moments that he did. 'Oh, it
doesn't matter.' He laughed. 'Ignore your old man. I've spent far
too long inside, that's my problem. I've had too long to think
about shit.'

As he brought the glass up to his lips, Austin caught Stevie's
eyes. The look of warning the other man shot him was more than
enough to make sure that he kept his mouth firmly shut – not
that he intended to spill the beans and tell his father all about his
criminal activities, the latest being the haul of coke he'd stolen
from Rosco. After his little speech tonight about gangs and peer
pressure, Austin had a sneaking suspicion that his old man might
well have turned soft. He might look the part, might have spent a
long stretch inside and might still have a reputation as a hard
man, but from what he could see and, more importantly, from
what he'd heard come out of his dad's mouth, that was all it was: a
reputation. With a heavy heart, he'd soon come to realise that his
dad wasn't going to take the news that his son had followed in his
footsteps quite as well as he'd always imagined he would.

## 15

Tina was sobbing and as she crawled out of Rosco's car, she looked as though she'd just gone ten rounds with Mike Tyson. Both eyes were bruised, her nose was bleeding, and her top lip had swollen to three times its usual size.

Clutching her stomach, she stumbled down the pathway to Frank's house and, collapsing against the front door, she began to cry even harder. For just over an hour Rosco had kept her a prisoner inside the car. He'd alternated between screaming, shouting and punching her until finally he'd had enough and kicked her out, literally.

No matter how much he'd terrorised her, she hadn't opened her mouth; she hadn't told him where he could find her son.

Feeling weak and nauseous, she could barely stand up, she was in that much pain. She thumped the palm of her hand on the door, hoping and praying that Jenny or Frank would hear her desperate attempt to be found. As the door opened, she slumped inside the hallway. From somewhere in the back of her mind she could feel herself being lifted up into the air and then carried inside the house before being gently placed down on the sofa. Through a haze of blurred vision she could just about make out Jenny's face looming over her; in the background she could hear the panic in Frank's voice as he shouted that they needed to phone for an ambulance.

She reached out her arm, her fingertips frantically trying to grasp hold of Jenny's hand as if the action would somehow save her from the pain Rosco's fists had inflicted. The movement caused a sudden shard of pain to shoot across her neck and shoulder blades. 'Rosco,' she whispered through swollen lips before her eyes rolled to the back of her head and her body became limp.

\* \* \*

Austin's mobile phone rang and, seeing his grandmother's name flash up on the screen, he was in two minds whether to answer or not.

'Are you going to answer that?' Fletch nodded down at the phone.

'It's Nan.' His finger hovered over the reject button.

'You'd best see what she wants, then,' Fletch answered with a smile.

'Yeah.' As he pressed answer, a wide grin was spread across Austin's face. 'Hello, Nan, I'm just having a drink with my dad.' With the phone pressed against his ear, the smile across his face slipped away. 'What?' His heart began to hammer inside his chest as he turned his back on his father. 'I'm coming,' he said, ending the call.

'Problem?' Draining his drink, Fletch placed the empty glass on the bar.

'No.' Staring into the distance, Austin shook his head. 'I've got to go.'

Fletch and Stevie shared a glance.

'Is everything all right?' Fletch asked, concern etched across his face. 'Has something happened?'

'No, of course not.' Austin attempted to smile, even though it was somewhat hollow to Fletch's eyes. 'I just need to go.' He placed his unfinished drink on the bar top. 'I'll give you a call later, Dad,' he said, his mind already elsewhere as he made his way towards the exit.

'Yeah, all right, son,' Fletch called after him. He waited a few moments, then, clapping Stevie on the back, he nodded his head in the direction his son had made off in. 'Something's going down. Come on, drink up – you can drive me over to my mum's.'

Downing the remainder of his pint, Stevie placed the empty glass on the bar then chased after his friend.

Austin had never felt so angry and as he put his foot down on the accelerator, he gripped onto the steering wheel so tightly that his knuckles turned a deathly shade of white. He dragged his free hand across his face; his skin felt cold and clammy to the touch and he wiped away the excess sweat on his thigh. To the majority of people who knew her, Tina was nothing more than a skank, a junkie, someone they looked down on with mistrust, but despite her problems she was still his mum and even after everything that had happened in the past, he still loved her.

Bringing the car to a screeching halt outside his uncle Frank's house, he flung open the car door, jumped out, then proceeded to race down the path. At the front door, he slipped his hand inside his jacket pocket and pulled out his mobile phone. Without even hesitating, he scrolled down to his sister's telephone number and pressed dial. They may have had their fair share of problems in the past, but Tina was still Kit's mother and if there was ever a time for them to make peace and put their differences aside, then it was now. 'Kit, it's me,' he growled. 'Mum's been done over; she's in a bad way. I'm at Nan's house. Meet me here.' He ended the call without giving his sister the chance to refuse his request, then hammered his fist against the front door.

It was his great uncle who answered, and as Austin stepped across the threshold, Frank tugged on his arm, bringing him to a halt.

'She's in a bad way, but she'll live,' he said in a low voice. 'She's not said much, other than...' He looked towards the lounge, then raised his eyebrows. 'She mentioned Rosco's name.' Frank held up his hands. 'What she meant by that, well, your guess is as good as mine,' he said, 'but if I was a gambling man I know exactly who I'd put my money on for having beaten the crap out of her.'

'Rosco?' Anger rushed to the fore. 'Are you telling me that cunt did this to her?' he growled.

Frank paused before answering and, glancing back in the direction of the lounge, he shook his head. 'All I'm saying is that she said his name before she blacked out.' He shrugged as he followed his nephew down the hallway. 'See if you can get any sense out of her; with a bit of luck she'll tell you who did it.'

Entering the lounge, Austin's face drained of all colour. His mum hadn't just been beaten; she'd been battered to within an inch of her life. She was so thin and so tiny it was incomprehensible that anyone would even want to lay their fists on her. 'I'm gonna have him.' The words came out in a low growl. 'I'm gonna string the bastard up by his fucking bollocks,' he said, backing out of the room and storming back down the hallway. 'I'm gonna fucking kill him,' he roared as he flung open the front door.

'Who are you going to kill?' Standing on the doorstep, blocking his son's path, Fletch's eyebrows were raised. 'Come on, son, who exactly are you planning to kill, and more to the point, why is this the first time I'm hearing about it?'

## 16

Switching off her mobile phone, Kit lay back on the bed and stared up at the unfamiliar ceiling of the hotel room.

'Who was that?' Beside her, Dennis pulled himself into a sitting position, leant back against the pillows and lit a cigarette.

'My brother.' She continued to stare up at the ceiling. 'It's my mum,' she said, turning her head to look at him. 'She's been attacked.' She took the cigarette from his fingers, took a deep drag, then blew out a thin stream of smoke. Passing back the cigarette, she sat up, pulled her knees up to her chest and rested her chin on her forearms.

It wasn't the first time Tina had found herself in trouble. It was in her nature to cause aggravation; she thrived on it and fully believed the world revolved around her. The majority of Kit's earlier memories were of her mum either screaming and shouting because she couldn't get her own way, or plotting and scheming so that she could be the centre of attention. She craved the limelight almost as much as normal, regular people needed oxygen to breathe.

Dennis twirled the gold chain that hung from his neck around his forefinger. 'Do you want to check up on her?' Stubbing out the cigarette in a small glass ashtray, he looked over his shoulder.

Kit shook her head. She and her mother hadn't spoken in years. Over and over again, she'd told herself that she didn't care, that it didn't bother her, that her relationship with her mother was toxic and that she was better off without her. It was a lie she had told herself so many times she almost believed it. Deep down, she still loved her mum – of course she did. She was her mum; how could she not love her? And scattered among the bad memories there were a few good ones, too. Admittedly, they were long before the drugs had taken hold and destroyed any sense of a normal life.

'It's no problem.' Dennis pulled her down beside him, and nuzzled his face into her neck. 'We can always do this another time; I'm not going anywhere.' He grinned. 'You already know that.'

Smiling back at him, Kit shook her head. She knew he would do exactly as she asked; he always did. It was one of the many reasons why their relationship worked. He was content to see her as often as he could, and the stolen moments they shared more than made up for the fact she was tied to Rosco's side.

Her eyes were drawn to the mobile phone sitting on top of the chipped MDF bedside cabinet. The hotel was hardly the Ritz; it was cheap and tacky and had only cost them thirty quid for the day. Still, as long as it had a bed then it was more than adequate for what they had wanted it for. 'Maybe I should go,' she sighed, gently pushing Dennis away from her and sitting up. 'I mean for Aus's sake, not for her, my mum,' she was quick to point out. She ran her fingers through her hair, pulling the thick mane into a loose bun at the nape of her neck. 'He's going to need me; he won't know how to deal with this.'

'Do you want me to come with you?'

'What, and risk Rosco catching us together?' Kit laughed. 'I think that would go down like a lead balloon, don't you?'

'I'm not scared of him.' Dennis gave a carefree shrug. 'I know how to handle myself, babe, and believe me, I've dealt with a lot worse than him in my lifetime.'

Kit fixed her gaze upon him. 'I know you're not afraid of him.' She slipped off the bed and made her way towards the adjoining bathroom. 'You wouldn't be here now if you were, but I need to do this alone.' She turned on the shower and threw him a small smile. 'I very much doubt my mum is going to welcome me with open arms and I'd rather not have an audience, if you don't mind.'

Dennis nodded his head. If he was disappointed, he didn't show it. 'And what about Rosco? He's still giving me grief; he's still got muscle out looking for Aus.' He waited for a moment or two to let his words sink in. 'He's not going to let this drop, darling. He's out for blood, and you know that as well as I do.'

'Fuck Rosco.' When she turned to face her lover, there was a steely glint in Kit's eyes. 'I'd sooner kill the bastard myself than ever hand my brother over to him.'

\* \* \*

'Answer the question, who are you going to kill?' Stepping over the doorstep, Fletch pushed his son none too gently back into the hallway.

'No one,' Austin said as he tried to block his father from entering the house. 'Just leave it, Dad.'

'No,' Fletch growled, 'I won't leave it. I knew something was going on with you, I could feel it in my gut, I've been saying for days that something wasn't right, and you are going to tell me exactly what's been going on around here.'

'Fletch.' Pulling on his friend's arm, Stevie's voice was low. 'Do as he asks and just leave it, mate.'

Fletch froze and, screwing up his face, he spun around and yanked his arm free. 'Are you in on this?' he asked, his tone accusing.

'Of course I'm not,' Stevie spat back. He held up his hands and took a step away in an attempt to create a reasonable distance between them. In his youth, Fletch had had a blinding right hook on him. Now fresh out of prison and bulked up, Stevie didn't think much of his chances should his friend decide to take a swing for him. 'There are just one or two things you don't know about yet.' He turned to look at Frank, his eyes silently beseeching him to help him out. As far as he was concerned, it wasn't his place to have to fill Fletch in on all the gory details.

'What things?' Fletch's voice began to rise, and he snapped his head around to look at his uncle. 'What's he going on about?'

'He's talking about Tina.' Entering the hallway, Jenny's back was ram-rod straight. 'It's all going to come out soon enough anyway,' she sighed.

Fletch narrowed his eyes. 'What about her?' he spat.

'She lives here; this is her home. It has been for a few years and if you don't like it, then I think it would be best that you leave.' She nodded towards the front door. 'I don't want her any more upset than she already is and you screaming and shouting at her isn't going to help the situation.'

'I feel like we're going around in circles. Why does everything have to revolve around Tina?' Fletch rubbed at his temples and as his gaze lingered on the faces staring back at him, a bitter laugh escaped from his lips. 'I can't get my head around any of this. You'd kick me out, your own son, over her?' He stabbed his forefinger in his mother's direction; his eyes narrowed until they were nothing more than two mere slits in his handsome face. 'You would rather put a junkie before your own family, before your own grandchildren, before your own son?'

'Tina needs me.' Jenny stood her ground. 'Now more than ever, that girl needs her family around her.'

'She's not family, though, is she?' Fletch roared. 'She's never been family and you know she hasn't. Tina fucking needs you? What about when my kids needed you, eh? Where were you when she was abusing them?' He turned to look at his son. 'I know all about it,' he told him, his voice becoming gentle. 'I know what she did to you and Kitty.'

'Dad.' Closing his eyes, Austin shook his head. 'You've got it—'

'Is she here?' Cutting off his son, Fletch snapped his head in the direction of the lounge, his mouth dropping slightly open as though the relevance of the question had only just dawned on him. 'She's here isn't she, she's in the house, that's the reason why you want to kick me out.'

Before anyone could stop him, Fletch had barged his way into the lounge. 'Where is she?' At his sides, his fists were clenched into tight balls. 'I'm gonna rip her head clean off her shoulders for what she's caused.'

The words had barely left Fletch's mouth when he reeled backwards, eyes open wide as shock resonated across his face. The trembling, bird-like woman sitting on the sofa wasn't someone he recognised; he would have walked past her in the street and not for a single second believed her to be the same woman who had birthed his children, the same woman he'd once shared a home with, for however brief a time that may have been. He continued to stare at the stranger. He was no expert, but even he could see she was taking a lot more than just coke. She began to cough; it was a deep, hacking cough, and as she swallowed down a mouthful of phlegm, Fletch turned his face away, his expression one of disgust.

'She was attacked,' Jenny explained as she came to sit on the sofa. Wrapping her arms protectively around Tina's painfully thin shoulders, she pulled her closer and gently rubbed her back.

Pushing her face into the crook of Jenny's arm, Tina's upper body heaved as she wept. Shame flooded through her and she put her hand out in an attempt to ward Fletch off. She didn't want him to see the damage Rosco had caused. She'd wanted to look nice for him; she'd wanted him to remember her as the vivacious woman she had been before he'd been sent down, and more than anything she wanted him to want her as much as she'd always wanted him, and in fact still wanted him.

'Attacked?' Still barely able to get his head around what he was seeing, Fletch turned to look at his uncle. 'Who did this to her?'

Frank gave a shrug and raised his eyebrows to the ceiling. 'Your guess is as good as mine; she hasn't told us yet.' He may have had his suspicions but at the same time Tina hadn't confirmed or denied Rosco's involvement.

'Someone must know who did it, why they did it. Was she mugged?' Fletch caught Stevie's eyes.

'I was with you all afternoon,' Stevie was quick to point out. 'I know as much as you do.'

'Aus?'

Austin shook his head and, shifting his weight from one foot to the other, he could barely look his father in the eyes. 'I don't

know, Dad,' he answered quietly. 'Same as what Stevie said – I
was in the pub with you, wasn't I.'

From behind them, a key turned in the lock and the front
door opened, bringing with it a blast of sweet perfume and
cold air.

'Kit.' Austin joined his sister at the front door and, grasping
her hand in his, he gave it a reassuring squeeze.

'How is she?' Kit slipped her door key back into her handbag.
'You said it was bad.' A movement from the hallway caught her
attention and she turned her head. 'What's he doing here?'
Looking her father up and down, she hissed out the words, slung
the leather strap of her handbag back over her shoulder, then
turned to give her brother an accusing stare. 'You didn't tell me he
was going to be here.'

'He just wanted to see if Mum was okay.' Blocking his sister's
view, Austin kept his voice low. 'Don't start, Kit; he's trying to look
out for us. He's actually all right once you get to know him. He's
not the bastard that Mum always said he was.' He lowered his
voice to a whisper and raised his eyebrows. 'I think he's actually
gone a bit soft.'

Kit rolled her eyes. Even at the best of times, her brother
wasn't the greatest judge of character; his relationship with
Sheree was testament enough to that little fact. Walking straight
past her father without so much as acknowledging him, Kit
greeted her great uncle with a warm hug. 'How is she? Aus said it
was pretty bad.'

'She's been better, darling,' Frank answered. He gestured
towards the lounge. 'Someone's done her over good and proper –
why don't you take a look for yourself.'

At the doorway, Kit hesitated. She turned back to look at her
brother.

'Go on,' he mouthed, nodding his head in encouragement.

With more than a hint of trepidation, Kit moved forward. She closed her eyes for a moment, took a deep breath, then stepped inside the room. 'Hello, Mum.'

Despite the pain that ravaged throughout Tina's body, she snapped her head around to face her daughter. 'You... you bastard whore.' Her fingertips gripped onto the sofa as she screamed out the words. 'Did he send you here to finish me off?'

Kit's stomach lurched; nothing could have prepared her for just how badly her mother had been beaten. The bruising was beginning to surface, and her swollen face was a mass of black and purple marks. It took all of Kit's effort not to wince.

'Well, did he?' Tina shrieked.

Instinctively, Kit knew exactly who her mother was referring to: Rosco. No one other than him would have dared touch a hair on Tina's head, not unless they were prepared for Austin to hunt them down and unleash his formidable temper. 'I don't know what you're talking about,' she said, turning to look at her brother and shrugging her shoulders.

'Mum.' Austin was quick to interrupt. 'Kit came to see if you were okay.' He spoke slowly as if he was talking to a child. 'It was me who called her...'

'Get her out,' Tina continued to scream. 'Get the dirty whore out of my sight.'

'Come on, Mum,' Austin implored his mother, 'don't do this.'

'It's okay,' Kit told her brother. 'Save your breath; I'm going.' Shaking her head, she let out a long sigh. 'I should have known she'd be like this; nothing ever changes with her, does it?'

'You should have known?' Clutching at her stomach, Tina gingerly got to her feet, the pain she'd felt just moments earlier numbed by the sudden explosion of outrage that her daughter's appearance had brought to her. 'More like I should have known, you mean, like I should have known that I'd bred a whore all those years ago.'

Staring around him at the car crash that was his family, Fletch had just about had enough. He wanted answers from them, and he wanted them now. He'd done enough pussy-footing around his family to last him a lifetime. 'Will someone,' he roared, 'just tell me what the fuck is going on here?'

* * *

Tina was smirking, a sight that Fletch was all too familiar with. Just one glance in her direction told him that nothing had changed, not really. Underneath the 'poor little me' act she liked to put on whenever she had an audience, she was still the same woman who had deliberately set out to trap him all those years ago. She was so transparent, she might well have been a pane of glass – he could see right through her. Even if she had pulled the wool over his mum's and everyone else's eyes. He'd marked her cards a long time ago and she couldn't fool him; she'd never been able to fool him. That was the difference.

'Oh, didn't you know,' Tina said turning her thin body around to face him, 'that me and you, between us, we bred a whore?'

'Tina,' Jenny warned, 'enough. I won't stand for you bad-mouthing my granddaughter.'

Taken aback, Fletch narrowed his eyes. 'What are you talking about?' He looked around him. 'What is she talking about?' He turned to look at his daughter and spread open his arms. 'Kitty?'

With his hands clasped behind his head, Austin's skin was ashen as he rubbed his thumbs across the nape of his neck. 'Mum, stop,' he begged of her. 'Don't do this, not again.'

Tina continued to smirk. Her swollen lips and blood-encrusted nose made her once-beautiful face, now ravaged by the drugs that over the years she'd either popped, injected or smoked, look grotesque. 'I won't stop,' she sneered at her son. 'It's about time your father knew the truth.' She shot her daughter a hard stare. 'Before she tries to take him away from me as well. Was that your plan?' she spat. 'To come here and take him away from me just like you took everything else from me?'

'You're sick, Mum, you need help,' Kit told her, her voice sincere.

As he tried to keep up with what was going on around him, Fletch's mind reeled.

Crossing her arms over her chest, Tina looked around her. She liked nothing more than to be centre stage, and to have her Fletch, as she still thought of him, in the same room was just about the icing on the cake. 'Our daughter...' Her tongue darted across her swollen lips and there was a wicked glint in her eyes. 'Our darling daughter...'

'Tina.' Cocking his head to one side, Stevie shot her a warning glare. 'Stop this, now.'

'No, wait.' Fletch put up his hand. 'I want to hear this; I need to know what's been going on.'

Tina continued to smirk and, not taking her eyes off her daughter, she swayed her body from side to side. 'Shall I tell him?' she mocked. 'Shall I tell him exactly what you did to me?'

Tears sprang to Kit's eyes as she swallowed down the hard lump in her throat and shook her head. Not for the first time did she wish that she'd listened to her gut instinct and stayed with Dennis in the hotel room. 'You spiteful bitch.'

Tina burst out laughing and, glancing around the room, she made sure that she had everyone's full attention. 'Me?' Her mouth dropped open in mock surprise. 'You've got the front to stand there and call me spiteful?' She poked a bony finger into her chest and, turning her wide eyes on Fletch, she sucked in her breath. 'I'm the victim here,' she cried. 'I had everything until our so-called daughter...' She pointed an accusing finger across the room. 'I was happy until the whore that we produced, stole my man, my home and my life.'

As soon as the words had left Tina's mouth, World War Three erupted.

## 17

It took all of Fletch and Austin's combined strength to hold Kit back. She was a lot stronger than she looked, and it was only after receiving a hard jab from Kit's elbow that Austin realised just how strong his little sister was. If he'd been in any doubt before about her being able to handle herself, he wasn't any more.

She fought them like a wildcat as she tried to reach the other side of the room. Her fists punched, slapped and pummelled at anything and everything that she could lay her hands on in her haste to reach Tina's side. The coffee table, fruit bowl and several bone china mugs filled with freshly made tea had been hurled up into the air as she kicked them out of her path, and still she didn't stop her attempt to reach the woman who had birthed her. Years of pent-up rage was being unleashed and it wasn't until Fletch had flung his arms around her waist and lifted her bodily into the air, then half carried and half dragged her, still kicking and screaming, from the room, that the tears finally came, even if they were more from frustration than anything else.

'You need to calm down,' he told his daughter as he slammed the kitchen door closed behind them. Leaning against it in a bid to stop anyone from entering and, more importantly, his daughter from exiting, he breathed heavily through his flared nostrils.

Kit paced the kitchen. Her movements reminded Fletch of a predator and for a brief moment he wondered where she had inherited her temper from. Himself, most probably, he rightly guessed. He'd been exactly the same when he'd been her age. Headstrong, his mum had called him – dangerous, others would say.

'Are you feeling calmer now?'

'What do you think?' Kit retorted as she paced the floor.

Fletch continued to watch her. Even in a temper with her dark brown hair sticking up all over the place and her cheeks flushed bright pink, she was a beautiful woman, far too beautiful for him to have fathered, yet he had, and the similarities, whether she would ever acknowledge them or not, were too strong to dismiss. She was him in a female form.

'Darling...'

'Don't call me that,' she snapped at him, her chest heaving as she tried to control the anger that rippled through her veins. 'You threw away the right to call me that a long time ago.'

'You're right, I did.' Nodding his head in agreement, Fletch held up his hands. 'I wasn't there for you or Austin when you were kids, and I should have been. I'll be the first to hold my hands up and admit that I was in the wrong, it was all my fault and I've only got myself to blame.'

'Shall I get the violin out?' Kit spat. 'Poor you for abandoning your children.'

'I didn't abandon you,' he answered, 'I would never have willingly walked away from you. I was sent down for a very long time; I had no control over that, and at the time I thought I was doing the right thing.' He looked down at the floor, remembering his brother Spencer and his subsequent murder. 'I was trying to avenge my brother's death, and yeah, maybe I did go about it in the wrong way, but no matter what, I'm still your dad,' he told her, 'and I have always loved you. When I was inside, not a day went by without me thinking about you, wondering what you were doing, if you were okay.'

'Yeah, and a fat lot of good that did us,' she snarled in return. 'A lot of good that did Aus when he was being battered on a daily basis.'

'If I could turn back time, I would,' Fletch told her, his voice gentle, 'but I can't.' He tilted his head to look at her. 'But I want to make it up to you, to both you and Austin.'

Still pacing the kitchen, Kit shook her head.

'What your mum said about her bloke...' He jerked his head behind him. 'We're not talking about Rosco here, are we? Not that it makes any difference to me,' he was quick to add. 'I mean, let's be clear on this, I don't like it,' he said, holding up his hands, 'but I just want to know what's been going on while I've been away.'

A bitter laugh escaped from Kit's lips. She stopped pacing and leant her weight on a wooden chair and faced her father. 'You don't know anything; you don't know what it was like for us,' she spat at him.

Fletch held up his hands. 'Then why don't you fill me in on the blanks.' He took a step towards her. 'She said you stole her bloke or something to that effect?'

'She's good at bending the truth, my mum, always has been.' She turned her back on him, moved across the kitchen and opened a drawer.

Fletch shifted his position to watch her. The last thing any of them needed was for her to pull out a knife; she was certainly angry enough to do just that.

Taking out the packet of cigarettes her nan kept in the drawer for emergencies, she took one out, lit up and took several short, sharp puffs. Exhaling a stream of smoke up into the air, she turned back to face her father. 'She likes to open that big trap of hers, but what she doesn't do is tell people the real story, the reason why I had to do what I did.'

Fletch gave a shrug of his shoulders. 'Well, I suppose...'

Kit tilted her chin in the air. 'It's okay, I'll wait,' she told him with more than a hint of sarcasm.

'Well,' he tried again, 'I don't know, I suppose how these things usually happen, you must have felt something for him.' He gave her a gentle smile. 'Don't get this twisted; I still don't like the idea of you and him together, and if you want to know the truth' – he held up his hands – 'the thought of it, of you and him, it makes me feel sick to my stomach, but I do understand what it's like, I really do. I've been there myself.'

Stubbing out the cigarette in a foil ashtray, Kit gave a half laugh. She moved across the kitchen and stood just inches away from her father. 'Then you must be even more stupid than I was led to believe.'

As his daughter left the kitchen, the smile slowly died on Fletch's face and, staring at the empty space her departure had created, his forehead furrowed as the front door slammed firmly shut behind her.

## 18

Making his way around the edge of the dance floor, Dennis shot a customary glance in the direction of the stripper up on the stage. Minus her stage costume, Marianne's black dyed hair framed her face as she gyrated up against a metal pole. She was a lot older than the majority of the girls who worked for Rosco and was the first to hold her hand up and admit that the stage make-up she'd layered on so thickly that it looked as though she'd used a trowel was her only saving grace – that and the club's strategic lighting. 'Dog rough' was how he would describe her. Still, it wasn't him handing over his hard-earned cash to watch her strip off and thrust her saggy tits in his face, so who was he to complain? She was only ever given the early slot for the sole purpose of warming up the punters, anyway, an agreement that suited everyone involved down to the ground.

It was still early afternoon and already a dozen or so of the usual regulars were in attendance and had taken ownership of the best tables as they waited for the star attractions, or the main earners as they were more commonly known, to climb up on the stage and begin their routines.

At the back of the premises, he slipped through a side door with the word 'private' emblazoned across it in large, bold letters, then made his way up to where the offices were located. Along the upper corridor, the floor beneath his feet vibrated. Night and day, the sound system from the club below pumped out endless tunes; it was enough to give him and anyone else who worked there a headache. Before he'd even reached Rosco's office, he could hear his boss's voice above the constant bass that came from the main floor and, groaning out loud, he pushed open the door.

With his mobile phone clutched to his ear, Rosco waved him in. Sitting behind the desk, he was animated as he barked orders into the mouthpiece.

Dennis's eyes were drawn to Rosco's knuckles, or to be more precise, his grazed knuckles. He waited for the man to end the call then nodded down at them. 'Trouble?'

'Trouble?' With a level of disbelief, Rosco shook his head. He downed his drink in one large gulp then smashed the glass down onto the desk. 'Unless it's escaped your notice, my merchandise has gone on the fucking trot.' His voice began to rise. 'The same merchandise that by rights should have been on the move over two weeks ago, the very same merchandise that should have been in Nathan Bannerman's greedy little hands by now.' Across his forehead was a layer of cold sweat, and he swiped away the clammy beads with the back of his hand. 'He's already been on the blower.' He glanced down at the mobile phone with a measure of anguish. 'There's only so many times I can tell the nutter that there's been a delay. He's like a rabid dog; I heard he once bit a man's ear off, actually chewed it in front of him and swallowed it down.'

Dennis raised his eyebrows. 'By all accounts, Nathan Bannerman is the least of your problems. Lee is the one you need to watch out for, the middle brother, the quiet one. Rumour has it that he's done far worse than chew off a man's ear. He once sliced off a man's testicles, all because he'd had the audacity to try and chat up his bird. The worst part about it was that he'd already planned to give her the elbow; poor bloke lost his nuts for nothing.'

The colour drained from Rosco's face and he physically blanched. Without giving pause, he unscrewed the lid of the whiskey bottle and refilled the glass. 'Why hasn't that little scrote been found yet?' He gulped at the drink as if the answers he craved were at the bottom of the glass. 'Why hasn't the bastard been brought to me?'

Rolling his lips together, Dennis shrugged. 'We're still looking for him.' Without a brain cell between them, it had been fairly easy to manipulate the men in Rosco's employment and steer them away from the usual haunts that he knew for a fact Austin frequented. Telling the men that he would personally search the flat where Kit's brother lived, they had accepted his commands without question. After all, he was Rosco's number two – why would they even doubt his intentions? As he glanced once more at Rosco's grazed knuckles, worry edged its way down Dennis's spine. He could only hope and pray that he was able to stay one step ahead of his boss. After all, it didn't take a genius to work out that Rosco was the culprit behind the brutal attack on Kit's mother. He was more surprised that Tina had actually kept her mouth shut; let's face it, she was hardly mother-of-the-year material.

\* \* \*

With a face like thunder, Kit barely paused for breath as she slammed her car door shut. Entering the club, she stormed across the dance floor without even stopping to say hello to the dancers and instead headed straight for the offices. She wasn't in the mood for pleasantries and as she charged up the carpeted staircase, it took every ounce of her willpower not to lash out, to kick, punch or scream at anyone who dared step into her path. No, it was Rosco she was saving her formidable temper for, and with her fists clenched at her sides, she shoved open the door to his office so hard that it bounced against the wall with a loud crash.

'You bastard!' she screamed at him. 'Do you know the fucking ructions you've caused?'

Lounging back in the chair, Rosco lit a cigarette and gave a nonchalant shrug of his shoulders.

'My mother,' she continued to scream. 'You've battered her to within an inch of her life; she looks like she's been in a train crash.'

'Yeah, and?' Rosco sneered. 'She's a fucking crackhead; what's the big deal? So I roughed her up a bit; it's not like it's the first time, is it?' A grin spread across his face. 'She used to love a dig, a ruck – it's how she's made. She loves nothing more than to cause aggro; she gets off on it.' He tapped his temple. 'She's sick in the head.'

Kit lunged forward and, grasping the edge of the desk, she bellowed in his face. 'What, you think this is funny?' she spat. 'You think it's funny to kick seven bells of shit out of my mother?'

'I think it's fucking hilarious,' he jeered. 'Like I said, she's a crackhead, a dirty skank.' He pointed the burning embers of the cigarette towards her. 'If you'd done as you were told and brought that prick of a brother to me, I wouldn't have had to go out looking for him, would I?'

'If I'd done as I was told?' The sheer audacity of the man made her laugh in his face. 'Despite what you might think of me, I'm your wife, not one of your paid lackies.' Gripping onto the desk even tighter, she could feel her hatred for the man oozing out of her pores. It was so strong, she was amazed that he was unable to feel it. 'My brother doesn't know anything about your poxy coke; why would he?'

Rosco jumped to his feet, his face turning almost purple with rage. 'Because he's a fucking weasel, that's why.' His breath came out in short sharp bursts and he smashed his fist down on the desk, upsetting the contents of the glass. The copper-coloured liquid sloshed over the sides, causing tiny puddles to form either side of the cut glass. 'This has got his name written all over it. He likes nothing more than to cause me grief; it's all he's ever done since the moment I clapped my eyes on him.'

'He was just a little kid.' Kit screwed up her face.

'He was no kid; he was a stroppy little bastard who always had something to say for himself. He wasn't content until he'd riled me up.' He stabbed his forefinger dangerously close to her face. 'I'm gonna have him for this; I'm gonna rip his fucking guts out for the grief he's caused me.'

Slapping his hand away from her, a shot of terror ran down the length of Kit's spine.

'Now I'm warning you, Kit, and I'm only going to warn you this one time, before I end up losing my fucking rag with you an' all. I want him dragged out from whatever rock he is hiding under, and I want him brought to me, kicking and screaming if need be, before I end up tearing apart your entire family looking for him. Because believe me, I will, if it's the last thing on this earth I ever do.'

Choosing to ignore the veiled threat, Kit was quiet for a few moments. 'Come on,' she said, spreading open her arms. 'Do you honestly think Austin has the intelligence to orchestrate something like this? He can just about tie his own shoelaces together and, believe me, that's him on a good day. How the hell would he have been able to steal that coke from underneath your nose?' She tapped her temple. 'He hasn't got the nous to do something like this and you know it. Like you've always said, he has the intelligence of a village idiot; you know full well he isn't clever enough to get one over on you.' She watched her husband's eyebrows knit together and allowed herself to relax. Like her father before her, keeping her elder brother safe was her one and only driving force. She would do anything and everything in her power to protect him; she always had done, and she always would. Growing up, all they had had was one another and as a result their bond was more than just tight, it was unbreakable, and no matter how much she might love Dennis, her brother was the only man she would ever well and truly love without question. She made a point of looking down at the thick scar that ran the length of Rosco's forearm. It was a calculated gesture, and the action had the effect she desired. 'No, you're looking too close to home,' she told him. 'Who else out there would take pleasure from getting one over you? Who else despises you enough to hold a grudge?'

As Rosco's fingers found their way to the scar, a scowl etched its way across his face and he kissed his teeth. The sound was loud in the otherwise quiet room. 'Your old man,' he spat.

Kit swallowed deeply and, digging her nails into the palm of her hand, she arched her eyebrows. 'My dad,' she said in agreement.

## 19

As Stevie drove his car through the streets towards his home in Upminster, he shot a sideways glance towards his oldest friend. Since climbing inside the car, Fletch had barely said two words.

He shifted his weight in the seat and cleared his throat. 'I'm sorry, mate,' he said, shooting Fletch a second glance. 'As soon as you came out of nick, I should have told you what was going down and, believe me, I wanted to. It was always there on the tip of my tongue, but I knew as soon as I opened my trap you'd end up kicking off and that was the last thing your mum wanted.'

Fletch remained silent and, tapping his thumb on the steering wheel, Stevie sighed. 'All right, I hold my hands up and admit I was in the wrong. We all were; we should have told you what was going on years ago when you were still inside.' The tapping on the steering wheel increased and he wanted to curse himself. If the tables had been reversed Fletch would have told him as soon as he'd an inkling his daughters weren't being cared for as they should be; that was the kind of mate he was.

They continued on in silence, the atmosphere in the car

becoming more and more uncomfortable with each passing second.

'Fletch.' Stevie turned his head. 'Come on, mate, say something.'

Staring through the windscreen, Fletch's voice was quiet as he spoke. 'I knew it was never going to be easy.' He snapped his eyes closed. 'Even before I came out, I knew they might not welcome me with open arms, that I'd have to work hard to gain their trust, and I was prepared to do that, I really was, but this...' He screwed up his face. 'This is like nothing I could have ever imagined. The whole situation, Tina, the kids.' He rubbed at his temples. 'My daughter is married to Rosco fucking Taylor, for fuck's sake; that right there alone is some fucked-up shit.' He turned his head. 'Are there any more surprises I should know about?'

Stevie took a moment to pause, then gave a slight shake of his head.

'Well, that's something to be thankful for, I suppose,' Fletch answered with a sigh. They had just reached Upminster high street and, unclipping his seat belt, Fletch jerked his head up ahead of them. 'Can you drop me off here? I'll take a cab back to the hostel.'

Pulling the car over to the kerb, Stevie switched off the ignition and leant back in the seat. 'Listen, mate, they just need more time. As I've told you before, let them get used to the idea of you being out and then take it from there, see if you can build a relationship with them. You're already halfway there with Austin; he's made up to have you back.'

Fletch looked into the distance and, opening the car door, he climbed out. He took a moment or two to think the situation through. 'I can't do this any more.' He closed the car door, leant his forearms on the roof and looked through the open window.

'They don't need me in their life; I'm not so sure they even like me.'

Stevie's forehead furrowed. 'You don't mean that, mate; you can't walk away from them, not now, not like this. All you've talked about for the last twenty years is your kids and how much you wanted to be on the outside with them.'

'My own daughter hates me.' Fletch's voice wavered, and he shook his head. 'And I can't make that right; I don't know how to.'

'Of course she doesn't. Yeah, I admit she's headstrong – she takes after you in that department.' He laughed in an attempt to make light of the conversation. 'But she doesn't hate you; you're her dad, how can she?'

'You didn't see the look on her face.' Fletch cut him off. 'She despises me and the worst part about all of this is that I've only got myself to blame. I should have been there for them, but instead' – he slowly shook his head – 'I was more concerned with hunting down my old man rather than looking after my own kids. What kind of a father does that make me?'

'Come on, Fletch.' Shifting his weight, Stevie hunched his upper body over the steering wheel so that he could get a better view of his mate. 'Back then we were only kids ourselves; you couldn't have predicted what would happen years down the line. How could you have known that Tina would spunk the money you gave her, or that she would turn into a junkie?'

Fletch lifted his shoulders. 'It's no excuse; I should have put them first. Nothing I could have done was ever going to bring Spencer back, but my kids, they were still here, and they needed me.' He exhaled loudly, tapped the car roof, shoved his hands into his jacket pockets and made off down the street, his shoulders sagging.

As Stevie watched him go, his heart went out to his oldest friend. He'd never seen Fletch look so despondent. Even when he'd been sent down he'd still had some fight left inside of him and no matter what he'd done in the past, Fletch was a good bloke, and he better than anyone else knew that to be a fact. After all, he'd known him long enough to know. When the shit hit the fan, Fletch was the kind of bloke you would want on your side. Closing his eyes, Stevie rested his head against the headrest. He wanted to kick himself; they should have been upfront from the start, the very moment Rosco had come onto the scene. It was only the fact they knew Fletch would have kicked off that had made them keep schtum in the first place and in all honesty they hadn't expected Rosco to stick around for any length of time. They certainly had never expected him to go from Tina to Kit; how could they have known? The very notion was not only sickening but downright disturbing.

* * *

The atmosphere in Rosco's office was charged and as she stared at her husband, Kit's heart beat a tattoo inside her chest. She'd never despised anyone as much as she did the man she was married to. Everything about him, from his bloated face to the heavy-set physique and permanent scowl, turned her stomach.

'I knew that little scrote was responsible,' Rosco snarled. 'All along, I said he had a hand in this.'

Kit's blood ran cold. 'No.' Her voice took on a desperate tone and she flicked her gaze between her husband and lover. 'No, Austin didn't have anything to do with this. You said yourself it was my dad; you know that Aus wouldn't have been able to pull this off.'

'Of course he had something to do with it,' Rosco roared. 'It was him who tipped your old man off; how else would he have known about the merchandise? I was hardly broadcasting the fact I was harbouring twenty kilos of coke, was I?' He poured out a tumbler of whiskey and downed it in one large gulp. 'That brother of yours' – he thrust the empty glass in her direction – 'he's crossed me one too many times.' His entire body was rigid, so intense was the rage that coursed through his veins. 'He's gone, do you hear me, Kit? I'm gonna kill the fucking bastard over this.'

'No!' As her husband charged around the desk, Kit reached out to grasp at his shirt. 'It wasn't him,' she cried.

Rosco batted her away from him as though she were a mere fly and made for the door. 'Round everyone up,' he ordered his right-hand man through gritted teeth. 'I want that little bastard found; I want him and the old man both found today.'

As her husband stormed out of the office, Kit turned to face Dennis. Her eyes were wide, her skin was ashen, and her hands shook so violently that she had to clench them into tight fists to stop the tremor from convulsing throughout her entire body.

'What have you done, Kit?' Shaking his head from side to side, Dennis stared at her. 'What the fuck have you done?'

After saying goodbye to Stevie, Fletch had thoroughly intended to get a taxi back to the hostel. Instead, he'd found himself outside Suzy's florist's shop, plucking up the courage to actually go inside.

Momentarily, he closed his eyes, then, opening them again, he blew out his cheeks and pushed open the door. What was the worst that could happen? he asked himself. She could either tell him to fuck off or that she was happily married, and then tell him to piss off. Bottom line was, nothing she said or did could make him feel any worse than he already did.

As he entered the shop, Susan looked up. For a moment, they

stared at one another, both of them at a loss for something to say. He watched the vein at the side of her neck throb and gave a small smile.

'Hello, Fletch.' It was Susan who spoke first. Her voice was just as gentle as he remembered all those years ago and her pale blue eyes still had the capacity to look into his very soul. 'I was hoping that you would come back.'

'Suzy.' He couldn't take his eyes away from her and, glancing at her wedding finger, he noted that she didn't wear a band. The knowledge made his heart beat that little bit faster. Remembering her daughter, he looked expectantly towards the back of the premises.

'Harri isn't here; it's her day off,' Susan volunteered.

'You named your kid Harri.' Shaking his head, Fletch gave a bitter laugh. Susan had been one of only a few people who'd ever known him by his birth name, Harry, and the fact she'd given her daughter his name was like a kick in the teeth as far as he was concerned. 'And there was me thinking you'd want nothing to remind you of me, the fuck-up you'd made – those were your words, weren't they? That was what you called me when you ended our relationship: a fuck-up.' As soon as the words had left Fletch's mouth, he wanted to kick himself and, rubbing the palm of his hand over his face, the stubble covering his jaw felt rough to his touch. 'I'm sorry.' He held his hands up. 'I have no right to say that.'

Susan tilted her chin in the air and there was a defiant gleam in her eyes. She had always known that this day would come, that it was inevitable that their paths would at some point in time cross. After all, it was the only reason she had bought the shop. Situated just a few miles down the road from where Fletch had grown up, as much as it terrified her, she'd hoped for this moment, prayed for it in fact. She'd even called the flower shop Suzy's, his nickname for her, in the hope that he would one day stumble across it. 'I named her Harriet for her father.'

'Yeah, I guessed as much.' Fletch looked down at the floor. After a moment or two, he jerked his head up to meet her eyes, his forehead furrowed. 'Her father – what do you mean by that?'

Susan gave a gentle sigh. 'Now maybe you'll understand why I had to run, why I had to leave England. I couldn't risk anyone finding out what had happened to Billy; I couldn't go to prison for what we did to him. I was pregnant. I had to put my baby first, our baby.'

'Our baby?' Taking a sharp intake of breath, the colour drained from Fletch's face and he clasped onto the table in the centre of the shop in a bid to stop himself from falling flat on his face. A fleeting image of Susan's daughter sprang to his mind and he tried to pull from his memory her features. Did they share any similarities?

'Is she definitely mine?' As her face fell, he gripped onto the table even harder. 'I'm sorry, but I have to ask, you know I do; I mean, you and Billy...' he said, referring to Susan's husband. 'Could she be his?'

Susan shook her head. 'Billy never wanted children.' Her cheeks flushed red and she averted her eyes. 'He always used protection.'

Fletch's mind reeled; of all the things he'd expected, this definitely wasn't one of them. 'Fuck me,' he said. 'A daughter.'

\* \* \*

With a heavy heart, Stevie twisted the key in the lock and pushed open the front door to his home.

'Daddy!' His youngest daughter ran into the hallway to greet him. 'Look what I made.' She held up a sheet of brightly coloured paper.

Hauling his daughter up onto his shoulder, he took the artwork from her and pretended to study it.

'It's upside down.' Megan giggled.

Turning the paper, he frowned. He could barely make out what it was she had painted, and sincerely hoped the pink blob in the centre of the page wasn't intended to be an interpretation of himself. 'That's smashing, darling.' He gave her a wide grin. 'You deserve a gold star, two gold stars even.'

From the corner of his eye he caught a glimpse of his wife as she entered the hallway. Just from her stance alone he could sense an argument was brewing and, kissing the top of his daughter's head, he placed her on the bottom step. 'Come on, up you go.' He grinned down at her. 'Give me and your mum five minutes to have a chat,' he added when his daughter stuck out her bottom lip. 'And then me, you and Rachel can watch a movie together.' He lowered his voice conspiratorially. 'We'll even make popcorn and sprinkle on lots of sugar, but don't tell Mummy.' He grinned.

He waited until his daughter had reached the top of the staircase, then reluctantly turned to look at his wife.

'Where have you been?' Jess's voice was hard.

Stevie sighed. Before he'd even opened the front door, he'd already known what was awaiting him: the five missed calls and subsequent text messages from his wife were his biggest clue that he was in the doghouse. 'I had some things to sort out with Fletch.' He gave a slight shrug of his shoulders. 'He's had some family shit to deal with.'

Jess rolled her eyes. Her dislike of his friend was written all over her face; she didn't even pretend to hide it any more. 'Yeah, I should have guessed,' she snapped back at him. 'Well, your dinner is in the bin,' she said, crossing her arms over her chest.

'It's been sitting on the kitchen table going cold for the past two hours.'

'I'm not hungry anyway,' he answered with a sigh. Pushing past her, he walked through to the kitchen, opened the fridge door and peered inside.

'Is this how it's going to be from now on? You barely coming home, spending all your time with him.'

'What's your problem, Jess?' After taking out a can of lager, Stevie slammed the fridge door closed and turned to face his wife. 'I'm here now, ain't I? I am home, not that it's done me any good,' he muttered underneath his breath.

Jess's back stiffened. 'Ever since he came out, me and the girls have been pushed to the background; we might as well not exist. It's embarrassing the way you run around after him. If I didn't know better, I'd think you were his lapdog.'

'Leave it out.' Snapping open the pull ring, Stevie shook his head. 'And he,' he said, emphasising the word, 'has a name, it's Fletch, and he also happens to be my best mate.' He took a long swig of the lager. 'Now, I swallowed the way you behaved around him the first time I brought him here, but don't for a single second think that I didn't notice,' he said, stabbing his finger towards her. 'You didn't even want to shake his hand, and I can tell you this for nothing: it's not something I'm going to put up with for much longer.'

'Oh, I am sorry,' Jess held up her hands, sarcasm clearly audible in her voice. 'Maybe I should take a leaf out of your book and bend over backwards for him, for the murderer that you allowed to breeze into our home. Would that be more to your liking?'

'He's done his time,' Stevie growled. 'He deserves a fresh start.'

Jess gave a bitter laugh. 'He killed his own father,' she spat. 'Is that the kind of man you want around our daughters? I mean, are the girls even safe? For all you know, he could creep in here in the dead of night and slit our throats while we sleep.'

'Hey, enough of that.' Stevie stalked forward until his wife was backed up against the kitchen table. 'You don't know anything about Fletch, nor the things he's had to do to survive.'

'You mean he's done more than just kill his father? Oh my God,' Jess cried, 'and you've allowed this man into our home; you've given him access to our daughters.'

'Figure of speech.' Stevie glanced away. She may have been his wife but he didn't trust her with the knowledge that long before Fletch had killed his father, he had also murdered their boss, Billy King. At the time it had been a matter of life and death and Fletch had had no other choice but to end the man's life. 'You don't know what happened that day; you weren't there.' His eyes held a steely glint to them. 'But I was, and I know exactly how it went down. We were lucky to walk away still in one piece and if Fletch hadn't topped his old man then he would have finished us off, it's as simple as that, so don't you dare stand there and look down your nose at him. If it wasn't for him, I'd be dead. So wind your neck in and lay off my mate. I'm all he's got; he needs me.'

His mobile phone began to ring, and he pulled the device out from his jacket pocket.

'I suppose that's him, is it?' Despite her husband's little speech, Jess was unable to keep the annoyance out of her voice. 'Can't he leave you alone for five minutes? You've got your own children up there to think about' – she pointed to the ceiling – 'and they need you a whole lot more than he ever will.'

'No, it's not Fletch.' Narrowing his eyes, Stevie stared down at the phone. 'It's Kit.'

'I suppose you're off out again, then?' Jess rolled her eyes. If it wasn't the murderer who wanted her husband's attention, then it was his kids. Not for the first time throughout her marriage did she wish that they would just leave him alone and allow him to live his life without constantly having to run around after them.

'Enough.' Stevie blew out his cheeks. 'Enough now, babe, you've made your point.' He fished his car keys out of his pocket, then leant forward and planted the briefest of kisses on his wife's cheek. 'I'll be back as soon as I can.' He gave a half smile and jerked his thumb towards the ceiling. 'Besides, I've already promised Meg we can have a movie night and you know me,' he said, becoming serious. 'I never go back on a promise.'

## 20

It was late afternoon by the time Stevie pulled his car into a lay-by on the fringe of Epping Forest. Switching off the ignition, he flung open the door, climbed out and made his way across the mud-splattered ground to where a black Mercedes was parked.

The Mercedes car door opened, and Kit stepped out. 'Stevie.' She gave him a small smile. 'Thank you for meeting me.'

'Bit cloak-and-dagger all this, ain't it?' He placed his foot on the grass verge and looked out across the darkened forest they had parked beside.

'It was the safest place I could think of,' Kit sighed.

Stevie's back stiffened and he swung his head around to look at her. 'What do you mean by that?'

Kit swallowed and, turning away, she slammed her eyes shut and took a deep breath.

'What's going on, Kit?' There was a harshness to Stevie's voice, and he glanced around him. For the briefest of moments he wondered if he'd been led into a trap and that Rosco was lurking in the shadows ready and waiting to pounce on him. Nothing would surprise him where the man was concerned; he was as much a coward as he was a bully.

'It's Austin.'

As he felt himself relax, Stevie gave an irritated sigh. 'What has he done now?'

'He's in so much shit.' Her voice cracked. 'And I can't help him this time.'

Stevie dipped his hand into his pocket and took out a pack of cigarettes. Leaning back against the car, he lit up, took a deep drag and blew out a cloud of smoke. 'Well, come on, spit it out – what's he done? I'm guessing it's something heavy if you had to drag me all the way out here.'

'It's Rosco.' She took a deep breath. 'He's going to kill Aus, I mean really kill him this time. It's more than just anger or spite talking; he's going to do it.'

'No surprise there; that cunt has had it in for him since day dot.' He continued to smoke his cigarette. 'I'm not being funny, Kit, but are you going to tell me what he's done or not?' Propelling himself away from the car, Stevie glanced at his watch. 'I haven't got all day. As it is, Jess is on the war path because apparently' – he used his fingers as quotation marks – 'I'm out all day and night running around after your dad.'

Rolling her lips together, Kit's voice dropped to a whisper. 'I tried to divert him away from Aus, I really did, but it only made the situation ten times worse and now he's out for blood and he's not going to stop until he's killed him.'

'For fuck's sake, Kit, will you just answer the question?' Staring at his best friend's daughter, Stevie fought down the urge to shake her. Whether she liked it or not, she had more of her father in her than she would ever realise. Fletch had been exactly the same when it came to Spencer.

'He stole something from Rosco.' Kit looked out at the forest;

eerie shadows danced across the trees and in the distance she could just about make out the roof of a public house. 'He hijacked a van, Rosco's van; it was transporting twenty kilos of coke.'

The blood drained from Stevie's face and he took a sharp intake of breath. 'Is this a wind-up?'

Kit shook her head. 'I wish it was.'

'Twenty kilos of coke.' Stevie whistled through his teeth. 'I know he might not always be the sharpest tool in the box, but this is taking things more than a step too far. Is he out of his tiny little mind?'

'Maybe.' Kit raised her eyebrows at the slur on her brother; if it had been anyone else other than Stevie, she would have laid into them. 'The thing is...' She swallowed deeply. 'I thought if I told Rosco it wasn't Aus, then he would... I don't know.' Her breath caught in the back of her throat and she lifted her shoulders in a helpless gesture. 'I thought he would back off and leave him alone.' She grabbed Stevie's arm and looked up at him. 'You have to help him.'

'I ain't got to do fuck all. I told him the last time he fucked up that I wasn't going to help him out any more; I'm getting sick and tired of cleaning up after him.' He gave her a sidelong glance as he flicked the cigarette to the floor and ground it out underneath his boot. 'And believe me, Kit, I meant every word. He has to learn to stand on his own two feet; he can't keep causing shit and then expect me to sort it all out for him.'

Tears sprang to Kit's eyes and she collapsed back against the car. 'Please,' she begged of him, 'Rosco is serious this time, he's even sent his goons out searching for him and if they find him...' She left the sentence unfinished, not that she really needed to say it; they both knew what Rosco was capable of when it came to Austin. The hatred between the two men went back years and as far as Rosco was concerned, it had been a case of loathing at first sight. The fact Austin was the image of his father had been more than enough of a reason for Rosco to go on and systematically abuse his adversary's son.

Stevie closed his eyes and sighed. Somehow she always managed to wrap him around her little finger; it was a particular knack of hers. 'I warned you not to marry him; how many times did I tell you that this would happen? I really thought you had a bit more sense than this.'

'I had no other choice; you know that I didn't.'

'Of course you did,' Stevie shouted. 'Time and time again, I told you that marrying the man wasn't going to stop him from going after Austin – any fool could have told you that. Did you honestly believe you would all play happy families once that ring was on your finger?'

Kit's cheeks flushed red. In reality, she'd never really thought that far ahead. At the time, all she'd wanted to do was get Rosco off her brother's back and when he'd made her a proposition to lay off Austin if she married him, as much as Rosco repulsed her, it had taken her all of ten minutes to agree to his proposal. 'I did it to save my brother,' she cried, 'you know I did.' Tears welled up in her eyes and she wiped them away with her fingertips. 'How was I to know it was all part of his game, that he only wanted to marry me to hurt Aus even more than he already had? And now look at me, I'm stuck with him, I hate him; you don't know what it's like for me. In here' – she pointed to her chest – 'I'm as miserable as sin but every day I have to smile, I have to pretend that I'm okay, that I'm happy; I have to do all of that for Aus's sake.'

Shaking his head, Stevie sighed. 'You could always divorce him.'

'How can I?' Kit threw her arms up into the air. 'He'll go after Aus if I even mention the word "divorce", you know he will.'

'Austin is a big boy now, Kit. Despite his faults, he knows how to take care of himself. Look,' he said, his voice becoming gentle, 'I'll see what I can do, okay, but I'm not going behind your dad's back on this one. He's already fucked off with me for not being straight with him and if I keep this from him as well it will just about tip him over the edge and it's me that'll end up getting it in the neck. And trust me, your dad isn't the type of man you wanna try and mug off twice.'

Kit looked away.

'What?' Stevie cocked his head to one side as he studied her. 'Whether you like it or not, he is your dad, and he loves you. Fair enough, he fucked up in the past but he's admitted this fact and apologised for it time and time again. He's trying to make things right; he deserves the chance to get to know you.'

Shaking her head, Kit bit down on her lip so hard that she could taste blood. Guilt was written all over her face.

'What have you done?' Stevie hissed out the words.

As she averted her gaze, Kit continued to shake her head.

'What have you done?' He grasped her by the shoulders and gently shook her.

'I told him it was my dad,' she choked out.

The words tumbled out of her mouth so fast that for a moment Stevie was unsure if he'd heard her right.

'Say that again?' His mind reeled as he tried to make sense of what she'd just told him.

'I told Rosco it was my dad. I thought it would divert him away from Aus—'

'No, back up a minute.' Stevie held up his hand, cutting her off. 'You told Rosco your old man stole that coke?'

A lone tear slipped down her cheek and as she swiped it away with the back of her hand, Kit gave a tiny nod of her head. 'I was trying to help Austin.'

Stevie's face fell and as the severeness of the situation hit home, he brought his hands up to his head. 'Are you trying to get your dad killed?' he roared at her.

'I was trying to protect my brother,' Kit retorted, 'and you told me yourself my dad would have done anything to keep his brother safe.'

'Not if that meant signing someone else's death warrant.' Stevie continued to roar at her, his eyes blazing with fury. 'He would never have put someone else's name in the frame for something Spencer had done.'

Kit lowered her head. 'I was trying to help Aus,' she repeated.

'Yeah, you keep telling yourself that.' Wiping away the film of cold sweat that covered his forehead, Stevie glared. 'If you were a bloke I'd lamp you one for the shit you've caused.' He clenched his fists into tight balls. 'What do you think your dad's going to say about this, eh, when he finds out that you've put a price on his head? The poor bastard has done fuck all wrong.'

'I don't know.' Kit gave a nonchalant shrug. 'I barely know the man; if it wasn't for the few photographs I've seen, I wouldn't have even recognised him.'

'He's still your dad.' Her words were more than enough to make Stevie see red and as he took a step towards her, she lifted her chin in the air. They both knew he wouldn't lash out; it wasn't in Stevie's nature to take his fists to a woman.

'Get in your car and follow me,' he spat at her. 'You can be the one to explain to your old man why he's got Taylor and half a dozen of his goons searching all over London for him.'

\* \* \*

Returning home from his grandmother's house, Austin climbed out of his car, locked up and swaggered casually towards the block of flats. He was just about to let himself in when something, or to be more precise someone, crashed heavily into his side and almost knocked him off balance. He could feel the air whoosh out of his lungs as he stumbled and before he'd even had the chance to retaliate he was being dragged away from the communal door, and seeing as he had some considerable bulk behind him the culprit had to be strong. It was no chancer, no little runt off the estate trying his luck. For a start, they wouldn't dare; his reputation alone was enough to guarantee him of that.

'Are you really that stupid?' As he slammed Austin against the brickwork, Dennis bellowed in his face.

Austin felt his insides relax and as a surge of adrenalin pounded through his veins, he shoved Dennis roughly away from him. 'What's your fucking problem?'

'What's my problem?' Disbelief could be heard in Dennis's voice. 'You've brought Kit in on the deal, your own fucking sister – are you fucking crazy? Isn't it bad enough that Rosco wants your blood on his hands? Are you trying to get her killed as well? Have you stopped taking your meds?' He tapped the side of his head. 'Is this a case of the lights are on but no one's home?'

'Watch your fucking mouth.' Austin's breath streamed out ahead of him as he squared up to Rosco's right-hand man. 'That trap of yours might impress those little pricks on Rosco's payroll, but it doesn't wash with me. I don't answer to you or anyone else, for that matter. If I want my sister or an entire marching band in on the deal then that's my prerogative.'

'You're becoming a liability and you're going to bring Kit down with you.'

Austin gave a nasty laugh. Dennis was beginning to get right on his tits; he was always whinging and whining about something or other. How his sister could even contemplate shagging the wanker, he'd never understand. Still, at least he was a step up from Rosco and that was saying something – the fat fucker reminded him of a sweating pig. Over the years he'd more than piled on the pounds and didn't look to be stopping any time soon.

'Yeah, and so what?'

'Is this all a big joke to you, a fucking game?'

'Do I look like I find this funny?' Austin pulled himself up to his full height. Just like his father, he had a formidable presence about him. 'My pal is on the missing list, and now to top it off I've got you in my earhole acting the billy big bollocks, shouting the fucking odds.'

'Someone has to; someone has to try and get through to that brain of yours. Which part of this don't you get? Rosco is out for revenge; he won't stop until he's hunted you down and dished out his own form of retribution, regardless of who gets in his way, and that makes my position in his firm that little bit more precarious. I'm hanging on by my fingernails all the while trying to cover your arse.'

'More like cover your own,' Austin sneered. 'Look at you, quaking like a fucking pussy; you're actually bricking it. Oh no, big bad Rosco might find out I'm fucking his wife,' he mocked.

Dennis narrowed his eyes. 'Fuck off, Aus, that's your sister you're talking about.'

'Yeah, that's right, she's my sister, so do yourself a favour and back off.' He made to walk towards the block of flats. 'In fact, why don't you run back to Rosco and lick his arse while you're at it.'

'You just don't get it, do you? You're putting her in danger.'

'Me?' Austin spun around, bounded forward and stood nose to nose with Rosco's right-hand man. 'It's not me who's creeping around behind that sweating pig's back,' he growled. 'If anyone's putting her in danger, it's you.'

'I'm trying to look out for her,' Dennis reasoned. 'I love her.'

'Go tell someone who gives a fuck,' Austin retorted as he walked away.

* * *

Now that he'd given himself the time to allow Susan's bombshell to actually sink in, Fletch allowed himself to relax.

Two hours earlier, Susan had closed the shop on the premise that they needed to talk and after sitting in the storeroom, surrounded by freesias, lilies, green leafy plants, rolls of ribbon in an assortment of colours, and blocks of oasis, any old feelings that he'd felt for her had resurfaced – not that he was sure they had ever left him. In fact, he knew they hadn't; she was still the only woman he would ever want. She held a piece of his heart and had done so from the very first moment he'd clapped eyes on her.

The conversation between them flowed easily, just as it always had in the past. He ached to hold her in his arms, to kiss her. Reluctantly he looked down at his watch, then set his coffee cup on the workbench. 'I should make a move.'

Disappointment was etched across Susan's face, although she tried her best to hide it. 'Will you come back, meet Harri properly?'

Fletch hesitated. Austin and Kitty hadn't taken his release from prison well; what was to say he wouldn't get the same reception from his second daughter? 'Does she know about me?' he asked.

'Of course.' Susan gave him a gentle smile. 'I've never hidden the fact you are her father. She would love to meet you.' She looked around the shop. 'It's because of her that we're here; for years she wanted to come to England, to be nearer to you.'

Fletch sighed and as much as a bubble of hope filled him, a little voice at the back of his head told him to err on the side of caution. 'She doesn't hate me?' he probed. 'I mean, for not being there for her growing up?'

'No, of course not,' Susan gasped. 'Harriet has never felt hatred towards you.'

They made their way across the shop and as they neared the door, Fletch involuntarily caught hold of Susan's hand. It was so unexpected that for a brief moment, they both stared down at their entwined hands with a level of surprise.

'I still love you,' Fletch said softly. 'I have always loved you.'

Tears filled Susan's eyes, and, waving her hand in front of her face, she turned her head away.

'Hey.' Fletch stepped forward, and lifted her chin up to meet his gaze. 'Don't ask me not to,' he begged of her, wiping away a stray tear from her cheek. 'I can't not love you; it's ingrained in me, in here.' He poked a finger into his chest. 'In here you are the only woman I will ever want.' He inched his face closer and as his lips brushed across her damp cheek, he breathed in her scent. 'I love you, Suze.'

Susan closed her eyes and as he swooped in for a kiss, she melted into him, their bodies slotting together like a missing piece of a jigsaw.

\* \* \*

Bringing the car to a halt outside the bail hostel, Stevie switched off the ignition, brought his mobile phone out of his pocket and dialled Fletch's number. There was no answer, not that he'd expected one. Fletch rarely used the phone that he'd given to him and he had a sneaking suspicion that after being locked up for twenty-two years the technology of today was beyond Fletch's comprehension. Tapping his thumb on the steering wheel, he studied the halfway house, then, flinging open the car door, he jumped out, made his way around to Kit's car and gestured for her to wind down the car window.

'He isn't picking up.' He placed the palm of his hand on the car roof and looked through the window. 'Where the fuck is he?' Worry was etched across his face and, biting down on his lip, he stabbed his finger through the open gap. 'If Rosco has nabbed him off the street, there'll be hell to pay,' he warned her. 'This will be on your head.'

Kit didn't answer; she wasn't stupid, and knew for a fact that she needed to keep Stevie on side. The last thing she wanted to do was antagonise him any more. As it was, she was skating on thin ice where he was concerned and without him, Austin would be left at Rosco's mercy.

Forty minutes later, Stevie's shoulders sagged with relief as Fletch rounded the corner of the street.

'Where the fuck have you been?' he called out to him.

'What?' Screwing up his face in consternation, a hot flush crept up Fletch's neck. He could hardly tell Stevie that he had just spent the afternoon with his Suzy, the love of his life, and that up against a wooden workbench, surrounded by freesias and green leafy plants, they had rekindled their relationship.

'Listen, Fletch.' Stevie cleared his throat and glanced back towards his car. 'We've got a situation, mate.'

Fletch followed his friend's gaze. 'Is that Kitty?' He nodded to the Mercedes parked behind Stevie's Land Rover.

'Yeah.' Stevie paused. 'There's something you need to know...'

Fletch craned his neck to get a better view of his daughter. Despite what he'd said about backing away from his children, a sliver of hope rippled through his veins. If Kitty was here then that could only be a good sign; maybe now that she'd had the chance to calm down, she'd come to realise he wasn't the enemy. Fletch tore his gaze away from his daughter to look at his friend. 'What the fuck is going on?'

'I need you to come with me.' There was an urgency to

Stevie's tone as he glanced up and down the street. 'Right now, mate.'

Fletch narrowed his eyes. It had been a long time since he'd last seen his friend looking so rattled. 'You need to tell me what the fuck is going on first, and while you're at it you can explain to me why my daughter is here.'

## 21

Talk about being on a high one minute and a low the next. As he listened to Stevie explain the situation, Fletch's blood ran cold. Deep down he'd had more than just an inkling that his daughter despised him, and this latest escapade was just about all the proof he'd needed. He was so hurt he couldn't even think clearly. Over and over again, Stevie's words played on a loop. She'd accused him of something he knew nothing about, let alone could have committed, all the while knowing that by doing so she was putting a price on his head.

'Mate.' Stevie gave him a sidelong glance.

Fletch turned his head. He was so consumed with what his own daughter had done to him that he'd barely been listening to a word Stevie said.

'I don't know how we're going to get out of this.' Stevie's eyes were wide.

'We?' Fletch asked, his voice strained.

'Yeah, we, as in you and me.' Stevie threw him a second glance. 'You didn't think I'd let you deal with this shit alone, did you?'

Fletch shook his head. If truth were told, he hadn't even thought that far ahead. The fact his daughter hated him was the only thing that registered inside his brain. He glanced in the wing mirror, checking that she was still following on behind. 'Why did Austin pull a stunt like this?'

'I don't know; you'll have to ask him yourself.' Stevie blew out his cheeks. 'If it ain't one thing with that kid then it's another.'

Screwing up his face, Fletch rubbed at his eyes. 'He's done this before, then?'

'Nothing near as serious as this.' Stevie flicked the indicator for the Barking turnoff. 'Like I said before, he's had his problems in the past.'

'You said he had anger issues, that my mum had needed to take him to a psychologist.'

'Yeah.' Stevie nodded. 'She did. But...' He paused for a moment. 'He doesn't think of the consequences; he never has done. He thinks he can do whatever the fuck he likes and that I'll be there to clean up his shit afterwards. But as for this, nah.' He gave a slight shake of his head. 'He knew what he was doing; he knew by taking that coke he'd cause fucking ructions with Rosco, and if he didn't then he's more stupid than I thought.' He turned his head. 'No offence, mate, I know he's your son and all that, but he can't keep pulling crap like this, and look at what he's caused.' He flicked his gaze up to the rear-view mirror and scowled. 'What they've both fucking caused.'

As he took a second look in the wing mirror, Fletch shook his head and sighed. It seemed like he was going to have to have a serious word with his boy; he could only hope and pray that he would be able to keep his temper at bay while doing so.

\* \* \*

Charlie Withers was sitting cross-legged on the floor. In his hand was a games controller and beside him on the floor, in an over-filled glass ashtray, was a joint.

He was engrossed in playing his game when a knocking at the front door broke his concentration. He'd recognise the knock anywhere; Austin was the only person he knew who knocked like he was the old bill about to execute a dawn raid.

'I'm coming,' he called out.

He pushed himself up from the floor, bent down to retrieve the joint and as he padded across the room, he flicked the lighter and lit up. The sweet pungent scent of cannabis filled the room as he took a deep toke. Above his head, a cloud of smoke drifted lazily across the small bedsit. He reached out for the door handle and pulled down. In a matter of milliseconds he'd been smashed up against the wall and a hand was wrapped around his throat so tight that his windpipe was almost crushed.

'Where is he?' a gruff voice barked out.

Charlie's face turned bright red, his eyes bulged and his lungs fought for air. To his shame, he actually wet himself and as the hot urine trickled down his leg and stained his tracksuit bottoms, the gruff voice bellowed in his face, spraying him in spittle as it did so.

'Where is that little scrote Austin?'

Charlie for his part did the only sensible thing he had ever done in his life and passed out.

\* \* \*

As he climbed out of Stevie's car, Fletch could barely look at his daughter. He didn't want to look at her, that was the problem – he didn't want to see the hatred she felt for him reflected back in her eyes. Instead, he concentrated on the low-rise block of flats where his son lived. The place was a shithole and that was saying some-thing, considering he lived in a dingy bail hostel. Every morning he had to fight his way into the bathroom that he shared with fifteen other residents. As for the kitchen, one glance inside had been more than enough to tell him not to ever attempt to cook in there; every available surface was covered in a thick layer of grease and as for the floor, it was littered with food particles, spilt sauces and what looked suspiciously like mouse droppings. He hadn't stepped foot inside since.

Stevie led the way around what appeared to be a children's playground. A death trap was how Fletch would describe it, if the broken swings and rusting climbing frame complete with several missing bars was anything to go by.

At the entry door, Stevie tapped in a series of digits and after a few moments the heavy door sprang ajar. As they walked across the lobby, Fletch shook his head. His son hadn't even bothered to enquire who was entering the property – a rookie mistake that could have made the difference between life and death back in his day.

At the top of the stairs, their footsteps were heavy as they walked along the corridor. Again, it was Stevie who thumped his fist on the flimsy wooden door.

'Yeah?' Austin cracked open the door. On seeing his father, the cocky grin he shot them slipped away and he stepped aside to allow them entry.

As they walked through the flat, Fletch looked around him. The inside was just as much a shithole as the outside. How the fuck had his son, his own flesh and blood, ended up in a place like this? All that money he'd left for them and they had nothing to even show for it.

'Is this about Mum?' As Austin flopped down on the rickety sofa, it creaked underneath his weight. 'She doesn't mean the things she says; she's not well.' He turned to look at his sister. 'You know she doesn't mean it, Kit, not really, not deep down. She was beside herself after you left, couldn't stop crying for what she'd caused.' It was a lie and they both knew it; in actual fact, Tina had continued on for well over an hour berating her daughter, blaming Kit for every thing that had gone wrong in her life.

'This ain't about your mother,' Fletch growled. He took note of the large zip bag filled with cannabis on the coffee table and wrinkled his nose at the unmistakable sweet, pungent stench that permeated the property. He shot a look at the woman sitting at the far end of the sofa, and rightly guessed that this was his son's girlfriend. For the life of him, he was unable to recall her name – Sheryl, Shelly, Sherry or at least something along those lines. On her lap she held a small child, his grand-daughter. She was wearing just a vest and a bulky nappy that was fit to bursting. He suspected she had more than likely needed changing hours ago. Question was, why hadn't she been? As he continued to study the little girl, Fletch's heart melted; Lacey was even more beautiful than he'd anticipated. She was simply stunning. The child's eyes were closed, and thick black lashes splayed out across her rosy cheeks. His throat constricted; she was around the same age Austin had been when he'd been sent to prison. It made what he'd done to his own two children that little bit more despicable. Guilt engulfed him. Where the hell had his head been at to even contemplate leaving his children, let alone actually seeing it through. As she drank from the bottle clasped in her chubby little hands, she made soft sucking sounds. Even from where he was standing, he could see that the bottle hadn't been cleaned out in days, maybe even weeks, if the layer of ground-in limescale staining the inside of the plastic was anything to go by. Disgust was etched across his face and, tearing his eyes away from the child, he caught her mother's eyes. He noted that as she looked away, her cheeks flushed pink.

'Shouldn't she be in bed by now? It's a bit late, isn't it?'

Austin looked up at his father. For the first time since their arrival, he sensed the anger that radiated from him and, picking at a loose thread on his tracksuit bottoms as though it was the most interesting thing he had ever done, he turned his head to look at the woman beside him. 'Yeah, it is.' He jerked his head towards the door. 'Put her to bed, Ree.'

Sheree opened her mouth to argue back, then, thinking better of it, she snapped it closed again and edged her body forward on the sofa, careful not to wake her sleeping daughter. Lacey had never had a bedtime routine and most nights they left her to sleep on the sofa until they themselves went to bed. With difficulty she managed to get to her feet. The child was a dead weight in her arms and as she exited the room, she gave her visitors one final glance before heading for the bedroom.

'They know, Aus,' Kit told her brother once Sheree was out of earshot. 'They know about the coke.'

For a few short moments, Austin stared at his sister, his expression hard. Then, jumping up from the sofa, he bellowed in her face, 'You had no right to open your trap. Who else have you told, eh?' He spat the words out with a measure of venom. 'Did Maguire put you up to this? I know you're shagging him.' He turned to look at Stevie. 'I bet you didn't know anything about that, did you? That's she's fucking Rosco's right-hand man.'

'Shut your mouth and sit down.' Fletch shoved his son none too gently back onto the sofa.

'She had no fucking right.' As Austin fell back in a crumpled heap, the sofa buckled underneath his weight. 'You need to learn how to keep your legs closed,' he screamed at his sister.

'Hey, I've already warned you once, that's enough.' At the side of Fletch's head, a vein began to pulsate, a sure sign that he was fast on his way to losing his temper. 'That's your sister you're talking about.'

'And the shit you've caused, boy,' Stevie was quick to add, 'you've no right to talk. You never learn, do you?' He balled his fists. 'I should batter you and not stop until I've knocked some sense into that thick skull of yours.'

'Yeah, all right, in your fucking dreams.' As he rolled his eyes, Austin gave an irritated sigh.

Running his tongue over his teeth, Stevie turned his head. 'Do you see now what I've had to put up with from this lairy little fucker? All he ever does is open that big trap of his and cause aggravation.' He took a step closer to the sofa. 'If you weren't his son' – he jerked his thumb in Fletch's direction – 'I would have kicked your arse to the kerb years ago. Once again, because of you and your fucking stupidity and the ructions you've caused, Rosco has put a price on your dad's head.'

As he looked up at them, any anger that Austin had felt was long gone and in its place genuine confusion spread across his face. 'My dad had nothing to do with it.'

'I already know that!' Stevie retorted. He turned to look at Kit. 'Do you wanna fill him in or shall I?'

'Fill me on what?' Looking from Stevie to his sister, Austin's eye's widened.

'I did what I had to do,' Kit hissed at her brother, her expression hard. 'Although I've got to admit, I'm beginning to wonder why I even bothered now.' She crossed her arms over her chest. 'Right from the start, Rosco suspected it was you, and I had to divert him somehow, the only way I knew how.'

'She told the fat cunt it was your dad who hijacked the van,' Stevie said.

Austin's eyes widened and he flicked a glance in his father's direction.

Fletch put up his hand and as they all turned to look at him, he addressed his son. 'This is getting us nowhere. Where have you stashed it?'

Austin swallowed, shifted his weight on the now-broken sofa and averted his eyes.

'Don't fuck us about,' Stevie said through gritted teeth. 'Your dad asked you a question – where the fuck is it?'

'He's hidden it at Nan's house,' Kit volunteered. 'It's underneath the floorboards in his old room.'

'You've done what?' Fletch screwed up his face.

'I don't fucking believe this.' Throwing up his hands, Stevie shook his head. 'Don't you ever think, boy?'

'What?' Austin asked, looking from his father to Stevie.

'What do you mean by "what"?' Fletch roared. 'You know full fucking well what – that's my mum's house.'

Austin shrugged. 'It's only temporary, until Mark can arrange the sale for it. What are you getting out of your pram for? It ain't a big deal; as soon as I can, I'll shift it. Nan will never even know it was there.'

Talk about clueless. Fletch may not have wanted his son to follow in his footsteps but he'd at least expected his offspring to have the common sense to stash the goods far away from where he or any of his family members actually lived. But to know he'd actually stashed the cocaine in his own grandmother's house was more than enough to make Fletch see red. In a matter of seconds, he'd hauled his son to his feet and shoved him roughly in the direction of the front door. 'You stupid, stupid bastard; this isn't some game you're playing.' As he stabbed a stiff finger against his son's temple, it took all of Fletch's strength not to batter his boy.

'Are you really so cocksure of yourself that you actually think you're untouchable?'

For the first time in his life, Austin had the sense not to answer back.

\* \* \*

Charlie's arm hung loosely at his side and as blood slipped past his wrist, through his fingers and onto a dusty linoleum floor covering, he highly suspected that he may have a compound fracture. The fact that bone fragments had pierced through the skin and soft tissue was more than enough to tell him that his suspicions were correct. He'd never known pain like it and as he screamed out in both agony and paralysing fear, his feet kicked out in front of him as he tried in vain to scoot across the Portakabin floor.

Rosco had barely broken out in a sweat. In his fist he held a claw hammer and streaks of Charlie's blood were splattered across the iron head. 'I asked you a question – where is he?' He stalked forward, the hammer in his fist swinging backwards and forwards as he did so.

'I don't know,' Charlie screamed back at him. 'If I knew, I'd tell you.' Tears stained his cheeks, and his panic-stricken eyes were drawn to the door as it opened. 'Dennis, help me out,' he pleaded.

The tiny hairs on the back of Dennis's neck stood up on end and as he cocked his head to one side, a sickening thought sprang to his mind. Did Charlie know about him and Kit? Had Austin somehow found out about them and told all his mates? Nothing would surprise him where Austin was concerned; everything in life was one big joke to him.

'Dennis, come on, man, help me.'

Moving forward, Dennis snatched the hammer out of Rosco's

hand. As he stood over Charlie, he raised the weapon and gave him a hard stare. 'Why are you bringing my name into this?' He kicked his foot out and executed a sickening blow to Charlie's ribs. 'Why the fuck would I want to help you out?'

The impact catapulted Charlie onto his back. 'You know, man,' he gasped as pain reverberated through his chest. 'You know why.'

Dennis's grip tightened around the hammer. 'No, I don't fucking know.'

Not taking his eyes off the weapon, Charlie raised his good arm above his head in a desperate attempt to protect himself. 'Yeah, you do,' he screamed as the hammer sliced through the air. 'You and—'

The attack that followed was both brutal and frenzied. As far as Dennis was concerned, he had to stop Charlie from opening his trap and blurting out the truth about him and Kit. Amid Charlie's screams, he used as much force as he could physically muster to rain the hammer down over and over again, and it wasn't until he was spent and out of breath that he allowed the weapon to slip to the floor with a loud clatter. When he finally turned his head to look at his boss, a snarl was etched across his handsome face. 'Torch the fucker.'

Rosco raised his eyebrows. He glanced down at the bloodied mass on the floor; the shallow rise and fall of Charlie's chest alerted him to the fact he was still alive, if only just. 'What the fuck was that all about?'

The muscles across Dennis's shoulders were rigid as he grasped Charlie by the ankles and began to drag the dead weight with relative ease across the linoleum floor, leaving a long, thick smear of blood in his wake.

'Oi, I asked you a question. What the fuck is going on here?'

Rosco narrowed his eyes until they were nothing more than two mere slits in his bloated face.

'The bastard,' Dennis spat through gritted teeth. As he dropped Charlie's ankles, they landed on the floor with a loud thud. The fact Charlie had even mentioned his name was enough to bring him out in a cold sweat, and his fingers automatically searched for the gold cross that hung from a thin chain around his neck. For the first time in his adult life, he sent up a silent prayer. What should have been a simple night's work was spiralling out of control and he had a sinking feeling that this was only the beginning of the bloodshed that was to come. 'He's no pal of mine; why the fuck would I help him out?'

As his number two resumed the task of dragging the blood-ied, broken body out of the Portakabin, Rosco watched him go. Dennis, for his part, had asked a valid question, one that Rosco would very much like to know the answer to. Why exactly would the little bastard have thought that his right-hand man would help him?

## 22

After a lot of persuasion, Jenny had finally convinced Tina to have an early night and go to bed. If truth be told, as of late she was feeling her age. Not only did her bones ache but her mind felt equally as weary. All she wanted was an easy life – not that she had much chance of getting what she wanted with Tina around – and yet she couldn't help but feel responsible for her grandchildren's mother. Tina had no real family to speak of, no siblings, and her parents had all but disowned her in recent years.

Handing over two painkillers and a tumbler of water, she'd watched as Tina had swallowed the pills down then helped her get to her feet, promising her that when she woke in the morning the situation wouldn't seem half so bad. It was an empty promise, of course. Nothing was going to change the circumstances, and she better than anyone knew that to be a fact. Kit would still be married to Rosco, Tina herself would still be an addict, and Fletch would still be out of prison, or at least she hoped he would, anyway.

The lounge was in darkness and, sitting on the sofa, Jenny

stared at the mantelpiece. The light from the streetlight illumi-
nated the photographs she had lovingly placed there.

Her gaze lingered on one of her younger son's school
portraits. She would give anything to see Spencer's lopsided grin
one last time, to hold him in her arms, for him to play one of his
practical jokes on her. Her heart ached for him as much today as
it had when he'd been so cruelly taken from her. It was a grief
that consumed her, a loss that she didn't believe she would ever
fully recover from. In the aftermath of his murder, she'd found it
difficult to remember to breathe, the ache in her heart numbing
her mind and body, so much so that she longed to join her son.
Even the fact she had a surviving son wasn't enough to deter her
from her dark thoughts, but eventually she had somehow
managed to get through the days, until the days had turned to
weeks, and then the weeks had turned to months. Before she
knew it, years had passed – twenty-two of them, to be exact.

From an early age, all her two sons had ever known was
violence. They had witnessed their own father's terrifying temper
first-hand, and on a regular basis they had watched him raise his
fists and beat her until she was black and blue. By the time they
could walk and talk, the boys were being subjected to the same
terror. Was it any wonder they had taken the path they had?
Perhaps it was inevitable that they would follow in their father's
footsteps and become criminals themselves. The way of life was
ingrained inside of them; it was all they had ever known, despite
her best efforts to raise them knowing right from wrong.

Perhaps everything was her fault. She should have left her
husband the first time he'd raised his fists and battered the boys –
no, long before then. She should have left him the first time he'd
lashed out and given her a split lip and blackened eye. If only
she'd have found the courage to leave him, it would have saved
her from all the heartache that was to follow.

The headlights from a car lit up the room, breaking her reverie and, sitting forward on the sofa, Jenny craned her neck to look out the window. From her position she could just about make out her son, followed by Stevie and her two grandchildren, making their way down the path.

Her heart was heavy as she stood up and made her way across the room. More than anything, she hoped that their arrival wasn't going to bring more trouble. There was only so much she could stomach in one day and as it was she'd already had a gutful.

A key turned in the lock and as the front door opened she could hear their hushed voices as they entered the hallway. Seeing as the house was in darkness, it didn't take a genius to work out that they thought she and Tina were in bed fast asleep and that Frank had slipped out to the pub for a pint.

As they crept along the hallway, their feet as light as tiny mice, their looming shadows were cast across the lounge wall. Jenny held her breath, and as they came closer to the open doorway, she snapped on the light switch and stepped out into the hallway.

'Jesus, Mum, what are you doing creeping around in the dark?' Recoiling away from his mother, Fletch's voice was raised.

'I could ask you the same thing.' Jenny couldn't help but notice how shifty they all looked, not that she expected anything different from them. They had been caught red-handed, creeping into the house, after all. When she spoke, her voice held a note of authority to it. 'You've all got some explaining to do and, believe me, it had better be good.'

Fletch hesitated. Ever since he was a kid, his old mum had been able to see right through him, and for a split second he considered actually telling her the truth, that they had come to collect twenty kilos of cocaine that had been hidden underneath the floorboards in what used to be Spencer's room. He flicked a glance at the mantelpiece, and his gaze lingered on the photograph of his brother. In some respects, Austin reminded him of Spencer; for a start, they both never thought through the repercussions of their actions.

'Well?' Jenny narrowed her eyes. 'Because let me tell you now, if you've come here to cause more aggravation then the lot of you can turn around and walk back through that door. I've had more than I can take for one day, and I won't let you, any of you,' she said in a warning, ''cause any more bloody ructions.'

'Don't be daft, Mum, it's nothing like that. We just wanted to make sure everything had calmed down here.'

Jenny cast her eyes over her grandchildren and Stevie. The three of them grinned at her and nodded in agreement. In fact, they reminded her of nodding dogs and she would have sworn blind they were up to no good. What they were actually up to, though, for the life of her she had no idea.

'And then when Aus said he wanted to collect something from his old room, we all thought why not come along for the ride.'

'Collect what?' Jenny snapped her head towards her grandson. 'You took everything with you when you moved in with Sheree.'

Flicking a nervous glance towards his father, Austin opened his mouth to speak.

'He needs his birth certificate,' Kit blurted out. 'He thinks it might have fallen through the gap in the floorboards, ain't that right, Aus?' She tilted her head towards him, silently beseeching him to play along.

'Yeah, that's right.' He moved towards the staircase. 'I'll just nip up and get it.'

'Oh, no, you will not.' Jenny's body bristled. 'Your mum's asleep up there, and I don't want you waking her up; that's the last thing we all need.'

'I'll be quiet.' Before his grandmother could answer him, Austin was halfway up the stairs.

'Aus,' Jenny hissed, 'get down here, now.'

'Mum, why don't you put the kettle on?' Guiding Jenny towards the kitchen, Fletch threw her a wide smile. 'I've missed your tea.' He winked. 'And compared to the cat's piss they pass off as tea inside, I could really do with one.'

'I suppose you'll be wanting biscuits as well?' Jenny sighed as she reluctantly flicked the switch for the kettle to boil.

'I wouldn't say no,' Stevie piped up.

Jenny rolled her eyes; she should have guessed. Stevie never said no when it came to food.

\* \* \*

Ever so carefully, Austin pushed open the door to what was once his bedroom. The room was in darkness and the soft snores that came from the direction of the bed told him that his mum was in a deep sleep. He crept across the room, bypassing the creaky floorboards and, at the foot of the bed, he sank to his knees. Stealing a glance back at the bed, he held his breath as his mother stretched out then rolled over. After a few moments, she resumed snoring and he gave the frayed edges of the carpet a gentle tug. With relative ease he was able to lift out the three floorboards nearest to the wall, revealing the open space underneath.

Pushing his arm into the gap, he felt around. Within moments, his fingertips came into contact with a hard object and with another hesitant glance towards the door, he lifted the object out. It was a semi-automatic pistol, the one he had used during the hijack. The firearm was cold and heavy in his hand

and, placing it on the floor beside him, he delved his hand into the hole a second time.

The holdall containing the bags of coke was wedged further back into the gap than he'd first thought and he needed to use some considerable force to retrieve it. Finally, and with a loud plop, the bag was free from its confines. Glancing towards his mother, Austin held his breath; he'd made enough noise to wake the dead. When Tina didn't stir, he blew out his cheeks, picked up the firearm and shoved it back into the hole before replacing the boards and re-laying the carpet.

\* \* \*

A few moments later, Austin walked back down the stairs with a dark-coloured holdall slung over his shoulder.

'Did you find what you were looking for?' Jenny asked, eyeing the bulging bag. She was pretty certain he hadn't been carrying one before he'd gone up to Jenny's room.

'Yeah, it was exactly where I thought it would be.'

Lifting a china cup to her lips, Jenny sipped at the scalding-hot liquid. They were definitely up to no good, she knew that for a fact. She also knew there was no way Austin could have found his birth certificate; she kept it in a box on top of her wardrobe along with any other important paperwork.

\* \* \*

Whistling through his teeth, Stevie stared down at the holdall that had been slung into his car boot. 'Fuck me.' He poked a package of cocaine with his forefinger. 'No wonder Rosco is doing his swede; this lot must come to at least...' He tilted his chin in the air as he tried to calculate how much the cocaine was worth at street value.

'Just over one and a half million pounds,' Kit volunteered.

Stevie's eyes widened. 'Fuck me.'

'How much was Taylor selling it for?' With his arms crossed over his chest, Fletch tore his eyes away from the bag to look at his daughter. 'What's this little lot worth to him?'

'Just under a million.' Kit shrugged.

Catching Fletch's eyes, Stevie blew out his cheeks. He slammed the boot down. 'Right then, so what do we do with it now?'

For a few moments they were all silent.

'We hide it underneath Rosco's nose, in the last place he would ever think of looking for it: we take it to the Portakabin.' As she thought the situation through, Kit nodded; in her mind, the cabin was the ideal hiding place. 'There are a few abandoned cars there. He would never even think of looking inside them – why would he? – and as far as I know, the cars haven't been touched in years. I know for a fact that they aren't roadworthy. I just need to nip home and get the spare key for the gates. It shouldn't take me any longer than an hour if I put my foot down.'

Stevie and Fletch shared a glance.

'It's not a bad idea,' Stevie conceded. 'Not entirely ideal, I admit, but if it means we get one over on that fat cunt in the process, then I'm all for it.'

'There is no "we",' Kit spat. 'This is mine and Austin's deal.'

'This ain't your deal, Kit; this is fuck all to do with you,' Austin stated.

Kit's body bristled, and she shot her brother a look of anger. 'That's not what you said. You told me I was in.'

'Only because you were doing my nut in,' he groaned.

'Cheers, Aus, thanks a lot for that,' Kit spat at him. 'I'm supposed to be your sister.'

Austin rolled his eyes. 'Anyone would think this is a free-for-all. I'll tell you what, why don't you ask the bloke next door if he wants in an' all,' he sighed.

'Enough.' Fletch held up his hands. 'This isn't the time for the pair of you to be bickering. Kitty, go and get the key.' He turned to look at his mother's house, then glanced down at his watch; he had just under two hours until his curfew kicked in and he needed to be back at the hostel. 'You can meet us back here.'

'Good idea,' Stevie agreed. He gave the house a wistful glance. 'I wonder if your mum has got any more of those biscuits in?'

Fletch screwed up his face. 'Is your stomach the only thing you think about?'

'Nah, of course not.' Stevie's cheeks flushed pink.

'Right then, that's settled. Kit, we'll meet you back here in an hour.'

* * *

Dennis was filling a metal bucket with cold water. He'd already emptied in two bottles of bleach and the strong scent of chemicals was enough to make his eyes stream.

'Make sure it's clean.'

Glancing over his shoulder, Dennis didn't bother to answer. At times, Rosco treated him not only like the hired help but also like an imbecile to boot. As if he wouldn't make sure all traces of Charlie Withers' blood had been wiped clean. At the end of the day, it was his neck on the line just as much as it was Rosco's. After all, it had been him who'd dished out the fatal blows.

He lifted the bucket, threw half the contents across the

linoleum floor, then, getting to his hands and knees, he began to scrub.

It took almost eight buckets of water, twelve bottles of bleach and a scrubbing brush to finally clean the floor and erase all traces of the crime that had taken place. Standing back, he pushed the sleeve of his sodden shirt up his arm and slammed his bare forearm over his nose and mouth as he inspected his handiwork. The chlorine scent that filled the Portakabin was enough to make his chest wheeze and his eyes sting.

'You've missed a bit.'

Dennis turned to face his boss. Was Rosco taking the piss? The fat bastard hadn't even moved a muscle to help clean up the aftermath of the brutal murder that had been committed, and it had been brutal; the amount of blood left behind was more than enough to prove that.

From outside the Portakabin, Rosco's so-called foot soldiers were standing around their cars, chatting and smoking cigarettes, while he had just spent the best part of an hour on his hands and knees scrubbing the floor. He was no skivvy; he was meant to be Rosco's number two, his right-hand man, and this was what he'd been reduced to.

'Couldn't you have got one of that lot to do this?'

Standing up, Rosco waved his hand. 'I wouldn't trust them to have a wank, let alone clean this. Come on.' He glanced at his watch. 'Get a move on; I want to get to the club.'

Dennis rolled his eyes, and as he watched his boss leave the Portakabin, not for the first time did he regret ever getting himself involved with Rosco Taylor.

\* \* \*

'Listen, Fletch.' Stevie stuffed a biscuit into his mouth, chewed, swallowed, then washed it down with a long slurp of his tea. 'A million quid, that's a lot of dough; this could set us up, and you can't deny that you could do with some cash in your back pocket.'

Fletch's mouth dropped open. 'Are you out of your mind? I'm not doing a drugs deal with my kids.'

'What, and you trust Austin to deal with this?' He picked up a second biscuit, then, thinking better of it, he dropped it back into the biscuit tin and replaced the lid. 'Let's look at the facts here, Fletch: he didn't even have the sense to stash the gear in a safe place, let alone have the capacity to sell it on. How the fuck do you expect him to deal with a firm of heavies? You know as well as I do that big fucking trap of his will run away with him and he'll be lucky if they don't end up gutting him like a pig, and that's if Rosco doesn't get his hands on him first.'

Fletch continued to shake his head. As far as he was concerned, he had too much to lose. He couldn't lose his kids again, couldn't lose Susan; as it was, he'd already sworn to her that the life of crime he'd once led was in the past, that he'd gone straight and was fully intending to stay on the right side of the law. 'No, I'm not doing it, no fucking way. I've just done a lump; I'm not doing time again. I've still got that probation officer on my back and, as I keep on telling you, I'm a changed man. I don't want any part in that way of life. No good can come from it; it's a slippery slope that leads to nowhere. We better than anyone know that to be a fact.'

'Yeah, how could I have forgotten.' Stevie rolled his eyes. 'You did a sociology course and turned over a new leaf. Next you'll be telling me that you found God while you were at it.'

Fletch narrowed his eyes.

'Please tell me you haven't?' Stevie's eyes widened. 'Jesus Christ, Fletch. Excuse the pun, mate, but fuck me, I never thought

I'd see the day when you of all people would turn into a holy Joe. You would have laughed if anyone had tried to preach to you before you went inside.'

'Leave it out, of course I haven't,' Fletch retorted, although it wasn't for the want of trying on the prison chaplain's behalf.

'Thank fuck for that.' Stevie exhaled loudly. 'Listen, mate, this turning over a new leaf business wasn't going to stop you an hour ago when you vowed to kill Rosco.'

'That's different and you know it,' Fletch spat out. 'That's personal; that's about my kids.'

'What, and this isn't? For fuck's sake, Fletch, think logical. We can't walk away from a million quid; we'd be crazy to even consider it,' Stevie persevered. 'And what's the alternative, eh? Take your head out of the sand; you know Austin can't handle something like this, but with me and you by his side, he might just be able to walk away from this with not only some bunce in his pocket but with his life still intact.'

'I said no,' Fletch growled. He narrowed his eyes as he studied his friend. 'Are you really willing to risk everything you have, your wife, your kids, your life? Because that's exactly what will happen if you end up going down this road. You're gonna end up inside, and I'm not talking about for a few months or even a few years; I'm talking about doing bird, proper bird, a life sentence, and trust me, it's not all it's cracked up to be. In fact, it's hell on earth.'

Stevie shrugged. 'We did all right before and if you hadn't killed your old man, we would have still been doing all right. The old bill never came near us; you know they didn't.'

'What are you talking about? I was sent down for six months for assaulting that copper.'

Stevie waved his hand in an attempt to dismiss Fletch's words. 'That was a set-up and you know it.'

'I'm not listening to this.' Fletch shook his head and made to walk away. 'You've got a short memory, mate.'

'Wait,' Stevie said, his cheeks flushing pink.

'What?'

'I need the money, mate.' He looked Fletch in the eyes and gave a half smile. 'Like I said, working the doors pays peanuts and with Jess not working we only have my wages coming in. I'm behind on the mortgage payments and if I don't think of something and fast, I'm going to lose the house. The bank is already talking about repossession. I've not even told Jess; I can't, I don't know how to.'

Closing his eyes, Fletch groaned. He rubbed at his temples and softly shook his head. 'Don't ask me to do something like this; I can't end up inside again, I just can't.'

'I have to.' There was a hint of desperation in Stevie's voice. 'I don't have any other choice; I need the money.'

Reluctantly and against his better judgement, Fletch nodded. 'It's not me you have to convince, it's them.' He jerked his head in the direction of the kitchen door. 'I don't think it's going to go down too well if we try and muscle in. As it is, my daughter already despises me.'

A wide grin crept across Stevie's face and for the third time that evening a sense of relief washed over him. 'You just leave them to me,' he said with confidence. 'It'll be a piece of cake.'

* * *

Fifty minutes later, once Jenny had gone to bed and Kit had returned with the keys to the Portakabin, they crowded into the kitchen.

'No.' She placed her hands on her hips and shook her head from side to side so fast that Fletch wouldn't be surprised if she had given herself concussion. 'No, this is our deal; you're not muscling in. Tell them, Aus.'

'What, and you honestly think he can handle something like this?' Stevie persisted. 'He didn't even have the sense to stash the goods somewhere safe.'

'He'll have me,' Kit answered. She took a step closer to her father's friend, her face contorted with rage. 'I'll be the one to handle everything.'

'Hey, hold up a minute, I didn't agree to that,' Austin protested.

Kit ignored her brother. 'He's already got a buyer anyway, so as you can see we don't need you.'

'Who's the buyer?' Fletch's voice was controlled as he spoke and they all turned to look at him.

'Yeah, good point, who's the buyer?' Stevie asked.

'A firm in Manchester.' Austin gave a nonchalant shrug.

'Which firm?'

'I dunno.' Austin shifted his weight from foot to foot. 'Just some firm. Mark's been dealing with them.'

'Who's Mark?' Fletch narrowed his eyes.

'My pal.' He reached into his pocket and toyed with his mobile phone.

'Well, get him on the blower and find out who they are.' Fletch nodded down to the outline of a phone in his son's pocket.

Pulling out the device, Austin shook his head. 'He hasn't been answering my calls. I don't know where he is; no one has seen him since the night of the hijack.'

Kit's cheeks flushed red and she rubbed at the back of her neck. 'We don't need Mark,' she said quietly. 'All we need to do is find a new buyer.'

Blowing out his cheeks, Stevie threw his arms up into the air. 'And you reckon you've got this under control?' He told Kit. 'From where I'm standing, you don't have a clue what you're doing. A deal has already been made; you don't go back on it now. What are you trying to do, start a war?'

'Yes, a deal was made with Mark,' Kit answered. 'Not with us, was it?'

'A buyer is the least of your problems.' Fletch swallowed deeply in an attempt to keep his temper in check. He could seriously maim his boy for his stupidity, and if he'd been anyone else, some random geezer, he would have punched his fists into his face and not stopped until he was begging for mercy. 'You need to get the gear into this Portakabin without being seen, first.'

'That won't be a problem.' Kit pulled out her mobile phone and as her fingers flew over the keyboard, she tapped out a text message. Within seconds of pressing send, her phone pinged back a reply. 'Rosco just arrived at the club. Dennis is going to let me know when it's safe to shift the merchandise.'

'And what about me and your dad?' Stevie asked. 'Are we in?'

'You already know what I think,' Kit retorted.

'Aus?'

Austin looked to his sister and shrugged. 'It can't hurt, can it?'

'Right then.' A grin spread across Stevie's face and he rubbed his hands together before Kit had the chance to sway Austin's mind. 'That's settled, then; me and your dad are in, so do us all a favour, Kit, and wipe that look off your face. It doesn't suit you, darling, and if I'm being truthful, it's more than enough to curdle milk.'

Kit rolled her eyes and as she leant up against the washing machine, she crossed her arms over her chest. As much as she hated to admit it, to have someone else take part of the burden away from her shoulders was a welcome relief.

## 23

As he followed Rosco through the club, Kit was at the forefront of Dennis's mind. Keeping her out of harm's way was his number one priority, and he had a sneaking suspicion that Rosco's feelings towards his wife were beginning to wane, not that he was so sure Rosco had ever felt much for her in the first place. She was nothing more than a tool to get at Austin, a way for him to exude even more power over his brother-in-law than he already did. No, Rosco didn't love her, certainly not in the same way as he loved himself.

In a short space of time, Kit had become Dennis's whole world, his everything, the very reason that he lived and breathed. He'd never felt such a strong connection to a woman before and the mere thought of her being tied to Rosco's side was enough to make him want to commit murder. All he wanted was for her to be free from her husband's grasp. He wanted her to be solely his; he even wanted her to meet his family. Still, before he could even contemplate introducing her to his parents, they would need to survive the fallout from Rosco's wrath. Not that he was overly concerned; as he'd already told Kit, he could handle himself, and it was no lie, he could. His father, Brandon Maguire, a bare-knuckle boxer, had taught him everything he needed to know – not only how to think fast on his feet, but also how to defend himself.

No, all Kit had ever been to Rosco was a bargaining tool, and he knew for a fact she had only married the man on the premise that he would give her brother a swerve. Right from the very beginning, Rosco had badgered, bullied and threatened her into marriage, and as much as he'd understood her reasons for going through with the wedding, he couldn't help but think she'd been a fool to take him up on the offer. Rosco was never going to stop his bid to destroy Austin; any idiot could have told her that. The hatred Rosco felt for Austin went way further than just skin deep; it was a hatred that consumed his every waking thought.

Despite the early hour, the club was in full swing, the tables were all occupied and as a result the club was now standing room only. Music blared out from the speakers, and as he stormed past the stage he glanced in the direction of Tiffany Blue, one of the club's star attractions. She was midway through her routine and was already minus the sky-blue sparkly bra top that was part of her signature outfit.

Amid the party atmosphere, he sensed an underlying current of danger, it was so thick it had smacked him in the face as soon as he'd entered through the doors. The fact Rosco's foot soldiers were running around like headless chickens was more than enough to tell him and anyone else with half a brain cell that some serious shit was going down.

They made their way up to where the offices were situated, and after a quick glimpse inside Kit's darkened office, he continued to follow Rosco along the corridor.

Taking a seat behind the desk, Rosco leant back in the chair. The buttons on his shirt strained against his flabby belly and looked as though they were in danger of popping apart at any minute. Without giving pause, he poured himself out a stiff drink and chugged back the contents. 'Where's Kit?' he asked, using the cuff of his sleeve to wipe across his slack lips.

Dennis shrugged. He took a seat opposite his boss and rubbed his hand over the dark stubble that covered his jaw.

Rosco snarled and a low growl escaped from his lips. 'You can bet your fucking bollocks that she's tipped that little prick off.' He stabbed his finger forward. 'He can't hide forever; I'm gonna have him. He'll make a mistake, and when he does...' He made his hands into the shape of claws and mimicked throttling someone. 'I'll be there, ready and waiting for him.'

On the desk, Rosco's mobile phone vibrated and *The Great Escape* theme tune filled the air. Rosco's choice of ring tone couldn't have been more ironic if he'd tried, and as the tune continued to play out, they both stared down at the device.

'It's Bannerman,' Rosco spat. His skin paled and as he breathed heavily through his flared nostrils, beads of cold sweat broke out across his forehead. 'That's the eighth call today; you'd think the bastard would take the hint by now that I'm avoiding him, wouldn't you? As if I actually want to talk to the nutter.' The call rang off and in his pocket, Dennis's own mobile phone began to vibrate. Without even looking at the caller ID, he knew exactly who it would be – Kit – and as much as his fingers itched to fish the device out of his pocket, he chose to ignore the call.

'I'd best get back out there looking for him.' He jerked his thumb behind him.

Absentmindedly, Rosco nodded his head. 'Oi, wait a minute.'

Almost at the door, Dennis turned around.

Rosco's beady eyes were narrowed. 'You have checked his flat, haven't you?'

'Yeah.' Dennis licked at his dry lips. 'I went there personally.'

'And he definitely wasn't hiding out there?'

'Nah.' Dennis shook his head. 'Like I told you, there was no sign of him and his missus said she hasn't seen him in weeks.'

'But you did go inside and check?'

'Yeah, of course I did. What do you take me for?' He reached out and curled his fingers around the door handle. 'It was just her and the kid at home; the place was a right shithole.'

'Right.' Rosco continued to study him. 'Oh well.' He blew out his lips. 'Was just a thought – go on.' He nodded towards the door. 'Go and find that little scrote.'

It took all of Dennis's strength to walk calmly from the office, and as he made his way back through the club, he glanced nervously over his shoulder. It wasn't until he was seated inside his car that he pulled out his mobile phone, tapped in a series of digits and brought the device up to his ear. 'I think he's on to us,' was all he said before ending the call and starting the ignition.

*  *  *

Slipping her mobile phone back into her coat pocket, Kit's face paled. The fact Dennis had sounded so rattled not only unnerved her but made the task in hand all the more urgent. 'Let's get this over and done with, shall we, and as quickly as possible.'

'And you trust him, this Dennis geezer?' Fletch nodded down at his daughter's pocket. 'It just seems a bit suspect to me; I thought he was meant to be Taylor's right-hand man. Everything about this screams out "trap".'

Kit shook her head. 'No.' She pushed open the car door and stepped outside. 'He wouldn't do that to me.'

'Right, come on then.' As he followed suit and climbed out of the car, Stevie made his way around to the rear of the vehicle. He glanced up and down the street, then unlocked the boot.

With the help of Austin, together they hauled out the holdall. It was a lot heavier than he'd anticipated and as it clattered to the floor with a loud crash, he cursed underneath his breath.

'Careful,' Fletch warned. His gaze flicked around them. 'Come on, and don't slam the boot.' He winced as his son did just that and he threw him a glare. 'Think,' he spat at him. 'The last thing we want to do is bring attention to ourselves.'

The forecourt was in darkness; only the streetlight picked out the six-foot steel fence that surrounded the property like a fortress. At the steel gates, Kit aligned a key in the padlock. It sprang open with a click and, pocketing the keys, she slowly pushed the gate ajar.

'Here, Fletch,' Stevie whispered, 'what does this remind you of?' He lifted his eyebrows and nodded across to the Portakabin. 'Our first introduction to the life was breaking into a Portakabin. We must have been, what, fifteen at the time?'

'We'd just turned fourteen.' Fletch was thoughtful for a moment. 'Spence was twelve.'

'Just kids really.'

'Yeah,' Fletch agreed, 'we were.'

Once they were through the gates, Kit led the way across the forecourt. Situated behind the Portakabin, just as she'd predicted there would be, were three abandoned cars. They were minus wheels and had obviously been sitting there, neglected and left to rot, for quite some time.

'I just need to get the keys for the cars.' She flicked her head towards the Portakabin.

Fletch followed on behind her.

As she unlocked the door, the overwhelming scent of bleach hit their nostrils, making their eyes water.

'Fuck me.' Pulling the cuff of his jacket over his nose, Fletch narrowed his eyes. 'Stevie,' he called out in a low voice, 'over here.'

'What's up?' Stevie peered into the still dark cabin. 'Fucking hell.' He began to cough and splutter. 'What the fuck is that?'

'Bleach would be my guess,' Kit said.

'What's going on?' Austin made his way over.

Fletch turned to face his son. 'When was the last time you saw this Mark bloke?'

Austin screwed up his face. 'I dunno, two, maybe three weeks ago. It was the night of the hijack. Why?'

Fletch shook his head.

'What do you reckon?' Stevie asked him.

'This is too fresh.' Fletch continued to shake his head. 'This was done a day or two ago, tops.' He closed his eyes and turned towards his son. 'When was the last time you heard from the other one, what's his name, Charlie?'

'Yesterday morning, I went to see him – why?'

Fletch raised his eyebrows and as he and Stevie shared a glance, he shook his head. 'Nothing. Come on, we need to stash the gear and then get out of here.'

As they walked back to the abandoned cars, Stevie spoke privately in Fletch's ear. 'Are you thinking what I'm thinking?'

Fletch shrugged. 'Depends. If you're thinking that one by one, Taylor is picking off Austin's mates, then yeah, I am.'

Stevie let out a soft whistle. 'Fuck me, Fletch, this is some heavy shit.'

'You can say that again.' Fletch glanced over his shoulder and as he spoke, worry churned in the pit of his stomach. 'Who is he going to target next? Because we both know he isn't going to stop until he's found my son.'

Stevie raised his eyebrows; his mate had a made a valid point and the very notion was as terrifying as it was sobering.

\* \* \*

Fifteen minutes later, once they had returned to their cars, Fletch turned to look at his daughter. 'I'm not happy about you going back to Taylor; it's not safe.'

Kit rolled her eyes. 'Oh, here we go again, the caring father act. I've already told you, you're twenty-two years—'

'Too late.' Fletch finished off her sentence. 'Yeah, maybe I am, but I'm here now and I'm telling you it's not safe; I don't trust the sly bastard.'

'It's a lot safer than if I don't,' Kit sighed. 'He's expecting me and if I don't turn up, all hell will break loose.'

Fletch exhaled loudly and rubbed the palm of his hand over his face. No matter what he did or said, he had a sinking feeling that his daughter would never forgive him for not being there for her and Austin while they were growing up. 'Fair enough.' He turned to look at his son. 'Tomorrow, after I've finished my shift at the shop,' he said with a level of irritation, 'you and me are gonna go and check out this Mark and Charlie.'

'What for?' As Austin chewed on his lip, a sliver of panic rippled through his veins. 'I've already told you, Mark's not been answering my calls.'

'Yeah, and that's exactly what worries me,' Fletch answered.

## 24

The door to Charlie's bedsit was ajar and as Austin gingerly pushed it open, he stared around him at the chaos that had been created.

The bedsit had been trashed beyond recognition; furniture was overturned and the stuffing from the mattress that doubled as both a bed and a sofa spilt out of a series of man-made slits and trailed across the floor in clumps. The television and games console had been smashed to smithereens and every drawer had been emptied out; even the cutlery drawer that he knew for a fact only held a handful of knives, forks and spoons had been pulled out from underneath the worktop in the kitchen area.

'What the fuck happened in here?' There was a level of shock in Austin's voice as he brought his hands up to his head.

Fletch's heart went out to his boy, and as he answered, his voice was gentle. 'I've already told you this is no game you're playing, son.'

Austin turned around; across his face, horror resonated. 'No.' He shook his head. 'No, he ain't, he can't be...'

'Taylor has already been here,' Fletch stated with a sigh as he looked around him at the devastation that had been left behind.

'No!' Hurling the shattered pieces of the games console through the air, Austin went on to destroy what was left of the bedsit. 'I'm gonna kill the cunt,' he roared. 'I'm gonna slice the fat bastard from ear to fucking ear.'

Out of breath, he finally fell to his knees and, grasping at the carpet fibres, he began to sob. Not for a single second had he assumed that any one of them would end up losing their life.

Turning away from his son, Fletch walked across the bedsit and leant against the door frame. From behind him, his son's pitiful sobs broke his heart and, lifting his fist to his mouth, he slammed his eyes shut tight.

Even as Stevie was coaxing Austin to his feet, Fletch was unable to turn around and reach out for his boy and offer comfort. Instead, he was transported back in time to when he himself had found his brother's body floating in a lake more than two decades earlier. The raw grief his son was exhibiting haunted him, and as Stevie bundled Austin past him and out of the bedsit, Fletch still remained rooted to the spot.

'Come on,' Stevie called out to him. 'We need to get out of here; the last thing we need is for the old bill to turn up; this doesn't exactly look good on us, does it?'

It took all of Fletch's effort to put one foot in front of the other and even as he followed Stevie down the short flight of steps, his mind was elsewhere.

\* \* \*

As he stepped his foot on the brake outside the low-rise block of flats where Austin lived, Stevie flicked his gaze up to the rear-view mirror. For the entire journey, Austin had sat huddled with his back against the door, his eyes shielded by his forearm.

'We can't leave him like this,' he stated.

'I don't plan to,' Fletch answered. He turned his body to face the back seat. 'Come on, son,' he coaxed, 'you're home now.'

Austin looked up; his eyes were red raw from the tears he'd shed. 'Do you think it was quick?'

Underneath Stevie's knowing stare, Fletch nodded. 'Yeah, I'm sure it was.' It was a lie and he had a feeling that they all knew it. Rosco would have tortured the boy, would have wanted information from him before dealing the final blow. 'Come on, me and Stevie will come up with you for a bit.'

They climbed out of the car and as they walked in the direction of the block of flats, Fletch looked around him on the lookout for anything out of the ordinary. Satisfied that no one was lurking in the shadows, he allowed his body to relax. All along, Stevie had been right; his son couldn't handle a situation as heavy as this and if he was being entirely honest with himself, he wasn't so sure that he could either. He'd been out of the game for too long and his instincts weren't as sharp as they had been in his youth.

* * *

Sheree could barely believe her luck. After watching the three men climb out of a car, she'd run into the lounge and draped herself over the sofa in what she hoped was a sexy pose. One of the springs dug into the small of her back but she ignored it; beauty was pain, she reminded herself as she shifted her position slightly.

As Austin's key turned in the lock, she held her breath, sucked in her stomach and tried her best to look as though she always resumed the position to watch television.

As the men walked through to the lounge, she took one look at Austin's face and sat bolt upright. All thoughts of trying to look sexy went out the window as she detangled her legs from underneath herself.

'What's happened?' She placed her hands on her hips and her voice came out as a high-pitched shriek. 'What have you done to him?' she asked, throwing them an accusing stare.

'Leave it out,' Stevie growled. 'I've known him since he was a fucking baby.'

'He's had some bad news,' Fletch said, giving her a knowing wink.

It was enough to make Sheree's cheeks blush a deep shade of pink. There and then she practically swooned at Fletch's feet. Remembering her boyfriend of three years was in the same room, she gave him a soft smile. She had to keep up the pretence of the doting girlfriend. 'Can I get anyone a drink?' She almost skipped out of the room when they silently nodded their heads.

Oh yes, Sheree decided, Fletch was definitely the man for her. *Sorry, Aus, but it's time to step aside.* She was done with the boy; she wanted the man now.

## 25

From across the street, Fletch was staking out Kit's club in the hope that Rosco would show his face. It had gone nine p.m. by the time he'd left his son the previous evening, and after Stevie had dropped him back at the hostel he'd slumped on his bed and stared up at the ceiling until the early hours of the morning. All the while, Rosco Taylor had lain heavy on his mind. When he'd shanked the bastard in the shower block of Pentonville prison, he hadn't for a single second thought that after his release Rosco would worm his way into Tina's life. The very notion hadn't even entered his mind. Why would it? By rights, Taylor should never have been able to even find her.

Over and over again, he thought through every viable scenario he could think of. Had Taylor perhaps overheard one of his conversations with another prisoner? Or maybe he'd sneaked into his cell and found one of Tina's letters? He'd already caught the bastard once in his cell having a shufti through his belongings, hence why he'd gone on to shank the bastard, but what was there to say that had been the first time?

He balled his fists; not only had Rosco been likened to a

coward back in the day, but he'd also been a sneaky bastard, a rat who couldn't be trusted, and Fletch very much doubted anything had changed over the years. He wouldn't trust him as far as he could throw him, and from what he'd heard about Rosco's huge bulk, he knew for a fact it wouldn't be very far. In hindsight, he should have done more than mark him that day; he should have killed the ponce, should have stabbed him over and over again, safe in the knowledge that there weren't going to be any come-backs. Knowing what he did now, there was nothing he would love more than to have been the one to put the sly bastard into a wooden box. Instead, all he'd done was given him a direct pathway to his kids. Unknowingly, he'd given him the opportunity to terrorise his son, which by all accounts he'd done with vigour, all because they shared a striking resemblance. As far as Fletch was concerned, it just about summed Taylor up: face to face with a grown man, he was a coward; he could only take people on mob-handed or terrorise women and children.

Not only was Tina buzzing off her head, but since she had woken up she had been drinking steadily and had downed two bottles of wine. By early afternoon, she could barely even see straight and as she stepped off a double decker bus, she almost crashed heavily to her knees. It was only the fact she was still clinging onto the door handle that stopped her from causing herself some serious harm.

'Fucking pisshead.' From inside the bus, two teenage boys laughed at her predicament.

Straightening up, Tina stuck her middle finger up at them, causing the two boys to laugh even harder.

'Little fuckers,' she screamed at them. 'If my boy was here, he'd have you for talking to me like that.'

'Fuck off,' they chorused, and as the doors closed and the bus moved off, they banged their fists on the windowpane, still laughing at her.

Tears sprang to Tina's eyes. 'Bastards,' she muttered underneath her breath. She inched her way forward, oblivious to the stares being thrown in her direction. Her battered and swollen face, which was riddled with purple and black bruises, brought more than one gasp as she made her way down the street.

Up ahead of her was Rosco's club, the very same club that her money had helped him to acquire. If it wasn't for her, he'd have still been scrambling around in the dirt without so much as a penny to his name.

At the entrance to the club, she pushed the two doormen out of her path as she tried in vain to gain entry. 'I wanna see my daughter.' She squinted up at them, her eyes barely able to stay focused on their faces. 'Get that bitch out here,' she screamed at them. 'Go on, go, tell the whore her mother is here and wants a word.'

With ease, they pushed her back onto the pavement. It wasn't the first time that she'd turned up shouting the odds and they were well prepared for her.

'Get out of here,' they told her. 'You're not welcome, so piss off.'

Tears trailed the length of Tina's face and she used the cuff of her sleeve to wipe away the snot from under her nose. 'It should have been my club,' she sobbed. 'It was my money that paid for it; by rights it's mine.'

The doormen shook their heads. 'Come on now, go home,' one of them told her as kindly as he could.

Leaning forward, Tina grasped hold of her thighs as she continued to cry. 'The bitch,' she sobbed. 'She took everything from me.'

* * *

Fletch heard Tina long before clapping his eyes on her; there was no mistaking the familiar shriek to her voice. It grated on his nerves as much today as it had done when they had briefly dated. Groaning out loud, he propelled himself away from the glass-fronted shop window that he'd been leaning against and made his way across the street.

'It's okay, I'll take care of this,' he told the doormen. 'I'm an old friend of hers.'

Tina swayed on her feet as she gazed up at him with a pained expression. 'It should have been my club, the bastard,' she slurred. 'He took the money, all of it; he took everything from me and our babies.'

Fletch gave a stilted smile that was more for the benefit of the two doormen than the mother of his children and, grasping Tina by the elbow, he steered her away from the club.

'Have you got a death wish?' he hissed in her ear as he pulled her along.

Wrenching herself free, Tina swayed on her feet. 'Get off me,' she screamed at him. 'She got to you, didn't she? That whore of a daughter we made has done what she set out to do and turned you against me.'

The alcoholic fumes that came off her breath were enough to make Fletch wrinkle his nose in disgust and, keeping her at arm's length, he continued to drag her towards the corner of the street. 'This is nothing to do with Kitty. This was all your doing; you brought that fucking scumbag into my kids' lives.' He slammed her none too gently against the wall and her head thudded against the brickwork with a loud crack. 'I could fucking kill you for what you've done. My fucking kids, Tina, and you allowed that sneaky, low-life bastard to terrorise them.' He grabbed her by her chin and forced her to look up at him. 'One thing I asked you to do for me, just one thing, and that was to look after my kids, to keep them safe from harm, and you couldn't even do that. Tell me what you did to try and stop him, and I'm warning you now, it had better be fucking good.'

His words instantly sobered Tina up and as she continued to sway on her feet, fear gripped at her heart. As always, she was only looking out for number one and as tears sprang to her eyes, she rubbed at her sore head. 'I didn't know what he was doing.' She clutched at his arm as she implored him to believe her. 'I swear to you I didn't.'

'What, you didn't know what was going on when Austin ended up with broken ribs; or how about every other time he was being battered? Because from what I've heard, you were there; you knew exactly what was going down. What was it you said?' He tilted his head slightly, forcing her to look into his eyes. 'That's right, you told everyone that he was accident-prone. Fucking accident-prone – are you for real, Tina?' He closed the gap between them so that their faces were almost touching. 'My son,' he hissed, 'and you allowed him to be used and abused by that sick cunt.'

Tina opened her mouth to speak. Of course she had known what was going on; Austin had been a mouthy kid, and as a teenager he'd become a law unto himself. Nothing she'd ever said or done could rein him in or calm him down, and God only knows how many times she'd tried. Time and time again he would deliberately set out to provoke Rosco, and in her mind he'd fully deserved the good hidings he'd received. She was partly relieved when he'd been taken into care, just so that she didn't have to deal with his attitude any more. A wave of nausea hit her and, jerking herself away from her children's father, she bent over and promptly vomited.

'Jesus fucking Christ.' Fletch screwed up his face and as Tina straightened up and wiped the cuff of her sleeve across her open lips, a long tendril of vomit-stained saliva hung down from her chin as she continued to retch. 'Just go home,' he told her. 'Go home and sleep it off.'

Tears stung her eyes and she reached out for him. 'I still love you,' she howled. 'I've always loved you, and I want us to be together again. I want us to make a go of it; we could make it work, I know we could.'

Fletch backed away. 'How many times do we need to have this conversation? There is no "us"; there has never been an "us",' he snarled. 'In fact, I wish to God that I'd never laid my eyes on you.'

'Because of her, that woman, because you loved her?' She looked up at him with wide watery eyes, the pain she felt evident in her gaunt face. Her entire body ached for him; all she had ever wanted was for him to love her back. She longed for them to be together, to be a couple.

'Just go home.' Shaking his head, the fight had left Fletch. Tina would never understand the way he felt about Suzy, how much he loved her, that she owned a piece of his heart. As for Tina, he'd never taken pleasure from hurting her; he just hadn't loved her, and it was as simple as that.

Not for the first time was Tina's heart breaking in two. Her sobs were pitiful as she moved off down the street, holding onto the wall for support as she went.

As angry as he was with her for the way she'd haphazardly raised his children, Fletch couldn't allow her to make the journey home alone. There was no saying what would happen to her in the state she was in, and as useless as she was as a mother, he didn't want his kids to have to deal with the fallout should she end up attacked a second time or something far worse, murdered. He glanced back in the direction of the club and blew out his cheeks. Rosco could wait; the fat bastard wasn't going anywhere.

## 26

Sitting at the breakfast bar in the flat above the shop, Harriet threw her mother a sidelong glance. As of late, Susan had a spring in her step. In fact, she was positively glowing.

As she rinsed her cup under the hot tap, Susan was humming softly to herself.

'You seem happy, Mum.'

'Do I?' Looking over her shoulder, Susan's cheeks flushed a deep shade of red. 'You know me, darling.' She gently smiled. 'I'm always happy.'

Harriet raised her eyebrows and, blowing on a cup of hot tea, it briefly crossed her mind that her mother's new-found happiness could all be down to meeting a man. The very notion was alien to her; up until now, her mother had shown no interest in men. She may have been on the odd date over the years but they had been few and far between and had never progressed beyond a second date – why, exactly, Harriet had no idea. Not only was her mother beautiful both inside and out, but she was also intelligent and had always had a steady stream of admirers, yet she'd been reluctant to settle down with any of them.

'Have you met someone?' Harriet probed.

Susan spun around. In her hand she held a saturated washing-up cloth and as the soapy water dripped to the floor, she tossed the cloth back into the sink and reached out for the roll of paper towels on the kitchen counter. 'What makes you ask that?' she said, swooping down to mop up the liquid.

'Just a hunch.' Sipping at her tea, Harriet studied Susan over the rim of the cup. 'I don't mind if you have.' She placed her cup on the breakfast bar and gave a tiny shrug. 'I only want you to be happy, Mum.'

Susan straightened up. It was on the tip of her tongue to tell her daughter that her father had walked back into their lives. She knew it was what Harriet wanted, what she had always wanted; for years she'd talked endlessly about meeting Fletch, yet something was stopping Susan. Just like the hunch her daughter claimed to have, Susan too had a niggling worry that for the life of her she was unable to shake off. Oh, she knew Fletch loved her, that he would never willingly leave her, but what if the choice was taken away from him? After telling her about the murder he'd committed and then his subsequent imprisonment, over and over again Fletch had sworn to her that he'd turned over a new leaf, that he'd learnt from his wrongdoings and that nothing and no one could entice him back into his old line of work, nor his old life. Although she wanted to believe him, and she really did want to, uneasiness ate away at Susan. After his release from prison she could only hope and pray that the lure of easy money didn't become too much for him to be able to resist. After all, it was all he'd ever known. From a young age, like a lamb to the slaughter he'd been thrown into Billy King's firm and had worked his way up the ranks. He'd been more than just one of Billy's hired muscle; he'd been a well-respected firm member. Was he really prepared to walk away from the only way of life he'd ever known?

As much as she loved Fletch and as much as she knew he was the only man she would ever want, she wasn't prepared to drag her daughter into the murky existence that was the criminal underworld. She'd already been there, done it, and had been lucky enough to escape with her life intact, but not without her husband intent on trying to kill her first. Still to this day she had flashbacks of Billy's hands wrapped around her throat as he'd tried to squeeze the life out of her.

'Well, have you?'

'No, of course I haven't.' Behind her back, Susan crossed her fingers. She'd never lied to her daughter before and the fact that she now had lay heavy on her conscience.

After dropping Tina off at his mother's house, Fletch made his way over to his son's flat.

Seeing how gentle and patient his old mum was with the mother of his children had broken his heart. Until now he'd never given Jenny the credit nor the respect she deserved. She'd buried a child and the mere thought of losing one of his own children was enough to bring him out in a cold sweat. How she'd coped with such a tragedy was beyond his comprehension, and then to top it off, within a matter of weeks she had also lost him – Fletch being sent down must have been equally as devastating for her.

No wonder his mother had clung to Tina. Before today, he'd never understood her reasoning; he hadn't wanted to. Perhaps Tina had become the daughter she'd never had, or maybe keeping Tina close had brought her comfort, a substitute for the sons that she had lost?

The truth was he was a selfish bastard, always had been. He'd never cared for anyone other than himself. Even as the thought popped into his mind, deep down he knew it wasn't true. He'd loved his brother; he would have done anything for him. He'd looked out for him, he'd tried to protect him, and more than anything he'd tried to save him; even when he'd found Spencer that fateful day, face-down in the lake riddled with bullet wounds, he'd still tried in vain to save his life.

As for his kids, of course he loved them. They were a part of him, and fair enough, he hadn't been there for them growing up but he was doing everything he could to make amends. Until his dying day he would never stop trying to make things right between them.

His thoughts turned to Suzy. He loved her too, loved her with a passion he hadn't even known was possible. Just the mere thought of her made his heart soar and, now that he'd found her again, he knew that he never wanted to let her go.

'We need to think about a buyer, Fletch.'

Stevie broke his reverie. Good old Stevie; he was the only mainstay in his life. He gave a half smile. Stevie was more like a bad penny; he couldn't get rid of him even if he wanted to.

'What are you grinning at?'

'Nothing.' Fletch shook his head. 'Yeah, you're right, we do – any ideas?'

As Stevie puffed out his cheeks, Fletch could see his mind ticking over. Stevie was as clueless as he was. Who were they trying to kid? They had been out of the life for too long, their contacts had long since dried up and they were nothing more than has-beens.

'I'll think of something,' Stevie told him with an air of confidence.

Fletch raised his eyebrows and, tapping in a series of digits on the entry call system, he waited patiently for the door to spring ajar.

'Here, Fletch.' As they walked across the lobby, Stevie caught hold of his arm. 'It'll cause ructions with Jess but...'

'What?' Fletch narrowed his eyes.

'Aus.' He flicked his gaze up the staircase. 'If things get dangerous, if he needs to leave this place, well, I've got a spare room – it's his if he ever needs it.'

'Cheers, mate.' Clasping his friend's hand, Fletch gave him a warm smile. 'Let's hope it never comes to that.'

They trudged up the stone staircase and waiting for them at the front door was Sheree.

'Aus has just popped over to his nan's. He won't be long – come on in.' She pushed the door open wider and led the way down the passageway.

'I must have missed him, then.' As he followed Sheree through to the kitchen, Fletch was relieved to see that the flat looked cleaner than it had on his last visit. It smelt much better, too.

'Where's Lacey?' Fletch searched around him for his granddaughter.

'She's at my mum's; Aus insisted that she went there for a few days.' She gave a wide smile and began to fill the kettle. If truth were told, as much as Sheree loved her daughter, she was glad to see the back of her, even if it was only for a few days. At the best of times Lacey could be an annoying little cow and, ever since she had hit the terrible twos, if she wasn't screaming the house down then she was doing everything in her power to push Sheree's buttons. Over the past week Lacey had done more than test her patience and Sheree had quite literally had enough of her. Not only that, but she could do with a break and having some quality time to herself. The thought of being able to have a proper lie-in sounded like the equivalent of heaven; most mornings little Lacey had her out of bed at the crack of dawn demanding her breakfast.

Fletch returned Sheree's smile. He was reassured that, if nothing else, his son had had the sense to send his daughter away for a while. Unlike himself, Austin was obviously a good father.

'Milk, sugar?'

'Yeah.' Fletch looked up. 'Both, please.' He turned to look at Stevie and raised his eyebrows questioningly.

'Just milk for me.' Stevie rubbed his hand over his protruding stomach. 'I'm on a diet.'

Fletch rolled his eyes; it was only a few days ago that he'd been stuffing biscuits into his mouth like there was no tomorrow. He turned back to look at Sheree. 'How is he? Aus, I mean.'

As she leant against the kitchen counter, it didn't escape Fletch's notice that at every available opportunity Sheree would flaunt her chest in his direction. He ensured his eyes stayed focused on her face as she answered him.

'He's all right, I suppose.' The kettle boiled and she gave a nonchalant shrug as she poured water into three mugs. 'Same old Aus, really.'

It was said in a carefree manner, and for a brief moment Fletch wondered if his son was bottling up his emotions, another thing he'd learnt about while inside.

'Can I use your toilet?' Stevie hopped from one foot to the other. 'Should have gone before I came out.'

'Yeah.' As she stirred the tea, Sheree glanced over her shoulder. Fletch watched him go.

'Here you go.' She passed across a steaming mug of tea and as she did so her fingers brushed against his.

Taking a sip of the scalding hot liquid, Fletch placed the mug on the worktop beside him and crossed his arms over his chest. 'I was just worried that he might be trying to suppress how he is really feeling.'

'No, I don't think so.' Flashing Fletch a wide smile, she stood just inches away from him. 'Like I said, he seemed fine this morning.' If nothing else, Sheree was a firm believer of not wasting time. Why bother skirting around the edges? When she wanted something, she went straight for the kill regardless of who she hurt in the process. As far as she was concerned, Austin was collateral damage, a stepping stone to his father. She reached out to touch Fletch's arm, her fingers caressing the skin below his wrist.

'Woah, what's your game?' Fletch stared down at her fingers then looked up. 'What the fuck are you doing? Take your hand off me,' he growled.

Sheree's smile froze, her skin paled and the fine hairs on the back of her neck stood up on end. 'I thought it was what you wanted?' There was a tinge of hope in her voice. 'I thought that you liked me; you winked at me last night.'

'No.' Screwing up his face, Fletch almost shouted out the word. 'Not like that.' Before today he'd barely said more than two words to her. How she could have come up with the idea that he was interested was beyond him; she was his son's girlfriend, and even if he had been attracted to her, which he wasn't, he wouldn't have touched her with a barge pole. She was off limits; she had to know that as much as he did.

'That's better.' Rubbing his hands together, Stevie walked into the kitchen.

Springing apart, they both swung their heads around to look at him.

'What?' he asked as he rocked back on his heels, suspicion etched across his face. 'What's going on?'

'Nothing, come on we're leaving.' Fletch all but pushed Stevie back out of the kitchen.

'What about my tea?' Stevie protested.

'I'll buy you a pint instead,' Fletch told him, more concerned with getting out of the flat than standing around drinking tea.

* * *

As she leant against the washing machine, Sheree wanted to kick herself. She was so sure that Fletch had wanted her just as much as she wanted him, if not more. The wink he'd given her the previous night had been a sign that he was interested, hadn't it? Instead all he'd done was humiliate her, made her look a fool, made her feel worthless, unattractive, ugly. No man had ever turned her down in the past; even Austin's mates fancied her like crazy.

A sliver of ice-cold fear ran down the length of her spine. What if Fletch told his son what she'd done? What if he told Austin that it'd been her who'd come on to him?

Tears sprang to her eyes and, darting across the kitchen, she took the untouched mugs, still full to the brim with steaming hot tea, and poured the contents down the sink.

As the liquid swirled down the plughole, in her mind she began to get her story straight. It was him who'd come on to her; that was what she would tell Austin. When Stevie had used the toilet it was then that the bastard had made his move and pounced on her. He'd tried to kiss her, no, he'd tried to stick his tongue down her throat, yes, that sounded better, and when she'd refused him he wouldn't take no for an answer.

By the time Austin arrived home ten minutes later, she almost believed her own lies, and as she ran sobbing into her boyfriend's arms, her performance was worthy of an Oscar.

\* \* \*

'What was all that about?'

As Fletch passed across a pint of lager, he shook his head. 'You don't want to know, mate.' They were in the Robin Hood pub in Dagenham and other than one or two customers propped up at the bar, nursing pints of beer, the place was as dead as a dodo.

'Yeah I do, what happened? I don't think I've ever seen you move so fast and I'm not counting that time we were being chased by dogs when we broke into that Portakabin as kids.'

Fletch gulped at his beer and, wiping away the excess froth from his upper lip, he continued to shake his head. 'She came on to me, like actually came on to me.'

'What do you mean she came on to you?' Stevie screwed up his face.

'What I said: she came on to me.'

'Are you sure?'

'Of course I'm fucking sure.' Fletch rolled his eyes. 'I know I've been away for a long time but I haven't forgotten how it all works.'

Stevie sipped at his lager and, eyeing Fletch over the rim of the pint glass, he raised his eyebrows. 'What did she do?'

'She put her hand on my arm.'

'Is that it?' Stevie exhaled loudly. 'That doesn't mean anything.'

'Nah, this was different. I know what I saw and she was definitely giving me the come-on.'

'You bastard.'

As the pub door banged open with such force that the glass panel rattled and looked ready to shatter at any moment, both Fletch and Stevie turned their heads.

'You bastard,' Austin roared. 'What did you fucking do to her?'

Before Fletch could even open his mouth to answer, Austin had swung back his arm and punched his father square on in the face. The pint glass Fletch had been holding was knocked out of his hand, the contents spilling over his shirt as it smashed to the floor. It took all of Fletch's strength to take the blows and not retaliate. He was determined not to fight back. He wasn't like his own father; he'd rather take the pounding, would rather become a punching bag then ever lash out at his son, regardless of whether or not it was warranted.

'Woah,' Stevie shouted as he wrapped his arms around Austin's chest and hauled him away from his father. 'Enough, your dad's done fuck all wrong.'

'No, it's all right.' Fletch dabbed at his bleeding lip; he shot a glance in the direction of the startled barmaid. 'I'm sorry,' he told her, 'I'll pay for any damages.'

Breathing heavily, Austin spat in his father's direction, 'All along Kit was right about you.' He screwed up his face. 'You're poisonous; I should have listened to her.'

His stomach plummeting, Fletch held up his hands. 'I don't know what she's told you, son, but I swear to you I didn't do anything.'

'You didn't do anything?' His father's words were the equivalent of a red rag to a bull and Austin tried to lunge forward a second time. 'You tried to shove your tongue down her throat, you had your hands all over her, you practically tried to rape her.'

'No.' As Fletch shoved his son roughly away from him, he exhaled loudly. 'I didn't touch her,' he protested.

'That's not what happened.' Open-mouthed, Stevie shook his head. 'I was only out of the room for a couple of seconds.'

'I'd rather shove wasps up my arse than do something to hurt you.' Fletch's voice took on a desperate quality. 'You're my son; the thought would never even enter my head.'

'He's telling the truth,' Stevie added as he tentatively released his arms from around Austin. 'Sheree's not his type. She's way too young, for a start; your dad always preferred older women.'

'Mate,' Fletch growled as he shot Stevie a sidelong glance, 'you're not helping matters.'

Holding up his hands, Stevie snapped his mouth firmly shut.

'Listen, Aus, I've done nothing wrong, I swear to you, son.'

'Just stay away from me.' As he began to back away, Austin shook the tension out of his fist. 'I mean it,' he said through clenched teeth. 'As far as I'm concerned, you're dead to me.'

As his son left the pub, Fletch rubbed at the nape of his neck, and just like that, with those few words, his whole world shattered into a million pieces.

'He doesn't mean what he said,' Stevie told him. 'He's angry; let him calm down and then he'll see that the whole thing was a big misunderstanding.' Stevie patted his shoulder in a reassuring gesture.

Deep in thought, Fletch sighed. Stevie meant well but he wasn't going to hold his breath; his son had seemed pretty convincing to him. His shoulders sagged and when he looked up, he spread open his arms. 'Do you know what, I'm done. If Taylor wants to find me, then let him. Bring it fucking on, because I've had enough of this bollocks to last me a lifetime.'

As his friend walked out of the pub, Stevie narrowed his eyes, unsure of what exactly Fletch had meant by the comment. Was he planning to kill Rosco or was he hoping that they found him first and that he himself was the one who'd end up in a shallow grave?

\* \* \*

Kit's forehead was furrowed as she listened to Sheree retell her version of events. Already her story had changed three times, a fact that Kit had immediately picked up on.

'You were right, Kit.' Austin's body shook, so intense was the rage that rippled through his veins. 'I should have listened; you warned me what he was like, but I couldn't see it. I didn't want to, I suppose.'

'It's not your fault.' As she gripped her boyfriend's hand, Sheree's voice was sugary sweet. 'How could you have known what he was like? He's a predator. Right from the start, he planned this. I knew he fancied me; I'd caught him giving me the eye more than once, but you know me.' She smiled up at him. 'I didn't want to say anything; I didn't want to cause any trouble between the two of you. I never thought for a second, though, that he would actually try it on.'

Kit continued to study her brother's girlfriend. In any normal circumstance Sheree was a mouthy cow with a trap that was bigger than Blackwall Tunnel. If she'd really been attacked, she would have screamed, hollered and shouted it from the rooftops; the whole estate would have known about it.

'I should have smashed him to the floor and not stopped until I'd caved his head in.' Austin clenched his fist into a tight ball. 'If I ever see him again, I'll finish him. I mean it, Kit; if he comes near me, I'll have the bastard for what he did to Ree.' He pulled his girlfriend underneath his arm, squeezed her tight and kissed the top of her head. 'He knows how cut up I am about Charlie and it still didn't stop him from trying it on with my bird. He's an arsehole.'

'And he just took it? He didn't attempt to fight back or defend himself?' Kit asked.

Austin shook his head. 'He did fuck all. He's a fucking pussy, a melt. Just proves I was right all along: he's as soft as shit. And I thought he was meant to be some kind of tough man,' he sneered.

'Yeah, and you know why he didn't fight back, don't you?' Sheree piped up, a smug grin spread across her face. 'It's because he's as guilty as sin.'

Kit narrowed her eyes. As much as she hated to admit it, she didn't believe a single word that came out of Sheree's mouth. It wouldn't surprise her if this was another case of the green-eyed monster rearing its ugly head. As it was, Sheree was already jealous of her and Austin's relationship. It stood to reason that she would resent the time her brother was spending with their father too.

## 27

Nathan Bannerman and his two brothers hit East London just after seven p.m. Fifteen minutes later, they pulled up outside the club Rosco had previously owned before he'd signed it over to Kit as a wedding gift. Mob-handed, they stepped out of the car, with the occupants of the cars behind swiftly following suit.

'Bit of a shithole this, ain't it?' Connor looked up at the dingy exterior of the building. The club looked as though it hadn't been modernised in years. Even the neon sign over the door that read 'Gentleman's Club' blinked intermittently as if the lightbulbs bringing it to life were about to give up the good fight at any moment.

'Did you expect any different?' Lee remarked. 'This,' he said, eyeing the club with a measure of distaste, 'just about sums Taylor up.'

Connor continued to look around him; the street they had parked on looked just as rough as the club itself. On one side of the street was the entrance to a council estate, boasting looming tower blocks that dominated the skyline. On the other side was a parade of rundown shops with colourful graffiti scrawled across the sheets of plywood that had been nailed over the windows. At first glance they appeared to be out of business, until, that was, he saw a customer laden down with plastic shopping bags emerge from a dimly lit doorway. And people had the front to say that the area where he had been born and raised in South London was a shithole; they had clearly never ventured to this part of East London.

They made their way towards the club and, without being questioned, they were granted entry, another no in Nathan's book.

On a daily basis, Taylor had no idea who was walking through his doors, and was in fact a sitting duck. Nathan was actually surprised the fat fucker had lasted as long as he had in their world.

As usual for an evening, the club was in full swing, and as they made their way inside, amid a fog of cigarette smoke and hazy stage lights, Tiffany Blue was midway through her routine.

Connor's eyes lit up. 'Wouldn't say no to her.' He nudged his eldest brother in the ribs.

'Leave it out,' Nathan chastised. 'Stop thinking with your dick for five minutes and use this instead.' He tapped his forefinger none too gently against his brother's forehead. 'We're not here for the sole purpose of you getting your end away.'

'Yeah, I know.' Connor looked back at the stage and as they made their way past, he got a better view of the stripper. Up close, she wasn't as attractive as he'd first thought, not that he would allow this fact to put him off. He'd been with some right old dogs in his time; surely one more wouldn't hurt, he reasoned. Stripped down to her thong, Tiffany Blue caught his eye and he flashed her a wide grin in return. With a bit of luck, he might be able to sneak backstage, although it was highly unlikely considering his elder brothers were the equivalent of snarling dogs on leashes. But you never know; if the business was concluded with the minimum of fuss then the opportunity might arise.

It took them all of five seconds to find the door to the offices and make their way inside. No one attempted to stop them and not for the first time did Nathan wonder what kind of outfit Rosco was running. It was something that he would never have allowed to happen on his own turf. If it did then heads would roll as a consequence.

They made their way along the upper corridor and after a swift glance inside a number of empty rooms they came to a halt in front of a closed door.

Jerking his head towards the door Nathan raised his eyebrows. In just under five minutes they had gone from exiting their cars to arriving outside Taylor's office. Not one single person had tried to bar them or question their intentions, and they had passed more than their fair share of heavies along the way. He gripped the door handle and, without hesitating, pulled down.

From behind the desk, Rosco looked up. Shock resonated across his bloated face and in the time it took for him to reach out for his mobile phone, Nathan had charged across the room and knocked the device out of his podgy hand.

'Don't even think about it,' Nathan snarled.

* * *

On leaving her brother's flat, Kit jumped into her car and drove straight to Stevie's house. She'd heard Sheree's version of events and now she wanted to hear her father's, or at least Stevie's.

Locking her car, she made her way down the path and knocked on the front door.

'Kit.' As she opened the door, Jess leant against the doorframe and gestured behind her to the staircase. 'Stevie's just saying good night to the girls; they refused to go to sleep until he was home.'

'Can I come in?'

'I suppose so,' Jess said with an irritated sigh. She stepped aside to allow Kit entry to the house. 'He's only just got home; he's been out with your dad for most of the day.' It was said with a degree of bitterness. 'The girls hardly see him these days – give them at least ten minutes with him.'

At the bottom of the stairs, Kit paused and looked up. A pang of jealousy tugged at her heart. Stevie saying good night to his daughters was such a simple act, something most children and parents took for granted. As a child she would have done anything for her own father to have read her a bedtime story. Fletch had never tucked her into bed or taken her to the park; he'd never wiped away her tears when she'd fallen over and grazed her knee, or even sat down and eaten a meal with her. He'd been imprisoned long before she'd even been born. As a child, she had only seen him a handful of times and even then a table had separated them. The few memories she had of him were vague; she wasn't so sure they were even real.

'Can I get you tea or coffee?'

'No.' Kit shook her head. 'I don't want to intrude.' She slipped her handbag off her shoulder and pushed her dark hair away from her face. It was a feminine gesture, almost dainty and at odds with the hard-nosed image she often portrayed. 'I just want to ask Stevie something and then I'll leave.'

Jess gave a stilted smile. 'Well, make yourself at home. He won't be long. I'll let him know that you're here.'

'Thanks.' As Jess left the room, Kit took a seat on the edge of the sofa. She had a sinking feeling that Stevie's wife didn't like her very much. In fact, she didn't seem to like any of Stevie's friends; she'd certainly never taken the time to get to know any of them.

'Kit.'

She looked up and as she began to rise from the sofa, Stevie held up his hand.

'Sit down. I'm guessing this is about your old man?' he asked with a sigh.

'Is it true?'

'What do you think?' He took a seat in the armchair opposite her and leant back against the soft cushions, his body weary.

Kit raised her eyebrows. 'I don't trust Sheree as far as I can throw her but that wasn't the question I asked. Did my dad attack her?'

'No.' Stevie screwed up his face. 'I was out of the room for no more than ten seconds.' He sat forward in the chair. 'And I can tell you this for nothing: Sheree's too much like your mum. There ain't a chance in hell that your dad would look at her twice. She isn't his type, for a start.'

Tilting her head to one side, Kit narrowed her eyes. 'What do you mean by that? My mum always claimed she was the love of his life.'

'She would.' Stevie laughed. 'Believe me, it was very much one-sided.' He sat forward in the chair. 'I know she's your mum, but you better than anyone know what she's like. Back in the day she may have been a looker but believe me, on the inside she was as ugly as sin. All she has ever done is cause your dad grief.'

'Yeah, don't I just.' Kit raised her eyebrows and gave a bitter laugh. 'I've been on the receiving end of that tongue of hers enough times to know that she's toxic.'

'She always has been. From day one your dad didn't want to be with her. The relationship just kind of steamrolled and if she hadn't deliberately set out to trap him, I know for a fact he would have had it away on his toes first opportunity he could, but he didn't. When he found out she was pregnant, he stuck around, and he did that for you and your brother.'

Sinking back on the sofa, Kit screwed up her face. 'That's not the story I was told.'

'That's because your mum's deluded.' He held up his hands and gave a slight shake of his head. 'I've already said too much, so let's change the subject now, okay?'

'No, I'm not a kid any more; I deserve to know the truth.' For the first time in her life, Kit felt as though she was getting an insight into her father. 'He must have wanted to be with her at some point, otherwise me and Austin wouldn't exist. We wouldn't be here now, would we?'

As he studied his friend's daughter Stevie sighed. 'All right.' He held up his hands. 'But this didn't come from me, do you understand what I'm telling you?'

Kit nodded. She was more than intrigued, and as Stevie took a deep breath she sat forward in the chair, eager to hear a different side to the story than the one her mother and grandmother had always told her.

'How did you get in here?' There was a slight tremor to Rosco's voice as he spoke. His heart was beating ten to the dozen and as he looked up at Nathan Bannerman, he actually felt his insides turn to liquid. The man standing in front of him was big, huge in fact, with hands the size of shovels. Standing well over six feet tall, Nathan not only had a muscular physique but he also had a menacing presence about him, as did his two younger brothers. Sticky, cold sweat pooled underneath Rosco's armpits and it took all of his strength not to swipe his hand across his clammy forehead. Any sign of fear that he gave away would be his downfall.

'We had a deal.' Ignoring the question, Nathan placed his hands on the edge of the desk and leant forward. 'Where the fuck is my merchandise?'

A nervous laugh escaped from Rosco's lips and as the sweat rolled down his temples, he dragged his hand over his forehead then wiped the excess moisture down the length of his thigh.

'Have I said something funny?' Straightening up, Nathan looked back at his brothers. 'Is he taking the piss out of me or am I missing the punchline here?'

Lee and Connor shook their heads, an amused expression spread across their faces. They found it quite entertaining when their elder brother lost his temper. It was definitely a sight to behold, not that it took very much to rile Nathan; even the most innocent of slights was enough to make him erupt with fury. He was well known for it and more often than not was, as a result, given a wide berth by those who knew of him.

'I'm gonna ask you one last time before I end up losing my rag and, trust me, you don't want me to do that, so think of this as your first and only warning. Where is my merchandise?' He launched himself forward and, grasping Rosco by the front of his shirt, he dragged him across the desk towards him. 'Where is it?' he bellowed in his face.

Rosco did what he did best and cried out in fear. Underneath the bravado he liked to put on around people he considered weaker than himself, deep down he was nothing but a coward and a bully. It didn't take a genius to tell him that he was in over his head with the Bannermans and as Nathan's fist came dangerously close to his face, he screamed even louder and slammed his eyes shut tight.

'I've had enough of this bollocks,' Lee stated. 'Give me five minutes alone with him and I'll have him singing like a fucking canary.'

Rosco's eyes snapped open. Out of the three brothers it was Lee who terrified him the most, and seeing as Nathan and Connor terrified him at the best of times, that was saying something. 'No,' he cried. 'There's no need for that.' His face turned bright red and as he willed his heart to return to its usual rhythm, his body shook, so intense was the fear that the Bannerman brothers instilled inside of him. 'There is no coke; it was stolen,' he blurted out.

'Do fucking what?' With his hands still grasping the front of Rosco's shirt in a vice-like grip, Nathan narrowed his eyes. 'What do you mean, stolen?' he growled. 'Who stole it?'

A crafty glint passed over Rosco's eyes and it took all of his effort to suppress the smirk that threatened to spread over his face. This was the moment he'd been waiting for, and when the Bannermans dished out their own form of retribution on the man who'd killed their uncle, he wanted more than just a front-row seat. He wanted to be in the thick of the action and more than anything he wanted vengeance for the brutal attack Fletch had bestowed upon himself, the attack that had left him scarred and forever disfigured. 'It was your cousin, Fletch, or Harry as you probably know him. It was him; he took it.'

Unbeknown to him, it was the worst thing Rosco could have ever said, and as he was dragged over the desk, he landed on the floor with a loud thud.

'I knew it.' Charging forward, Lee kicked out his heavy boot. There was so much ferocity behind the attack that, on impact, Rosco was lifted several feet into the air. 'I told you he was trying to get one over on us,' he said through clenched teeth. 'The no-good bastard went behind our back and did a deal with that murdering cunt.' He bent down and gripped Rosco's jaw in his fist. 'Do we look like mugs?' His grip tightened and his voice began to rise. 'Have you actually got the audacity to try and treat us like fools?'

Shaking his head, Rosco curled himself into a foetal position. A sharp pain ripped through his abdomen and back; the agony was enough to take his breath away, let alone the paralysing fear that gripped at his heart. 'How could I have been dealing with him?' He gasped for breath. 'I didn't even know he was out of nick.'

Lee kicked out a second and third time, each blow landing upon the same spot. Standing over Rosco's prostrate form, he ran a hand through his dark hair and turned to look at his brothers. 'He comes with us,' he snarled.

After being dragged to his feet, mob-handed, they marched Rosco down the staff staircase. He could barely stand. so intense was the pain in his gut, and as he faltered they shoved him forward through the crowded club. The men in his employment were nowhere to be seen; he'd already sent the majority of them out searching for the little scrote Austin and his father. They breezed past the two doormen at the entrance. To his dismay, they didn't try to intervene and save him. They had to know he wasn't walking out of the club of his own free will; the fact that Nathan Bannerman had his meaty fist grasped around the back of his neck as he was frogmarched forward should have been their first indication that not all was as it seemed. There and then, Rosco vowed to make sure the men suffered for their treacherous behaviour. They were meant to be loyal to him; it was him who paid their wages. The stark reality, of course, was very different. The Bannerman name alone instilled far more fear than his name ever could; there wasn't a chance in hell that the doormen were going to question the brothers and ask them what their intentions were.

Within a matter of minutes, he'd been bundled into a car and sandwiched between the two younger brothers like a sardine. As the car pulled out onto the road, he gave the premises a wistful glance. More than anything, he hoped it wasn't going to be the last time he ever saw the club again.

## 28

Not long after his sister had left the flat, Austin had followed on behind her. Earlier that day, he'd collected the handgun from underneath the floorboards in his old room and with the weapon firmly rammed into the waistband of his jeans, he walked towards Rosco's club with a determined swagger.

Revenge was at the forefront of his mind. Charlie and Mark hadn't deserved to die, and as his friends' faces flashed before his eyes, Austin's features twisted into a snarl. As far as he was concerned, only one man deserved to die and that was Rosco fucking Taylor. The fat, sweating pig who'd all but destroyed his childhood, had torn apart his family, and now terrorised his sister on a daily basis, had to go.

Bypassing the front of the club, Austin walked down the narrow alleyway that ran directly behind the parade of shops where the club was situated. The alleyway was used as nothing more than a dumping ground. Behind each premises, litter spewed out of the ripped plastic bin bags that had been carelessly discarded. He stepped over the offending litter: soft drinks cans, flyers, used condoms, cigarette butts and empty takeaway containers, the remnants of the meals inside still visible. It was no wonder the area was a haven for foxes and rats.

Outside the club, he surveyed his surroundings. A six-foot steel fence encased a small courtyard where empty crates had been haphazardly piled up on top of one another. He tested the gate, fully expecting it to be locked. To his surprise, it swung open. He gave a half laugh; Rosco the cunt wasn't going to know what had hit him.

* * *

Inside the club, Dennis was genuinely perplexed. Rosco was nowhere to be seen. Which in itself wouldn't have been unusual if his car had also been absent, but it wasn't. Rosco's BMW was parked outside the club in his usual spot. Rosco never walked anywhere – fact.

Walking back to the two men working the doors, he called out to them as he approached. 'Where's Rosco?'

Both men turned to look at him. They were big men and, as Dennis highly suspected, didn't had a brain cell between them. It just about summed up Rosco's firm, himself excluded, of course. Wearing black bomber jackets, black polo shirts and black trousers, they looked the part and that was about as far as it went.

'He's not here,' one of them called back to him.

Dennis rolled his eyes. 'I gathered that.' He gave a jerk of his head. 'Where is he?'

'Dunno.' They shrugged in unison. 'He left here with the Bannerman brothers, about...' They looked down at their watches. 'Two hours ago, maybe.'

Dennis stared at the men; hell would freeze over before Rosco willingly walked out of the club with the Bannermans in tow. 'You fucking muppets,' he growled.

'What?' they chorused back at him, looking and sounding more like Dumb and Dumber with each passing second.

Ignoring the question, Dennis marched back up to Rosco's office where the CCTV monitor screens were housed. Rubbing the palm of his hand over his face, he inwardly groaned. There, as brazen as you like, on the grainy screen was Kit's brother. 'Brilliant,' he muttered under his breath. On top of everything else that was going on, he needed Austin and his antics like he needed a hole in the head.

* * *

The semi-automatic pistol felt hard against Austin's skin, and as he stepped forward, his hand hovered above the waistband of his jeans. He was more than prepared to take the weapon out as and when it was required. He had no qualms about murdering his sister's husband. In fact, he was going to enjoy ending Rosco's life; the bastard had had it coming to him for years. Every put-down, every punch and every kick that he'd received spurred Austin on and, creeping closer to the door, his entire being was on high alert.

From inside the club, he could hear footsteps approaching the metal door and his heart began to beat that little bit faster. Moving back into the shadows, he slid his hand inside his jeans and gripped the handle of the gun.

The sound of bolts being slid across the door only served to heighten his senses and as his breath streamed out ahead of him, he readied himself to not only pull out the gun but to also pull the trigger.

'What the fuck do you think you're playing at?' Dennis hissed as he grabbed Austin by the throat and slammed him up against the wall.

Pulling out the gun, Austin shoved it into Dennis's side. 'Where is he?' he snarled, his face twisting with anger. 'Get that wanker out here.'

'Have you got a death wish?' Oblivious to the firearm that dug into his stomach, Dennis shoved Austin back across the yard towards the steel gate, the muscles across his shoulder blades tightening with each and every step he took. 'Are you seriously this fucking stupid that you've come here,' he growled, 'here to the fucking club. I've put my neck on the line for you, you ungrateful fucker. Are you trying to get us both topped?'

'Fuck you.' Using his shoulder as a battering ram, Austin shoved his way forward. 'He killed my pals; he killed Charlie and Mark. I'm not letting him get away with that.' He brought the gun up so that it was level with Dennis's face. 'And if I have to go through you to get to that bastard, then trust me, I will. I won't think twice about blasting your head clean off your shoulders.'

Momentarily, Dennis closed his eyes. It had been him who'd murdered Charlie, not Rosco. His shoulders ever so slightly drooped and he rubbed at the back of his neck. 'You're wasting your time. Rosco's not here.'

Austin glanced up at the club. 'You're talking bollocks,' he spat. He tried to push through a second time. 'He's here, I know he is. Oi, Rosco,' he bellowed at the top of his voice, 'get out here and face me, you fucking coward.'

Blood rushed to Dennis's face and as his cheeks burnt he rounded on Austin. 'I said he's not here.' He glanced nervously over his shoulder, expecting the two heavies working the doors to appear at any moment. 'So do yourself a favour and fuck off before one of that lot in there gets wind of you being here. The last thing either of us need is you causing ructions.' Using his considerable strength, he was able to successfully manoeuvre

Austin out of the yard and into the alleyway. 'And don't,' he warned, 'come fucking back.'

As the iron gate was slammed on him, then padlocked, Austin screwed up his face. 'I will have him, do you fucking hear me?' he hissed. 'He can't hide behind you forever.'

Dennis sighed. 'Just go fucking home,' he said as he walked back across the yard. 'And while you're at it, do us all a favour and put the gun away before you end up doing someone some damage or getting your collar felt.'

Watching as Dennis made his way inside the club, Austin rammed the gun back into the waistband of his jeans and screwed up his face. He'd have Rosco if it was the last thing he ever did, and as he stalked away from the club he kicked a discarded cola can out of his path, not for the first time wishing it was Rosco's head he was taking his anger out on.

* * *

Kit was enthralled as she listened to Stevie speak.

'Your dad...' He shook his head. 'Trust me when I say this: he might seem, I don't know.' He blew out his cheeks as he tried to find the right words. 'He might come across as—'

'Aus reckons he's gone soft, that he didn't even attempt to defend himself,' Kit interrupted.

Stevie chuckled. 'Let's put it this way: Aus is lucky that he's your old man's son. Your dad chose not to give him a dig. In my eyes, that doesn't count as being soft and let me tell you this for nothing – your dad has got a blinding right hook on him. If he'd wanted to he could have knocked your brother across the pub and not even broken out in a sweat. If your dad was soft, he would never have lasted in Billy King's firm for as long as he did.'

'Who's Billy King?' Kit tilted her head to one side to look at her father's friend.

'He was our boss – right hard bastard an' all he was. There weren't many men around like him; he was old school and could have a ruck when he needed to. Life was different back then. We didn't need blades or weapons like the kids of today do; men used their fists to end a dispute – it was how we did our business. Anyway, that,' he said with a sigh, 'brings me to Susan, Billy's wife, or Suzy as your dad called her.'

'I've never heard of her.' Kit screwed up her face.

'You wouldn't have. Susan King was one of your dad's best kept secrets; he rarely ever mentioned her back in the day. It would have been more than his life was worth.'

'I don't understand, what has this Susan got to do with my dad?'

'Maybe I've already said too much.' Having second thoughts, Stevie held up his hands and looked away. Fletch wasn't going to take it too kindly if he ever found out that he was spilling his deepest, darkest secrets, and to his daughter of all people.

'No, there's more – what are you keeping from me?' Arching her eyebrows, Kit sat forward. 'You agreed I deserve to know the truth.'

Stevie hesitated.

'Come on,' she urged him, 'I'm not a little kid any more.'

'Your dad...' He glanced away. Fletch would kill him if he ever found out he'd opened his trap. As it was, he was already skating on thin ice where his best mate was concerned. 'Promise me this goes no further than this room?'

Kit nodded.

'Well, he loved her – Susan, I mean. He idolised her. In fact, he still does,' he sighed.

Kit's mouth dropped open.

'To be fair, she was a beautiful woman.'

'Was?' Kit sat up a little straighter.

'Figure of speech.' Stevie laughed. 'She probably still is a beautiful woman; she had a touch of class about her as well, maybe that was the attraction. Right from the start I told your dad not to get involved with her, that it would all end in tears, and I was right, not that it did me any good, mind. He wouldn't listen to me; he never did back then. That's where your brother gets his pig-headedness from. Anyway, Billy, like I said, he was one hard fucker, and believe me he makes Rosco look like a pussy cat in comparison. Not that I think the fat bastard has got much going for him in the first place; he's all piss and wind, for a start,' he was quick to add. 'Get him on his own with a real man and the fucker would shit himself.'

'So, what happened?' Kit sat forward in the chair.

'Well, she was married, wasn't she?' Stevie raised his eyebrows. 'Your dad was besotted with her, and then one day out of the blue she ended the affair. Personally I think she was scared Billy would find out. She was petrified of him; he controlled her. All she ever was to him was a possession. She may have well been his car or house for the way he treated her. It just about broke your dad; he was devastated, and not long after that he met your mum. She was never meant to become a permanent fixture and as I've already said the relationship just kind of steamrolled. But for your mum's part' – his face twisted into a grimace – 'she knew what she was doing and she purposely set out to trap him by getting pregnant. From day one that had been her plan and your dad being the kind of bloke he is stuck it out with her; I suppose he had no other choice, really. At some point he must have decided to give the relationship a second chance otherwise as you rightly said you wouldn't be here now. In fact, his last words to me as he was being led away in handcuffs were "Look after my kids."

Even then all he could think about was you and Austin.' He slumped back on the sofa and sighed. 'Not that I did a very good job of it. I let your dad down, and I let you and Aus down; maybe that's why I put up with Austin's attitude as much as I do, because I feel guilty for not stopping Rosco from battering him.'

Kit shook her head. 'No one could have stopped what happened. By then it was already too late; he had my mum under his control. She would never have left him. She needed him for her next fix.'

'Your dad would have stopped him,' Stevie told her, his expression serious. 'Believe me, darling, if your dad had been on the outside, he would have ended Rosco the second he'd laid a finger on either of you. Your dad loves you, he always has and he always will.'

Staring into the distance, Kit nodded her head. Deep down she'd always known that her dad loved her and Austin. Her nan had told her so enough times, her dad himself had even told her, yet she couldn't help but feel anger towards him. All she'd ever wanted growing up was a dad who was there for her, just like her friends' dads were. So many times over the years she'd imagined him taking her out to the park or taking her to a Wimpy bar for a chocolate milkshake. It was never going to happen; how could it, when he'd been locked up her entire life.

'Why don't you give him a chance and get to know him? When I used to visit him in the nick all he ever talked about was you and your brother, how much he missed you, how much he longed to be on the outside with you both. If he fucks up a second time, at least you know you gave him this one chance to make things right. If nothing else he deserves that, sweetheart.'

'I don't think I can.' Kit shook her head. 'It's not as easy as that, is it?'

'Course it is,' Stevie persevered. 'What have you got to lose?'

'My pride.'

Stevie blew out his cheeks. 'Now you're talking out of your arse,' he chastised. 'Go and see your old man, get to know him, and see for yourself what he's like before you sit there judging him. You never know, you might actually find that you're a lot more similar than you think.'

* * *

In one of the Bannermans' rented factories in South London, the faint scent of chemicals lingered in the air. It was a scent Rosco knew all too well: cocaine. As he looked around him, he took a wild guess that this was where the brothers conducted their business, or at least they had. Other than the solid wooden workbenches that ran the length of the rear wall, the factory was devoid of any other fixtures and fittings. It was also spotlessly clean.

For just over an hour, Rosco had been tied to a chair, and his gaze flicked between a pair of rubber-handled bolt cutters that had been placed on one of the workbenches and then to the three brothers, who were standing huddled together having what could only be described as a deep, hushed and animated conversation. The bombshell he had dropped regarding their cousin's release from prison had clearly rattled them and although he couldn't hear exactly what they were saying, from their stances alone he could tell that they weren't happy bunnies.

After they had trussed him up, Rosco had assumed that they would immediately begin their torture of him, but they hadn't, and for the past hour they had barely even glanced in his direction, other than when the youngest brother, Connor, had rolled a bottle of water towards him. He guessed that this was Connor's idea of a joke, since Rosco's arms had been bound behind his back with cable ties. There was no way he could pick the bottle up even if he wanted to and, despite the fact he would give anything to be able to swallow the liquid down in greedy gulps and quench his thirst, hell would freeze over before he ever asked for their help. He wouldn't give them the satisfaction of laughing in his face, or refusing his request, because he knew without a doubt that they would. It would amuse them to see him beg; he could only hope and pray that by the end of the night he wouldn't be begging for his life.

The anticipation of waiting for them to begin their attack on him almost drove Rosco out of his mind and every sudden movement they made was enough to make his pulse quicken, and the tiny hairs on the back of his thick bull neck stand up on end. It was a mind game on their part, one that was working to their full advantage, and as a result Rosco was terrified.

By the time they turned around to face him, Rosco almost screamed out in fear. He recalled Dennis's story about Lee slicing off a man's testicles, and glanced nervously towards the workbench. To his relief he couldn't see an actual blade but that didn't mean to say the bolt cutters wouldn't be able to do the same job.

'You all right there, Rosco? You're looking a bit peaky, mate. Is it just me, or' – Connor tilted his head to one side and rolled his lips together as he studied him – 'does he look a bit grey around the edges to you?' He gave a raucous laugh. 'It's all gone a bit Pete Tong for you, mate, ain't it?'

It was the youngest brother again, clearly the one out of the three who thought of himself as a comedian. Of course he was looking a bit grey around the edges; he'd been tied to a chair for the past hour. And as for things going wrong, Connor could say that again; he'd fully expected the brothers to take him on side, that together as equals they would plan Fletch's demise.

The cable ties were biting into Rosco's flesh and the pain in his gut and back had intensified, so much so that he wouldn't be surprised if he was pissing out blood for the foreseeable future. That was, if they even let him survive through the night. His shoulders felt as if they had been pulled out of their sockets and he couldn't feel his hands any more; the tight bonds that bound him had cut off the blood supply a long time ago. And if that wasn't enough, he also needed to go to the toilet. Just the mere thought of his life being at their will was enough to make his bowels loosen.

Walking across to the workbench, Nathan picked up the bolt cutters and, turning them over in his hand, he gave Rosco a side-long glance. 'You can do a lot of damage with a pair of these,' he said, pushing the handle open and closed in quick succession. The metal blades snapped together with a loud snip. He then turned to look at his brothers. 'Hold the treacherous bastard's hand out.'

As the two brothers advanced towards him for the first time that night, Rosco's screams reverberated around the factory.

Kit was the last person Fletch had expected to see on his doorstep and as he led her out of view of the CCTV camera, his mind raced. Her expression was unreadable and there and then he braced himself for her to lash out, for her to say the same words her brother had already said to him, that he was dead to her too.

Leaning against the wall, Fletch dug his hands into his pockets as he watched his daughter look up at the hostel. He'd never felt more ashamed. Not for the first time did he pick up on the tension between them. She was his daughter and he knew for a certainty that he would love her until the end of his days; he would even be prepared to lay his life on the line for her, yet for her part he was nothing more than a stranger to her. He didn't even have anything to offer his children: no prospects, barely any money, no real belongings to speak of and even the clothes on his back, although clean, were just the basics. His life was poles apart from the one he'd left behind all those years ago. Before he'd been sent to prison, he'd had everything his heart had ever desired: a flashy car, money in abundance, designer clothing, a prestige position in Billy King's firm, and he'd even had the woman of his dreams. For a while life had been more than just good; it had been everything he'd ever dreamt it could be. Until, that was, the day his Suzy had ended their relationship; from then on his life had spiralled out of control. Tina had clung to him like a limpet and then deliberately set out to trap him, his brother had been murdered and then, as if that wasn't bad enough, he'd gone on to commit a crime so heinous that the life sentence he'd been handed out was no more than he'd deserved. He looked down at his feet and as he swallowed deeply, he gave a slight shake of his head. 'I didn't touch her.'

'I know.'

Fletch snapped his head up to look at his daughter, his forehead furrowed.

'Sheree is a lying bitch; she loves nothing more than to be the centre of attention and Aus falls for it every single time.'

For a few moments they stood in silence, the awkwardness between them growing larger by the second.

'Stevie said that I should come here.' Breaking the silence, Kit stole another glance up at the hostel – anything other than look at her father.

'I'm glad that you listened.' Fletch gave his daughter a gentle smile. 'You might not believe me, and I get it, I really do. You don't know me, and I only have myself to blame for that, but I do love you. You're my daughter, and keeping you and your brother safe is my number one priority; it always will be.' He momentarily closed his eyes and sighed. 'I take it you've been told about Charlie?'

Kit nodded. She looked down for a moment, debating within herself whether or not she should utter out loud the words that had plagued her ever since she'd set foot inside the Portakabin with Rosco. 'Mark is dead,' she said quietly. 'Rosco shot him.'

'I thought as much,' Fletch sighed. The fact his daughter was trusting him with the information was a huge step in the right direction as far as he was concerned. 'Austin doesn't know yet?'

'No.' She shook her head and as tears sprang to her eyes, she swiped them away with the back of her hand, angry at herself for coming across as weak. It was imperative that she stayed strong, that she stayed in control of her emotions; it was down to her to keep her brother safe and she wouldn't be able to do that if she cracked. 'It's going to destroy him when he finds out.'

'Hey.' Stepping forward, Fletch opened his arms to embrace her.

Shaking her head, Kit moved away and crossed her arms over her chest in a bid to ward him off.

Fletch held up his hands. 'I'm sorry – too soon.'

Kit nodded, rested her back against the wall and sighed. 'Aus doesn't think. He never thinks; that's his problem.'

Fletch joined her, making sure there was a reasonable distance between them. 'Spencer, my brother...' He gave her a sad smile and started again. Of course she would know who Spencer was; his mother's house was full of photographs of his younger brother. 'Your uncle, he was exactly the same; I spent the majority of my life looking out for him.'

'Austin hasn't always been like this. When we were kids, he looked out for me.' She gave a light laugh as a memory sprang to her mind. 'I must have been, I don't know, about six or seven and it was my birthday. Mum had bought me a birthday cake but I think I'd been playing her up; I could be a right little madam at times, especially when I couldn't get my own way.' She laughed. 'And anyway, she said I couldn't have my cake, that I didn't deserve it, and so she put it up on top of the kitchen cabinet, where I couldn't reach it. When she wasn't looking, I climbed up there, took it down and hid it underneath a bush in the back garden but when I went back to collect it ants had found their way into the box and were crawling all over the icing. I was absolutely devastated. To cheer me up, Austin made me jam sandwiches. He placed one on top of the other so that they were about this high.' She placed her thumb and forefinger three inches apart. 'We pretended it was my cake; that was the kind of brother he was – thoughtful, caring. It wasn't until Rosco came along that I had to start looking out for him.' She became serious. 'Rosco ruined him. From day one he had it in for him, only Mum couldn't see what was going on underneath her nose. She blamed Aus, said that he was naughty, that he deserved the good hidings he received, but he didn't. He was just a little kid and all of a sudden there was this man in our home, shouting the odds, ruling the roost. Rosco did everything he could to be spiteful. He even banned Aus from kicking a ball about in the back garden, said it was ruining the lawn, and Mum, because she was so weak, agreed with him. I think I can count on one hand how many times Rosco actually ventured into the garden. He didn't give a shit about it. Why should he? He'd already done what he'd set out to do and that was take something away from Aus, something he'd loved.' She gave a thin smile. 'Up until then, wherever Aus was you could be sure that a ball was nearby. He never left the house without one tucked under his arm; he'd had dreams of playing for England one day, and he was good, really good. He could have made it. Up here' – she tapped her temple – 'Aus is fucked up. He doesn't mean half the things he says or does. He lives for the moment; he doesn't think his actions through.'

As he listened to his daughter speak, Fletch's blood began to boil. It took all of his strength to not charge down the street and end Taylor there and then. Fuck his curfew, fuck the probation officer; he'd happily go back to prison for the remainder of his life if it meant avenging his son. He'd always vowed his own children would never suffer in the same way he and his brother had, that his children would never witness violence, that they would never be terrified in their own home. The stark reality, of course, was that he'd let them down. 'I can't put right what has already been done, but I swear to you, Taylor will pay for what he did.'

Kit raised her eyebrows. She could only hope and pray that it wasn't yet another empty promise.

'Why did you marry him?' Fletch's voice was gentle as he asked the question.

With a shrug of her shoulders, Kit gave a sad smile. 'I had no other choice. He made me a proposition that he would lay off Aus if I married him and because I'm obviously stupid, I took him up on it. I should have known nothing would change and by the time I came to realise what a big mistake I'd made' – she looked away and blew out her cheeks – 'it was already too late.'

Closing his eyes, Fletch sighed. 'Do me a favour, darling: don't go home to him tonight.'

Kit opened her mouth to speak.

'Yeah, I know,' Fletch interrupted her. 'Like you keep reminding me, I'm twenty-two years too late for the caring father act, and you're right, I am, but it's not safe for you to go back to the house alone.' He looked into her face. 'Go and stay with Aus or a friend, or maybe even this Dennis geezer.'

Kit bit down on her lip. She could hear the genuine concern

in her father's voice and the ice wall that imprisoned her heart ever so slightly melted. 'I'll stay at Austin's tonight.'

As Fletch nodded, a wave of relief flushed over him and he felt as though a lead weight had been lifted from his shoulders. The less she was around Taylor, the better, as far as he was concerned.

## 29

Rosco was sweating like a pig and as the bolt cutter came closer to his restrained hand, he screamed out in fright. Much to his dismay, once they had sliced away the tight cable ties that had cut off his blood supply and wrenched his hand out in front of him, the numbness he'd felt was beginning to fade. Pins and needles were still present in his fingers, but he could feel their touch; therefore, to his horror, he would feel pain. 'I've done nothing wrong,' he cried.

'You sound just like a tart. In fact, my old mum would have more bollocks than this. I thought you were meant to be a tough man,' Connor mocked.

Tearing his eyes away from the bolt cutter, Rosco glanced up at the youngest of the Bannerman brothers. The mere mention of testicles made his heart beat that little bit faster. As for 'tough man', he was the first to hold his hand up and admit that he was only tough when it came to terrorising women and children or when he had his firm behind him.

'Wait.' Just below the knuckle on his left hand, the sensation of cold steel enveloped Rosco's pinkie finger. Tears rolled down his cheeks and sheer terror gripped at his heart; he needed to think of a way out of the mess he'd found himself in, and fast.

It was too late and as the bolt cutter sliced through skin, tissue and bone, stars exploded behind Rosco's eyes and he let out a roar of pain. Using both hands, Nathan applied pressure and squeezed down on the tool; a loud crack could be heard and for a brief moment Rosco thought that his heart would actually stop beating.

Blood gushed from the stump where Rosco's finger should have been and in a wild panic he tried in vain to escape from the chair. The colour had drained from his face and his eyes were so wide they were almost popping out of his head. In all his life he'd never screamed so loud and as they fought to regain control of him, he actually wet himself. The hot urine ran down his legs, soaking the crotch of his trousers in the process, and he began to wail even harder.

'This is just a taste of what's to come.' Nathan waved the bloodied tool in front of Rosco's face, and with a jerk of his head he indicated for his brothers to hold the man still. 'Just in case you weren't aware by now of what happens to people who cross us.'

'No, wait.' Tears mingled with snot trailed down past Rosco's lips. He was bleeding out, and from what he could see there was a lot of claret covering not only himself, but also the workbench and floor. He tore his eyes away from his severed finger, which sat in a puddle of blood. 'I've got a bargaining tool.' He looked up at them, his wide eyes going from one brother to the next. 'My wife…'

'You've got a wife?' Connor raised his eyebrows, the hint of a grin threatening to crease his face. 'Fuck me, and there was me thinking you wouldn't be able to pull a canary, let alone a bird.'

He motioned to his elder brother. 'Here, Lee,' he said, tongue in cheek, 'have you heard this? There's hope for you yet, bruv.'

Amid his brother's laughter that echoed off the factory walls, Lee grunted in disapproval.

Rosco swallowed deeply, ignoring the barb. He already knew that he was no oil painting and in any normal circumstances a woman with Kit's beauty would never have looked at him twice. 'She's Fletch's daughter. Do whatever the fuck you want with her; she's nothing to me, but to her father,' he said craftily, 'she's worth more than her weight in gold. He'll do an exchange, I know he will.'

Narrowing his eyes, Nathan glanced towards his brothers. Just when he'd thought Rosco couldn't sink any lower than he already had, he'd thrown them another gem. 'A daughter?'

'Kit.' As he swallowed, a sliver of hope filled Rosco. 'She's yours; take her, use her as bait.'

Nathan laughed. It was a low laugh that resembled a rumble, and as his fist shot out he punched Rosco so hard that the chair he was sitting on toppled over. 'You treacherous cunt, you'd serve up your missus just to save your own skin.'

Lying in a crumpled heap on the floor, blood oozed from both Rosco's nose and severed finger. Blinking rapidly up at them, he brought his arm across his chest and tucked his injured, bleeding, throbbing hand into his armpit, in the hope that it would stem the bleeding. As the brothers began to discuss their next move, his shoulders ever so slightly relaxed; just maybe he would live to see another day after all.

* * *

It wasn't until early evening that a chance arose for Jenny to sneak into the room that Tina was occupying and have a snoop around.

The fact her grandson had lied about what he had collected had sparked her curiosity and as soon as she heard the familiar slosh of water as Tina lowered herself into the tub, she tiptoed up the stairs.

Tina's bedroom was a fair size and overlooked the back garden, and as she entered she wrinkled her nose at the bitter stench that permeated the room. The smell reminded her of sour milk and for a moment she wondered if Tina had spilt a drink and not cleaned up afterwards. Nothing would surprise her where Tina was concerned; at the best of times, she could be a lazy mare. Yet again she would need to have another word with her grandchildren's mother and remind her to air the room out once in a while.

Looking around her, Jenny searched for anything out of the ordinary. In front of the single wardrobe, Tina had carelessly discarded her shoes and soiled clothes. The chest of drawers held a selection of personal effects, perfume, deodorant, make-up and a faded photograph of her eldest son.

There was nothing at all to set alarm bells ringing inside Jenny's head and as she went to walk out of the room, she paused, stole a glance towards the closed bathroom door, then knelt beside the single bed. She was about to lift the mattress when out of the corner of her eye she caught sight of the frayed carpet edges. Crawling a few paces forward, she sat back on her haunches and lifted the thin carpet with a measure of trepidation.

Jenny wasn't sure exactly what she'd expected to find, but there was nothing visible underneath the carpet to cause her alarm, only bare floorboards. She dropped the carpet, then moved back to the bed and lifted the corner of the mattress.

Hidden underneath the mattress was a cloudy crack pipe, the bulb scorched and blackened. Beside it lay a tiny scrap of tin foil.

The concealed stash was more than enough to make Jenny's heart plummet. Time and time again, Tina had promised her that she was clean, and she, like the silly old fool that she was, had believed her every word.

Snatching up the items, she made her way back down the stairs, her expression set like thunder. As far as she was concerned, Tina had run out of chances, and to think she had been prepared to kick her own son out of the house for the likes of a lying drug addict. She should have known it was all lies; after all, it wasn't as though it was the first empty promise Tina had made.

* * *

True to her promise, after leaving her father, Kit drove straight to her brother's flat. Exiting her car, she locked up and made her way towards the communal door. After tapping in a series of digits on the entry pad system, the door sprang ajar and she made her way across the lobby. At the foot of the stairs she fished her mobile phone out of her pocket and sent off a text message to Dennis, letting him know where she was, then promptly switched off her phone before making her way up the stone staircase.

'Kit.' Barefoot and dressed in only a pair of tracksuit bottoms, Austin opened the front door. 'What are you doing back here?'

'Can I stay here tonight?'

'Why?' Austin's forehead furrowed and as he stepped aside to allow his sister entry, his entire body was rigid as he scrutinised her face for any tell-tale signs of swelling or bruising. 'Has that fat bastard hurt you?'

Kit shook her head. There was an edginess in her brother's stance that she'd never seen before and she had a sneaking suspicion that just one wrong word from her would tip him over the edge. 'I thought it would be nice to spend some time with Lacey,' she lied. 'I hardly ever see her these days and she is my only niece.'

Austin screwed up his face. 'Lacey is with Sheree's mum and dad; I told you that when you came over earlier.'

Entering the kitchen, Kit leant against the counter. She'd totally forgotten that Lacey was with Sheree's parents.

'What's going on, Kit? This ain't like you; you've never wanted to stay the night before.'

'I went to see Dad.' She turned her head as Sheree entered the kitchen. Wearing just a pair of cotton shorts and a matching cropped top, it was obvious that Sheree had been in bed asleep before she'd arrived. Her hair was dishevelled and thick black gloops of mascara were still clinging to the corners of her eyes. It was so typical of Sheree; she couldn't bear for Kit and Austin to be left alone for any longer than five minutes.

'Why would you do that?' Austin hissed. 'Right from the start you made your feelings clear about him. Why go and see him now after what he did to Ree?'

'Because' – she took a deep breath and braced herself for her brother to kick off – 'I wanted to know the truth.'

'You already know the truth.' Austin's voice was hard as he pulled Sheree protectively underneath his arm. 'The bastard attacked Ree.'

'She doesn't believe me.' Wrapping her arms around her boyfriend's waist, Sheree sniffed back her tears, albeit crocodile tears. 'I'm the victim here. He tried to kiss me, he tried to shove his tongue down my throat, but I suppose that doesn't mean anything to you, does it? You've never liked me; all you've ever done is look down your nose at me. Anyone would think that your own shit doesn't stink the way you carry on.'

'Of course she believes you.' Kissing the top of his girlfriend's head in an attempt to allay her tears, Austin pulled Sheree even closer. 'Don't you, Kit?' He tilted his head to one side as he studied his sister, his eyes hard. 'You know the truth; he tried it on.'

As she stared at her brother's girlfriend, there was a steely glint in Kit's eyes. Her dislike of Sheree was so strong she could almost taste it. She had to give it to her, though – she was a good actress, and if she hadn't have known any better she would have fully believed her lies just as Austin did. How he couldn't see how manipulative she was, Kit would never understand. He was the same when it came to their mother; he took what they both said at face value. 'Yeah, you're right, I do know the truth,' she answered matter-of-factly.

Austin's shoulders relaxed and, reaching out for the bag of cannabis, he began building a joint. 'Well, you can still stay the night, ain't that right, Ree?'

For a split second, Sheree's expression faltered. Then, composing herself, she gave a sweet smile. 'Course you can. You're welcome any time; you know that, Kit.'

There was a hint of sarcasm to her voice that Kit immediately picked up on and she returned an equally false smile.

Sparking up the joint, Austin leant against the kitchen counter. 'I could do with you being here, to be honest, sis, after what's happened to Charlie and Mark.' He shook his head and through the haze of smoke, Kit could see the tears well up in her brother's eyes. 'I don't trust you being around Rosco.' He paused for a moment. 'I went to the club today, but the fat fucker wasn't there.'

'What?' Kit's mouth dropped open and she stole a glance in Sheree's direction. 'Why would you do that? You know if he'd found you there he would have killed you.'

Austin sneered. 'I didn't plan on giving him the chance.' He lifted two fingers and pointed them at the side of his head, then mimicked pulling the trigger of a gun.

Kit's blood ran cold and, tilting her head to look at her brother, she narrowed her eyes. 'What are you talking about?'

'I went there to kill him.' He gave a nonchalant shrug. 'The sooner that arsehole is dead, the better it will be for everyone.'

'Did you know about this?' Kit threw Sheree an accusing stare.

'Me?' Sheree's mouth dropped open and she bounced on her feet, reminding Kit of a boxer preparing to go twelve rounds inside a canvas ring. 'Sounds about right, you always blame me for everything,' she huffed.

'Ree didn't know anything about it,' Austin butted in before the two women ended up at loggerheads. 'And you can thank your boyfriend for the fact Rosco is still breathing, talking and shitting.'

Kit's body stiffened and she shot a second glance in Sheree's direction. The smug expression across the other woman's face was enough to tell Kit that she'd been told everything there was to know about her and Dennis. 'You told her?' Kit spat, emphasising the word. 'Her, of all people.'

'I am still here, you know.' Sheree raised her eyes to the ceiling, concealing the spark of jealousy that rippled through her. Dennis was hot; not in the same league as Fletch, mind, but he was still a good-looking man with a toned, muscular body that rippled beneath his shirts. What he saw in Kit with her constant sour, miserable countenance, for the life of her she would never understand.

Relighting the joint, Austin looked up at his sister. 'She is my missus, Kit, and Ree isn't going to say anything. Your secret is safe with us.' He grinned.

'This isn't funny, Aus.' The fine hairs on Kit's arms stood to attention and goose flesh covered her skin, making her involuntarily shudder. 'This isn't a game we're playing. Just one wrong word to Rosco and my life will be over.'

The smile slid from Austin's face. 'It won't come to that,' he answered, his voice serious. 'I'd kill him stone dead long before he ever laid a finger on you.'

'It had better not,' Kit retorted. Even as she said the words, a prickle of fear ran down the length of her spine. At the best of times Rosco could be a spiteful, vicious bastard; there was no saying what he would do if he found out about her and Dennis. She knew for a fact he wouldn't think twice about killing them; he would take pleasure from it.

As Nathan Bannerman brought his car to a halt outside Rosco's home, he took a moment or two to look the house over. The house, a terraced cottage, wasn't exactly what he'd been expecting. Knowing how flash Taylor was, he'd thoroughly expected to see something ostentatious, something that reflected Rosco's gaudy, egotistical personality.

He stepped out of his car and, from the back seat, his brothers followed suit. Between them Rosco was sandwiched. Still the snivelling bastard complained about his severed finger; anyone would think he'd had his arm ripped off, the way he was carrying on.

Ignoring Rosco's whimpers, Nathan led the way down the path.

'She's not here.' Rosco sniffed. 'Her car isn't here.'

Nathan looked back at Rosco's bloated face. His voice was hoarse, his skin blotchy and his eyes red-rimmed from the tears he'd shed. 'We'll have to wait for her then, won't we?' Nathan grinned. 'But don't you worry, we'll make ourselves at home; we always do,' he said with a wink.

There and then, Rosco's heart plummeted.

* * *

The anticipation of what was to come caused Tina's heart to beat hard and fast. After drying herself and then hastily dressing, she'd begun the task of preparing her nightly fix, one that would send her happily off to sleep.

She'd already closed the bedroom door and slid across the six-inch bolt. Placing her hand under the mattress, her fingers reached out to clasp the cloudy crack pipe and scrap of tin foil that contained the tiny crystals.

Her hand glided across the smooth divan base. When she couldn't find what she was looking for, she knelt down, heaved the edge of the mattress up onto her shoulder and felt around.

Panic slid through Tina's veins and, jumping to her feet, she hauled the mattress to the floor. Much to her horror and just as she'd suspected it would be, the divan base was empty.

*No*, she wanted to scream at the top of her lungs, *no, no, no.* Flinging the duvet, pillows and sheet across the room, her eyes were wide and her skin had drained of all colour. She sank to her hands and knees, hoping against hope that somehow the pipe and tin foil had slipped off the bed, even though she knew it was a long shot. Her stash had been placed in the middle of the base, where she could easily reach it; there was no way it could have rolled to the floor.

As she got to her feet, a snarl filtered across Tina's face and, sliding across the bolt, she rushed out of the room and thundered down the staircase. In the kitchen, she found Jenny. Her need for a fix was all-consuming and knowing that she couldn't lay her hands on the drug that her body so desperately craved made the dull ache in her belly gnaw away at her until it had engulfed her entire being. It was more than just a desire; it was a craving that threatened to drive her out of her mind.

Tina's thin, emaciated body shook and as she lunged forward she grasped a handful of Jenny's hair in her fist and dragged her around to face her. 'Where is it, what have you done with my stash?' she screamed in Jenny's face, covering her in foul-smelling spittle as she did so.

Shock resonated across Jenny's face, and, prising Tina's hands out of her hair, she forcefully pushed the mother of her grand-children away from her. Considering her tiny size, Tina was strong, a lot stronger than any of them had ever given her credit for and as Tina bounded forward a second time, her ragged fingernails were ready to claw at Jenny's face.

'Stop.' Using her hands as a shield, Jenny screamed, 'Stop this now.'

Tina's cheeks were bright red from the exertion and her chest heaved so hard that she could barely catch her breath. She stabbed a nicotine-stained finger forward. 'Where is it?' she gasped. 'I'm fucking warning you, tell me what have you done with it.' Swinging from anger to despair, her voice took on a pleading tone and she wrapped her arms around her trembling frame. 'I need it, please, Jenny, give it back to me.'

'You've been lying to me,' Jenny cried. 'You swore to me that you were clean.'

Despite her predicament, a bitter laugh escaped from Tina's lips. As far as she was concerned, Jenny was not only as stupid as they came, but also naïve. She was clueless to everything and everyone around her. Talk about blind; her own grandson had been dealing drugs from the house for years and not once had she clocked what he was getting up. 'Where is it?' she spat.

As she eyed Tina warily, Jenny shook her head and smoothed down her ruffled hair. Her lips were set into a thin line. 'You promised me, Tina,' she said in a stern voice, 'and I can't have drugs in the house – I'm sorry, but I can't. Right from the very start, before you even moved in, you knew that was the only stipulation we had. Me and Frank, we won't put up with it and if you can't abide by our rules' – she swallowed deeply, her heart breaking in two for what she was about to say – 'then I think it would be best that you found yourself somewhere else to live.'

'Your rules.' Tina stalked forward until she had backed Jenny up against the kitchen counter. 'What about when Aus was dealing right underneath your nose? Where were your precious rules and stipulations then?'

Jenny's mouth fell open. 'No,' she cried, 'Austin would never do something like that. He's had his problems in the past, I admit, but he wouldn't sink so low, he wouldn't.' She took a quick glance around the kitchen as though the answers she craved were staring back at her from the walls. 'Not here, not in the house, not in our home.'

'Oh, but he did.' A wicked glint was in Tina's eyes. 'Who do you think supplies it to me?' She gave a nasty chuckle, revealing nicotine-stained teeth. 'Aus is up to his neck in all of this; he's a dealer, has been for years, even when he lived under your roof.'

Across Jenny's chest, a pain begun to grow. In that instant, she recalled the bulging bag her grandson had fetched from Tina's room. 'No.' She continued to shake her head. 'Please God, no, he wouldn't.'

Clenching her teeth, Tina's eyes were mere slits in her pale face and as she spoke there was a whine to her voice that bordered on desperation. 'What have you done with my fix?'

Following Jenny's gaze towards the plastic waste bin, the sight before Tina was enough to make her see red. Sitting on top of the potato peelings and remnants of the meal they had eaten earlier that evening was her crack pipe. It had been snapped clean in half and the bulb of the pipe had been smashed to smithereens. 'You bitch!' She ran across the room and delved her hands into the bin, oblivious to the shards of glass that nicked at her skin. Digging deeper, she searched for the scrap of tin foil containing the tiny rocks. Tears of frustration slipped down her cheeks and in the pit of her stomach the all-familiar ache intensified. 'No,' she cried as her hands delved deeper.

'You won't find what you're looking for.' Jenny lifted her chin in the air. 'I tipped the poison down the sink.' Her voice became gentle. 'It's for your own good, darling. I'm only thinking of you. You're killing yourself; you need professional help.'

'No,' Tina roared. She charged forward. Her hands, which still held traces of gravy, mashed potato, blood and a squashed pea, were raised, ready to attack.

Before Tina could strike out, she was lifted off her feet and carried from the kitchen. 'Enough,' Frank roared. He dumped Tina down in the hallway and with his hand still gripped around her arm in a tight vice, he flung open the front door and shoved her none too gently outside. 'Now fuck off, and don't darken my door again.' Without saying another word, he slammed the door closed on Tina's face.

In the kitchen, Jenny began to sob. She slumped down onto a chair at the kitchen table and held her head in her hands. 'She's got nowhere to go; this is her home, Frank.'

Frank sighed and, after closing the kitchen door in the hope it would drown out Tina's pitiful cries, he pulled out a chair and sat down. 'She isn't your problem; you need to remember that. She's got her own family; let them worry about her for a change.' He leant across the table and clutched his sister's hand in his. 'Besides, she's never been short of somewhere to stay in the past when she's been on a bender and disappeared for days on end, sometimes even weeks, has she?'

Jenny sniffed back her tears. There was some truth to Frank's words. On more than one occasion, Tina had disappeared only to return days later as if nothing had ever happened. A fresh set of tears filled her eyes. 'Where did I go wrong?' she wept. 'First the boys and now Austin.'

'I don't know, girl,' he answered, and it was true: he didn't know where it had all gone so very wrong. Jenny had been a blinding mother to her sons. She had only ever put their needs first, even when that had meant going without herself, which she had done so often. 'It's in their blood.' He gave her a sad smile. 'It's in their DNA; no matter what you did or didn't do, it was never going to be enough to change who they are. They have too much of that bastard Bannerman running through their veins for them to be anything different.'

George Bannerman had been the epitome of evil, and as Jenny looked up at her brother, his words were the equivalent of a ten-ton truck smashing into her. Now with a sudden clarity she knew what he said was the truth. No matter what she'd said or done over the years, she would never have been able to change the course of events that had plagued her family. Her sons had been the outcome of a wicked, evil man, a man who'd lived by the sword and ultimately died by the same sword, a man who had run a criminal empire through fear, destruction and malevolence.

She sat up a little straighter and closed her eyes tight. A saying she'd once heard ran through her mind with a speed that frightened her to the very core. *What was bred in the bone will come out in the flesh.*

## 30

Early the next morning, Fletch made his way over to Susan's flat in Upminster. Susan had decided to take the day off from work after feigning a headache meaning that she would have the flat to herself for the majority of the day. He rubbed his hand over his face. He still couldn't get his head around the fact that he had fathered a third child, a daughter who was not only beautiful but, as her mother had pointed out, kind-hearted, intelligent and talented. Having been raised in Spain, she was also fluent in the language.

As he climbed the short flight of steps up to Susan's flat, she was waiting for him at the front door. He gave her a wide grin and as she smiled back, his heart soared.

'I've fucking missed you.' He placed his arms around her waist, lifted her off her feet and planted a kiss on her lips.

'Fletch!' She let out a shriek and playfully slapped his arm. 'Put me down.'

'Never.' He laughed.

Entering the flat, he kicked the front door closed behind him, carried her through to the bedroom then gently dropped her onto the double bed and began stripping off his clothes. 'We've got some making up for lost time to take care of.' He beamed.

Susan's eyes sparkled and a husky laugh escaped from her lips. How she had lived without this man by her side, for the life of her she would never fully comprehend. As he lowered himself down on top of her and kissed her neck, all she could do was hope and pray that he was never ripped away from her again. She was certain that her heart wouldn't be able to cope with losing him a second time.

\* \* \*

As she watched her brother and Sheree tuck into a full English breakfast, Kit nibbled at a slice of buttered toast. She had no appetite and couldn't actually remember the last time she had sat down and eaten a meal that consisted of more than what most people considered to be a snack.

'I should make a move.' She placed the uneaten toast on the edge of the plate and reached out for her handbag.

About to cram half a sausage smothered with egg and tomato sauce into his mouth, Austin looked up. 'Bit early, ain't it?' He looked down at his sister's breakfast plate; she'd hardly eaten a thing. 'Are you not eating that?'

Kit shook her head. She slipped the strap of her handbag over her shoulder and stood up. 'I need to get home, have a shower and change clothes before heading to the club.'

Scraping his sister's breakfast onto his plate, Austin nodded. As Kit made her way towards the front door, he called after her. 'Remember to be careful around that fat cunt,' he said in a warning. 'He's a slippery bastard and I don't trust him.'

Kit sighed and, turning around, she gave her brother a tight smile. 'You know me,' she said, 'I'm always careful.'

With those parting words, she left the flat and as she descended the stone staircase her heart was heavy. Pretending to be happier than she actually felt was not only draining but also beginning to take its toll on her.

Thirty minutes later, she pulled up outside her house. It should have been her marital home, a place where she and her new husband could plan out their future, and if she had been married to anyone other than Rosco she may well have done just that. Instead, the house was like a prison, a place where she felt so suffocated, so trapped that at times she couldn't breathe.

Noting that Rosco's car wasn't parked outside the house, a wave of relief flushed over her. The last thing she wanted or needed was to see the man she was married to; she loathed him with an intensity that at times frightened her.

As soon as she opened the front door, Kit sensed that something was different – wrong, even. In the air was an unfamiliar scent of cologne and she knew for a fact that it wasn't coming from her husband. Rosco hardly ever wore aftershave and when he did it was a cheap and nasty scent; he had no class and actually believed the cologne that reeked to high heaven was enough to make her want to drop her knickers and drool all over him. No, this scent was expensive, woody with a hint of citrus, similar to the one she had bought Dennis for his birthday.

With a measure of trepidation, she stepped further into the hallway. 'Hello,' she called out.

At the bottom of the staircase, she sensed a presence watching her and, spinning around, Kit's breath caught in the back of her throat. 'Who are you?' she asked Connor. Standing at well over six feet tall, he was young, mid to late twenties perhaps, and if it wasn't for the hard glint in his eyes she would have considered him to be handsome. There was also something familiar about him, although she was pretty certain they had never met before.

She racked her brain, wondering if he was a friend of Austin's, maybe an old school friend? 'I asked you a question.' She pulled herself up to her full her height, all five feet four inches of it, her voice coming across a lot stronger than she actually felt. 'Who the fuck are you and what are you doing in my house?'

'That's not very nice, is it? Is that how you greet all your guests?' Nathan asked.

Kit spun around to look at a second man. He looked so similar to the first that she was convinced they had to be related – brothers, perhaps – same height, same build, same dark hair, same features. Her pulse began to quicken. 'Where's Rosco?'

'Through there.' He gave her a bright smile and gestured towards the lounge.

The door to the lounge was open just a crack and as she tried to peer through the gap, unease gripped at Kit's heart.

'Shall we?' Nathan put out his hand as though he was in his own home and she was the guest.

Left with no other choice, Kit stepped forward and pushed open the lounge door. Sitting on a hard-backed chair beside the open fireplace, Rosco looked up. In a matter of seconds she took in his swollen nose and the smear of dried blood across his cheek. His hand, which was wrapped in a bloody tea towel, was held at an angle across his chest. Behind him, a third man was standing guard – another relative or brother, she rightly guessed.

Her senses went into overdrive. From the moment she had set foot inside the front door she had known something was wrong. In that instant she decided to make a run for it and bolted across the lounge. She had almost reached the patio doors that led out to the enclosed courtyard garden before the two men she'd met when entering the house were upon her. She tried to scream but a hand was slammed over her mouth so hard that her head was jerked back and she bit down on her tongue. Wincing at the sudden, sharp pain, Kit could taste blood and as she was dragged back from the patio doors, her arms flailed around her and her feet attempted to kick out at them.

Her attempts to escape were fruitless; the men were far too strong, and a stinging back-hander sent Kit careering across the room. Landing with a heavy thud in front of the glass coffee table, jarring her spine in the process, tears of frustration welled up in her eyes and, pressing the back of her hand against the side of her face, her cheek smarted and felt hot to her touch. 'What do you want from us?'

'What do we want?' Nathan asked. 'We want your old man, sweetheart, and Rosco here, well...' He crouched down beside her and waved his hand in Rosco's direction. 'He's sold you out, darling.' A hint of a smile played out across his lips. 'In fact, this,' he said, getting to his feet, 'was all his idea. You're the bait that's going to lure your old man to us.'

'My dad?' Prickles of fear ran down the length of Kit's veins and as much as she tried not to, she couldn't help but shudder. Alongside her father's name, it was only a matter of time until Austin was brought into the equation. 'You bastard,' she hissed at her husband. She looked up at the man standing over her. 'My dad had nothing to do with the stolen coke.'

Nathan gave a nasty chuckle; it was a low, throaty, callous laugh that only exacerbated Kit's terror. 'This isn't about the deal any more.' Grasping her by the elbow, he yanked her roughly to her feet. 'This is personal.' He looked her up and down with a sneer as though she was nothing more than a piece of meat laid out on a slab for him to feast his eyes upon. 'You could even say it all boils down to revenge,' he said with a menacing wink. 'In fact, that old chestnut, "an eye for an eye, a tooth for a tooth," springs to mind.'

'Get your hands off me.' Trying in vain to escape from his grasp, Kit screamed out the words.

To her dismay, his grip tightened and as she was dragged from her house and into a waiting car, terror gripped at her heart and her legs almost buckled underneath her.

* * *

As he lay back on the bed, Fletch placed his hands behind his head, watching as his Suzy walked from the room, dressed in just a short, pale pink silk kimono that only just brushed past her pert backside; it was a sight that he could never tire of. 'Don't be long,' he called after her.

Looking over her shoulder, Susan laughed. 'You're insatiable.'

Fletch grinned. 'You make me insatiable.' He winked.

From the tangled heap of clothes on the floor, his mobile phone began to ring. It took him a few moments to actually realise it was his phone; he rarely used the device and only a handful of people had the phone number.

Reaching out his arm, he scooped the phone up. A withheld number flashed up on the screen and with a slight shrug, he pressed answer then placed his free arm behind his head, making himself comfortable.

'Hello.'

'Hello, Harry.'

Sitting bolt upright, the hairs on the back of Fletch's neck stood up on end. Only his immediate family, Stevie and Susan knew him by his birth name. 'Who is this?'

At the end of the line came a menacing chuckle, a chuckle that sounded so familiar, yet it couldn't be – only one other person he knew had had the same low, throaty laugh and he had been dead for more than twenty-two years. He knew this to be a fact because it had been Fletch who'd killed him: his father.

Fletch clambered off the bed and peered through the window blinds down onto the high street below, his eyes scanning the horizon for anything out of the ordinary. 'I asked you a question – who is this?' he growled into the phone.

Again, another throaty laugh.

'Who the fuck is this?' His raised voice brought Susan rushing back into the bedroom and as she opened her mouth to speak, Fletch held up his finger, silencing her. 'Now, I don't know who the fuck you are' – he craned his neck to take a second look out of the window – 'but you'd best start fucking talking, and fast.'

'See, the thing is, Harry,' said the voice at the end of the line with a hint of amusement, 'you're not in a position to demand anything. I think you'll find that it's me who has the upper hand. In fact, I have something that belongs to you; something, or should I say someone, who I think you'll be keen to have returned in one piece.'

Fletch's blood ran cold and as the line went dead, he stared at the phone in his hand.

'Fletch?' There was a slight tremor to Susan's voice. 'What's wrong?'

Looking up, Fletch's face had drained of all colour. An image of his son flashed before his eyes and, pulling on his clothes, he rammed the phone into the pocket of his jeans.

'Fletch?'

'I've got to go, sweetheart, I'm sorry.' He paused to look at her, then, bounding forward, crushed her to his chest and kissed her forehead.

'Is something wrong? Has something happened?'

'No.' Fletch swallowed deeply for the lie he was about to tell.

'No problem.' He gave a smile in an attempt to make light of the conversation. 'It's nothing for you to worry about, darling.'

Susan's eyes narrowed and as she stepped back a pace, she looked up at him. 'You sound just like Billy,' she said, referring to her deceased husband. 'Those are the exact same words he would say when he was trying to hide something from me.'

Fletch's smile died and, momentarily closing his eyes, he shook his head. He was nothing like Billy; for a start, he genuinely loved Susan, and would never willingly do anything to harm her. 'I can't, Suze.' He sank onto the bed and began pulling on his socks.

'What can't you do?' The tremor in Susan's voice intensified.

Pushing his feet into his shoes, Fletch ignored the question.

'Tell me,' she demanded. Two pink spots appeared on her cheeks and her eyes were full of hurt. 'You can't spend the morning in bed with me and then just leave as if this' – she gestured towards the unmade bed, where just fifteen minutes earlier they had made love – 'meant nothing to you.'

'Is that what you think of me?' Fletch jumped to his feet and stalked forward. 'That this, what me and you have, means fuck all to me?'

Susan swallowed deeply and, biting down on her lip, she shook her head, too afraid to look at him, too afraid that there was some truth to her words.

'Hey.' He gently placed a finger underneath her chin, bringing her face up to look at him. 'You know how I feel about you; I shouldn't even have to say it. You know that you're the only woman I have ever loved.'

'Then why the hurry to leave?'

'My son,' Fletch sighed.

'Austin?' she asked.

'Yeah.' He took a deep breath, knowing full well that the

promise he'd made her just a week earlier had already been shattered. He'd fully intended to stay on the straight and narrow and would have done if Austin hadn't masterminded the drugs haul. Over the years, he'd stayed in more than his fair share of prisons and as much as he had no intentions of seeing the inside of a cell again, he wasn't prepared to leave his son high and dry and let him deal with the fallout of his stupidity alone. 'He's got himself into some trouble and—'

'And you need to deal with it?' Finishing off his sentence, Susan closed her eyes in despair and the nagging worry at the back of her mind began to intensify. All along she had feared that the life he'd once led would be too much for him to resist.

'Yeah, that's about the crux of it.' Fletch patted himself down, checking that he had his wallet, keys and mobile phone.

'And just like that' – she gave a bitter laugh – 'you're straight back into the life.'

Fletch looked up and narrowed his eyes. 'I didn't plan this. I've already told you I want no part in that world; I'm a changed man.'

'And the minute you walk out that door,' Susan protested, 'you are back in that world.'

'He's my son; I can't leave him to deal with this alone. He'll end up getting himself killed.'

Tilting her chin in the air, Susan crossed her arms over her chest. 'Then don't come back,' she warned him. 'I mean it; if you do this, then what we have is over. I can't go back to that way of life and I will not allow Harriet to get mixed up in the criminal underworld.'

'Are you being serious? You're actually giving me an ultimatum?'

For a moment, Susan paused, then, biting down on her lip, gave a curt nod of her head.

'You can't make me choose.' Screwing up his face, Fletch's voice began to rise. 'He's my son, for fuck's sake – how can I turn my back on him now? I've already let him down once; I can't leave him out to dry a second time. What kind of father would that make me?'

'I'm not asking you turn your back on your son,' Susan told him. 'I'm asking you not to do whatever this is that you're planning on doing.'

'I don't have a choice.' He patted himself down a second time and shook his head. 'I have to go.' He came to stand in front of her and lifted a lock of hair from her face. 'Come on, Suze,' he said, tilting her face up to meet his. 'Don't be like this; don't make me choose between you and my kids. I love you but I can't walk away from them again, you know I can't.'

As he walked from the flat and closed the front door gently behind him, Susan slumped onto the bed. Her heart was heavy and, looking down at the crumpled sheets, she fought down the urge to weep. She should never have asked him to choose between her and his son. Austin would come first each and every time, and rightly so.

## 31

Bringing his car to a screeching halt on Upminster high street, Stevie barely gave Fletch the time to jump in and slam the door closed behind him before swiftly pulling away from the kerb.

'You and Susan, eh?' Stevie glanced sideways. 'I have to admit I didn't see that one coming.' He gave a shake of his head, disbelief clearly audible in his voice. 'What's with all the secrecy? It's not like you have to creep around any more, is it? It's not like Billy's going to come back from the grave and haunt the two of you.'

Without answering, Fletch dug into the pocket of his jeans and pulled out his mobile phone. The truth was, he had no idea where to even start. How was he supposed to explain to Stevie, let alone Austin, Kitty and his mum, that he'd fathered a third child who until a week ago he'd known nothing about? It was because of Harriet that he and Susan were keeping their newly reacquainted relationship quiet. They wanted to wait until the time was right to break the news to their daughter, even though Susan had reassured him over and over again that Harriet would be thrilled to finally have him in her life.

'She hasn't remarried, has she?' Stevie looked up and studied the flower shop in the rear-view mirror. 'This ain't a case of history repeating itself, is it? Because I'm really not in the mood for disposing of another body.'

'Leave it out,' Fletch growled. 'You're making her sound like she's a slapper; she's not like that and you fucking know it.'

Stevie raised his eyebrows but decided to wisely keep his mouth firmly shut. When it came to Susan, Fletch could be a touchy sod; he'd always been the same. He cleared his throat and hastily changed the subject. 'So who was it that made this phone call? Did you recognise his voice – was it Rosco?'

Fletch paused, he wanted to say it was his father but even he wasn't foolish enough to believe that George was alive and kicking. Besides, the voice had sounded way too young; his father would have been well into his sixties had he lived. 'It wasn't Taylor; I would recognise that ponce's voice anywhere. I don't know who he was,' he admitted, 'but there has to be a connection, I can feel it in my gut.' He scrolled down his contact list, located his son's phone number and pressed dial. The call rang off. In quick succession, he pressed redial a further four times; each time the result was the same. Austin, it seemed, was unsurprisingly blanking his calls. 'For fuck's sake,' Fletch growled as he hit redial a fifth time. 'Answer your fucking phone.' Panic was beginning to set in and as he chewed on the inside of his cheek, beads of cold sweat broke out across Fletch's forehead. He began tapping out a text message, the pads of his fingers clumsily banging away at the smooth screen.

After a few moments had gone by, Stevie tapped his thumb impatiently against the steering wheel. It was actually painful to watch Fletch fumble with the phone and his fingers itched to snatch the device out of his mate's hand and finish the task. 'Do you want me to text him?' They'd stopped at traffic lights and he held out his hand; it would be a whole lot quicker, he knew that much.

Shooting Stevie a glare, Fletch shook his head. 'I can do it,' he barked out. 'I'm not completely useless.' After another minute or so of trying to type out the message, he gave up. 'Why the fuck is this so hard?' he complained. 'Phones weren't this difficult back in the day. They had actual buttons to press, not fucking this.' He dragged his finger across the glass screen to prove his point. 'And you reckon the kids of today are falling over themselves to buy this shit. What the fuck is wrong with them?'

Stevie shrugged. 'Technology has moved on since you've been banged up; you'll get used to it.' Putting the car into gear, he eased his foot off the brake. 'We're nearly there now, anyway.' Up ahead of them, as he turned the car onto the A13, was the Barking turnoff.

Slipping the phone back into his pocket, Fletch nodded. 'Do me a favour, mate, and put your foot down.'

* * *

With still no sign of Rosco, Dennis had been repeatedly trying to contact Kit to let her know that her husband was on the missing list. Since her text message the previous evening, she'd dropped off the grid and her mobile phone in turn had been switched off, which in itself was highly unusual. She also hadn't turned up at the club, and as he wandered from Rosco's empty office to Kit's, he bit down on his lip. Where the fuck was she?

From the club below, the sound system kicked in and, after a quick glance at his watch, he guessed that Marianne had taken to the stage. He could envisage her gyrating against the pole, her black dyed hair falling around her face as she teased the handful of punters who'd already taken up residence in the best seats with her saggy tits and wrinkled skin. This fact alone only served to heighten his concern. Kit should have shown her face by now; it was unheard of for her not to at least pop in and check up on the dancers, making sure that everything was as it should be.

He made his way down the stairs and, after giving the main floor a quick once over, he made for the exit. It had now been fourteen hours since he'd last heard from her; fourteen hours too many, in his opinion.

* * *

Taking the concrete steps two at a time, Fletch and Stevie raced up the communal staircase.

As they reached the upper hallway, Austin was waiting for them at the front door. His fists were clenched at his sides and a snarl was plastered across his face.

Seeing that his son was safe, Fletch's shoulders sagged with relief and he wiped the palm of his hand over his clammy face. On the short drive over to Austin's flat, his imagination had run away with him and with each passing second the scenarios he'd imagined were like something straight out of one of his worst nightmares, each of them ending with the same result: his son's brutal death. 'You're all right, thank fuck for that.'

'Of course I'm all right,' Austin spat. 'No thanks to you. I can't believe you've got the front to turn up here. I should have finished you off in that boozer; I should have caved your fucking head in for what you did to my missus.' He made to lunge forward, only to be blocked by Stevie. 'Come back to have another crack at her, have you?' he said through clenched teeth.

'Leave it out,' Stevie growled. 'Your dad never touched her and she fucking knows it.'

'Are you calling her a liar?' Spittle gathered at the corners of

Austin's snarled lips. 'Are you trying to say that she made all of this up?' He placed his hands on Stevie's chest and shoved him roughly across the landing. 'Are you trying to say that she's sick in the fucking head?'

'Don't fucking test me, boy.' Pulling back his fist, Stevie's body shook, so intense was the rage that coursed through his veins. For as long as he could remember, Austin had been a thorn in his side and as much as he loved his friend's son, there was another part of him, a much bigger part, that wanted to give him a good hiding. It was only his loyalty to Fletch that had stopped him from doing so over the years.

'Hey, enough.' Putting himself between his son and his friend, Fletch forced Stevie to look at him. 'There's no need for this, mate.'

'Nah,' Stevie snarled, looking past Fletch, his face almost purple with rage, 'I've had enough of this lairy little prick to last me a lifetime. For years I've put up with him and his big fucking trap.' He stabbed a stiff finger forward. 'All you've ever done is treat me like I'm a fucking joke,' he said, addressing Austin. 'Well, no fucking more, I'm done, and I can tell you this for nothing: I stood side by side with your dad in Billy King's firm, I've done things that would make your fucking toes curl, so do yourself a favour and show me some fucking respect. For once in your life, use this.' He thumped a forefinger against his temple. 'Get it into that thick skull of yours and actually start thinking for once. Your dad has done fuck all wrong. Sheree, the fucking bastard that she is, has spun you a load of old bollocks. I was here and I know exactly how it went down. She came on to him, not the other way around. Your old man wouldn't look twice at her. I wouldn't look twice at her; no decent man would. She's as bad as your mother, and you,' he roared, 'are too fucking stupid to see what's staring you back in the face.'

Austin's breath streamed out ahead of him. He swallowed deeply, allowing Stevie's words to sink in. 'Nah, Ree wouldn't do that.' As he spoke, his voice was low and his cheeks were flushed pink. Stevie having a pop at him had been a long time coming and he was the first to hold his hands up and admit that not only had he treated his father's friend like a mug, he'd also taken advantage of his good nature, not to mention his loyalty. More than once over the years Stevie had needed to help him out of the precarious situations he'd got himself into and he'd never even thanked him, not properly. All he'd ever given him was a half-hearted promise not to fuck up again. 'She wouldn't lie to me.'

'If it makes you feel any better, then you keep telling yourself that,' Stevie retorted. He rubbed at his temples, the anger leaving him as quickly as it had arrived. 'Right,' he said, blowing out his cheeks, 'now that I've got that off my chest, can we all just calm the fuck down?'

Begrudgingly, Austin nodded. He was no fool and knew when to keep his mouth firmly shut.

'Right then.' Stevie jerked his thumb behind him in Austin's direction. 'Seeing as this one over here is all right, then what the fuck was that phone call all about?'

'You tell me.' Fletch chewed on his lip, racking his brain as he tried to recall the conversation. Maybe he'd misheard or misunderstood what had been said, although he was pretty certain this wasn't the case. He knew exactly what he'd heard and there had been no mistaking the threat that had come down the phone line.

Footsteps ascending the concrete staircase made all three men turn their heads, their muscles rigid.

'Oh, here we fucking go,' Austin growled. 'I need you like I need a hole in the head.'

At the top of the stairs, Dennis paused. Gripping onto the banister rail, he eyed the men warily. 'Where's Kit?' he asked.

'How would I know? I'm not her keeper.' Austin rolled his eyes. 'Try the club.'

'She hasn't shown up, her phone has been switched off all day, and as for Rosco' – Dennis lifted his eyebrows – 'he's been on the missing list since last night.'

As he and Stevie shared a glance, the blood drained from Fletch's face and his heart began to pound so hard and so fast that for a brief moment he fully believed that he would black out and fall flat on his face. He'd been so focused on Austin that he hadn't given his daughter a second thought; there and then he wanted to berate himself. He brought his hands up to his head and rubbed at his temples as though he could wipe away the anguish that tore through him at a pace that actually took his breath away. 'He's got Kitty.'

'Who's got Kit?' Austin screwed up his face, looking from Dennis and then to his father. 'What the fuck is going on?'

'Your dad had a phone call.' Holding up his hand in a bid to silence Austin, Stevie hastily explained the situation. 'We don't know who it was, but he said he had someone who your dad would want returned in one piece. We wrongly assumed they meant you.'

Austin turned his attention back to Dennis. 'This is your doing,' he spat. Charging across the landing, he swung a punch forward. 'I knew this would happen,' he screamed as his heavy fist connected with Dennis's jaw. 'I told you that you were putting her in danger.'

'Pack it in,' Fletch roared, hauling his son away. 'You going in all guns blazing isn't going to help matters, is it?'

'It's him,' Austin continued to bellow. 'I warned him this would happen.' He shook his head. 'If anything happens to my sister, I'm gonna kill you, do you hear me? I'm gonna fucking kill you.'

Rubbing at the side of his face, Dennis opened his mouth wide and moved his jaw from side to side, checking that everything was still in working order. The punch had been hard, not that he'd expected any different. Austin wasn't exactly a pushover; he could hold his own and, despite the bravado he put on, even Rosco wasn't stupid enough to try and take his brother-in-law on single-handed, hence why he sent his firm out mob-handed to do his dirty work. 'This is nothing to do with me. This is about the drug deal that you,' he said through gritted teeth, 'fucked up; they want their merchandise and they're not going to stop until they get it.'

'Who's "they"?' Fletch narrowed his eyes, scrutinising Dennis.

'The Bannerman brothers,' Dennis sighed. 'Rosco was last seen leaving the club with them. They want their coke and they couldn't give a shit who gets in their way. It's all one big game to them, a blood sport; they're like fucking animals. I told Rosco not to deal with them, that they were out of his league, but he wouldn't listen to me. He was hell-bent on doing this deal; he reckoned it would be the making of him. To be fair, there's a lot of dough involved.'

Shock resonated throughout Fletch and as his breath caught in the back of his throat, every inch of him bristled. Of all the names he'd been expecting, Bannerman wasn't one of them. The only Bannerman brothers he knew were his father and his uncle Albie, and he knew for a fact that they were both dead. Long before he'd shot and killed his father, Spencer and their boss, Billy King, had brutally murdered Albie. For days they had tortured the man before Spencer had been instructed to dish out the final blows and kill him. Albie's corpse had then been transported to a breakers' yard, dumped into the boot of a rusting car and subsequently crushed.

Stevie visibly paled and, catching Fletch's eye, he shook his head. 'Bannerman brothers? It can't be, can it?'

Feeling sick to his stomach, Fletch's mind reeled. To his knowledge, his father had never remarried or gone on to have any more children. From somewhere in the back of his memory, he recalled being told his uncle had children, three of them, sons perhaps, or was it daughters? 'They've got to be Albie's kids,' he stated. 'They have to be.'

'I don't know about that, but what I do know is that they're proper nutters,' Dennis answered. 'Right hard bastards – "unhinged" springs to mind, if you know what I mean.' He tapped the side of his head to emphasise his words. 'They're not a firm I would willingly deal with and, believe me, I don't scare easily.'

'Sounds about right.' Fletch raised his eyes to the ceiling and sighed. His own father had been more than a little bit unhinged; he'd been the epitome of evil and that was putting it mildly.

'Dennis Maguire.' Moving forward, Dennis thrust out his hand. 'Kit's...' He paused, unsure of who exactly he was to her. 'Friend.'

'I know exactly who you are, son.' Fletch shook the proffered hand, noting that the grip was strong. 'I also hear that you're Taylor's right-hand man.'

Underneath Fletch's hard stare, Dennis squirmed and lowered his eyes. 'Yeah.' He shifted his weight from foot to foot. 'Supposedly.'

'Good. In that case, you can get us into his club with the minimum of fuss. I want the shithole torn apart; anything we find that helps brings my little girl home, the quicker the fucking better, as far as I'm concerned.'

## 32

Earlier that morning, Kit's captors had brought her and Rosco to what appeared to be a remote warehouse on the outskirts of South London. Barely uttering a single word to her, the men had then gone on to secure her wrists behind her back with cable ties before proceeding to bind her to the wooden chair she'd been forced to sit down on with a thick rope. The bonds were tight and the thick plastic dug into her flesh. No matter how much she tried, she was unable to free herself and as a result her wrists were fast on their way to becoming red raw; the skin underneath the tight plastic was already bruised and bleeding. Rosco, she noticed, hadn't been subjected to the same treatment. There and then she hated her husband that little bit more, if that was even possible. The whine in his voice as he spoke sickened Kit to her stomach. Austin had been right all along; the sooner her husband was dead, the better it would be for them all.

Running her tongue across her teeth, she tore her eyes away from her husband and focused on the men. There was something so familiar about them and in a way they reminded her of her brother: same height, similar build, same dark hair. Right there, she decided, was where the similarities ended. Austin would never harm a woman; he didn't have it in him.

'I need to go to the toilet,' she called out.

Snapping his head around, a sneer creased Nathan's face. 'You can wait.'

'I can't.' Kit smiled sweetly up at him and made a point of jiggling her body from side to side. 'I really need to go.'

Nathan gave an irritated sigh. 'Deal with this,' he ordered his youngest brother, 'and make it quick.'

'Me?' Connor's eyes widened and he tapped at his watch. 'I've got plans; I have to be somewhere.'

'Since when?' Nathan narrowed his eyes.

As Connor gave a nonchalant shrug, his smug smirk told Nathan everything he needed to know. 'I won't be long.' He grinned. 'Couple of hours, tops.'

'This here' – Nathan gestured around him – 'is a bit more important than you getting your fucking dick wet, don't you think?'

Connor's grin increased. 'Needs must and all that, bruv.' He winked.

'I'll do it,' said Lee. Slowly rising from his chair, he snatched up a Stanley knife from the workbench in order to cut the cable ties.

Kit's heart sank. Out of the three men it was this one who scared her the most; there was something detached about him, something that told her he could be cruel. His dark brown eyes that bordered on black had been emotionless when he'd stared at her and she briefly wondered if he would be the one they chose to finally kill her. She had a feeling it would be something he would not only enjoy but would take great pleasure from.

Nathan nodded and as his brother made to walk past, he

grabbed him by the elbow, bringing him to a halt beside him. 'Be nice,' he said in a low voice. 'She's worth nothing to us dead.'

Lee gave a low chuckle. 'And you reckon she's worth anything to us alive?' he stated. 'Her old man won't put in an appearance and you fucking know it.' He glanced in Kit's direction and twisted his lips into a menacing snarl.

'He'll show up.' Following his brother's gaze, Nathan shook his head. Unlike Lee, he could see Kit's worth and as Rosco had already pointed out, to the right man she was worth more than her weight in gold. 'So be fucking nice to her and that's an order.'

Lee gave a carefree nod; he didn't take orders easily but for now would play along to his elder brother's tune. 'Okay.' Holding up his hands, Lee gave a smile that instantly transformed his hard expression, making him look not only handsome but also harmless.

A few moments later, after Lee had dragged her into the toilet area, Kit shook herself free from his grasp and made to close the cubicle door, only for it to be blocked by his heavy boot jammed in the doorway.

'Are you going to stand there watching me?' she hissed at him.

A slow smile crept over Lee's face. 'That's the general plan.' He laughed. Leaning against the door frame, he jerked his head in the direction of the toilet. 'So do us both a favour and get a move on.'

'Fine.' Rolling her eyes, Kit slid her trousers and knickers down to her knees then sat down on the toilet seat, all the while her cheeks burning with shame.

She could feel his eyes watching her and lifted her head to meet his. 'Is this how you get your kicks?' she snarled at him. 'Watching women urinate?'

Lee's expression clouded over and for a brief moment Kit wondered if she'd just hit the proverbial nail on the head.

'You do, don't you?' She screwed up her face in disgust. 'You get off on this.'

Within seconds, Lee had bounded inside the cubicle and yanked Kit to her feet. 'That trap of yours is going to be your undoing,' he growled in her ear. 'One more word and I'll see to it that you're brown bread, do you understand me?' He shoved her roughly away from him with such force that Kit almost smashed head first into the mirrored wall. 'Because right now, sweetheart, the only person standing between you and me is my brother, and trust me when I say this: not only does he have a short fuse but he also has a short attention span to go along with it. He'll grow tired of you just like he does with everything else in his life, and when the time comes, I'll be there ready and waiting. In fact, I'm going to take my time with you and have some fun while I'm at it, just like your old man did when he killed my uncle.'

Fear grasped at Kit's heart and as he frogmarched her back through to the main warehouse, it took all of her strength not to break down and cry.

* * *

'I don't like this,' Stevie stated as he started the ignition.

'What, and you think I do?' Fletch answered. 'This is my daughter we're talking about.'

'No.' Stevie shook his head. 'I'm talking about these Bannerman brothers.' He took a deep breath and gave Fletch a sidelong glance. 'If they are Albie's sons, then...'

'What?' Fletch asked.

'Spencer,' Stevie sighed.

'Yeah, what about him?' Fletch screwed up his face.

Stevie cast a second glance in his friend's direction. 'Spencer killed their old man, didn't he?'

Rubbing the palm of his hand over his face, Fletch shook his head. 'They won't know about that. Other than you and me, no one else knows what Spencer and Billy did; even my old man wasn't a hundred per cent sure.'

'How certain are you of that? I mean, could Billy have talked, could Spencer have opened his trap? Let's face it, he barely knew right from wrong. What's to say he didn't brag about what he and Billy had done?'

'Spencer wouldn't have blabbed.' Fletch's voice was hard, the protectiveness he'd always felt for his brother rushing to the fore. 'He wasn't stupid; he knew when to keep his mouth shut.'

'I didn't say he was stupid.' Flicking the indicator, Stevie shook his head. 'I'm just saying maybe, and I do mean maybe, before you jump down my throat again,' he said, holding up his hand, 'maybe he told someone, and somehow this someone went back to these Bannerman brothers and told them what went down that night.'

For a few moments, Fletch was silent. 'Nah, this is nothing to do with Albie; this is about my old man and revenge. This ain't even about the coke deal any more, and that,' Fletch said, sitting up a little straighter, 'is the reason Taylor was so hell bent on dealing with them in the first place. He knows they have a connection to me. Our fathers were brothers and that makes us...'

'Cousins,' Stevie volunteered.

'Yeah.' Fletch swallowed deeply. 'That makes us cousins.'

Blowing out his cheeks, Stevie shook his head. 'This is some serious heavy shit.'

'Tell me about it.' Fletch turned to look out of the car window. 'Listen, change of plan: swing by Kit's house first, just to check she isn't there,' he said with a measure of hope in his voice.

Stevie raised his eyebrows and, flicking the indicator, he looked up at the rear-view mirror to where Austin and Dennis were following on behind them. 'You'd best get on the blower, then, mate, and let them two know that we're taking a detour.'

As he dug his hand into his pocket, Fletch groaned. First opportunity he had, he would be buying himself a decent phone, one with actual buttons.

* * *

It took Tiffany Blue all of ten minutes to drop her knickers. She knew money when she saw it and the man who was currently pumping away inside of her positively reeked of it.

Once he'd finished and was pulling up the zip of his jeans, she quickly cleaned herself up, threw the soiled tissue paper down the toilet and pulled the chain before sitting on the edge of the closed lid.

'I'm glad you came back,' she said, smiling up at him.

'Yeah, and why's that?' Glancing down at her, Connor flashed a grin.

Standing up, Tiffany squeezed past him, walked through to the changing room and leant back against the dressing table that held an array of cosmetics, cans of deodorant and several boxes of tampons. 'Because...' She swallowed down a large gulp of cola that had been laced with speed. 'You and me, we have a connection, don't we? I felt it last night when you were here.'

'Is that so?' Connor chuckled. Stalking forward, he placed his hands on either side of the table where Tiffany was standing. 'I can't say I feel the same way myself.' He smirked. 'But if it makes you feel any better, sweetheart, you keep on believing that.'

Tiffany's face fell; it wasn't often men turned her down. She was a stunner with the body of a goddess and was used to men falling at her feet. 'You bastard.' She raised her hand in the air to slap him across his face.

Connor chuckled even louder and as he caught her wrist, he lifted her arm above her head, his free hand snaking out to stroke the soft flesh between her thighs. 'We both know what this is all about.' He winked. 'So get your knickers off; I don't know about you, but I'm ready for round two.'

Tiffany didn't need to be told twice. Even the looming threat that Kit could walk into the changing room at any given moment and subsequently give her the boot wasn't enough to deter her. As far as she was concerned, despite Connor telling her that he didn't feel a connection between them, she was more than willing to prove him wrong.

## 33

Kit's house was silent, too silent for Fletch's liking, and after rattling the door handle up and down several times, he moved across to the bay window and peered through the wooden slatted blinds.

'I can see fuck all,' he complained.

'There's got to be a back door, right?' Looking up at the house, Stevie spoke. 'I mean, all houses have one, don't they?'

'Yeah, you're right, they do,' Fletch answered.

Together, all four men walked around to the rear of the property that was enclosed by a six-foot brick wall.

'Aus.' Fletch flicked his head in the direction of the wall. 'Get over there and have a butcher's, will you? If you can get into the house, let us in through the front door.'

Austin happily obliged. Within a matter of seconds, he'd launched himself up and over the wall. Just moments later, he was into the house and had let them in.

'One of the chairs has been overturned,' Austin stated as he led them back through to the lounge, 'and there's some blood, not a lot, just a few drops beside the fireplace.'

As they entered the lounge, they inspected the dark droplets. As Austin had already told them, there wasn't much but still it was enough to put the fear of God into Fletch.

'Check every room,' Fletch instructed his son and Dennis, and as they eagerly walked from the lounge he caught Stevie's eyes. 'Whatever they've done to her, she was bleeding.'

Stevie looked down at the blood. 'You don't know that for certain, mate; this could be Taylor's blood, or maybe she hit out and this belongs to one of the Bannermans. Let's face it, she's got a temper on her; she would have fought them like a wildcat, you know she would have.'

Rubbing at his temples, Fletch shook his head. 'This is all my fault. First Spencer and now my own daughter.' He looked up at Stevie and, opening his mouth to speak, he quickly snapped it closed again. Now wasn't the time to tell him about Harriet; once he had found Kit and he knew for sure that she was safe, he would tell them all that he had fathered a second daughter.

'So where to now, then – the club?'

'Yeah.' Taking one last look around the lounge, Fletch momentarily closed his eyes. He was going to kill Rosco and enjoy every last second of doing so.

Kit recalled Lee's words over and over in her mind. *'Just like your old man killed my uncle.'* To her knowledge, her father had only ever killed one man: her grandfather, George Bannerman. With a sudden clarity, Kit sat up a little straighter. No wonder the men had seemed so familiar. They were her father's cousins; they were family, albeit a family she'd had no knowledge of or had had any dealings with.

She turned her head to look at her husband and wondered if

Rosco had known about the connection. He must have done; for all his faults, and there were plenty of them, Rosco wasn't stupid. He had an obsession with her father, a relentless hatred that burnt inside him day and night.

'What are you hoping to achieve by doing this?' She addressed her husband, her voice low so that only he could hear.

When he turned his bloated face on her, Rosco's forehead was furrowed. 'What are you talking about?' he snapped, his eyes automatically looking nervously from the brothers and then back to his wife.

'This.' Kit nodded around her. 'What is this really about?'

Rosco made a hawking sound in the back of his throat then swallowed down a mouthful of phlegm. 'I'm the innocent one,' he told her, lifting his injured hand in the air. The tea towel had been discarded and the bright red stump where his pinkie finger should have been was swollen to twice its usual size, and, if she wasn't very much mistaken, also infected. The yellowing, green pus that oozed from the stump was a dead giveaway to that little fact. Give it a day or two and it would start to smell, if it didn't already, that was. 'I'm the victim in all of this.'

Kit snorted with derision. Victim? Rosco didn't know the meaning of the word. Her brother had been a victim; the cruel treatment he'd suffered growing up had scarred him for life. She herself was a victim, forced to marry a man old enough to be her father just to keep Austin safe from his clutches. Even her mother in a roundabout way was a victim. It had been Rosco who'd introduced her to drugs; it had been him who'd convinced her to sell the house in Rainham, so that he could buy the club, leaving her mother both homeless and penniless. 'This is about my dad, isn't it? You despise him that much that you decided to make his family suffer.' It was the first time she had ever outwardly confronted her husband and as a smug smirk spread across his face, she wanted to charge out of the chair and batter him. She would have done, too, if she wasn't being restrained. 'You're scared of him – my dad, I mean. That's why you need them.' She nodded across to the two brothers. 'You knew about their connection to my family and you've used it to your full advantage.'

The smile was gone from Rosco's face. 'That bastard,' he spat, 'he scarred me for life; he deserves to pay for what he did to me.' He tilted his head back slightly to look at her, his sly eyes narrowed into slits. 'Your dad' – he scowled – 'is nothing, do you hear me, nothing.'

As she raised her eyebrows, a tight laugh escaped from Kit's lips. 'We'll see about that. When my dad finds me, which he will, he's going to destroy you.'

It was Rosco's turn to laugh, a huge belly laugh that began in his stomach and forced its way up and out of his throat. 'Do you honestly believe they'll keep you alive long enough?' He wiped the tears of laughter from his eyes. 'They've got their own agendas to fulfil, an eye for an eye and all of that old bollocks. All you are to them is the bait; as soon as your old man puts in an appearance, it'll be curtains for you and with a bit of luck they'll take out that little scrote you like to call a brother while they're at it.'

Kit's stomach dropped. Lee's threat to kill her was still fresh in her mind and she gave an involuntary shudder. She squeezed her eyes shut tight. Her own death she could deal with, make sense of even, but Austin, her poor brother, who as a child had only ever had dreams of playing football for England, didn't deserve the same death sentence. Admittedly, he'd fucked up in the past and if she was being totally honest, more than once, but in his defence only because over the years Rosco had systematically damaged him.

With Rosco's laughter still ringing loudly in her ears, Kit

dug her fingernails into the palms of her hands. She still had one final ace up her sleeve, one that was going to wipe the smile from her husband's face, and with a bit of luck his life with it.

* * *

As he stepped out of his car, Fletch looked up at the strip club.

'You all right, mate?' Stevie followed his friend's gaze and looked upwards. The neon sign above the door had finally given up the good fight, the redundant bulb as dead as a dodo.

'Have to be, don't I?' Fletch answered with a sigh.

From behind them, the sound of car doors closing made them both turn their heads. Approaching them were Austin and Dennis, who had been joined by his father, Brandon.

'Fletch.' Brandon held out his hand. 'It's been a long time, mate.'

Fletch shook the proffered hand. The grip was strong and not for the first time did he notice that Brandon's hands were the size of shovels. 'Fuck me.' He let out a laugh that was tinged with a hint of disbelief, a laugh that until now he would never have believed he had inside of him. He'd known Brandon Maguire even longer than he'd known Stevie and, even though he didn't consider them to be close friends, they shared a mutual respect that had kept them in good stead over the years. Under the circumstances, he was somewhat relieved to have Brandon on side. He was a bare-knuckle champion and could more than handle himself if the need arose. 'This isn't your son, is it?' he asked, referring to Dennis.

Brandon Maguire puffed out his chest. Like his son, he was a good-looking man, tall with a muscled body that hinted to the fact he still liked to work out. 'That he is.'

'I should have guessed,' Fletch answered. 'The name Maguire is a dead giveaway.'

'I told him,' Brandon said, jerking his head in his son's direction, 'to steer clear of Taylor, but he wouldn't listen to me. You know what the kids of today are like; give 'em a bit of bunce in their back pocket and they think they're billy big bollocks when in reality they're barely off their mother's tits and know fuck all about the life.'

Dennis's cheeks flushed pink and, shoving his hands into the pockets of his jeans, he lowered his eyes. 'Leave it out, Dad.'

'Leave it fucking out?' Brandon chastised. 'You're lucky I don't knock some sense into that brain of yours.' To prove his point, he lifted his meaty fist in the air and waved it in front of his son's face, then turned back to look at Fletch. 'I hear that there is a problem with your daughter, that she's missing?' he said gently.

'Yeah.' Fletch tore his eyes away from his old friend to look up at the club. 'I want this shithole torn apart, brick by brick if need be.' He screwed up his face, pushing away the familiar sense of panic that threatened to envelop him. 'I want my daughter found.'

Storming through the club mob-handed, Fletch's face was set like thunder. All thanks to Dennis's association to Rosco, they had been granted entry with the minimum of fuss, a bonus as far as he was concerned. The last thing any of them needed or wanted for that matter was for the old bill to be called. From the sound system, 'Insomnia' blared out from the speakers, it was a tune he recognised from back in the day when he, Stevie and Spencer had gone out clubbing. The music did nothing to soften his mood; in fact, it did the complete opposite. His little girl was missing yet around him people were oblivious to the torment that ran through his veins.

He turned his face upwards. 'Start with the offices,' he growled. 'Look for anything that links in with the Bannermans.' He clenched his fists into tight balls. 'We need an address for those bastards.'

* * *

A knocking on the changing-room door caused Tiffany to curse under her breath. It was typical; just when things were beginning to get interesting between her and Connor, they were rudely interrupted.

'Who's that?' Leaning against the table with his trousers still around his ankles, Connor quirked an eyebrow.

'One of the other dancers,' Tiffany grumbled.

'You'd best let her in, then.' Connor's eyebrow rose a notch, a smirk plastered across his face.

'Are you going to get dressed first?' she huffed, glancing down at what was dangling between his legs.

Connor chuckled. When it came to women, he'd never had any inhibitions. Half-heartedly, he began pulling up his jeans and once he was dressed, Tiffany dragged away the chair that she had jammed underneath the handle and yanked open the door.

'Nice timing,' Tiffany said, giving the dancer in question the evil eye. 'Cheers for that.'

Looking from Tiffany to Connor, Amber Monroe's perfectly plucked eyebrows were arched. 'Well, well, well.' She laughed, causing her light brown curls to dance around her shoulders. 'What's being going on here, then?' Dumping her bag on the velvet chaise longue, she placed a hand on her hip. 'You're lucky it was me instead of Kit,' she said, giving Tiffany a knowing wink.

Tiffany's lips turned down at the corners. She understood perfectly the hidden meaning behind Amber's words. Wherever she went, Kit turned heads. She didn't even have to try; she was the type of woman who could wear a bin bag and still look stunning, something that secretly annoyed Tiffany, and although she would never say it out loud, she was jealous of her boss, jealous of her lifestyle, jealous of the attention she created.

Clearing his throat, Connor held up his hands. 'Looks like this is my cue to love and leave you,' he said, flashing both women a wide grin.

Tiffany pouted. If she wasn't careful, she could end up losing her meal ticket, and to Amber of all people. 'You don't have to go yet,' she purred. 'I'm not due on stage for another hour.' She reached out to caress his forearm. 'We've still got time to finish what we started.'

From the corridor outside the changing room came the sound of raised voices and, unless Connor was very much mistaken, they didn't sound overly welcoming. Pushing Tiffany aside, he poked his head outside the changing room door, groaning out loud as he did so. He was no pushover but even he could see when he was outnumbered. 'For fuck's sake,' he grumbled. Closing the door, he leant back against the wooden panels and chewed on his bottom lip. He should never have come back; time and time again, Nathan had warned him that chasing after pussy would be his downfall. 'Is there another way out of this place?' he asked.

Tiffany nodded. 'The back yard leads out onto the alleyway; the gate is never locked. Why, what's going on?' she asked, her voice rising several decibels.

'Nothing.' He held up his hand for her to keep her voice down, then inched open the door and listened. 'How do I get to the yard?' he asked.

'Turn left – the corridor will lead you straight there.'

'Right.' He opened the door, checking that the coast was clear, then slipped outside. 'See you around, sweetheart,' he told Tiffany before casually walking away.

Unfortunately for him, his presence had already been clocked.

* * *

By the time Connor reached the back yard, evening was beginning to draw in and the hour he had promised his brother he would be absent for had turned into three. Reaching the metal gate, he made to yank it open. To his dismay, it didn't budge. He tried a further three times, each with the same outcome.

'Bollocks,' he muttered under his breath.

'I'd say you were fucked.' There was a menacing tone to Fletch's voice.

Inwardly groaning, Connor turned around. He gave a half grin and shook his head, knowing full well that he'd been caught bang to rights. In a matter of seconds, he'd assessed the situation. One on one, he had a high chance of winning, maybe even two against one, but five on one and his hopes of emerging as the victor were significantly reduced.

'What do you want?' He jerked his head towards the men, his eyes searching around him for a weapon he could use – an empty beer bottle, perhaps; even the plastic crates that were haphazardly stacked on top of one another in the corner of the yard were beginning to look promising.

Fletch took a step forward. Despite not wanting to, he could see the family resemblance. The man before him was the image of his father, even more so than he was. The knowledge made him despise Connor that little bit more. 'I want to know where my daughter is.'

Connor screwed up his face and gave a nonchalant shrug. 'How would I know where she is?'

Fletch's lips curled into a snarl. 'We've got a comedian on our hands,' he spat, shortening the gap between them, 'only the situation isn't funny, is it? I'm going to ask you one more time before I do you some serious damage: where is my daughter?'

Taking several steps back, Connor's gaze darted around him. 'I've already told you, I don't know where she is.' In a split-second decision, he darted to his left in an attempt to reach out for one of the plastic crates. As he did so, Fletch swung out his arm and his fist connected with the side of Connor's face. The sound of bone cracking against bone was loud in the otherwise quiet courtyard.

Just one punch, that was all it took for Connor to plummet face-first to the floor. Landing in a crumpled heap on the concrete, he lay motionless.

As Fletch stood over Connor's prostrate form, Austin stared at his father open-mouthed.

'And you thought your old man had gone soft,' Stevie remarked, patting Austin on the back. 'Bet you're glad he didn't whack you one back, now, aren't you?' he said with a knowing wink.

Shaking out the tension in his fist, Fletch looked over his shoulder, his expression one of utter contempt. 'Get this piece of shit out of here,' he growled.

* * *

In a lock-up in Ilford that was owned by Brandon Maguire, Connor's arms had been tied behind his back, the skin surrounding his right eye had swollen to twice its usual size, and the tiny thread veins in his left eye were broken, making the white of his eye appear blood-red. His jawline was a mass of purple and black bruises and blood was encrusted around both nostrils. Still, Fletch pounded his fists into him; the violence he meted out was relentless and, as far as he was concerned, also warranted.

Twice already Stevie had needed to pull him away, warning him that dead Connor was nothing to them, but alive they could use him as a bargaining tool for Kit's safe return.

Each time Fletch tried to calm himself down, he'd glance in Connor's direction, feel the anger well up inside himself again and charge forward.

'Enough,' Stevie roared after pulling him away a third time. 'You're angry and I get it,' he said, forcing Fletch to look at him, 'but you need to start thinking clearly. Kill him and it's over; we don't even know where Kit is being held yet.'

Breathing heavily through his flared nostrils, Fletch nodded and rubbed his hands over his face, all the while staring at the man responsible for his daughter's disappearance. 'Hose him down,' he instructed his son.

As Austin turned on the hosepipe and sprayed icy cold water over Connor's unconscious form, Stevie threw his arms up in the air. 'Fletch,' he warned.

Fletch held up his hands. 'I'm not going to touch him,' he said with a level of calmness. 'I just want to know where my daughter is and the quicker he tells me, the better it'll be for him.'

Roused from his unconsciousness, Connor groaned. He couldn't see out of his right eye, he could taste blood and his chest painfully heaved with each and every ragged breath he took. It didn't take a genius to tell him he was fucked, nor that his chances of walking away from the situation were slim.

As he stood over his so-called cousin, it took all of Fletch's strength not to lash out, to kick his heavy boot into the man's gut or to smash his head against the concrete floor.

Crouching down, he grasped a handful of Connor's hair in his fist and jerked his head back so that he could look into his eyes. 'Where is my daughter?' he growled.

Connor closed his eyes, or at least his good eye; the other was already swollen shut.

'I asked you a fucking question.' Jerking Connor's head back even further, Fletch spat out the words.

Opening his good eye, Connor held Fletch's gaze. 'Fuck you,' he groaned.

Fletch snarled and, throwing Connor away from him, he jumped to his feet and lifted his heavy boot several inches off the floor.

'Fletch,' Stevie warned, ready and waiting to pull his mate off a fourth time if need be. 'Think rational,' he yelled at him.

'Think rational?' Fletch roared back, the heel of his boot poised just inches away from Connor's head. 'How the fuck am I supposed to think rationally? He knows where Kitty is.'

'I know,' Stevie agreed. He looked over his shoulder to Brandon for support. 'But killing him won't give you the answers you want. Listen, mate,' he said in a low voice, 'as it is, it's already getting late.' He tapped his watch, reminding Fletch of his curfew. 'Go home and get some sleep, let this pile of shit stew in his own juices overnight and then in the morning interrogate him again.'

'Go to sleep,' Fletch exclaimed. 'Are you fucking crazy? Do you honestly think I'd be able to sleep not knowing where my daughter is?'

'No, probably not,' Stevie agreed, 'but it's better than the alternative: you miss your curfew and you'll be recalled back to nick so fast that your feet won't even touch the floor.'

'Stevie's right,' Brandon piped up. 'You're no good to anyone banged up. Go home – I'll keep this piece of shit warm for you,' he said, jerking his head in Connor's direction. 'In fact, it'd be my fucking pleasure.'

Fletch sighed and, with one final look in Connor's direction, he reluctantly agreed. 'Okay.' He held up his hands. 'First thing tomorrow morning, we start all over again.'

'Good man.' Brandon nodded. 'You know it makes sense, and me and Dennis here will babysit him for you. We won't let him out of our sights.'

'Yeah, and you can count me in as well.' Austin crossed his arms over his chest. 'I'm staying here; the bastard won't be going anywhere.'

As Fletch and Stevie left the lock-up, Stevie turned his head. 'We're gonna find her, mate.'

Fletch nodded, not trusting himself to answer. As it was, a hard lump filled his throat and no matter how much he tried to swallow it down, it wouldn't budge and the tears that he'd held at bay for the majority of the day threatened to well up in his eyes. If anything happened to his daughter, he would never forgive himself; he knew that as well as he knew his own name.

## 34

Tapping his fingers in a steady beat against the wooden work-bench, Nathan was becoming increasingly agitated. Six hours his youngest brother had been on the missing list for, and as the minutes ticked by he fought down the urge to smash his fists into Connor's face, when and if the reckless bastard decided to finally show up. There and then he vowed to put the hard word on his brother, to rein him in, to show him once and for all who was the boss.

'Try him again,' he said, turning to look at Lee.

'He's not answering,' Lee answered, toying with the phone in his hand. He gave a carefree shrug. 'You know what the randy little fucker is like; he's probably balls deep in some dirty slag as we speak.'

Nathan rolled his eyes. Ever since he'd hit his teenage years, Connor had been the same; women were his weakness and on more than one occasion he'd warned his brother that they would be the death of him. 'Try him again,' he ordered.

Lee sighed and made a great show of pressing redial before bringing the device up to his ear, all the while staring at his brother with a cold expression. 'Like I said,' he remarked as the call rang off, 'he isn't picking up.'

'Where the fuck is he?'

Stretching out his legs, Lee lounged back in the chair. 'I've already told you, he's probably balls deep. Give him another hour or so,' he said with a bored tone, 'before sending out a search party.'

Nathan continued tapping his fingers against the workbench. From across the warehouse he caught Kit's eyes and for the briefest of moments he thought he saw the flicker of a smirk play out across her lips.

\* \* \*

The next morning, as he and Stevie entered the lock-up, Fletch's eyes were automatically drawn to the badly beaten man who lay on the floor in pretty much the same position he'd left him in the previous evening.

'Has he talked?'

Brandon shook his head. 'Hasn't said a fucking dicky bird.'

Shrugging off his jacket, Fletch walked across the concrete floor, his footsteps heavy. 'Oi.' Using his foot, he propelled Connor onto his back, then, crouching down, he grasped a handful of the man's hair in his fist and dragged his head up towards him. 'Where is my daughter?'

Slowly, Connor opened his good eye. Despite the pain he was in, he managed to screw up his face. 'Fuck you,' he groaned.

White hot fury coursed through Fletch's veins. He ran his tongue across his teeth, threw Connor away from him and stood up. 'Hose the bastard down,' he instructed his son.

Austin did as his father bade and, switching on the cold water tap, he pointed the hosepipe towards Connor's face.

Coughing and spluttering as the icy water burnt his eyes and nose, Connor gasped to catch his breath.

After thirty seconds had gone by, Fletch held up his hand, indicating for his son to cut out the water.

'Right.' Pulling up his shirtsleeves, Fletch advanced forward. 'I'm done playing games,' he stated. 'Now start fucking talking.'

For the first time since he'd arrived, Connor hesitated and as he opened his mouth to speak, Fletch held up his hand to quieten the men down.

'Quiet,' he shouted as he crouched down, 'he's gonna say something.' He turned his head back to Connor. 'Where is she?'

Connor opened his mouth a second time and as Fletch leant in closer, he whispered in his ear. 'Fuck you.'

The beating that followed was not only severe but brutal in every aspect. He had to hand it to Connor – as much as he despised the man, and he really did despise him, lesser men would have talked at the first hint of a beating of this magnitude.

Finally spent and out of breath, Fletch kicked out one last time, his heavy boot connecting with Connor's gut. He then began to pace the lock-up. Rubbing at his temples, he sucked in his bottom lip and chewed on it. He was running out of options, and more importantly running out of time.

A name sprang to his mind, the name of a man who until now he'd been reluctant to even consider as a viable option but, seeing as he was at the end of his tether, the time had come when he had no other choice but to seek him out. He stopped pacing and turned his head in Stevie's direction. 'I need you to take me somewhere, mate.'

'Where?' Looking from Fletch to Connor and then back to Fletch again, Stevie narrowed his eyes.

Fletch sighed, straightened out his shirt, then shrugged on his jacket. 'To see a pal of mine,' he said, not quite looking his friend in the eye. 'My old cellmate.'

Stevie's forehead furrowed. 'And has this cellmate of yours got a name?' he asked.

Catching the look Stevie shot him, Fletch blew out his cheeks. 'Ginger... Ginger Parmar.'

Stevie's eyes widened. 'Fuck me, Fletch, now you're talking about some serious muscle.'

'Yeah,' Fletch muttered under his breath, 'tell me something I don't already know.'

* * *

It had just gone midnight when Nathan had sent out a search party to look for his errant brother. Seven hours later, there was still no sign of him and as he paced the warehouse, Nathan was ready to do someone some serious damage.

'Get back out there,' he bellowed at the men in his employment, 'and this time, fucking find him.'

As the men turned to look at one another, Nathan bestowed his menacing glare on them. 'What are you waiting for?' he growled.

Averting their gaze the men shifted their weight from one foot to the other. When it came to Connor Bannerman, they knew from experience that he could be absolutely anywhere. As it was, they had trailed every pub and club south of the river with no positive sightings of him.

'You heard my brother.' Lee got to his feet, his chest muscles straining against the shirt he wore. 'Get out there and find him.'

'Where else are we supposed to look?' one of the men asked, his eyes blinking rapidly as though trying to ward off an incoming fist from smashing into his face. 'We've already searched his usual haunts and he hasn't put in an appearance.'

'The stupid bastard.' Screwing up his face, Nathan growled out the words. 'He's gone back to the club for that fucking slapper, that fucking whore who was on stage stripping.'

Lee snapped his head in Kit and Rosco's direction; within seconds, he'd bounded across the warehouse and grasped Rosco by the front of his shirt, yanked him bodily towards him and pulled back his heavy fist. 'Where is my brother?' he spat.

'How would I know?' Rosco slammed his eyes shut tight and cowered away. 'I've been here the whole time, haven't I?'

Throwing Rosco away from him, Lee ignored the man's piercing shriek of pain and turned his attention towards Kit. 'What do you know about this?' he said in a low growl. 'It's common knowledge you bitches all stick together.'

'Don't touch me,' Kit warned. She lifted her foot in the air, fully intending to kick out if he so much as laid a finger on her.

Lee slowly looked her up and down, an all-too-familiar smirk playing out across his lips. 'Don't flatter yourself, darling.'

'Why are you doing this?' Kit protested as she lifted her chin in the air to meet his gaze. 'We're cousins; whether we like it or not, we're family. My grandfather and your father were brothers.'

'First cousins once removed,' Lee corrected. Using the Stanley knife, he lifted a lock of auburn hair away from her forehead, then teased the blade gently down her nose and across her cheek. 'It would be such a pity to ruin this pretty face.' He leant in closer, his breath hot on her face. 'Not that I give two fucks; I'd slice you wide open and not bat a fucking eyelid,' he hissed in her ear.

Kit's heart beat wildly inside her chest and, leaning her body as far away from him as she possibly could, she brought her knee up hard and fast, catching Lee unexpectedly in the groin. 'I warned you not to fucking touch me,' she screamed at him.

As he let out a howl of pain, Lee was bent over double, his hand clutching at his tender testicles, which, if he wasn't very much mistaken, were lodged somewhere up in his stomach. When he finally managed to catch his breath and look up at her, his expression was murderous.

There and then, Kit's heart sank and as she shrank back against the chair, she steeled herself for his onslaught.

## 35

'You bitch.' Lee's eyes were almost black as he yanked Kit towards him with so much force that her backside was lifted several inches off the chair, almost snapping her restrained wrists in half in the process. The scream that she let out was deafening, which only served to fuel Lee's fury.

'Shut up.' With one hand clutching the front of Kit's cotton shirt, almost tearing it from her body, his other hand slammed over her nose and mouth. 'Shut the fuck up,' he hissed in her ear.

'What the fuck is wrong with you?' Hauling his brother away, Nathan spat out the words. 'Which part of this don't you get?' He gave Kit a quick once-over. Slumped in the chair, her head was flung back, her eyes slammed shut and her chest heaving as her lungs fought for air. 'She's worth nothing to us dead.'

Pulling himself out his brother's grasp, Lee adjusted the crotch of his jeans, the ache between his legs making him feel nauseous. 'She means fuck all to us dead or alive. She's that wanker Harry's offspring; I say we kill the bitch and dump her corpse on his fucking doorstep. It's what he deserves – payback for what he did to George.'

Nathan wearily shook his head. How many times did they need to have the same conversation before it sank in? Even Connor, for all his faults, had managed to grasp the importance of keeping her alive. 'We don't touch her; it's her old man we want, not her,' he spat. 'All she is to us is bait; she'll be the one to lure that no-good fucker here, so I'm warning you now, don't fuck this up.'

Kissing his teeth, Lee moved away. 'Then you'd better keep her out of my face,' he warned, 'otherwise I'll kill the bitch, and fuck the consequences.'

As he watched his brother limp across the warehouse, Nathan turned his attention back to Kit. Her breathing had returned to its normal rhythm and the colour had returned to her cheeks. He studied her for a few moments, noted the defiant look in her eyes and shook his head. She would never understand just how close she had come to a certain death.

As they drove through a set of electronic gates on the outskirts of Havering-atte-Bower, Greater London, Stevie whistled through his teeth.

'Fuck me,' he stated, 'this is some fucking gaff.' He shook his head in wonder. 'You've got to have some wedge to own a place like this; how much do you reckon it's worth? Five million, ten million?'

Fletch shrugged. If he was being honest, the house, or rather the mansion, was exactly what he'd expected. You didn't get to the top of your game and still scramble around in the dirt, and Ginger was most definitely at the top of his game. He was solely responsible for the majority of drugs being sold in and around the South East, and that was without the bank and post office robberies that he either bankrolled or took a cut from, all because they were on his so-called turf, and even by his own admission his turf was vast. To put a finer point on things, Ginger controlled the whole of Essex and East London and didn't look to be downsizing his empire any time soon.

At the front door they were met by four heavies, subsequently patted down, then led into a large sitting room. Two four-seater pale-blue damask sofas with matching armchairs took centre stage in the room. On the floor was a cream-coloured carpet that had cost more than what most decent hardworking men earned in a month.

A few moments later, the man in question entered the room. Ginger was not, as his name indicated, red-haired. No, in actual fact he had light brown skin, hard eyes that were as black as onyx and a shaved head that he liked to rub scented oil into, giving the bald pate a slight sheen. Where his name had derived from was anyone's guess and had often been a topic of speculation. His mother had once told him it had come from her love of ginger while pregnant, but seeing as his mother had never been exactly what he would call maternal he often wondered if she'd chosen the name as a cruel joke. He was in his early fifties and a larger-than-life character. Six foot four in height, he was also, as many unfortunate people had had the misfortune to find out, as dangerous as fuck. In fact, he not only exuded danger, but it actually seeped out of his pores; he may well have been holding a neon sign above his head warning people to give him a wide berth.

After shaking Fletch and Stevie's hands, Ginger indicated for them to take a seat, then, following suit, he lounged back in an armchair, crossed one leg over the other and steepled his long fingers in front of his chest, all the while giving them an amicable smile that showed off a row of perfect white teeth.

'What is it I can do for you, Fletch?' Ginger asked in a gravelly voice that indicated he was a heavy smoker.

Fletch shot a sidelong glance at a man who'd taken a seat on the far end of the sofa. Although they had never been formally introduced, he'd seen him enough times when he'd visited Ginger in prison.

Sensing Fletch's discomfort, Ginger momentarily paused before giving a half smile. 'You can speak freely in front of Ron,' he stated. 'Ron here will take your secrets to the grave, ain't that right,' he said, turning his head to look at the man in question.

Ronnie Knox was a large man with cropped hair and a broad chest that he'd squeezed into an expensive white linen shirt. He grunted out a reply that Fletch could only guess was meant as an agreement.

'So what is it I can do for you?'

Fletch took a deep breath. 'Our mutual friend,' he said with a rise of his eyebrows.

Ginger tilted his head to one side, his eyes narrowed. 'And which friend would this be?'

'The same one who turned Queen's evidence and was the cause of you being sent down for a lump,' he said, referring to Rosco Taylor.

A nerve at the side of Ginger's jaw twitched. After a moment or two, he leant back in the chair and lit a cigarette, never once taking his eyes away from his visitor. 'What about him?' he asked, exhaling a cloud of smoke up into the air.

Sitting forward in the chair, Fletch rested his forearms on his knees. 'I know you,' he told Ginger, 'and I know you will have been keeping tabs on him.'

Ginger chuckled. It was a menacing laugh that was enough to put the fear of God into those around him. 'You've got me all wrong.' He spread open his arms. 'I keep my nose clean these days; I mind my own.' He tapped the side of his nose to emphasise his point. 'Why would I need to keep tabs on anyone, least of all our mutual friend?'

'Because, like I said, I know you,' Fletch persevered, 'and I know for a fact that you've been biding your time.'

As he smoked his cigarette. Ginger continued to study Fletch. 'Why the sudden interest in Taylor?' he asked with a carefree shrug.

Fletch paused. He could feel Stevie's eyes boring into the back of his skull and, ignoring his friend, he tilted his chin in the air. 'I'm interested in his business dealings with a certain firm, three brothers who go by the name of Bannerman.'

Ginger's eyes ever so slightly widened. 'I've got no beef with the Bannerman brothers. In fact, I've concluded many a business deal with them myself,' he said, emphasising the word 'business'. 'They're good men, reliable, a bit like yourself.'

Fletch's heart sank and his mind wandered to Brandon Maguire's lock-up, where the youngest Bannerman brother was not only being currently restrained but had also been half beaten to death and was as a result lying in a puddle of his own blood, urine and vomit on the concrete floor.

'So.' Stubbing out his cigarette in a crystal ashtray, Ginger resumed his position and steepled his fingers once more in front of his chest. 'Let's get to the chase, shall we? Why are you really here? And no pussy-footing around the bush this time, because I'm really not in the mood to be playing guessing games. I leave that kind of thing to Ron over there,' he said with a wry grin.

Swallowing deeply, Fletch sighed. 'These Bannerman brothers, they've taken my daughter. They have Taylor too, not that he's important in the grand scheme of things. All I want is an address for them; I want my daughter back, unharmed.'

Ginger took a few moments to think this over. 'I don't

condone what has happened to your daughter. Terrorising women has never been my scene, but...' He allowed the word to linger in the air for a few beats before continuing, 'I can't be seen giving out the contact details of my associates to all and fucking sundry, you should already know that. It'd be bad for business and as you well know I have a reputation to uphold. Unlike our mutual friend, I didn't get to where I am today by becoming an informer.'

Fletch's heart sank even further. For a brief moment, he considered pleading with Ginger's better nature, that was if he even had one. Fletch couldn't recall ever seeing any evidence of him having a gentler side. Looking up, he narrowed his eyes. 'You don't seem surprised by Taylor's capture.'

A low chuckle escaped from Ginger's lips. 'Nothing gets past you, does it?' he said, pointing a finger forward. 'You always were astute and I like that in a man. That's why me and you got along so well; you're no fucking muppet, no pushover.' He rolled his lips together, his expression for all intents and purposes contrite. 'I have heard one or two whispers,' he admitted, holding up his hands. 'Like I've already said, the Bannerman brothers are good men; they've got a head for the business and believe me, they're good fucking earners. They keep me in the know and as you well know, nothing happens on my turf without me knowing about it first.'

'You fucking knew.' As Fletch jumped to his feet, the tiny hairs at the back of his neck stood up on end. If Ginger knew about Kit's disappearance then the likelihood of him finding her alive were growing slimmer by the minute.

Ronnie Knox slowly rose to his feet, ready to intervene when and if the need arose, not that Ginger needed his or anyone else's help, for that matter. He could more than handle himself and everyone in the room knew that to be a fact.

Ginger, for his part, didn't so much as flinch and as he looked up at Fletch, a lazy smile filtered across his face. 'Sit down,' he ordered. He held out his hand, indicating to the empty seat beside Stevie. 'And then we will talk.'

Fletch looked around him, sighed, then reluctantly sat back down.

'As you well know, our mutual friend owes me, owes me big time. I spent the best part of ten years banged up all because of him, the fucking grass that he is, and that's without the deal he made with the Bannermans, the same deal he failed to deliver on, the very same deal that was going to pocket me a great deal of cash. At the end of the day, a million nicker isn't to be laughed at.' He gave a wry grin. 'You could say it's a drop in the ocean, considering,' he said gesturing around him at his opulent home, 'but dollar is still fucking dollar in my book and like my mother always said, I'm a greedy bastard, and she should know, the fucking whore that she is.'

Fletch shook his head, his teeth gritted as he spoke. 'Now we're getting to the truth of the matter. There never was a deal, was there?'

'Oh, the deal was real enough.' Ginger paused to tap a cigarette out from its packet, lit up, then pointed the smouldering embers in Fletch's direction. 'Whether or not our mutual friend would ever see a penny from it is another matter entirely.'

'And what about my daughter?' Fletch spat. 'She's innocent; she's nothing more than a bystander.'

Ginger continued to smoke his cigarette. 'I'd like to help, I really would...'

'Then give me an address.' There was an urgency to Fletch's voice. 'Tell me where I can find them.'

Ginger's gaze lingered on Fletch, then, flicking his head in Ronnie's direction, he indicated for him to close the lounge door so that the men could speak in private. 'I knew your father,' he said, sitting forward. 'Did I ever tell you that?'

Swallowing deeply, Fletch shook his head. For just over a year, he'd shared a cell with Ginger. Not only had he eaten his meals with him and worked out beside him in the gym, but they had talked, really talked, and not just idle chit-chat to pass away the time of day; he'd talked about his children, how much he loved them, how much he missed them. He'd even told him about Susan, but not once in all that time had Ginger ever let on to the fact that he'd known George Bannerman.

'He was a hard fucker, ruthless, didn't give two shits about anyone other than himself and maybe his old mum and his brother, Albie, but I expect you already knew that?'

Fletch's back stiffened. George had been an evil man who'd taken pleasure from terrorising his wife and sons. For years, Fletch had wrongly blamed himself for the brain injury Spencer had suffered at his father's hands. All his life he'd been plagued with guilt, riddled with it; he'd hated himself for what he'd caused. It was him, not Spencer, who George's fists were intended for that fateful day. If only he'd have taken the beating instead of trying to escape, then Spencer would never have been caught in the crossfire.

'And like I said, I don't condone terrorising women or children.' Ginger's words were loaded with meaning. 'And believe me, I will be having words with the brothers.'

'Then help me,' Fletch pleaded. 'All I want is my little girl home safe.'

'What more can I tell you other than the Bannerman brothers are your father's kin.' He sat back slightly and lifted his chin in the air, waiting for the penny to drop.

As his heart sank, Fletch threw up his arms. 'Don't you think I already know...' The words caught in the back of his throat and he momentarily closed his eyes. How could he have been so stupid? The answers he desperately craved had been right underneath his nose the whole time. Shaking his head, he rubbed a hand across his forehead. Other than himself and his two children, Albie's sons were his father's only living relatives and the fact he had murdered his father meant that George's estate had bypassed him and his own children and instead had been inherited by the three brothers. 'My old man's house.'

'What about it?' Stevie asked, looking from Fletch to Ginger.

'My old man's house,' Fletch repeated. 'They fucking inherited it, didn't they? That's where they'll have taken Kit, they're bound to have.'

'Well, what are we waiting for?' Stevie jumped to his feet.

'Hold up.' Holding up his hand, Ginger gave a flick of his head back to the sofa.

Warily, Stevie sat back down.

'Our mutual friend.' Lounging back in the chair, Ginger resumed his position and steepled his fingers in front of his chest. 'He's mine,' he said, his expression becoming hard. 'I wasted ten years of my life all because of that ponce; did you really think I'd take that lying down? As you've already correctly pointed out, I've bided my time and, believe me, when I finally show my cards, the cunt isn't going to know what's hit him.'

Fletch opened his mouth to protest.

'You get in the way of that,' Ginger warned, 'and then me and you are going to have a problem.'

Closing his eyes, Fletch sighed. 'He abused my kids; I can't let him get away with that.'

'And I did a lump,' Ginger roared, his eyes blazing. 'That bastard is fucking mine.'

Fletch took a moment or two to think the situation through. Inside of him, a war was raging. One side told him to give in to

Ginger's demands; then there was the other, the more stubborn side of him that wanted to dish out his own form of retribution. For years, his children had suffered at Taylor's hands. Was he supposed to just let that slide?

'Well?'

Reluctantly Fletch held up his hands. 'Okay.' He nodded. 'But understand me on this: if you don't end him, then I fucking will.'

Ginger chuckled. 'You know me well enough to know there'll be nothing left of the sly bastard once I get my hands on him.'

Fletch nodded a second time. Inching his way across the lounge, he jerked his head for Stevie to join him and as they reached the door, he paused. 'Cheers for the heads up,' he said, reaching out to clasp the door handle.

Waving his hand in the air, Ginger tilted his head to one side. 'No need to thank me; you worked it out all by yourself,' he said with a knowing wink.

\* \* \*

Looking up at the house where he had spent his early childhood, Fletch sneered. If he'd had his way, the house would have been bulldozed with George still residing inside it. Why waste the time, money and effort on burying the bastard? They should have left him to rot underneath the rubble and timber.

'You're not thinking of knocking on the front door, are you?' Stevie asked, fixing his gaze on the house.

'Leave it out,' Fletch answered. Sucking in his bottom lip, he moved forward. 'We're going around the back. You said it yourself: all houses have a back door and I know for a fact this one does.'

The rear of the property had barely changed over the years. Towering conifer trees still lined the six-foot fence that surrounded the garden. Within seconds, Fletch had launched himself up and over the fence. It was only as he landed on the other side that he wondered if the Bannermans owned dogs. Ever since he'd been bitten by a stray dog as a child, he'd been afraid of them. Standing stock-still, he took a moment to listen for the familiar bark or growl to back up his fear. All the while, his eyes were frantically searching the mown lawn for any evidence of dogs roaming free.

'Give me a hand,' Stevie puffed. 'I'm stuck.'

Fletch turned his head.

With his legs straddling either side of the fence, Stevie's upper body lay across the top of the panel, his hands gripping on for dear life in case his weight brought the wooden fence crashing to the ground.

'For fuck's sake,' Fletch groaned. 'Fat lot of good you'd be if we had to get out of here pronto.' He stole a glance back at the lawn, satisfied that there were no dogs in the near vicinity.

'Enough with the fat-shaming,' Stevie groaned as his fingers held on that little bit tighter. 'I'm a fat fucker, I already know that. I love me grub too much to be anything different.'

Fletch rolled his eyes. If the situation surrounding his daughter's disappearance hadn't been so serious, he would have been on the floor roaring with laughter at Stevie's predicament.

'Come on, then.' Pushing his way back through several large bushes that had sprouted up in front of the fence, he gave Stevie's leg a hard tug.

'Leave it out,' Stevie yelped as the wood swayed underneath his weight. 'You're gonna make it collapse.'

'Are you being fucking serious?' Fletch growled. 'It's a six-foot drop, if even that – you could roll off.'

Looking down at the bushes below him, Stevie assessed the situation. 'Yeah, you're right.' He heaved his leg over the fence and awkwardly slipped to the ground, landing face first in the bush nearest to him.

'Are you ready now?' Fletch asked with a shake of his head as he watched Stevie scramble to his feet and then brush himself down.

'I never said I wasn't ready,' Stevie grumbled as he looked back at the fence, hoping more than anything that they wouldn't be leaving the same way they had entered.

## 36

As she lifted a glass to her lips, the sound of movement coming from the kitchen made June Bannerman's eyes spring open wide. Her heart began to beat faster and a sliver of cold fear ran down the length of her spine. She strained her ears to listen, her pulse thumping so loudly that she could barely hear anything else above it.

Ever so slowly, she inched her way forward on the chair, gently placed the glass on the coffee table and reached out for the empty wine bottle. If nothing else, it would make the perfect makeshift weapon, one that she was unafraid to use. She hadn't been married to Albie for all those years without learning a trick or two along the way.

There it was again: another movement, no, a footstep; it was definitely a footstep. Getting to her feet, she raised the bottle above her head. She wouldn't go down without putting up a fight first. After all, she was June Bannerman, not some wilting wallflower.

As the door to the lounge inched open, June held her breath, tightened her grip around the bottle neck, then charged forward.

* * *

'Woah.' Instinctively, Fletch held up his hands as June advanced towards him, her peroxide-blonde hair flying out in all directions, the bottle raised in her fist.

'Who are you,' she screamed, 'and what are you doing in my house?'

With his hands still held up in front of him, Fletch gave a cautious smile. 'Mrs Bannerman?' he enquired.

June narrowed her eyes. 'Who the fuck wants to know?' She bristled.

Thinking fast on his feet, Fletch took a moment to assess the situation. It was evident that neither Kit nor the Bannerman brothers were at the house but what he did have in the form of the brothers' mother was a bargaining tool. Fletch's expression became sorrowful. 'I'm here about your son, Mrs Bannerman.'

June's eyes narrowed even further. 'Which one?'

Fletch hesitated for a moment. 'The youngest one,' he told her.

'Connor,' she gasped, lowering the bottle to her side. 'What's happened to him?'

'That's right, Connor, he's...' He looked back at Stevie and raised his eyebrows, at a loss for something to say.

'He's been in an accident.' Stevie jumped in. 'Nothing too serious but we've come to take you to him.' Noting the look Fletch shot him, Stevie gave a slight shrug. Under the circumstances, what else was he meant to say?

'And what, you couldn't have knocked on the front door?' June's eyes were narrowed again as she stared at the two men. 'You had to break into my house to give me the news?'

Stealing a glance at the wine bottle held in her fist, Fletch raised his eyebrows. 'We did knock, Mrs Bannerman, several times in fact, but there was no answer.' He gave a discreet nod to the wine bottle held in her fist. 'Maybe you didn't hear us?'

A pink tinge crept up June's neck. 'I'm not usually one to drink during the day,' she told them, 'and don't you go informing my sons about this either.' She placed a hand on her hip and raised her eyes to the ceiling. 'I'll never hear the effing end of it if they find out. As it is, they think I'm in my dotage.'

Fletch afforded her a bright smile. 'Your secret is safe with me.' He winked. 'Shall we?' he said, putting out his hand towards the hallway.

June couldn't help but smile back, feeling at total ease. Whoever the stranger was, he was a charmer all right. In a way, he reminded her of her Albie; he'd been a charmer too. In fact, he'd been able to charm the birds from the trees, much to her dismay.

\* \* \*

Connor's breathing had become laboured and as he stared down at him, Brandon shook his head. 'This doesn't look good,' he stated. 'If we're not careful, the fucker's gonna croak on us.'

'Let him,' Austin sneered. He raised his foot in the air, contemplating giving the youngest Bannerman a swift kick to his head. With a bit of luck, if he put some force behind the attack, it would put the bastard out of his misery.

'Don't even think about it,' Dennis yelled from across the lock-up. 'Leave him.'

'What are you worried about him for?' Austin growled, turning his head. 'It's because of him Kit's on the missing list.'

'Exactly.' Dennis stalked forward, his fists clenched at his sides. 'He,' he said with a nod of his head at Connor, 'is the only one who knows where she is. Kill him and we may never find her.'

Returning his foot to the floor, Austin took a few moments to mull over Dennis's words. Dennis, for his part, wasn't looking too clever, in his opinion, his face pinched and his skin drained of colour. Every few minutes or so he rubbed at his forehead as though the knowledge that they may not find Kit in time was more than he could bear. 'We're gonna find her,' Austin said, more for his own benefit than anyone else's.

Brandon stole a concerned glance towards his son. His voice, when he spoke, was gentle. 'Of course we are,' he answered, patting Dennis sympathetically on the back. 'Your dad's gonna make sure of it.' Discreetly, he looked down at his watch. As it was, Fletch had been gone for almost three hours. If they weren't careful, by the time he arrived back it would be too late. 'Help me to sit him upright,' he told Austin. 'The more air we can get into him, the better.'

* * *

June's eyes were wide. From the back seat of the car, she noted that they had just driven past the turnoff for the hospital. 'Here, what's your game?' she called out to them. 'The hospital is back there.'

From the front seat, Fletch and Stevie shared a glance.

'We're not heading to the hospital,' Fletch answered. 'Connor's at a friend's house.'

'What do mean, he's at a friend's house? Which bloody friend?'

'Just a friend,' Fletch called back. his voice calm.

'Well, we'll see what my Nathan has to say about this.'

Blowing out her cheeks, June opened her handbag and took out her mobile phone. Squinting down at the device, she began to tap away at the buttons.

'No phones.' Scrambling over the front seat, Fletch knocked the device out of June's hand and as it landed in the passenger footwell, he reached down and snatched it up.

June's eyes widened even further. 'Who are you?' she cried, fear and shock clearly evident in her voice. 'You don't work for my boys; they would never allow me to be disrespected like this.'

Resuming his position on the front seat, Fletch didn't answer.

'Let me out.' On entering the car, the central locking system had been activated and, to her horror, as she yanked down on the handle, the door didn't so much as budge. 'Let me bloody out,' she screamed at them.

Fletch turned his head. The smile he'd afforded her was long gone and in its place was a snarl. 'We're taking you to your son,' he said matter-of-factly, 'so do us all a favour and shut the fuck up. You're beginning to give me a headache.' To prove his point, he rubbed at his temples.

A sob lodged in the back of June's voice and she racked her drink-addled brain as to who the two strangers could be. 'Are you the police?' she asked, her voice tinged with hope.

From the front seat, Fletch gave a menacing chuckle. 'Do we look like old fucking bill to you?'

June's heart sank even further. If they weren't the police, then who the hell were they and more to the point, what did they want from her? Biting down on her lip, she stared out of the window, her mind going into overdrive. 'You're George's boy,' she finally said, sitting upright. 'The minute I saw you, I knew you looked familiar. You've got the Bannerman look about you; you must be Harry.'

Fletch didn't need to answer. The way his shoulders tensed was enough to alert June to the fact she was right.

'Why are you doing this?' she pleaded with him. 'You must remember me from when you were a little boy; you used to call me Auntie Junie,' she said gently.

'Shut up,' Fletch hissed.

'I used to buy you and Spencer sweets when I visited, do you remember? Sherbet lemons were always your favourite.' She smiled.

'I told you to shut up.' Launching himself over the front seat, Fletch's face was poised just inches away from hers. 'I don't know you,' he spat. 'I've never seen you before.'

'Yes, you have,' June persevered, her voice calm. 'It was me who cleaned Spencer up after your father attacked him; it was me who cleaned up his blood. I helped you all to escape that night. I drove you to the telephone box, and I waited with you until your uncle Frank showed up, and you' – she gave him a gentle smile as she pulled the memory from somewhere in the back of her mind, where she had kept it hidden away – 'you cried as we said our goodbyes. You were nothing more than a terrified little boy who held onto my legs, begging me to come with you. You told me that you loved me.' She shook her head. 'It broke my heart to have to say goodbye. I loved you like my own son.'

Fletch screwed up his face. 'You're lying,' he spat.

June shook her head. 'I've no reason to lie to you, Harry,' she said, 'ever since that night, I've kept my mouth firmly shut. I've never told anyone about the part I played in your escape. I kept it a secret. I didn't even tell my Albie; how could I have? In here' – she tapped a finger against her temple – 'I knew what George was capable of, and if he'd ever found out that I was involved, that I knew where you were living, he would have hunted you down and made it his mission to destroy you, all of you, myself included.'

The memory of his childhood came flooding back to Fletch. Still to this day he could recall the smell of the blood that had seeped out from his brother's head after their father had punched him so hard that he'd rebounded off the corner of the kitchen cupboard. He could still hear his mother's screams, could hear his own screams; he could even hear his father frantically trying to wake Spencer up, his voice becoming more and more desperate as the seconds ticked by, and then there was the blonde woman, the one who had finally taken charge of the situation. His next memory was the car journey. His mother's face had been ashen, Spencer had been quiet, too quiet, and then he could recall himself crying, begging the woman, the one who he'd lovingly called Auntie, not to leave them.

'He killed my brother.' Hurt was clearly audible in Fletch's voice and, swallowing down the hard lump in his throat, he returned to his seat and stared out of the windscreen.

Catching Stevie's eyes in the rear-view mirror, June nodded. 'I guessed as much.' She was quiet for a few moments. 'Is my Connor okay?' she asked. 'As big as he is, he's still my boy, my baby.'

Fletch closed his eyes and, rubbing the palm of his hand over his face, he chose to ignore the question. Instead, he turned his head to look at Stevie. 'Do me a favour and put your foot down, mate.'

\* \* \*

As the door to the lock-up sprang open, all three men inside turned towards it.

'About fucking time,' Brandon yelled out. 'Any longer and this fucker would have been brown...' On seeing the tiny woman sandwiched between Fletch and Stevie, the words died in Brandon's throat and he snapped his mouth closed. He watched her face pale and her eyes widen, then cleared his throat, rightly guessing that this was the Bannermans' mother. 'It's not as bad as it looks,' he said in an attempt to allay her fears.

'Not as bad as it looks?' June shrieked, her voice bordering on hysterical. Crouching down beside her son, she turned her head to look at Fletch. 'What have you done to him?' Tears filled her eyes as she clasped Connor's limp hand in hers. 'What have you done to my baby?'

Shifting his weight from one foot to the other, Fletch rubbed at the back of neck. 'He knows where my daughter is. He and your other sons took her in revenge for what happened to George.'

June's mouth fell open and she shook her head. 'No,' she gasped, 'no, they would never do such a thing.' Her cheeks were wet as she looked back at her son. 'He needs help; he needs to go to hospital,' she pleaded with them.

All eyes turned towards Fletch. They couldn't help but notice the change in him. For now, the anger was long gone, leaving in its place a great sense of sorrow.

Conflicted, Fletch shook his head. 'I need to know where my daughter is,' he told June, 'and we're not leaving here until he starts talking.'

As she cradled her son's head to her chest, June sobbed. 'How is he meant to tell you anything?' she cried. 'He can barely lift his head, let alone speak.'

'Shall I hose him down again?' Indicating to the length of rubber tubing that had been carelessly discarded, Austin made to move forward.

Shooting his son a glare, Fletch shook his head, all the while averting his eyes away from the look of horror that creased June's face.

'And you reckon you've got nothing of your father in you?' June hissed as she pulled her son closer. 'This here' – she gestured around her – 'has got his bastard name written all over it.' She got to her feet and, with her head held high and her shoulders flung back, she walked across the lock-up and came to stand just inches away from the man she'd once regarded as her nephew. 'I'm taking my son to hospital,' she said, placing her hands on her hips, 'and if you don't like it, then you can fucking well lump it, because let me tell you now, you don't scare me. I stood up to your father and if I can stand up to him, then believe me, I can stand up to anyone.'

From behind them came a groan.

'I'm here.' Rushing towards her son, June crouched down beside him. 'It's okay,' she soothed, 'Mum's here.'

With a lot of effort, Connor slowly lifted his head.

As the youngest of the Bannerman brothers opened his mouth to speak, Fletch moved forward.

The lock-up was so quiet that a pin could be heard dropping and as Fletch spun around, the men physically jumped.

'Well,' Stevie urged him, 'what did he say?

'We've got an address.' A laugh escaped from Fletch's lips. 'We've got a fucking address,' he repeated.

The relief was immense and, punching his fist in the air, Austin grinned from ear to ear.

'And what do we do about them?' Brandon asked as he jerked his head in Connor and June's direction.

Fletch looked back at the woman who'd been responsible for saving his family. 'We take them with us. Once Kit has been returned, they can get him the medical help he needs.'

From the floor beside her son, June gave a curt nod of her head. Words were not needed and instinctively she knew this was Fletch's way of trying to make amends for the beating her son had suffered at his hands – not that she would ever fully forgive him, but she had a sneaking suspicion he didn't expect her to.

## 37

Rosco wrinkled his nose at the foul stench that appeared to be permeating from him. Lifting his armpits, he had a quick sniff. He didn't exactly smell fresh but his body odour wasn't the source of the problem, either. Lifting his hand in the air, he inspected his pinkie finger, or rather the lack of a pinkie finger in his case. Swollen to at least twice its usual size, the skin felt tight and hot to his touch. More alarming, though, was the yellowy green pus that oozed out from the tip where it had been severed. Five times in as many minutes he'd needed to wipe the finger down his shirt to clean the pus away. As quickly as it was gone, beads of yellow moisture oozed and began to trickle down the length of the stump. Tentatively, he brought his hand up to his nose and recoiled instantly as the stench hit his nostrils. The smell was bad enough to make him want to gag. He narrowed his eyes; he was no quack but even he could tell when something was wrong, very wrong, in fact. Fear clutched at Rosco's heart. What if the infection spread? What if he went on to lose his hand, or, God forbid, his arm?

From across the warehouse, he watched the two brothers. He

and Kit had been at their mercy for just over twenty-four hours with still no sign of his adversary putting in an appearance. If truth were told, he was becoming bored waiting around for something to happen. Fletch should have shown his face by now, and even more importantly than that he should have been dead, his corpse dumped in a shallow grave, or fed to pigs. He actually knew of a pig farmer should the brothers need his input on how to dispose of the body.

Stretching out his legs, he stole a glance in Kit's direction. Ever since Lee's attack on her, she'd grown quiet. It was a good thing in his mind. She'd always been vocal; she was like her brother in that respect. He was another one who had a bit too much to say for himself. 'Cocky' was one way of characterising him, although, in Rosco's opinion, 'lairy little bastard' was a much more apt way of describing Austin Fletcher.

A grin settled across Rosco's face. He couldn't wait for the show to start. It was going to be legendary, and with a bit of luck he'd be able to dine out for free on his version of events for weeks to come, maybe even months, or perhaps, if luck was on his side, years.

He turned back to look at Kit. The hard look she gave him was enough to make his wistful expression slip away. She may have learnt to keep her mouth shut but the look in her eyes said a thousand words, all of them pointing to the fact that she despised him.

'What?' he asked.

Shaking her head, she screwed up her face and promptly turned away from him. *Fuck her*, Rosco decided. All she'd ever been to him was a means to an end. It wasn't as though he actually loved her. No, he wasn't fool enough to fall into that old trap. In fact, there was only one person on this earth who he loved and that was himself.

\* \* \*

From the outside, the remote warehouse in South East London looked nothing out of the ordinary. It was a fairly old building, Victorian, and a lot smaller than Fletch had imagined it would be, maybe only a few hundred or so feet larger than Brandon Maguire's lock-up, and if it wasn't for the fleet of cars parked on the unkempt forecourt, he would have assumed the warehouse was derelict and ready for demolition.

'What do you reckon?' Stevie asked with a nod towards the cars. 'There could be a lot of manpower inside.'

As he sat forward in the passenger seat, Fletch chewed on the inside of his cheek. Stevie was right; there were six cars parked, and assuming each car had been filled with hired muscle, they were talking about at least twenty-five men inside, not including the two remaining Bannerman brothers.

'I say we steam in.' From the back seat, Austin peered out of the car window. 'Take the fuckers by surprise.'

Fletch shook his head. Without knowing how many men they were dealing with, steaming in was the equivalent of suicide. He looked in the rear-view mirror, studying Brandon's car where Connor and June were being held. 'We do this the easy way and we keep calm.'

'Keep calm,' Austin repeated, screwing up his face. 'They've got Kit in there; she could be hurt.'

'And that,' Fletch said, turning to look at his son, 'is exactly why we do this as calmly as possible. Going in all guns blazing will only serve to put Kit and ourselves at risk.'

Blowing out his cheeks, Austin slumped back in the seat. After a few minutes had ticked by, he shifted his weight. 'Are we gonna sit here all day, then?'

'No,' Fletch answered through gritted teeth. Rubbing at his

temples, he swallowed down his irritation, Austin may have been his son, and God knows how much he loved him, but at times he got on his tits. The boy had a lot to learn, as far as he was concerned, and once again Stevie was right: up against a real firm, Austin wouldn't have lasted more than five minutes. 'Wait here,' he told them as he opened the car door and stepped outside.

'What have we got?' Brandon asked as Fletch approached.

Leaning his forearms on the car roof, Fletch looked back at the warehouse. 'We don't know how many are inside. Worst-case scenario, we're looking at more than twenty men, easily.'

'Yeah.' As he followed Fletch's gaze, Brandon did his own calculations. 'So what's the plan? I'm assuming you have one?'

Fletch nodded and, catching June's eyes from the back seat, he said, 'We do this the easy way. We keep calm and propose an exchange; the least casualties there are, the better.'

'Yeah, makes sense,' Brandon said in agreement. 'Just give us the nod when you're ready to make your move.'

With a tap of his hand on the car roof, Fletch walked back to Stevie's car, all the while keeping tabs on the warehouse for any movement or signs that their presence had been clocked.

'Remember,' Fletch said, addressing his son, 'we do this my way.'

Austin rolled his eyes and as he climbed out of the car, he groaned under his breath. They should have been using brute force, not going in all softly, softly. Fat lot of good that approach was going to do them; they'd be dead within the first five minutes.

'I mean it, Aus,' Fletch reiterated, stabbing a finger in his son's direction. 'My way.'

'All right,' Austin growled. 'Fuck me, I get the picture; you don't need to keep on reminding me.'

At the entrance to the warehouse, Fletch paused, hoping more than anything that he was doing the right thing, and more importantly that he wasn't about to make the biggest cock-up of his life. And let's face it, he'd made plenty of those over the years.

'Remember: calm.' Fletch held up his hands, his voice low. He waited for them to agree, then turned back to the iron door and pushed it open.

\* \* \*

Lee had been toying with his mobile phone when the door to the warehouse swung open. Within seconds, he was up on his feet, his eyes flashing with anger. 'Looks like we've finally found Connor,' he spat.

From across the warehouse, Nathan turned his head, fully expecting to see his brother's cocky grin aimed back at him. He'd been about to shower him in a tirade of abuse when he rocked back on his heels. His brother's face that was so like his own was almost unrecognisable, bruised and swollen to twice its usual size. Sweat drenched his hair. He'd taken a beating, that much was evident, and if it wasn't for the fact he was being held up, Nathan rightly guessed that his little brother would have fallen flat on his face, but it was seeing his old mum sandwiched between the group of men that really made Nathan's blood boil. With a quick glance in Lee's direction, he advanced forward, as did the men in his employment.

\* \* \*

Fletch held up his hands. 'Tell the ankle-biters to back off,' he said, referring to the hired muscle, 'and then me and you can talk.' He shot a glance in his daughter's direction, the anger in the pit of his stomach intensifying. From what he could see of her, other than a bruised cheekbone she looked unharmed, but that wasn't to say she hadn't been touched, hadn't been forced upon. The mere thought was enough to bring bile rushing to his throat.

'Talk?' Nathan barked. 'There ain't nothing to talk about – you killed my uncle.'

'That's right, I did.' Fletch nodded his head in agreement. 'And he murdered my brother, his own son. I did what any man would have done in the circumstances: I took the bastard out.'

Nathan narrowed his eyes. For the briefest of moments, the hint of shock resonated across his face. As quick as a flash, the expression was gone, leaving in its place a snarl.

'Listen to him, son,' June pleaded. 'George was an evil man; he doesn't deserve any of this and he doesn't deserve your loyalty to him.'

'You've got brothers.' Fletch jerked his head behind him to where Connor was currently being held up by Brandon and Dennis. 'Don't tell me you wouldn't have done the same for one of them.'

'You know fuck all about what I would or wouldn't do,' Nathan spat.

'You're right, I don't,' From across the warehouse, Fletch picked out Rosco. The smug smirk he gave was more than enough to make Fletch want to kill the man stone dead, but he wouldn't; he'd leave that honour to Ginger. After all, he'd given his old cellmate his word. 'But I know what it's like to have a brother, to care about them, to want to protect them.'

\* \* \*

From where he was sitting, Rosco watched the scenes unfolding before him with more than a healthy level of interest. This was what he'd been waiting for, this very moment when Fletch would finally get his comeuppance. Years he'd waited for the jumped-up prick to get what was coming to him, fucking years, and as he sat back and watched the scene play out, he could honestly say that the wait had been worthwhile.

\* \* \*

'Are you actually gonna listen to this bollocks?' Lee snarled at his elder brother. 'Kill the bastard, finish him off.'

'No, son.' Narrowing her eyes, June stepped forwards. 'There'll be no killing done here today. All Harry wants is to talk. He wants his daughter back unharmed, and Connor needs medical help.'

'Fuck Connor,' Lee roared. 'This ain't about him; it's about that murdering cunt.' He turned his head to look at his brother. 'What are you waiting for? Do him.'

Rolling his lips together, Nathan shook his head. 'You don't know what you're talking about, Mum. He killed George,' he said with a flick of his head in Fletch's direction. 'He's got to pay for what he did; it's what Dad would have done if he was here.'

June sighed. 'As much as I loved him, your dad was a silly old fool. He was blinded by his brother; George could do no wrong in his eyes, but I witnessed first-hand the damage your uncle inflicted. I saw him treat his own children, two little boys, no better than he would have treated an animal. It was me who helped Harry, his mother and brother escape. I put my own neck on the line because I knew that if they'd have stayed, George would have killed them and I couldn't stand by and let that happen. They were innocent, just like that young woman is back there,' she said, giving a nod of her head in Kit's direction. 'So let her go, son. Let's walk out of here and get Connor the help he needs before we end up losing him too.'

'This is un-fucking-believable.' Shaking his head, Lee gave a bitter laugh. 'You're not actually falling for all of this old fanny, are you?' he goaded. 'If you're not careful, she'll have you fucking crying in sympathy for him next. It's all bollocks, all lies; if Dad was here, that fucker would have been dead by now and you know it.'

'Dad ain't here, though, is he?' Nathan growled. He took a moment to look over at his youngest brother. Connor wasn't looking too good; to be more precise, he looked as though he was at death's door.

'Nah, but we are,' Lee said, 'and if you won't finish him, then I will.'

'Don't you dare,' June hissed. 'Look at you, you're like bloody animals. I'm ashamed of the pair of you, but as for you' – she pointed a finger towards her middle son – 'you've got too much of your uncle inside of you, that's your trouble. For years I've watched you, hoping, praying even, that you'd grow out of it, that it was nothing more than a phase, but I can see now that it wasn't. This is who you are: a bloody monster.'

Taken aback, Lee screwed up his face. 'Don't say that, Mum.'

'Don't say what?' June roared. 'That you're missing something up here?' She tapped a finger against the side of her head. 'That you're a nasty piece of work?' She let out a bitter laugh. 'And to think it was this one I used to worry about.' She jerked a thumb in her eldest son's direction. 'But believe me, he is worth ten of you.'

Lee raised his eyebrows, the hint of a smirk playing out across his lips. If only she knew just how dangerous her eldest son was. Nathan wouldn't think twice about beating a man to death; in fact, he had done so already and on more than one occasion.

'Leave it out, Mum,' Nathan remarked, his voice low. 'You're taking his side over ours, your own sons.'

'I'm not taking anyone's side.' June's body shook with anger.

'But this is wrong, all of it is wrong. Now let that girl go, and let us get our Connor to hospital.'

As he took a second glance back at Connor, anger began to build inside of Nathan and by the time he turned his eyes on Fletch, steam was practically coming out of his ears. Not only had he beaten his brother beyond recognition but he'd managed to turn their mother against them in the process.

June's scream was loud as her son bounded forward, his fists clenched into tight balls and his face a mask of anger. 'No,' she cried, 'stop.'

## 38

Rosco sat up a little straighter in the chair. This was more like it; much to his horror, he'd actually thought the cousins were going to hug it out, bringing with it his hopes of Fletch suffering for what he'd done to him crashing down around his ears.

He craned his neck to get a better view of the action, the excitement he felt reaching fever pitch. As fists began to fly, and punches were thrown, he clenched his uninjured hand into a tight ball and punched the air as though he were in the thick of the action, or at least as close to the action as he would ever want to be.

'Go on,' he encouraged as he moved his neck and shoulders from side to side, 'hit him, finish the wanker off.'

\* \* \*

Forcing her way in between her eldest son and nephew, June slammed a hand on each of their chests. 'Enough,' she screamed at them as tears rolled down her cheeks. 'Stop, the pair of you, just bloody stop,' she cried. 'What are you trying to do – kill one another? You're cousins, for Christ's sake. You share the same blood.'

'He's no blood of mine,' Nathan said, spitting on the floor. 'I'm warning you, Mum, get out of my fucking way,' he growled, his face white with anger.

'Or what?' June's forehead was furrowed. 'What are you going to do, batter me next?' Using as much force as she could physically muster, June shoved her son an inch or two back. 'I won't let you do this.'

Breathing heavily through his flared nostrils, Fletch dabbed at his lip. Taking away his hand, he saw a smear of blood.

'You all right, Fletch?' Stevie asked him.

Fletch nodded, not taking his eyes away from Nathan should he decide to go for round two. He'd had his fair share of scraps over the years and this one was no different. One of the few lessons in life his father had taught him was to never take your eyes off the ball. In other words, watch your opponent at all times otherwise the sneaky bastard would land one on you and it'd be game over.

'Well, well, well,' a low gravelly voice said. 'Is this a mother's meeting or can any fucker join in?'

All heads turned. Standing there, as large as life and flanked on either side by his heavies, was Ginger Parmar.

* * *

As he looked around him, Ginger's onyx-coloured eyes fell upon June. 'Hello, darling.' He grinned. 'Long time no see – you're looking as lovely as ever.'

'Ginger.' June straightened up and looked him up and down with a sneer. 'I wish I could say the same about you. You're looking...' She placed a finger to her lips as she pretended to study him. 'Old.'

Ginger chuckled. 'You always were a comedian,' he said. 'I guess that's where young Connor gets it from.' His eyebrows knitted together. 'Speaking of which, where is he?'

As he and Stevie shared a glance, Fletch sighed.

'Oh dear.' Ginger tutted when he finally spotted the youngest Bannerman brother, who was still being propped up between Dennis and Brandon. 'Now that does look nasty; so who's the culprit?' he asked, looking around him. His eyes fell upon Fletch and he shook his head. 'We didn't discuss this. I don't recall giving you the nod that you could batter young Connor half to death.'

Fletch ran his tongue across his teeth, taking his time to answer the question. 'I didn't realise I needed your approval.'

Ginger laughed. 'You do when you're on my fucking manor,' he stated. 'But,' he said, spreading open his arms, 'seeing as we're in South London, I'll let you off, but only this once, mind.'

'Cheers,' Fletch muttered with a roll of his eyes.

'So, then.' Pulling out a chair, Ginger sat down. 'Let's get down to business, shall we?' He lit a cigarette, exhaled a puff of smoke up into the air, then said, 'Where's my fucking coke?'

* * *

Rosco felt as though his heart would actually stop beating, he was that shocked. He'd always been so careful and had never purposely conducted any business deals that would put himself on Ginger's radar.

For years he'd looked over his shoulder, half expecting the man to catch up with him, and now he finally had, today of all days, when by rights he should have been able to sit back and watch Fletch get what was coming to him, he should have been celebrating, not quivering with fear.

He slunk down even further on the chair, trying to make himself as invisible as he could, half contemplating whether or not it would be feasible for him to get on his hands and knees and crawl away unseen.

'Well?' Ginger said, cupping a hand around his ear. 'I can't hear anything.' He turned his head to look at Ronnie Knox. 'Can you hear anything, Ron?'

Ronnie shook his head. 'I can hear fuck all,' he grunted in reply.

'That's exactly what I thought,' Ginger said, lounging back in the chair as though he was holding court. 'I'll tell you what,' he said with a glance at his watch, 'you've got roughly two minutes to start talking before I end up blowing my fucking gasket, and believe me, you really don't want me to do that.'

Rosco's ears pricked up. Just maybe he would be able to redeem himself after all. If he told Ginger who it was who had stolen the coke then the knowledge might earn him some brownie points, and God only knew how much he needed them. With a bit of luck, Ginger might have even forgotten all about the fact that he'd given evidence against him, that it had been his word and his testimony alone that had put him behind bars for ten years. It was a long shot, he knew. From what he could remember of the man, Ginger had the memory of an elephant, and never forgot a slight made against him, especially one as damning as the one he had happily made.

A smug smirk slid across Rosco's face and before he could stop himself, his hand had shot up in the air as though he was back at school and vying to get the teacher's attention.

'Who's that?' Feigning ignorance, Ginger sat up a little

straighter and peered into the corner of the warehouse. All eyes followed his gaze.

'Well, fuck me, if it ain't my old mucker Rosco,' he said, grinding out the cigarette underneath his boot. 'Have you got something to say?' he asked.

Rosco nodded.

'Well, stand up, then, man, so that we can all hear.'

Ginger flicked his head towards one of his foot soldiers indicating for him to sever the ropes that restrained Rosco to the chair.

Once he'd been released from the thick binds Rosco cautiously got to his feet. 'It's about the coke.'

'Say that again?' Ginger asked as he leant forward on the chair.

'I said it's about the coke.' Rosco cleared his throat. 'I know who took it.'

\* \* \*

Fletch inwardly groaned. He could feel Stevie stiffen beside him and silently willed him to keep calm. The last thing they needed right now was to bring attention to themselves or make themselves appear any guiltier than they already were.

He shot a glance back at his son. Austin looked like the equivalent of a rabbit caught in headlights; his eyes were like stalks and his skin had paled. Raising his eyebrows, Fletch shot him a warning to keep schtum.

\* \* \*

'So are you going to enlighten me, then, or is this the part where I'm supposed to guess?' Ginger's booming voice asked.

Rosco gave a nervous chuckle. He licked at his dry lips, wishing that he'd saved himself some of the bottled water instead of guzzling it down like the greedy bastard he was. 'It was him,' he spat, pointing his finger in Fletch's direction. 'He stole it.'

As he turned his head to look at Fletch, Ginger's eyes were narrowed. 'What's super-grass talking about?' he growled.

Fletch swallowed deeply. 'I dunno, he's talking bollocks. You know what he's like – he can't be fucking trusted, can he?'

Ginger's eyes remained firmly fixed on Fletch. 'Well, that depends,' he said. 'Do I trust the fucker as far as I can throw him? No, I fucking don't.' He rubbed at his chin. 'Did the ponce testify against me? Yes, he did, and that,' Ginger said, getting to his feet, 'is where the problem lies. You see, I was guilty of those offences. I hold my hands up,' he said with a roguish grin. 'Guilty as fucking charged, me, which brings me to question why our mutual friend would need to start lying now.'

'I told you, I don't know what he's talking about.' Beads of cold sweat broke out across Fletch's forehead. 'Your guess is as good as mine.'

'I don't play guessing games,' Ginger roared, making those around him recoil. 'As I've already stated, I leave that kind of thing to Ron over there.' He stalked forward, his large frame dominating the space.

Fletch sighed. In his mind's eye, he recalled the day his son had been born, the joy he'd felt as he'd held the tiny newborn in his arms. That day, he'd vowed to always protect Austin, no matter what, and all these years on nothing had changed. He'd move heaven and earth for his son, he'd lie for him, he'd give him an alibi, he'd even take the blame for him. 'You're right.' Slowly, he raised his hands in the air, resigned to the fate that awaited him.

'Fletch.' Stevie's mouth fell open. 'What the fuck are you doing?'

'No, Dad,' Austin gasped, 'don't.'

'It's all right.' Fletch turned to give his son a reassuring smile, a smile that didn't quite reach his eyes. At the best of times, Ginger could be brutal. Violence meant nothing to him; it was in his nature, and it was also a known fact that he'd killed men for doing far less, let alone stealing twenty kilos of cocaine. 'It'll be all right, son,' he said.

Ginger pulled himself up to his full height, his eyes narrowed until they were nothing more than two mere slits. 'What do you mean by I'm right?' he hissed.

Fletch took a deep breath. 'The coke, it was—'

'It was Rosco!' Kit screamed out the words.

Fletch's heart hammered inside his chest as he jerked his head in his daughter's direction.

'Who said that?' Ginger spun around.

'I did,' Kit answered, yanking at the restraints that confined her to the chair. 'Rosco took it. He hid it in the boot of a car at his Portakabin.'

## 39

Rosco's face drained of all colour. 'She's lying,' he roared. 'It wasn't me; why would I need to steal my own deal? I'm the innocent one here; I'm the victim in all of this,' he whined, shoving his septic finger in the air for them all to see.

With a flick of his head, the men in Ginger's employment barged past June and her sons and stormed across the warehouse to where Kit and Rosco were being held captive.

'Don't touch her,' Fletch screamed. 'You lay a finger on her and I'll fucking kill you with my bare hands.'

A slow smile swept across Ginger's lips and he gave a shake of his head. 'Give me some credit,' he said with a wink.

All the while, Rosco continued to loudly protest his innocence. 'It wasn't me,' he cried as he was prised none too gently away from the chair. 'I didn't do anything, I swear.' Sweat pooled underneath his armpits and dripped down his face in rivulets as he began to cry, great sobs that made his shoulders heave and his chest feel so tight that he could barely breathe.

After she'd been released from the cable ties, Kit barely paused for breath as she darted across the warehouse straight into her brother's arms. Her body shook so violently that Austin had to hold her tight in a bid to stop the tremor.

'It was him,' she cried as she glared towards her husband. 'He told me himself right from the very beginning what he was planning to do. I witnessed him stash the haul in the boot of one of his cars with my own two eyes.'

Ginger's expression was murderous, and as he swung back his fist, knocking Rosco to the floor with one heavy punch, he stood over the man whose testimony alone had put him away for the best part of a decade. 'For years I've bided my time,' he roared, kicking out his heavy boot, 'fucking years.'

Cowering on the floor, Rosco positioned his arms across his face and head in an attempt to defend himself, all the while whimpering, 'It wasn't me, I would never have tucked you up.'

The words were more than enough to make Ginger see red and as a black mist descended over him, he pummelled his fists into Rosco's soft flesh with an intensity that shocked even those around him. 'You wouldn't have tucked me up?' he spat between each punch. 'You treacherous cunt, it was because of you I was sent down.' As he continued punching, years of pent-up rage and hatred were finally being unleashed.

After what seemed an age, Ginger straightened up, his breath coming hard and fast, his expression a mask of hatred. 'Get him out of here,' he instructed his heavies.

Sheer horror resonated across Rosco's face. Instinctively, he knew that his would not be a quick death. No, if Ginger had his way, he'd be tortured, perhaps for days, maybe even weeks before his life was prematurely extinguished. 'No,' he screamed. And as he was dragged from the warehouse, he became hysterical; bubbles of snot billowed from his nostrils, his cheeks were wet from the tears he'd shed and his eyes, which were wide and terror-stricken, pleaded for help. Not that anyone would come rushing to his aid; the damage he'd systematically caused over the years was enough of a guarantee to know that his fate was sealed and that no one would bat an eyelid at his demise, especially his wife and brother-in-law. 'Dennis, help me,' he cried in a last-ditch attempt for salvation.

Dennis screwed up his face and, spitting in his one-time boss's direction, he shook his head. 'I wouldn't piss on you if you were on fire, let alone help you.'

Rosco's face fell and as he was dragged through the warehouse door, he took one last look at his wife. He watched her grasp his right-hand man's hand and his eyes ever so slightly widened as realisation finally took hold. All this time the whore had been playing away, more than likely laughing behind his back as she did so.

The warehouse fell silent and, kissing his teeth, Ginger looked between Nathan and Fletch. 'The floor's yours,' he said with a flick of his hand, 'but try not to kill one another, and while you're at it you'd best get him to hospital.' He jerked his thumb in Connor's direction. 'He ain't looking too clever, if you want my opinion, and let's face it, one death is more than enough for us to contend with tonight, don't you think?' With those parting words, he walked from the warehouse.

June let out a shaky breath and as she looked up at her sons, she nodded her head. 'As much as I despise the old fucker, he's right. Connor needs medical help before it's too late.' She looked towards Fletch. 'You have your daughter – now give me my son.'

Fletch sighed and with a jerk of his head he indicated for Connor to be brought forward.

The exchange completed, Fletch's instincts were on red alert, not fully trusting the two remaining brothers not to charge forward now that they had their brother back.

From where she was standing, June closely watched the man

who she had once loved like a son, and as if reading his mind, she spoke. 'There'll be no comebacks, not while I'm still breathing. This family has been through the mill and back as it is. Let bygones be bygones; let the destruction George caused end with his death. Make your peace and move on.'

There was more than a hint of truth to June's words. For the majority of his life, Fletch had been riddled with guilt, all because of his father's wickedness. Spencer's life had been cruelly cut short and even his own children had known abuse; it was time to break the cycle, time to heal and time to put the past behind them. 'There'll be no comebacks on my part,' he stated with sincerity.

June gave a gentle smile, then looked up at her sons. 'Make amends,' she urged them. 'George doesn't deserve your loyalty; he never has done. If he could terrorise his children and kill his own son, then what kind of a man did that make him?'

Nathan blew out his cheeks. For a moment he closed his eyes. A part of him still wanted to smash his cousin's face in for what had befallen his uncle and youngest brother, but an even bigger part of him pitied Fletch. He'd only ever known love from his own father; he'd never been raised surrounded by fear or hatred. He shot Lee a look of warning. 'There'll be no comebacks from us,' he promised.

Closing her eyes, June sighed. 'Now let's get your brother to hospital.'

## 40

Standing in the kitchen at Kit's house, Fletch stared out of the window that overlooked the garden. He was so deep in thought that he didn't hear his daughter approach him.

'Dad.'

Fletch turned his head. He gave her a small smile and shoved his hands into the pockets of his jeans. From his position, he could see into the lounge where Stevie, Dennis and his son were in deep conversation.

'Why don't you go to her?'

'Who?' Taken aback, Fletch narrowed his eyes.

'Susan.' As she opened the fridge door, Kit shielded her face from his view. 'Stevie told me about her,' she said, taking out a bottle of wine.

Fletch sighed and, looking down at his feet, he closed his eyes, debating within himself whether or not now was the right time to tell her his secret. 'You have a sister,' he eventually told her with a level of caution. 'I only found out myself a few weeks back.'

Kit's face lit up and she shook her head in wonder. 'I don't know what to say,' she said. 'It's a bit of a shock, I suppose.' She glanced over her shoulder to look at Austin. 'It could have been worse; you could have told me there was another one of him out there,' she said with a grin.

'God forbid.' Fletch chuckled. 'I think it's safe to say that Austin is more than enough for us to contend with.'

'Go.' Reaching out her hand, she placed it on Fletch's forearm and gave a gentle squeeze. 'Go on, go to her – you deserve to be happy.'

'How can I?' Tearing his eyes away from the bruises and welts that circled his daughter's wrists, Fletch shook his head. 'I can't leave you here, not now, not like this, not after what happened.'

'Course you can.' She rubbed her fingers over the bruises. 'They don't even hurt.' It was a lie and they were both well aware of that fact. 'Go on, go, I'm fine, and besides, I've got Dennis and Aus to keep me company.' She leant slightly forward. 'I've got a feeling Aus isn't in a rush to get back to Sheree. I think after the shit she's caused, he's finally going to give her the elbow.' She blew out her cheeks and shook her head. 'It's about time he saw her for who she really is.'

Stealing a glance towards his son, Fletch nodded. As for Susan, after her ultimatum he wasn't so sure that she even wanted him. 'Are you sure you're going to be okay?' He tilted his head to look at her. 'Because it's okay to admit otherwise if you're not. I mean, Taylor...' He took a deep breath. 'He is still your husband... or at least was,' he quickly amended. 'Whether you want it to or not, his death is bound to have an effect on you.'

'I'm fine, honest.' She began to fill a wine glass, careful not to let him see the slight tremor in her hand. 'As for Rosco, I despised him. He destroyed my family.' She stole a glance towards her brother. 'For the first time in a long time, I actually feel free. I don't have to worry about Aus any more; I'll be able to go to sleep at night knowing he isn't in danger, that Rosco won't ever be able to harm him.'

Fletch sighed. He only wished he'd been able to feel the same sense of freedom regarding his own brother. Pushing himself away from the counter, he made to walk away. Reaching the kitchen door, he paused and looked over his shoulder. 'There's something I want to ask you,' he said. 'When you suggested stashing the coke at the Portakabin, did you plan to set Taylor up from the off?'

Looking up at her father, Kit shrugged, her expression unreadable. 'I knew Aus couldn't handle it,' she answered after a moment of thinking the question through, 'and so I did what I had to do to keep him safe.'

Fletch gave a chuckle. 'I'm gonna have to watch out for you,' he said with a wink. 'You've got too much of your old man inside of you.'

Together they shared a grin.

'Could be worse.' She winked back. 'I could take after my mum.'

'Nah, you're nothing like her,' Fletch answered, his voice serious. With one last smile, he turned to walk away.

'Dad, wait.'

Fletch paused.

'Thank you, for, you know... what you did. You were prepared to sacrifice yourself for Aus. You would have died for him.'

'That's what dads do.' Fletch shrugged.

Launching herself forward, she wrapped her arms around his waist and leant her head against his chest.

For a brief moment, Fletch froze. It was so unexpected that he didn't know how to respond. Finally, he hugged her to him and kissed the top of her head. 'I love you, Kitty; don't you ever forget that, darling,' he said softly in her ear.

\* \* \*

As Stevie drove them towards Upminster, Fletch was thoughtful. 'I'm sorry, mate,' he said.

Stevie narrowed his eyes. 'What for?'

'The coke deal,' Fletch answered. 'I know how much you were relying on that money.'

Waving his hand in the air, Stevie dismissed his friend's words. 'It's sorted.' He grinned. 'And you'll be pleased to know it's all legal and above board.'

Fletch narrowed his eyes.

'Kit,' Stevie explained. 'She's selling the club and is going to lend me the money. I'll have to pay her back, obviously, but that's a whole lot better than losing the house.' He tapped his fingers on the steering wheel. 'Plus it has the added bonus of Jess never having to find out about it.'

'Yeah, there is that.' Fletch laughed.

'Listen.' As he pulled up outside the flower shop, Stevie cleared his throat. 'The situation with you and Jess,' he said, his tone becoming serious. 'I think that you both got off on the wrong foot, and yeah, I know,' he said, holding up his hand, 'that you did nothing wrong. It's her,' he said, referring to his wife. 'She doesn't come from our world; she was scared and she doesn't know you like I do. She heard the word "murder" and, well, put two and two together and came up with five.'

'I get it.' Fletch gave his oldest friend a small smile. 'I'll tell you what,' he said, 'once the dust settles, why don't we all go out for a meal, start again, see if we can make amends.'

Stevie beamed. 'Yeah, I'd like that.' He looked over at the shop. 'Go on.' He nodded. 'Scarper – you're starting to bore me now.'

'Cheers.' Fletch laughed. Opening the car door, he climbed

out, closed the door behind him and looked through the open window. 'And thanks, mate, for everything. You did your best; you stepped up when I was away. I know my two aren't the easiest to deal with—'

'Too bloody right they're not,' Stevie interrupted. 'They're too much like bloody you.' He nodded once more towards the shop. 'I only hope and pray the third one has more of her mother in her.'

'Time will tell, mate.' Thumping his hand on the car roof, he stood back, watching as Stevie drove away before walking towards the entrance of the flat.

Susan had been having a tidy around when she heard a knock on the front door. Her pulse quickened and, straightening out her dress, she patted down her hair before making her way down the hallway.

As she pulled open the front door, Susan's heart was in her mouth. She wanted it to be Fletch, desperately wanted it to be him. With no word from him since he'd left the flat more than twenty-four hours previously, she ached to know that he was okay, that he was safe, that he still wanted her.

'Hello, Suze.'

On seeing him, Susan placed her hand across her chest. 'Fletch,' she cried, reaching up to gently touch the slit above his lip, 'I didn't think you'd come back.'

'You can't get rid of me that easily.' He winked, hiding the fact that it was only by a miracle that he had managed to come back at all.

Bending down, he brushed his lips against her cheek, breathing in her familiar scent.

'And everything is sorted out?' Susan probed. 'Austin is okay?

Fletch nodded. 'I think it's safe to say that Austin has learnt his lesson,' he answered.

Susan smiled. It was such a heart-warming smile that Fletch didn't think he could ever love her more than he did right now.

* * *

Two days later, with Susan at his side, Fletch walked through the gates of Upminster cemetery. In his hand he held a bouquet of white lilies and as they reached Spencer's graveside, Susan gave his hand a reassuring squeeze.

'I'll give you a few moments alone with him,' she said.

Nodding, Fletch watched her return to the pathway, then turned his attention back to the grave. For a few moments he stood just thinking, then, remembering the flowers he was holding, he laid them beside the headstone.

'I miss you, mate,' he said, resting his hand on the black marble that was inscribed with his brother's name, 'more than you could ever know.'

Squeezing his eyes shut tight, he swallowed down the hard lump in his throat in a bid to stop the tears from flowing. It was too late and as a lone tear rolled down his cheek, he swiped it away with the back of his hand.

'I'm sorry for not visiting before now.' He cleared the lump from his throat. 'I was scared,' he explained, 'scared that if I came here then I'd have to admit to myself that all of this was real, that you were really gone.'

Above him he could hear the sound of birds chirping and he gave a soft laugh. His mum had been right: Spencer would have liked it here; he would have approved.

Bending down, he kissed the stone. 'I'll come back soon, bruv,' he promised.

On the path, Susan gave him a gentle smile. 'Are you okay?' she asked.

'Yeah.' Taking a deep breath, Fletch answered, 'I actually am.'

Hand in hand, they walked away from the graveside. Later on that afternoon they were planning to sit Harriet down and explain to her that he was her father. Fletch was a bundle of nerves at the prospect, despite Susan telling him he had no need to be. Harriet was going to love him, she'd told him over and over again, and if it turned out that she didn't love him and that he had to work hard to gain his second daughter's trust, then he was okay with that. He was more than prepared to put in the time and the effort needed; after all, he'd had some practice. After a shaky start he'd finally won Kit and Austin around and he knew without a doubt that he would be able to do it all over again.

# ACKNOWLEDGMENTS

A huge thank you to Boldwood Books for believing in me. And to my partner, Jimmy, and my daughter, Lizzie – your support and patience over the past few months have been invaluable.

I would also like to take this time to say thank you to Deryl Easton, Sammee Hart, Sarah Warman, Sophie Doherty, Nikki Taylor and Darren Mitchell – your encouragement has meant so much to me. This book is for you.

Finally, a huge thank you to NotRights Book Club and LondonCrime: you have been with me every step of the way and I cannot thank you enough for your continued support and encouragement.

## MORE FROM KERRY KAYA

We hope you enjoyed reading *The Score*. If you did, please leave a review.

If you'd like to gift a copy, this book is also available as an ebook, digital audio download and audiobook CD.

Sign up to Kerry Kaya's mailing list for news, competitions and updates on future books.

http://bit.ly/KerryKayaNewsletter

Another gripping gangland read from Kerry Kaya, *The Price*, is available now.

# ABOUT THE AUTHOR

**Kerry Kaya** is the hugely popular author of Essex based gritty gangland thrillers with strong family dynamics. She grew up on one of the largest council estates in the UK, where she sets her novels. She also works full-time in a busy maternity department for the NHS.

Follow Kerry on social media:

 twitter.com/KerryKayaWriter

 instagram.com/kerry_kaya_writer

 facebook.com/kerry.bryant.58

## ABOUT BOLDWOOD BOOKS

Boldwood Books is a fiction publishing company seeking out the best stories from around the world.

Find out more at www.boldwoodbooks.com

Sign up to the Book and Tonic newsletter for news, offers and competitions from Boldwood Books!

http://www.bit.ly/bookandtonic

We'd love to hear from you, follow us on social media:

facebook.com/BookandTonic

twitter.com/BoldwoodBooks

instagram.com/BookandTonic